Harlequin Books is proud to offer classic novels from today's superstars of women's fiction. These authors have captured the hearts of millions of readers around the world, and earned their place on the bestseller lists with every release.

As a bonus, each volume also includes a full-length novel from a rising star of series romance. Bestselling authors in their own right, these talented writers have captured the qualities Harlequin is famous for—heart-racing passion, edge-of-your-seat entertainment and a satisfying happily-ever-after.

Praise for *New York Times* and *USA TODAY* bestselling author Heather Graham

"Heather Graham will keep you in suspense until the very end."
—*Literary Times*

"A fast-paced and suspenseful read that will give readers chills while keeping them guessing until the end."
—*RT Book Reviews* on *Ghost Moon*

"Heather Graham knows what readers want."
—*Publishers Weekly*

Praise for bestselling author Debra Webb

"Debra Webb is endowed with an incredible imagination and an impressive ability to create multidimensional, realistic characters."
—*The Romance Reader.com*

"Webb guarantees a nail-biting, one-sit read."
—*RT Book Reviews* on *Colby Justice*

USA TODAY Bestselling Author

THER GRAHAM

In the Dark

ISBN-13: 978-0-373-60579-8

IN THE DARK

This edition published by arrangement with Harlequin Books S.A.

For questions and comments about the quality of this book, please contact us at CustomerService@Harlequin.com.

Printed in U.S.A.

IN THE DARK

New York Times and *USA TODAY* Bestselling Author

Heather Graham

HEATHER GRAHAM

New York Times bestselling author Heather Graham has written more than a hundred novels, many of which have been featured by the Doubleday Book Club and the Literary Guild. An avid scuba diver, ballroom dancer and mother of five, she still enjoys her south Florida home, but loves to travel as well, from locations such as Cairo, Egypt, to her own backyard, the Florida Keys. Reading, however, is the pastime she still loves best, and she is a member of many writing groups. She's a winner of the Romance Writers of America's Lifetime Achievement Award, and is currently vice president of the Horror Writers' Association. She's also an active member of International Thriller Writers and Mystery Writers of America. She is the founder of The Slush Pile, an author band and performing group.

For more information, check out her websites, TheOriginalHeatherGraham.com, eHeatherGraham.com and HeatherGraham.tv. You can also find Heather on MySpace and Facebook.

Prologue

Alex nearly screamed as her foot hit the shell. She choked down the sound just in time but still stumbled, and that was when she fell.

She'd missed the shell, running in the dark. As she lay there, winded from landing hard on the sand, she damned the darkness. In just another few hours, it would be light.

In just a matter of minutes, the eye of the storm would have passed and the hundred-mile winds of Hurricane Dahlia would be picking up again. And here she was, lying next to the water, completely vulnerable.

She rolled quickly, gasping for breath, ready to leap back to her feet. She didn't dare take the time to survey the injury to her foot, as the constant prayer that had been rushing through her mind continued. Please, just let me reach the resort. Please…

A thrashing sound came from the brush behind her.

The killer was close.

She would have to run again, heading for the safety of the resort. Or would even that be safety now?

She needed to reach the resort without being seen, needed to reach the lockbox behind the check-in, where the Smith & Wesson was kept. She was almost certain no one else had taken the gun.

Move! She silently commanded herself. What was she waiting for?

There was no one who could help her, no one she could trust.

She had to depend on only herself, no matter how desperately she wanted to believe in at least one man….

It was then that, so near that she could recognize him despite the darkness, she saw Len Creighton, prone on the sand.

Another body, she thought, panic rising in her. Well, she had wondered where he was. And now she knew. He was lying facedown on the sand, a trickle of blood running down his face. The wild surf was breaking over his legs where he lay surrounded by clumps of seaweed. Already, little crabs were scouring the area, carefully eyeing what they hoped would be their next meal.

She choked back a scream. Above her, the clouds broke. Pale light emerged from the heavens.

And that was when the first man exploded from the bush.

"Alex!" he called. "Get over here."

He stood there, panting for breath, beckoning to her, eyes sharply surveying the area. And he was carrying a speargun, one that had been used on some living creature already—blood dripped from the tip. "Alex, you've got to trust me. Come with me now—quickly."

"No!"

He spun on a dime at the sound of the second voice.

A second man. This one carrying a Glock, which was aimed at the first man.

"Alex, come to me. Get away from him," the newcomer insisted.

The men faced off, staring, each one aware of the weapon the other was carrying.

"Alex!"

This time, she wasn't even sure which man spoke. Once she had trusted them both. One, she had loved before. The other had so nearly seduced her heart in the days just past.

"Alex!"

There was what appeared to be a dead man at her feet. A co-worker. A friend. She should be down on her knees, attempting to find life, however hopeless that might be. But one of the two men facing her was a killer. She couldn't look away. Seconds ticked by, and she stood frozen in place.

Her heart insisted that it couldn't be either man.

Especially not him.

She couldn't think. She could only stand there and stare, eyes going from one man to the other, everything within her soul screaming that neither one of them could be a killer.

But one of them was.

She could feel the ocean lapping over her feet. She knew these waters so well, like the back of her hand.

So did they.

No, not these waters. Not this island. She knew it as few other people could.

There was only one thing she could do, even though

it was insanity. The storm might have passed for the moment, but the sea was far from placid. The waves were still deadly. The currents would be merciless.

And yet…

She had no other choice.

She turned to the sea and dove into it, and as she swam for her life, she realized that a few days ago, she wouldn't have believed this.

That was when it had all begun. Just days ago.

She felt the surge of her arms and legs as she strove to put distance between herself and the shore.

Something sped past her in the water. A bullet? A spear?

People always said that in the last seconds of someone's life, their entire past rushed before their eyes.

She wasn't seeing that far back.

Just to that morning, by the dolphin lagoon, when she had found the first body on the beach.

The one that had disappeared.

Chapter 1

"The main thing to remember is that here at Moon Bay, we consider our dolphins our guests. When you're swimming with them, don't turn and stalk them, because, for one thing, they're faster than you can begin to imagine, and they'll disappear on you in seconds flat. And also, they hate it. Let them come to you—and they will. They're here because they're social creatures. We never force them to interact with people—they want to. Any animal in the lagoon knows how to leave the playing arena. And when they choose to leave, we respect their desire to do so. When they come to you naturally, you're free to stroke them as they pass. Try to keep your hands forward of the dorsal fin. And just stroke—don't pound or scratch, okay?"

Alex McCord's voice was smooth and normal—or so she hoped—as she spoke with the group of eight gathered before her. She had done a lot of smiling, while she first assured the two preteen girls and the teenage boy, who looked like a troublemaker, that she wasn't angry but they would follow the rules. A few of her other smiles had been genuine and directed at two of the five adults rounding out the dive, the father of the boy and the mother of the girls.

Then there were her forced smiles. Her face was beginning to hurt, those smiles were so forced.

Because she just couldn't believe who was here.

The world was filled with islands. And these days the world was even filled with islands that offered a dozen variations of the dolphin experience.

So what on earth was David Denham doing here, on her island, suddenly showing an extraordinary curiosity regarding her dolphins? Especially when his experiences must reduce her swims to a mom-and-pop outing, since he'd been swimming with great whites at the Great Barrier Reef, photographed whales in the Pacific, fed lemon sharks off Aruba and filmed ray encounters in Grand Cayman. So why was he here? It had been months since she'd seen him, heard from him or even bothered to read any of the news articles regarding him.

But here he was, the ultimate ocean man. Diver, photographer and salvage entrepreneur extraordinaire. Six-two, broad shoulders bronzed, perfect features weathered, deep blue gaze focused on her as if he were fascinated by her every word, even though his questions made it clear he knew as much about dolphins as she did.

She might not have minded so much, except that for once she had been looking forward to the company of another man—an arresting and attractive man who apparently found her attractive, as well.

John Seymore, an ex–navy SEAL, was looking to set up a dive business in the Keys. Physically, he was like a blond version of David. And his eyes were green, a pleasant, easygoing, light green. Despite his credentials, he'd gone on her morning dive tour the day before, and she'd chatted with him at the Tiki Hut last night and found out that he'd signed on for the dolphin swim, as well. He'd admitted that he knew almost nothing about the creatures but loved them.

She'd had a couple of drinks…she'd danced. She'd gone so far as to imagine sex.

And now…here was David. Distorting the image of a barely formed mirage before it could even begin to find focus. They were divorced. She had every right to envision a life with another man, so the concept of a simple date shouldn't make her feel squeamish. After all, she sincerely doubted that her ex-husband had been sitting around idle for a year.

"They're really the most extraordinary creatures in the world," Laurie Smith, one of Alex's four assistants, piped up. Had she simply stopped speaking, Alex wondered, forcing Laurie to chime in? Actually, Alex was glad Laurie had spoken up. Alex had been afraid that she was beginning to look like a bored tour guide, which wasn't the case at all. She had worked with a number of animals during her career. She had never found any as intelligent, clever and personable as dolphins. Dogs were great, and so were chimps, but dolphins were magical.

"You never feel guilty, as if the dolphins are scientific rats in a lab—except, of course, that entertaining tourists isn't exactly medical research."

That came from the last member of the group, the man to whom she needed to be giving the most serious attention. Hank Adamson. He wasn't as muscled or bronzed as David and John, but he was tall and lithe, wiry, sandy-haired, and wearing the most stylish sunglasses available. He was handsome in a smooth, sleek, electric way and could be the most polite human being on earth. He could also be cruel. He was a local columnist, and he also contributed to travel magazines and tour guides about the area. He could, if he thought it was justified, be savage, ripping apart motels, hotels, restaurants, theme parks and clubs. There was something humorous about his acidic style, which led to his articles being syndicated across the country. Alex found him an irritating bastard, but Jay Galway, manager of the entire Moon Bay facility, was desperate to get a good review from the man.

Adamson had seemed to enjoy the dive-boat activities the day before. She'd been waiting for some kind of an assault, though, since he'd set foot on the island. And here it was.

"The lagoon offers the animals many choices, Mr. Adamson. They can play, or they can retire to their private area. Additionally, our dolphins were all born in captivity, except for Shania, and she was hurt so badly by a boat propeller that she wouldn't have survived in the open sea. We made one attempt to release her, and she came right back. Dolphins are incredibly intelligent creatures, and I believe that they're as interested in learning about our behavior as we are in theirs." She shifted focus to address the group at large. "Let's begin. Is there any particular behavior you've seen or experienced with the dolphins you'd like to try again?"

"I want to ride a dolphin," the boy, Zach, said.

"The fin ride. Sure, we can start with that. Would you like to go first?"

"Yeah, can I?"

She smiled. Maybe the kid wasn't a demon after all. Dolphins had a wonderful effect on people. Once, she'd been given a group of "incorrigibles" from a local "special" school. They'd teased and acted like idiots at first. Then they'd gotten into the water and become model citizens.

"Absolutely. One dolphin or two?"

"Two is really cool," David said quietly, offering a slight grin to the boy.

"Two."

"Okay, in the water, front and center. Fins on, no masks or snorkels right now," Alex said.

The others waited as the boy went out into the lagoon and extended his arms as Alex indicated. She signaled to Katy and Sabra, and the two dolphins sleekly obeyed the command, like silver streaks of light sliding beneath the water's surface.

Zach was great, taking a firm hold of each fin and smiling like a two-year-old with an oversize lollipop as the mammals swam him through the water, finishing up by the floating dock, where they were rewarded as they dropped their passenger. Zach was still beaming.

"Better than any ride I've ever been on in my life!" he exclaimed.

"Can I go next?" one of the girls asked. Tess. Cute little thing, bright eyes, dark hair. Zach had been trying to impress her earlier. Tess opted for one dolphin, and Alex chose Jamie-Boy.

One by one, everyone got to try the fin ride. John Seymore was quieter than the kids, but obviously pleased. Even Hank Adamson—for all his skepticism and the fact that he seemed to be looking for something to condemn—enjoyed his swim.

Alex was afraid that David would either demur—this was pretty tame stuff for him—or do something spectacular. God knew what he might whisper to a dolphin, and what a well-trained, social animal might do in response. But David was well-behaved, looking as smooth and sleek as the creatures themselves as he came out of the water. The only irritating thing was that he and John Seymore seemed to find a tremendous amount to talk about whenever she was busy with the others. Then, during the circle swim, David disappeared beneath the surface for so long that the two parents in the group began to worry that he had drowned.

"Are you sure he's all right?" Ally Conroy, Zach's mother, asked Alex.

"I know him," Alex told the woman, forcing another of those plastic smiles that threatened to break her face. "He can hold his breath almost as long as the dolphins."

David surfaced at last. Macy, the staff photographer, just shrugged at Alex. They made a lot of their research funding by selling people photos of their dolphin experiences, but Alex and Macy both knew David didn't need to buy any photos.

At that point, David and John began talking quietly in the background, as Alex got the others going on their chance for dolphin hugs and smooches. She couldn't hear what the two men were saying, but she was annoyed, and became more so when Hank Adamson joined the conversation. She found them distracting, but had a feeling she'd look foolish if she were to freak out and yell at the lot of them to shut up. It looked like a little testosterone party going. They were probably chatting about diving—in a manly way, of course.

Why did it bother her so much? David was out of her life. No, David would never be out of her life.

The thought was galling. She had been able to see that the relationship wasn't working, that time wasn't going to change the facts about him, her or the situation. And they had split. She didn't regret the decision.

It's just that he was here again now, when she had a lovely minor flirtation going on, the most exciting thing she'd experienced since the divorce. And just because the object of her current affections seemed to be getting on with David as if they were long-lost friends…

"Hey," Zach whispered to her, his eyes alight, "those guys aren't paying any attention. The girls and I could sneak in and take their hugs, huh?"

She would have loved to agree. But no matter what it looked like Hank Adamson was doing, he was a reporter. One whose writing could influence the fate of Moon Bay. She had to play fair.

"I'd love to give them to you and the girls, but it wouldn't be right."

"Zach, you can take my place."

She hadn't known that David had broken away from his conversation.

She stared at him. "The girls would want an equal opportunity."

"Hey, I'll give up my time." That, amazingly, came from Hank Adamson. He grinned at Alex. "It's cool watching the kids have fun. Don't worry—you're getting a good write-up."

"I'll give up my hug, too," John Seymore told her, shrugging, a dimple going deep.

"Another round for the youngest members of the group, then," she said.

Finally the time was up. Alex went through her spiel about returning flippers, masks, and snorkels, telling the group where they could rinse off the brine and find further information on dolphins before heading off for whatever their next adventure might be.

John gave her a special smile as he stopped to thank her. "I was figuring I'd do it again, maybe check out a time when the groups weren't full. I don't have a thing in the world against hugs. Even from a dolphin."

She smiled in return, nodding.

"I think I have an in with the dolphin keeper," he added softly.

"You do," she assured him.

He turned, walking off. David had been right behind him. He'd undoubtedly heard every word. Now his dark blue eyes were on her enigmatically. She wished he wasn't even more appealing soaking wet, that thatch of impossibly dark hair over his forehead, bronzed shoulders gleaming. She wished there wasn't such an irresistibly subtle, too-familiar scent about him. Soap, cologne, his natural essence, mingled with the sea and salty air.

"Nice program you've got going," he said. "Thanks."

Then he walked away. He didn't even shake her hand, as the others had. He didn't touch her.

She felt burned.

"Thanks," she returned, though he was already too far away to hear her.

"You okay?"

Alex whirled. Laurie was watching her worriedly.

"So hunky-dory I could spit," Alex assured her, causing Laurie to smile.

Then her friend cocked her head, set her hands on her hips and sighed. "Poor baby. Two of the most attractive men I've seen in a long time angling for your attention, and you look as if you've been caught in a bees' nest."

"Trust me, David is not angling for my attention."

"You should have seen the way he was looking at you."

"You were reading it wrong, I guarantee you."

Laurie frowned. "I thought the divorce went smoothly."

"Very smoothly. I don't think he even noticed," Alex told her ruefully. She lifted a hand in vague explanation. "He was in the Caribbean on a boat somewhere when I filed the papers. He didn't call, didn't protest…just sent his attorney with the clear message to let me do whatever I wanted, have whatever I wanted…. I was married, then I wasn't, and it was all so fast, my head was spinning."

"Well, that certainly didn't mean he hated you."

"I never said he hated me."

"Well…want my advice?"

"No."

Laurie grinned. "That's because you've never been to a place like Date Tournament."

"What?"

"I told you I was going the other day," Laurie said impatiently. "It's that new club in Key Largo. They've been doing it all over the country. You go, and you keep changing tables, chatting with different people for about ten minutes each. The idea isn't bad. I mean, there are nice guys out there, not just jerks. Some are heart-broken—like me. And some are just looking. Imagine, the perfect person for me could walk by me in a mall, but we'd never talk. We never see someone and just walk up and say, 'Hey, you're good-looking, the right age, are you straight? Attached? Do you have kids? Do you like the water? We wouldn't last a day if you didn't.' So at Date Tournament, you at least get to meet people who are looking for people. Sexual preference and marital status are all straightened out before you start. You're not stuck believing some jerk in a bar who says he's single, gets more out of the night than a girl set out to give, then apologizes because he has to get home before his wife catches him."

Alex stared at her blankly for a minute. Laurie was beautiful, a natural platinum blonde with a gorgeous smile, charm and spontaneity. It had never really occurred to Alex that her friend had the least difficulty dating. Living at Moon Bay seemed perfect for Alex. She had her own small but atmospheric little cottage, surrounded by subtropical growth—and daily maid service. There was the Tiki Hut off the lagoons for laid-back evenings, buffets in the main house for every meal, a small but well-run bookstore and every cable channel known to man. She thought ruefully that just because she had been nursing a wounded heart all this time, she'd had no reason to think the others were all as happy with celibacy as she was.

She arched an eyebrow, wishing she hadn't spent so much time being nearly oblivious to the feelings of others.

"So…how was your evening at Date Tournament?"

"Scary. Sad," Laurie said dryly. "Want to hear about it?"

"Yes, but I want to get away from here first," Alex said. She could see across the lagoon, and the Tiki Hut was beginning to fill up for cocktail hour. Fishing parties returning, those who'd been out on scuba and snorkeling trips coming in, and those who had lazed the day away at the beach or the pool. She could see that Hank Adamson was talking to her boss, Jay Galway, head of operations at Moon Bay, and he was pointing toward the dolphin lagoons.

She didn't want to smile anymore, or suck up to Adamson—or defend herself. They were also standing with a man named Seth Granger, a frequent visitor, a very rich retired businessman who had decided he wanted to become a salvage expert. He signed up for dives and swims, then complained that they weren't adventurous enough. Alex had wished for a very long time that she could tell him not to go on the dives when he didn't enjoy the beauty of the reefs. Their dives were planned to show off the incredible color and beauty to be found on the only continental reef in the United States, not for a possible clash with modern-day pirates. Nor were they seeking treasure.

Well, if he wanted to talk about salvage or adventure, he could pin David down one night. They deserved each other.

Jay Galway seemed to be trying to get her attention. She pretended she didn't notice.

"Let's go to the beach on the other side of the island, huh? Then you can tell me all about dating hell," she said to Laurie.

"Mr. Galway is waving at you," Laurie said, running

to catch up as Alex took off down the beach. "I think he wants you."

"Then move faster," Alex told her.

She turned, pretended she thought that James was just waving, waved back and took off at a walk so brisk it was nearly a run.

The dolphin lagoons were just around the bend, putting them on the westward side of the island rather than on the strip that faced the Atlantic. There were no roads out here from what wasn't even really the mainland, since they sat eastward of the Middle Keys. A motorboat regularly made the twenty-minute trip from the island to several of the Keys, and a small ferry traveled between several of the Keys, then stopped at the island, five times a day. Moon Bay had only existed for a few years; before its purchase by a large German-American firm, it had been nothing more than a small strip of sand and trees where locals had come to picnic and find solitude.

The western side was still magnificently barren. White-sand beaches were edged by unbelievably clear water on one side, and palms and foliage on the other. Alex loved to escape the actual lodge area, especially at night. While their visitors were certainly free to roam in this direction, mercifully, not many did once it turned to the later portion of the afternoon. Sunbathers loved the area, but by now they were baked, red and in pain.

It was close to six, but the sun was still bright and warm. Nothing like the earlier hours, but nowhere near darkness. The water was calm and lazy; little nothing waves were creating a delicate foam against the shoreline that disappeared in seconds. The palms rustled behind them as they walked, and the delightful sea breeze kept the heat at bay.

Alex glanced up at the sky. It was a beautiful day, glorious. All kinds of tempests might be brewing out in the Atlantic or down in the Gulf somewhere, but here, all was calm and perfect. The sky was a rich, powdery blue, barely touched by the clouds, with that little bit of breeze deflecting the ninety-degree temperature that had slowly begun to drop.

Alex came to a halt and sat down on the wet sand. Laurie followed suit. The identical tank tops they wore—the words Moon Bay etched across black polyester in a soft off-white were light enough that Alex almost shivered when the breeze touched her damp arms. She had little concern for her matching shorts—they were made to take the sand, sun and heat with ease. It was comfortable clothing, perfect for the job, and not suggestive in the least. This was a family establishment.

A great place to run after a bad marriage, with everything she needed: a good job doing what she loved, water, boats, sand, sun, privacy.

Too much privacy.

And now…David was here. Damn him. She wasn't going to change a thing. She was going to do exactly what she had planned. Shower, dress nicely, blow-dry her hair, wear makeup…sip piña coladas and dance at the Tiki Hut. Flirt like hell with John Seymore. And ignore the fact that every single woman in the place would be eyeing David.

Over. It was over. They had gone their separate ways….

"Well?" Laurie said.

"I'm sorry. What?"

"Do you want to hear about Date Tournament? Or do

you just want to sit here, me quietly at your side, while you damn yourself for divorcing such a hunk?"

"Never," Alex protested.

"Never as in, you never want to hear about Date Tournament, or never as in…what, exactly? You are divorced, right?"

"Of course. I meant, I'll never regret what I did. It was necessary."

"Why?"

Alex was silent. Why? We were going different ways? We didn't know one another to begin with? It was as simple as…Alicia Farr? No, that was ridiculous. It was complex, as most such matters were. It was his needing adventure at all costs, her needing to be a real trainer. It was…

"Oh my God!" Laurie gasped suddenly, staring at her. "Was he…he was abusive?"

"No! Don't be ridiculous."

"Then…?"

"We just went different ways."

"Hmph." Laurie toed a little crab back toward the water. "Whatever way he was going, I'd have followed him. But then, I've had the experience of Date Tournament, which you haven't—and which I thought you wanted to hear about."

"I'm sorry. I'm being a horrible friend. I'm in shock, I think. Having this lovely time with John Seymore, and then…up pops David."

"So what?"

"It's uncomfortable."

"But you and David are divorced, so what are you worried about? Enjoy John Seymore. He's a hunk, too. Not like anyone I met at Date Tournament."

"There must have been some nice guys."

"If there were, I didn't happen to meet them. Now let's get back to your love triangle."

Alex grinned. "There is no love triangle. Let's get back to you. You're gorgeous, bright, sweet and intelligent. The right guy is going to come along."

"Doesn't seem to be too much wrong with Mr. John Seymore. Did you know he's an ex-navy SEAL? But there you go. Apparently, when my right guy comes along, he wants to date you."

Alex arched an eyebrow, surprised. "I hadn't realized that…that…"

"You hadn't realized 'that' because there was no 'that' to realize. I hadn't even talked to the guy until today. Then there's your ex-husband."

"He's certainly a free agent."

"He's your ex. That's a no-no."

"I repeat—he's a free agent."

"One who sends you into a spiral," Laurie noted.

"I'm not in a spiral. It's just that…I was married to him. That makes me…I don't know what that makes me. Yes, I do. It makes me uncomfortable."

"You never fell out of love with him."

"Trust me—I did. It's just that…"

"All you've had for company since your divorce has been a bunch of sea animals?" Laurie suggested, amused.

"Neither one of us has dated in…a very, very long time," Alex agreed.

Laurie sighed glumly, setting her hands on her knees and cupping her chin in them. "Think it might be due to the fact that we've chosen to live on a remote island where the tourists are usually married, and the staff are usually in college?"

Alex laughed. "Maybe, but you'd think…sun, boats, island—fishing. Oh, well."

"What do you mean, oh well? At least there's excitement in your life. You've got the triangle thing going. Husband, lover."

"Ex-husband and new acquaintance," Alex reminded her.

"Ex-husband, new almost-lover. Vying for the same woman. And you know guys. They get into a competition thing. What a setup for jealousy and…"

Her voice trailed off, and she stared wide-eyed at Alex, like a doe in the headlights.

"Oh my God!" Laurie gasped.

She stared at Alex in pure horror. Alex frowned. "What? Come on, Laurie. Believe me, it's not that serious. You think that they'll get into some kind of a fight? No, never. In our marriage…David just didn't notice. Didn't care. I can't begin to see him decking someone—and sure as hell not over me."

"Oh my God," Laurie breathed again.

"Laurie, it's all right. Nothing is going to happen between David and John."

Laurie shook her head vehemently and slowly got to her feet, pointing. "Oh God, Alex. Look!"

For a moment, Alex couldn't quite shift mental gears. Then she frowned, standing up herself.

"What?" she said to Laurie. She grasped her friend's shoulders. "Laurie, what in the world is it?"

Laurie pointed. Alex realized that Laurie hadn't been

staring at her at all during the last few moments—she had been staring past her.

She spun around.

And that was when she saw the body on the beach.

Chapter 2

"I've read about you," John Seymore told David. "In the scuba magazines. That article on your work with great whites...wow. I've got to admit, I'm astounded to see you here. This place must seem pretty tame to you. It's great to get to meet you."

"Thanks," David said.

Seymore seemed pleasant. He was good-looking, well-muscled probably naturally, since he'd said he hadn't been out of military service long. Despite his surfer-boy blond hair and easy smile, there was a rough edge about him that betrayed age, maybe, and a hard life. David had a feeling his military stories would be the kind to make the hair rise on the back of the neck. Just as he had a feeling that, no matter how pleasant the guy might seem, he had a backbone of steel.

They'd started talking during the swim, and when Seymore had suggested a quick drink at the Tiki Hut,

David had been glad to comply. He was interested in what would bring a man of John Seymore's expertise to such a charming little tourist haven.

"I know the people here," David told John. "The guy managing the place, Jay Galway, is a part-time thrill seeker. He's been on a few of my excursions over the years. I like coming here, but this is the first time I've stayed. The cottages are great. A perfect place to chill, with all the comforts of home, but you feel as if you're off somewhere in the wilds. What about you?"

"I know the water pretty well, but I've never had any fun with it. I've been out on the West Coast. I left the military…and, I'm afraid, a painful divorce."

"So you retired from the military," David said. "Living a life of ease, huh?"

Seymore laughed. "I did pretty well with the military, but not well enough to retire the way I'd like to. But my time is my own. I'm doing consulting work now. Because of my work in the service, I made some good contacts. But I needed a break, so I found this place on the Web. Seemed ideal, and so far, it has been."

Seymore was leaning on the bar, looking across the lagoon. Everyone was gone, but Seymore was staring as if someone was still there. Someone with features so delicately and perfectly proportioned that she was beautiful when totally drenched, devoid of all makeup, her hair showing touches of its radiant color despite the fact that it was heavy with sea water.

Despite himself, he felt a rise of something he didn't like. Anger. Jealousy. And an age-old instinct to protect what was his. Except that she wasn't his anymore.

He had no rights here, and when he had first seen Alex this morning, after the initial shock in her eyes had died away, they had been narrowed and hostile each time they had fallen on him.

He lowered his head for a moment. You were the one who filed the papers, sweetie. Not a word to me, just a legal document.

I didn't come here because of you, he thought.

Okay, that was a lie. There had been no way he wouldn't show once Alicia's message had whetted his curiosity. He had come expecting to find Alicia Farr, even though, after he had returned her call and not heard back, warning signals had sounded in his mind. He wasn't surprised that she wasn't here, but he was worried.

And now he was feeling that age-old protective-instinct thing coming to the fore with Alex again—whether he did or didn't have the right to feel it. He told himself it was only because he was already on edge over Alicia. And anyway, maybe nothing was going on here. Maybe Alicia had made other arrangements and gone off on her own.

Or maybe someone was dead because of something going on here.

Unease filled him again.

Whatever had happened between Alex and him, the good and the bad, he couldn't help the tension he was feeling now. Especially where his wife was concerned. Ex-wife, he reminded himself. He wondered if he would ever accept that. Wondered if he would ever look at her and not believe they were still one.

Ever fall out of love with her.

Impatience ripped through him. He hated fools who went through life pining after someone who didn't want them in return. He hadn't pined. His life hadn't allowed for it.

That didn't mean that she didn't haunt his days, or that he didn't lie awake at night wondering why. Or that he didn't see her and feel that he would go after any guy who got near her. Or that he didn't see her, watch her move, see her enigmatic blue-green eyes, and want to demand to know what could have been so wrong that she had pushed him away.

All that was beside the point now. Yes, he had come here to meet Alicia. But he had come to meet Alicia because of Alex.

And now he was going to find out what was going on. Alex, of course, would believe that he was here only to find Alicia, to share in whatever find she had made. In her mind, he would be after the treasure, whatever that might be. Wanting the adventure, the leap into the unknown. No, she would never believe his main reason for being here was her, to watch over her, not when the danger wasn't solid, visible….

"Well," David murmured, swallowing a long draft of beer before continuing. "So you had a bad breakup, huh? They say you've got to be careful after a bad divorce. You know, watch out for rushing into things."

"Yeah, well," John told him, a half grin curving his lips, "they also say you've got to get right back on the horse after you fall off. Besides, I've been divorced about a year. You?"

"The same. About a year."

John Seymore studied him, that wry, half smile still in place. "I admit it. That's half the reason I wanted to buy you a drink. I know you were married to our dolphin instructor. Her name and picture were in one of the articles I read. I guess I wanted to make sure I wasn't horning in on a family reunion."

David could feel his jaw clenching. Screw Seymore. Being decent. Man, he hated that. He leaned on the counter, as well, staring out across the lagoon. "We split up a year ago," he said simply. "Alex is her own person."

What the hell else could he say? It was the truth. He could only hope his bitterness wasn't evident. Yet, even as the words were out of his mouth, he felt uneasy. He was, admittedly, distrustful of everyone right now, but this guy was suspicious of him, too. Here was an ex–navy SEAL, a man who knew more about diving than almost anyone else out there, at a resort where the facilities were great for tourists, but…a man with his experience?

A thought struck him, and he smiled. He was an honest man, but maybe this wasn't the time for the truth.

"Well," he said, "as far as she knows, she is, anyway."

"What does that mean?" Seymore asked him.

David waved a hand dismissively. "That's one of the reasons I'm here. There's a little technicality with our divorce. I wanted to let her know, find a convenient time for us to get together with an attorney, straighten it all out. But, hey…" He clapped a hand on Seymore's shoulder. "It's fine. Really. I think I'll go take a long hot shower. I'm beginning to feel a little salt encrusted. Thanks for the beer."

Seymore nodded, looking a little troubled. "Yeah, I…I guess I'll go hit the shower, too."

"My treat next go-around," David said. Then he set down his glass, turned, and left the Tiki Hut.

* * *

It was definitely a body. Alex and Laurie could both clearly see that, despite the seaweed clinging to it.

Alex started to rush forward, but Laurie grabbed her arm. "Wait! If she's dead, and you touch her, we could destroy forensic evidence."

"You've been watching too much TV," Alex threw over her shoulder as she pulled free.

But she came to a halt a few feet from the body. The stench was almost overwhelming. It was a woman, but she couldn't possibly be alive. Alex could see a trail of long blond hair tangled around the face.

She had to be sure.

Turning, taking a deep breath and holding it, Alex stepped forward and hunched down by the woman. She extended a hand to the throat, seeking a pulse. A crab crawled out of the mound of seaweed and hair, causing her to cry out.

"What?" Laurie shouted.

"Crab," Alex replied quickly. Bile rumbled in her stomach, raced toward her throat. She gritted her teeth, swallowed hard and felt the icy coldness of the woman's flesh. No pulse. The woman was dead. Alex rose, hurrying back to Laurie.

"She's dead. I'll stay here, you go for help."

"I'm not leaving you here alone with a corpse."

"Okay, you stay, I'll go."

"You're not leaving me here alone with a corpse!"

"Laurie—"

"She's dead. She's not going anywhere. We'll both go for help."

"Yes, but what if someone…what if a child comes out here while we're gone?"

"What?" Laurie demanded. "You think I'm going to throw myself on top of a corpse to hide it? There's nothing we can do except hurry."

"I'm not afraid to be alone with a corpse."

"You should be. What if the person who turned her into a corpse is still around here somewhere?"

Alex felt an uneasy sensation, but it was ridiculous. She shook her head. "Laurie, she's drifted in from… from somewhere else. She's been in the water awhile."

"Maybe. Neither one of us is an expert."

"Laurie, that…stink takes a while to occur."

"Let's just hurry. We won't be long, and she won't go anywhere."

"All right, then, let's go."

They tore back along the path they had taken and minutes later, neared the Tiki Hut. Laurie opened her mouth, ready to shout.

Alex clamped her hand over it. "No!"

Laurie fought free. "Alex! Did you touch that corpse with that hand? Maybe she died of some disease."

Alex had to admit she hadn't thought of such a possibility. She winced, but said, "We can't just start shouting about a corpse. We'll cause a panic."

She scanned the Tiki Hut. The mothers who had been on the swim earlier were there—the teens were evidently off somewhere else. She would have liked to see John Seymore. Since he was an ex–navy SEAL, he would surely know how to handle the situation.

She would even have liked to see David, Mr. Competence himself. Cool, collected, a well of strength in handling any given situation.

"Let's find Jay," she said.

She caught Laurie by the elbow, leading her past the

Tiki Hut and along the flower-bordered stone pathway that led to the lobby of the lodge. They burst in, rushing to the desk. Luckily, no one was checking in or out. Len Creighton was on duty. Thirtyish, slim, pleasant, he smiled as he saw them, and then he saw their panic and his smile faded.

"Len, I need Jay. Where is he?"

Len cast a glance over his shoulder, indicating the inner office.

She headed straight back.

Jay wasn't there.

"He's not here," she called.

"I'll page him."

His voice was smooth as silk, hardly creating a blip against the soft music that always played in the lobby.

Moments later, Jay Galway, looking only slightly irritated, came striding across the lobby.

He was tall and lean, with sleek, dark hair, expressive gray eyes and a thin, aesthetic face. Patrician nose. His lips were a bit narrow, but they added to the look almost of royalty that he carried like an aura about him. She really liked her boss. They were friends, and he had always been ready to support her in her decisions, even if he didn't agree with them. She'd known him before she'd come to work here. In fact, he'd called her about the job when he'd heard about the divorce.

He paused in front of the counter, perfect in an Armani suit, and stared at her questioningly.

"What on earth is this all about?" he demanded.

He was still a short distance away from her, and a few guests had just come in and were heading in their direction.

"I need to talk to you. Alone." She glanced meaningfully at Len.

"I hide nothing from Len."

Alex glanced at Len and wondered if there was more going on between the two men than she knew. Not that she cared, or had time to worry about it now.

"There's a body on the beach," she said very softly.

"A body," echoed Laurie, who was standing behind her.

He stared at her as if she had lost her mind. "This is Florida, honey. There are a lot of bodies on the beach."

Alex groaned inwardly. "A dead body, Jay."

"A dead body?" Len exclaimed loudly.

They all stared at him. "Sorry," he said quickly.

Jay gave his full attention to her at last, staring at her hard, his eyes narrowing. His focus never left her face, but he warned Len, "Shut up. I mean it. That reporter is around somewhere. All we need is him getting his nose into this."

Alex stared back at him, aghast. "Someone is dead, Jay. It's not a matter of worrying about publicity. Will you call the sheriff's office—please?"

"Right. Len, call the county boys and ask them to send someone out. Someone from homicide."

"Homicide?" Laurie murmured. "Maybe she just… drowned."

"It still needs to be investigated," Alex said, still staring at Jay. His behavior puzzled her. They had no idea who the dead woman might be, where she had come from, or even if there was a murderer loose in paradise, and he seemed so blasé.

Finally he said, "Show me."

"Let's go."

Len started to follow, but Jay spun on him. "You're on duty. And you," Jay warned Alex, "make it look as if we're taking a casual stroll."

"Jay, honestly, sometimes—"

"Alex, want to cause a panic?" Jay demanded.

"Sure. Fine. We're taking a casual stroll."

They left the lobby, Alex leading, Jay behind her, Laurie following quickly. They took the path through the flowers, passed the Tiki Hut—which seemed unusually quiet for the time of day—and around the lagoon area.

"Alex, slow down. We're taking a stroll, remember?" Jay said.

She looked back, still moving quickly. "Jay, we're in shorts and you're in an Armani suit, about to get sand in your polished black shoes. How casually can we stroll?"

He let out a sound of irritation but argued the point no further.

They reached the pristine sand beach. The temperature was dropping, the sweet breeze still blowing in.

Alex came to a halt. Jay nearly crashed into her back. As if they were a vaudeville act, Laurie collided with him.

"What the hell?" Jay demanded.

"It's gone," Alex breathed.

"What's gone?" Jay demanded.

"The body."

Laurie was staring toward the thatch of seaweed where the corpse had lain. She, too, seemed incredulous. "It—it is gone," she murmured.

Without turning, Alex could feel the way that Jay was looking at her. Like an icy blast against the balmy summer breeze, she could feel his eyes boring into her back.

She didn't turn but ran down the length of the beach, searching the sand and the water, looking for any hint as to where the body had been moved.

"What, Alex?" Jay shouted. "You saw a corpse, but it rolled down the beach to catch the sun better?"

She stopped then, whirling around.

"It's moved," she said, walking back to where Jay stood.

"Your corpse got up and walked?"

She exhaled impatiently. "Jay, it was here."

"Really, Jay, it was," Laurie said, coming to her defense.

They all turned at the sound of a motor. A sheriff's department launch was heading their way. Nigel Thompson, the sheriff himself, had come.

Usually Alex liked Nigel Thompson. He looked just the way she figured an old-time Southern sheriff should look. He was somewhere between fifty and sixty years old; his eyes were pale blue, his hair snow-white. He was tall and heavy, a big man. His appearance was customarily reassuring.

He tended to be a skeptic.

A skeptic when rowdy, underage kids told their stories. A skeptic when adults who should have known better lied about the amount they had been drinking before a boating accident. He was never impolite, never skirted the law, but he was tough, and folks around here knew it.

He cut the motor but drew his launch right up to the beach. Hopping from the craft, he demanded, "Where's this body?"

Jay looked from Nigel to Alex.

"Well?" he asked her.

She lifted her chin, grinding down hard on her teeth. She looked at Nigel. "It was right here," she said pointing.

He looked from the sand and seaweed to her. "It was there?"

"I swear to you, it was right there."

He looked at Alex, slowly arching an eyebrow. "Alexandra, I was just about to sit down to dinner when the call came in. Tell me this isn't a joke or a summer prank."

"Had to have been a prank—and Alex fell for it," Jay said. He didn't sound angry with her, but he did sound aggravated.

"I'm here now," Nigel said, looking at Alex. "So tell me what you saw."

"A sunbather who thought it was one hell of a joke to fool someone into thinking she was dead," Jay said.

"She was dead," Alex said. "Nigel, you've known me for years. Do I make things up?"

"No, missy, you don't," the sheriff acknowledged. "But there is no body," he pointed out.

"It was here, right here. I got close enough to make sure she was…I touched her. She was dead," Alex asserted with quiet vehemence.

"She sure looked dead," Laurie offered.

Alex winced inwardly, aware her friend was trying to help. But her words gave the entire situation an aura of doubt.

"She was dead," Alex repeated.

"Cause of death?" Nigel asked her.

"I didn't do an autopsy," she snapped, and then was furious with herself.

"There was nothing that suggested a cause of death?" Nigel asked patiently.

She shook her head. "If she had washed up with a rope around her neck, I didn't see it. I'm sorry, I've dealt with dead dolphins, but I never interned at the morgue," Alex told him. "But I know a corpse when I see one."

"So you've seen lots of corpses?" Jay asked.

"I've seen enough dead mammals, Jay." She looked at Nigel. "I swear to you that there was a dead woman here, tangled in seaweed."

He sighed, looking at the sand and the water, then back to her. "No drag marks, Alex. She wasn't pulled into the bushes."

"She was here," Alex insisted stubbornly.

"Alex, I'm not saying this is what happened, but isn't it possible that someone was pulling a prank?"

"No," she said determinedly.

"So…what did happen? Why isn't she here?"

"I don't know. I thought she was far enough out of the water, so I don't think the waves could have pulled her back out… I think someone came and moved her."

"They were quick," Nigel commented.

"I'm telling you, she was here. Isn't there a way you can check? It will be dark soon. Can't you spray something around, see if there are specks of blood in the seaweed or on the sand anywhere? Better yet, take samples. Get more men out here and make certain that the only tracks around came from Jay, Laurie and myself?"

"There could be dozens of tracks around, and it wouldn't mean anything. The beach is accessible to all the staff and every guest," Nigel told her.

"Surely there's something you can do," Alex said.

"I can see if a body turns up again," he told her quietly. "Seriously, Alex. The most likely scenario is that the woman wasn't dead. Maybe she was unconscious but came to while you were up at the lodge. One of you should have stayed here."

Alex glared at Laurie.

Laurie looked back at her defensively. "Hey, how could I know that a corpse could get up and walk away?"

"A corpse can't get up and walk away," Jay interjected impatiently. "Unless the person you saw was not a corpse."

"We're going in circles here," Alex told him.

"This is ridiculous," he told her. "You pull me out here, make me ruin my good Italian shoes, drag Nigel away from his supper...because you saw someone passed out. Maybe someone in need of help, who you left. Or, more likely, someone playing a joke. A sick joke, yes. But a joke, and you fell for it."

Alex lifted her hands in exasperation. "All right, fine. There's nothing I can say or do to make you believe me. Nigel, I'm sorry about your supper. I owe you one. I'm going to take a shower."

"Wait a minute," Nigel said. "I'm not ignoring this. I'll make a check on passengers who took the ferry over today, and, Jay, you check your guest lists. We'll make sure that everyone is accounted for."

Alex stood in stony silence.

"Alex, that's all I can do since there's no body," Nigel said patiently. "We're not New York, D.C., or even Miami. I don't have a huge forensic department or the manpower to start combing every strand of seaweed, especially since the tide is coming in. Alex, please. I'm not mocking you. It's just that there is no body." He turned to Jay. "Get busy on the paperwork, Jay. I'll handle the ferry records. And, Alex…don't mention this around, all right?"

She frowned curiously at him. "But—"

"Don't you dare go alarming the guests with a wild story," Jay said.

"Actually, I was thinking that if there was a corpse and someone's hidden it, it might be a very dangerous topic of conversation," Nigel told her.

"He's right," Jay said. He pointed a finger toward Alex. "No mention of this. No mention of it for your own safety."

"Oh, yeah, right."

Nigel turned around, looking at the beach. He shook his head and started away.

"Where you going, Nigel?" Jay asked.

"To check on the ferry records," Nigel called back.

He reached his launch, gave it a shove back to the water and waded around to hop in, then gave them a wave.

Jay stared at Alex and Laurie again. "Not a word, you understand? Not a word. It doesn't matter if there were a dozen corpses on the beach, Alex, they're not here now. So keep quiet."

"Fine. Not a word, Jay," Alex snapped, walking past him.

"Hey! I'm your boss, remember?" he told her.

She kept walking, Laurie following in her tracks.

"I'm still your boss," he called after her. "And you owe me a new pair of shoes."

They were soon out of earshot. "Alex, there really was

a corpse, wasn't there?" Laurie asked. But she sounded uncertain.

"Yes."

"Perhaps…I mean…couldn't you have been mistaken?"

"No." She turned. "I'm going to go take a hot shower and a couple of aspirin. I'll see you later."

Laurie nodded, still looking uncertain. "I'm sorry. Jay has a way of twisting things," Laurie said apologetically.

"I know. Forget it. I'll see you later."

She lifted a hand and turned down a slender trail that led through small palms and hibiscus, anxious only to reach her little cottage.

She slid her plastic key from the button pocket of her uniform shorts and inserted it into the lock. The door swung open.

The air was on; the ceiling fan in the whitewashed and rattan-furnished living-room area was whirling away. The coolness struck her pleasantly.

She walked through the living area and into the small kitchen, pausing to pull a wine cooler from the refrigerator. She uncapped it quickly and moved on, anxious to flop down on the sofa out on the porch. She opened the floor-to-ceiling glass doors and went out, actually glad of the wave of warmth outside, tempered by the feel of the night breeze and the hypnotic whirl of another ceiling fan.

But even as she fell into a chair, she tensed, sitting straight up and staring across to the charming white gingerbread railing, too startled by a figure looming in the shadows of coming twilight to scream. Then she took a deep breath of relief when she recognized who it was.

It wasn't just anyone planted on her porch.

It was David.

He was wearing nothing but swim trunks, broad, bronzed shoulders gleaming, arms crossed over his chest as he leaned against the rail. He was very still, and yet, as it had always been with him, it seemed that he emanated energy, as if any moment he would move like a streak of lightning.

Her heart lurched. He was so familiar. How many times had she seen him like this and walked up to him, wherever they were, sliding her fingers down his naked back, sometimes feeling the heat of the sun and sometimes just that of the man? She had loved the way he had turned to her in response and taken her into the curl of his arm.

How many times had it led to so much more? There had been those days when, just in from the water, he had been speaking to a TV camera, holding her as he talked, then had suddenly turned to her, and she had seen a sudden light rise in his eyes. She could remember the way he would move, his attention only for her, as he excused himself, smiled and led her away. By the time they reached a private spot, they would both be breathless, laughing and pulling at the few pieces of clothing they were wearing. He could move with such languid, sinewy power; the tone of his voice could change so easily; the lightest brush of his fingers could evoke a thousand rays of pure sensuality. And she had been so desperately, insanely eager to know them all.

But then, that had been in the days when it had mattered to him that she was with him.

He didn't smile now. His deep blue eyes were grave as he surveyed her. She'd seen him cold and distant like this, as well, the light in his eyes almost predatory.

"David," she said dryly, pushing away the past, forcing herself to forget the intimacy and remember only what it had been like once she had determined to pursue her own career and he had begun to travel without her. Days, weeks, even a month...gone. Not even a telephone call, once he was with his true love. The sea.

And those who traveled it with him.

"Alex," he responded. "I've been waiting for you."

"So it appears. Well, how nice to see you. Here. On my porch. My personal porch, my private space. Gee, this is great." Her tone couldn't have held more acidity.

"Thanks." Her welcome hadn't been sincere. Neither was his gratitude. But there was no mistaking the seriousness of his next words.

"So," he said, "tell me about the body you found—the one that disappeared from the beach."

Chapter 3

"*What?*" she said sharply.

"You heard me. Tell me about the body." He uncoiled from his position, coming toward her, taking a chair near hers. He was close, too close, and she instantly felt wary and, despite herself, unnerved. They'd been apart for a year, and she still felt far too familiar with the rugged planes of his face, the bronzed contours of his hands and fingers, idly folded now before him.

She managed to sit back, eyeing him with dignity and, she hoped, a certain disdain.

"What the hell are you doing on my porch? There's a lobby for guests."

"Get off it. You must have been in a panic. And Jay probably behaved like an asshole."

"I don't know what you're talking about."

"I'm trying to help you out."

"If you want to help me out, get off the island."

"Am I making you uneasy?"

"You bet," she told him flatly.

That drew a smile to his lips. "Missed me, huh?"

She sat farther forward, setting her wine cooler on the rattan coffee table, preparing to rise.

"I assume you have a room. Why don't you go put some clothes on."

"Ah, that's it. Can't take the sight of my naked chest. It's making you hot, huh?"

"More like leaving me cold," she said icily. "Now go away, please."

His smile faded for a moment. "Don't worry. I know you want me to leave. I haven't forgotten that you had the divorce papers sent to me without a word."

"What was left to say?" she asked with what she hoped was quiet dignity.

"Hmm, let me think. Maybe your reasons for leaving me?"

She got to her feet. "You want the truth? I couldn't take it. I was so in love with you, it hurt all the time. You were all that mattered to me. My dolphins were far too tame for you—and far too unimportant. Our agreement that we'd spend time dedicated to my pursuits didn't mean a thing—not if a sunken ship turned up or a shark-research expedition was formed. Then it came to the point when I said you were welcome to go off even when you were supposed to be helping me—and you went. And then that became a way of life. There's the story in a nutshell. You were gone long before I sent those papers. And sometime in there, I got over you. I love working with dolphins. No, it isn't like finding a Spanish galleon, or even locating a yacht that went down ten years ago, maybe. But I love it. What you apparently needed, or wanted, was a different kind of wife. Either a pretty airhead who would follow you endlessly, or…someone as fanatic about treasure as you are. So go to your room and put some clothes on, or take a stroll over to the Tiki Hut and give someone else a thrill."

She started inside, hoping he would stop her. Not because she wanted to be near him, but because he knew about the body.

Her back to him, she suddenly wondered how he knew. The question left her with a very uneasy feeling.

"Alexandra, whatever anger you're feeling toward me, whatever I did or didn't do, I swear, I'm just trying to help you now."

She spun around. "How do you know about the body, anyway? Jay gave me very direct orders not to mention it to anyone."

He cocked his head slightly. "Jay's assistant talks."

"What did you do? Flirt with Len, too?"

He arched an eyebrow, curiously, slowly. She wished she could take back the comment. It made it appear as if…as if jealousy had been the driving factor in her quest for freedom. And it hadn't been.

Thankfully, David didn't follow up on her comment. "I don't think Len could contain himself. He tried to be smooth and cool, but I guess he feels he knows me and that I'm intelligent enough not to repeat what he said. He told me you'd all gone off in search of a body, and then it turned out to be gone. I overheard Jay tell him that part."

She stood very still, watching him for a long moment. "You know, I came back here to be alone."

"So talk to me, then I'll leave you alone."

"You know, this is very strange. Most people would

scoff at the idea immediately. Bodies don't turn up on a daily basis. And yet…it sounds as if you think that there…should have been a body."

"No," he corrected. "I didn't say I thought there should be a body."

Alex pressed her fingers to her temples. "I can't do this," she said.

She was startled when he suddenly moved close to her. "Alex, please. If there was a body, and you saw it—you could be in danger."

She sighed. "Not if no one knows about the body."

"But I know, so others could, as well."

"You said Len only told you about it because he trusts you."

"Others might have overheard."

"Just what do you want?"

He was no more than an inch from her. He still carried the scent of salt and the sea, and it was a compelling mixture. She looked away.

"I don't want anything. I'm deeply concerned. Alex, don't you understand? You could be in danger!" His hands fell on her shoulders then. It was suddenly like old times. "You have to listen to me."

She'd heard the words before. Felt his hands before. Memories of being crushed against that chest stirred within her. She didn't want to believe that she had once been so in love with him just because he was so distinctively male and sensual. There had been times when they were together when his smile had been so quick, and then so lazy, when just a finger trailing across her bare arm or shoulder had…

"David, let go of me," she said, stepping back.

His eyes were narrowed, hard. She'd seen them that

way before, when he was intent on getting to the bottom of something.

"Talk to me, Alex."

"All right. Yes, Jay acted like an asshole. Yes, I'm convinced I saw a body. A woman. A blonde. Other than that…I couldn't see her face. The angle of her body was wrong, and she was tangled in seaweed. When we went back, she was gone. Even Laurie, who saw the body first, wasn't sure we'd seen it anymore. She didn't actually go near the body even when it was there. Anyway, there was no corpse. So, are you happy?"

He didn't look happy. Actually, for a moment, he appeared ashen. She wanted to touch his face, but he was still David. Solid as rock.

"Please, will you leave me alone?" she asked him.

His voice was strange, scratchy, when he spoke. "I can't leave you alone. Not now," he said. And yet, contrary to his words, he turned and left her porch, disappearing along the back trail that led, in a roundabout way, to the other cottages and the lodge.

She stared after him, suddenly feeling the overwhelming urge to burst into tears. "Damn it, I got over you," she grated out. "And here you are again, driving me crazy, making me doubt myself…and not doubt myself," she finished softly.

She realized suddenly that twilight was coming.

And that she was afraid.

David had almost made her forget. No matter what anyone said, she'd seen a body on the beach. That was shattering in itself, but then the body had disappeared.

She slipped back inside, locking the sliding-glass door behind her. Then she looked outside and saw the shadows of dusk stretching out across the landscape.

She drew the curtains, uneasily checked her front door, and at last—after opening and finishing a new wine cooler—she managed to convince herself to take a shower.

David sat at a table at the Tiki Hut, watching Alex. Not happily. He had been sitting with Jay Galway, who hadn't mentioned Alex's discovery, naturally. There might be a major exodus from the lodge if word got out that a mysterious body had been found, then disappeared, and Galway would never stand for that.

During their conversation, David had asked Jay casually about recent guests, and any news in the world of salvage or the sea, and Jay had been just as cool, shrugging, and saying that, with summer in full swing, most of their guests were tourists, eager to swim with the dolphins, or snorkel or dive on the Florida reef. Naturally—that was what they were set up to do.

David had showered, changed and made a few phone calls in the time since he'd left Alex. He'd still arrived before her.

If she'd seen him at the table, she'd given him no notice, heading straight for the table where John Seymore was sitting with Hank Adamson. They were chatting now, and he had the feeling that part of Alex's bubbling enthusiasm and the little intimate touches she was giving Seymore were strictly for his benefit, her message clear: Leave me the hell alone, hands off, I've moved on.

How far would it go?

All right, one way or the other, he would have been jealous, but now he was really concerned.

A woman's body had been found on the beach, and

he had not heard back from Alicia Farr—who was a blonde.

David couldn't stop the reel playing through his head.

From what he'd overheard, Jay was convinced a trick had been played, or that Alex had assumed a dozing sunbather was a corpse. David didn't see that as a possibility. Alex was far too intelligent, and she wouldn't have walked away without assuring herself that the body no longer maintained the least semblance of a vital sign.

A trick? Maybe.

Real corpses didn't get up and walk away, but they could be moved.

If there had been a real corpse and it had been moved, it had been moved by someone on the island. That meant Alex could be in serious danger. After all, Len had told David what was going on, so who knew who else he might have told?

An ex–navy SEAL, maybe? The perfect blond hero—but was that the truth behind John Seymore being at Moon Bay?

Hopefully he would find out soon enough.

"So?"

"I'm sorry, what did you say?" David said, realizing that Jay had been talking away, but he hadn't heard a word.

"Well? Is it a photojournalism thing or a salvage dive?"

"What…?"

"Your next excursion," Jay said.

"Oh…well, I was looking into something, but my source seems to have dried up," David told Jay. My key source either dried up, or was killed and washed up on your beach, and then disappeared, he thought. Then his attention was caught by Alex again.

The band was playing a rumba. She was up and in John Seymore's arms. Head cast back, she was laughing at whatever he had to say. Her eyes were like gems. She was beautifully decked out in heels and a soft yellow halter dress that emphasized both her tan and her tall, sinewy length. Her long hair was free and a true golden blond, almost surreal in the light of the torches that burned here by night.

The lights were actually bug repellents. There was no escaping the fact that when you had foliage like this, you had bugs. But the glow they gave everything, especially Alex, was almost hypnotic.

David turned to Jay. "Sure you haven't heard about anything?" he asked him.

"Me?" Galway laughed. "Hell, I'm a hanger-on. The big excitement in my life is when I get a taste of something because of the big-timers—like you."

"Well, I'm looking at the moment," David told him. "So, if you do get wind of anything, anything at all, I'd like to know."

"You'd be the first one I'd go to," Jay assured him solemnly.

"Interesting that you'd say so—with Seth Granger here and ready to pay." And in the Tiki Hut at that moment, David realized. Granger was a big man and in excellent shape for his sixty-odd years. He was speaking with Ally Conroy, mother of Zach, at the bar. She was at least twenty years his junior, but he'd gathered from their bits of conversation before the swim that she was a widow, worried about rearing her son alone. Seth wasn't all that well-liked by many people, yet Ally seemed to be giving him the admiration he craved. Maybe they were a perfect fit.

"Seth…well, you know. He's always looking for something to bug his way into. Hell, why not? He's rich, and he loves the sea, and he'd like to make a name for himself in his retirement years. Don't you love it? Tons of money, no real knowledge, yet he wants to be right in the thick of things. Executive turned explorer."

"Why not?" David said with a shrug. "Most expeditions need financial backing."

"Yeah, why not? It's what I'd love to do myself. I've got a great job here, mind you—but I sure wish I had his resources. Or your reputation. Every major corporation out there with a water-related product to sell is willing to finance you—even on a total wild-goose chase."

"You know me—game for anything that has to do with the water," David murmured absently.

Alex was leaning very close to John Seymore now. In a moment she'd be spilling out of her dress.

"Excuse me," he said to Jay, rising, then went up to the couple on the floor. Alex wouldn't be happy, but if John Seymore was really such an all-right kind of guy—or even pretending to be one—he would show him the courtesy of allowing him to cut in.

A tap on Seymore's shoulder assured him that he had correctly assessed the situation. The other man, his eyes full of confident good humor, stepped back.

Alex gave David a look of sheer venom. But she wasn't going to cause a scene in the Tiki Hut. She slipped into his arms.

"What are you doing?" she asked him.

"Dancing."

"You know I don't want to dance with you."

He ignored her and said, “I guess you haven’t had a chance to talk with Seymore yet.”

“John and I have done lots of talking.”

“Well, I happened to mention to him one of the reasons I’m here.”

“And it has something to do with me?”

“Definitely.”

She arched a delicate eyebrow. “I guess you’re going to tell me—whether I want to know or not.”

“We’re not divorced.”

“Don’t be ridiculous,” she said sharply. “I filed papers, you signed them.”

“I don’t quite get it myself, but apparently there was some little legal flaw. I must not have signed on all the dotted lines. The documents were never properly filed, and therefore the decision was declared null and void. I know what a busy woman you are, but I need to ask you when would be a good time to get together with my lawyer and rectify the situation.”

She wasn’t even pretending to dance anymore. She just stood on the floor, staring at him. His arms were still around her, tendrils of silky soft, newly washed blond hair slipping over his hands, teasing in their sensuality. He knew he needed to move away, but he didn’t.

“That’s impossible!” she exclaimed.

“Sorry.”

She stared at him, still amazed. “I don’t…I…can’t…”

“Look, Alex, I know how eager you are to be completely rid of me. I’m sorry. But as of this moment, we are still married.”

He wondered if lightning would come out of the sky to strike him dead.

It didn't.

God must have understood his situation.

"It's…it's impossible," she repeated.

He shrugged, as if in complete understanding of her dismay. "I'm sorry."

Something hardened in the depths of her ever-changing, sea-green eyes. "I'll make time to see your attorney."

"Great. We'll set it up. Well, lover boy is waiting, so I'll let you go in a sec. But first I need you to listen to me. Alex, I'm begging you, listen to me. You've got to be careful."

She pulled back, searching his eyes, then shaking her head. "David, I understand why you're here, and frankly, I'm surprised you took the time to actually ask what would be convenient for me. But I don't quite get this sudden interest. Where's Bebe whats-her-name? Or the thin-but-oh-so-stacked Alicia Farr, the Harvard scholar?"

Her question sent an eerie chill up his spine. *I think she's your disappearing body.*

"Alex, I'm afraid you're in danger." His words, he realized, sounded stiff and cold.

She shook her head. "No one else believes I discovered a corpse. Why should you?"

He hesitated for a minute. "I know you," he told her. "You're not a fool. You would have looked closely enough to know."

"Well, thanks for the compliment. I wish Nigel Thompson felt that way. I couldn't get through to him that though it's improbable that a body was really there and somehow moved, it's not impossible. So if you'll let me off the dance floor…?"

He released her. But as she started to step past him, he caught her arm. She looked up, and for a moment, her eyes were vulnerable. Her scent seemed to wrap around him, caress him.

"Don't trust anyone," he said.

"I certainly don't trust you."

He pulled her back around to face him. "You know what? I've about had it with this."

"Oh, you have, have you?"

"I got a long lecture. You can have one, too. You read a lot that just wasn't there into a number of situations. You never had the right not to trust me. It was just that, to you, the minute a phone or a radio didn't work, I had to be doing something. With someone. And you know what, Alex? That kind of thing gets really old, really quick."

"Sorry, but it's over anyway, isn't it? You received the divorce papers and said, 'Hey, go right ahead.' You were probably thankful you didn't have to deal with any annoying baggage anymore. And now you're suddenly going to be my champion, defending me from a danger that doesn't exist?"

"Alex, you know me. You know what kind of man I am. Hell, hate me 'til the sun falls from the sky, but trust me right now."

"There are dozens of people here. I don't think I'm in any danger in the middle of the Tiki Hut. And trust you?" She sounded angry, then a slow smile curved her lips.

"What?"

"I just find it rather amusing that you're suddenly so determined to enjoy my company. There were so many times when…well, never mind."

He stared at her blankly for a moment. "What are you talking about?"

"It doesn't matter anymore. It's over."

"Actually, it's not," he said. Again he waited for lightning to strike. Not that it should. He was doing this out of a very real fear for her life.

She waved a hand in the air. "All over but the shouting," she murmured.

"Maybe that's what we were lacking—the shouting."

"Great. We should have had a few more fights?"

It was strange, he thought, but this was almost a conversation, a real one.

And then John Seymore chose that exact moment to return, tapping him on the shoulder. "Since you're on the dance floor and not actually dancing…?"

"And it's a salsa," Alex put in.

"Salsa?" John murmured. "I'm not sure I know what I'm doing, but—"

"I do," David said quickly, grinning, and catching Alex in his arms once again. "I'll bring her back for the next number."

"Since when do you salsa?" Alex demanded as they began to move.

"Since a friend married a dance instructor," he told her.

She seemed startled, but he really did know what he was doing. He'd never imagined the dance instruction he'd so recently received from a friend's wife would pay off so quickly. Alex was good, too. She'd probably honed her skills working here, being pleasant to the guests in the Tiki Hut at night.

After a minute, though, he wasn't quite sure what he had gained. They looked good together on the floor, and he knew it. But the music was fast, so conversation was impossible. At the end of the song he managed to lead her into a perfect dip, so at least he was rewarded by the amazement in her eyes as they met his.

In fact, she stayed in his arms for several extra seconds, staring up at him before realizing that the music had ended and the gathering in the Tiki Hut was applauding them.

He grinned slowly as she straightened, then pushed against his chest. "The dance is over," she said firmly, then walked quickly away.

"You really are a man of many talents."

Turning, he saw Alex's assistant, the pretty young blonde. She was leaning against the edge of the rustic wood bar.

"Thanks."

"Do you cha-cha?" she asked, smiling.

"Yes, I do," he said.

"Well, will you ask me? Or are you making me ask you?"

"Laurie, I would love to dance with you," he said gallantly.

As they moved, she asked him frankly, "Why on earth did you two ever split up?"

"Actually, I don't really know," he told her.

"I bet I do," she told him. "You must be pretty high maintenance."

"High maintenance? I'm great at taking care of myself. I may not be a gourmet, but I can cook. I know every button on a washing machine. I usually even remember to put down the toilet seat."

She laughed. "Well, there you go."

"Excuse me? How is that high maintenance?"

"You don't need anybody," she said. "So it's high maintenance for someone to figure out what they can do for you."

She wasn't making any sense, but she was sincere, and she made him smile.

Then the music came to an end, and he regretted that he had been so determined on proving his mettle with Alex, because he found himself being asked to dance by almost every woman in the Tiki Hut.

And somewhere, in the middle of a mambo, he realized that Alex had slipped away—and so had John Seymore.

Somehow, just when things had begun looking a little brighter, David had walked back into her life, and now he was ruining everything.

John's arm sat casually around her shoulders as they strolled toward her cottage. "Hate to admit it," he said casually, "but you two looked great out there. Did you spend a lot of time out dancing while you were married?"

"No. We didn't spend much time together doing anything—other than diving for treasure or facing great whites or experiencing some other thrill."

"Strange," he said.

"What?"

"The way you sound. You love the sea so much, too."

"Actually? I'm not into sharks. I was terrified every time I went into the water with them, but with the crew of hard-core fanatics that always seemed to be around, I didn't want to look like a coward. I love the sea, yes. But I'm into warm-blooded, friendly creatures, myself."

"You really love your dolphins, huh?"

She shrugged, liking the way his arm felt around her, but feeling a sense of discomfort, as well.

David. Telling her that they were still married. But they weren't; they hadn't been for a year. Not in any way that mattered. All he was talking about was legality. His words shouldn't mean a thing.

Except that…

She was traditional. She'd been raised Catholic.

Damn David. He would know her thought process, that she would feel that she shouldn't be with another man, that it wouldn't be right, and…

Just how many women had he been with in the last year? What was wrong with her that she couldn't see how ridiculous it was for her to be concerned over anything he had to say? Why had seeing him again made her uncertain, when she knew that an easy confidence and charm were just a part of his nature?

"I do love my dolphins," she said, realizing she had been silent for too long after his question. "They are the most incredible animals. What I like most is that they seem to study us just as we study them, and just as we learn their behavior, they learn what our behavior is going to be. Sometimes their affinity for man, especially in the wild, can be dangerous for them, but still, the communication we can share is just amazing."

"They are incredible," he agreed. "I've seen them used in the navy in the most remarkable ways. Never worked with them myself," he added quickly. "But I've seen what they can do."

They had reached her porch. Strange, her thoughts had been filled with David's behavior—she wished she could begin to understand the male of her own species half as well as she understood her dolphins—and then with John's company, which, she had to admit, she had found all the more intoxicating just because she knew that it disturbed David.

Now, despite the light burning on her back porch, it seemed that the shadows of night were all around her, and she remembered the body on the beach. It wasn't that she had ever forgotten, but despite her determination, the doubts of others had crept into her mind.

Was she insane, thinking the woman had been dead?

Or was she more insane now, trying to do what Jay had demanded, keep silent about the possibility of a body on the beach?

John had escorted her up the two wooden steps to her little back porch, with its charming, gingerbread railing. They were standing by her back door.

He was probably waiting to be invited in.

And just this morning, she had thought that if this moment came, she would invite him in.

She mentally damned her ex-husband again. Her almost-ex-husband.

She smiled up at John Seymore. His dimple was showing as he offered her a rueful smile.

"You're really something," he said.

"So are you," she murmured. Blond hair, handsome face, shoulders to die for, arms that were wonderfully secure…

She slipped into them. He lowered his mouth to hers, and she allowed herself the kiss, but she couldn't stop herself from analyzing it. Firm mouth, coercive, not demanding, fingers gently suggestive in her hair, tongue teasing at her lips, slipping into her mouth, warm, very warm, definitely seductive…

On a physical level, he was incredible.

So if she could just forget about David…

She couldn't. Not when he was here, on the island, so irritatingly in-her-face.

She stepped back, stroking John's cheek.

"You're around for a little while longer, right?" she inquired softly, hoping he understood her signals. I'm interested, but it's been a very long and strange day….

"I can arrange to be around for a very, very long time," he told her. Then he grinned. "I'd like to come in. But I understand perfectly. Okay, well, not perfectly, and I am disappointed, wishing I could be sleeping with you tonight."

She felt a flush touch her cheeks. "I didn't mean to… lead you on, to suggest…"

"You didn't. You're just the most fascinating woman I've met in aeons, and…hell, good night. I'll be around."

"I—well, I know you've been talking to David. We are divorced. There's just some ridiculous technicality."

"I'm not worried about a technicality," he told her.

"Neither am I."

"But I will step back if the technicality isn't just on paper, if it's something a lot deeper."

His words made her like him all the more. He wasn't about to step into the middle of a triangle, or be second-string to any other man.

"It's only a technicality—really." She meant to sound sincere. She wasn't sure if she really was or not. And she wasn't sure what he heard in her denial.

"Well…" he murmured.

He drew her to him, kissed her forehead. Then he walked down the steps, and started back along the foliage-bordered path.

She watched him disappear, realized she hadn't opened her door, and felt the pressure of the night and the shadows again. She quickly slid her key into the bolt for the glass doors, then stepped inside, feeling a rise of anger. She had never felt afraid here before, ever.

And now…

Though the image had faded for a moment due to skepticism and doubt, she could now vividly recall the corpse on the beach. A corpse that had disappeared.

She locked the door, making certain it was secure; then, still feeling an almost panicky unease, she walked through the little Florida room, kitchen and living room, assuring herself that windows were tightly closed and the front door was locked.

Damn David a million times over for both the trials haunting her tonight. If it hadn't been for him, John Seymore would be inside with her. Then she wouldn't be afraid of the shadows, or the memories stirring in her mind.

She slipped through the hallway to the first of the two bedrooms in the cottage, the one she used for an office area. She checked the window there and even opened the closet door.

David's suggestion that she might be in danger seemed to be invading her every nerve. But the office was empty and secure.

Finally she went to her own room, found it safe, then prepared for bed and slipped under the covers. The night-light she kept on in the bathroom had always provided her with more than enough illumination, but tonight it only added to the shadows.

Usually the sound of the waves and the sea breeze rustling through the trees was soothing, but tonight…

She lay there for several seconds. Waves…breeze… palms. Foliage that seemed to whisper softly in the night, usually so pleasant…

A sudden thumping sound startled her so badly that she nearly screamed aloud. She did jump out of bed.

She'd heard a thump, as if something heavy had just landed on her roof.

She stood dead still, waiting. And waiting….

Nothing, no sound at all. Had she been deceived? The sound might have come from elsewhere….

Or might not have come at all.

She almost let out a loud sigh of pure frustration, but swallowed it back, and slowly, silently, tiptoed from her bedroom.

Into the hall…through to the kitchen. From there she could see both the living room and the little Florida room and the glass doors that led out back. The curtain was partially open. Had she left it that way?

The noise had come from the roof. There was a fireplace in the living area of each of the cottages. Despite the fact that this was sunny Florida, in the winter, during the few days that dipped into the forties or even the thirties, a fire was incredibly nice. But the chimney was far too small for a man to slip through.

So she was safe. There was nothing.

She was letting the simple sounds of nature slip into her psyche and scare her because she was still so unnerved by the happenings of the day.

A coconut had probably fallen off a palm. Still, just to be sure…

She walked to the back, trying to stay behind the curtain, then peeked out the glass. She pulled the drape back just a little more….

And screamed.

Chapter 4

Everyone was gone, Laurie thought. First Alex and John, then David. There were people around, but the Tiki Hut seemed empty. The band had reverted to calypso, very pleasant but also, in her current state of mind, sleep inducing.

Alex was crazy. She'd been married to David Denham and divorced him.

Alex had never been to Date Tournament. Had she realized what was out there, she would undoubtedly still be married.

Maybe Alex thought that nights spent at a place like Date Tournament were simply not in her future. Then again, maybe she would never have such a night—because there was something about Alex that attracted men.

Laurie wished she had that innate…thing, whatever it was. Maybe it would come with age, but Alex was only three years her senior. Well, maybe things weren't as perfect as they seemed for Alex, either.

"You're up late, aren't you?"

She started. It was Hank Adamson. She hadn't seen him before, but the Tiki Hut had been hopping, earlier, so he could have been lost in the crowd.

She saw Jay Galway on the other side of the bar, conversing with Seth Granger and a few of the other guests. He was staring at her—glaring, really—and giving her a big smile. Sign language, Jay Galway style. She was supposed to be as nice as possible, suck up big-time.

She gave an imperceptible nod to Jay and smiled as instructed at Hank. He slid out the chair opposite her and sat. "Okay if I join you and ask a few questions?"

"Sure."

In his lanky way, he was actually very attractive, she realized.

He grinned. "You look so wary."

"Do I? Well, we all know that the pen is very powerful."

"Update to computer," he said dryly.

"Okay, the written word—no matter how it's written."

"Honestly, you don't have to be so cautious. I didn't come to do a simple review. I'm going to do a whole piece on the place."

"A good piece—or a bad piece?"

"Good, bad…truthful."

"We're a good place," she said.

His grin deepened. "Actually, yes, Moon Bay does seem to follow through on every promise it makes. That's what's important. A little mom-and-pop establishment can get a great write-up, as long as it delivers on what it offers."

"Um, we're not exactly mom-and-pop," Laurie murmured.

"No, but so far, I've gotten a good bang for my buck, and that's what matters."

Laurie smiled. "That's great. I love Moon Bay. It's not just that I work here—I really love it. It's a wonderful place for a vacation."

"With the happiness and well-being of the guests foremost in everyone's mind at all times?"

"Yes, of course…" Laurie murmured, looking down at her hands suddenly. Was that true? What if that hadn't been a prank on the beach today? If Alex had been right, and a woman had been dead—and what if the killer had come back, aware that the body had washed up, and moved it?

"What is it?" She suddenly knew why Hank Adamson was considered so good. He asked casual questions; people gave casual answers. So casual you didn't realize that your mind was wandering off and that you were about to betray your real thoughts.

"What is what?" she asked innocently.

"You were about to say something. Do you feel that maybe, just sometimes, management isn't as concerned with safety as they should be? I'd never quote you by name."

Laurie stared at him and smiled slowly. "Well…" She leaned on the table, edging closer to him.

He did the same, anxious to hear whatever dirt she had to dish.

She leaned back. "Sorry, I don't have a bad thing to say about the place."

Adamson sat back, as well, obviously disappointed. He shook his head. "If there was something going on… something big, do you think that the employees would get wind of it?"

"Like what? The president arriving, or something like that?"

"No…like Moon Bay being involved in…something."

"Drugs? Here? Never," she assured him.

"I wasn't referring to drugs," he assured her.

She laughed softly. "Illegal immigrants? Not with Jay around. He wouldn't hire an illegal if his life depended on it."

"Not illegals," Hank said.

"Just what are you getting at?" she demanded.

"I don't know," he said. "I was hoping you did."

"That makes no sense. This is a resort, specially licensed for work with sea mammals. What could be going on?" Other than a body that appeared on the beach, then disappeared.

"Have you ever heard of a woman named Alicia Farr?" Adamson asked her.

"Sure. She's almost like a young, female Jacques Cousteau."

"Have you ever met her?"

"Nope. I think she's friends, kind of, with Alex. She's worked with David Denham. I'm pretty sure Jay Galway has worked with her, too."

"She hasn't been here, then, in the last couple of weeks?"

"Not unless she's been hiding in the bushes." Laurie was actually enjoying her conversation with him now. She'd had a few Tiki Hut specials, but she always watched her drinking here. And she could stand up to a grilling by a man like Hank Adamson. "Is she supposed to be here?"

"There was a rumor she was going to be, but I guess it wasn't true."

"I guess not."

"You're sure she's not here?" he persisted.

"There are private cottages here, twenty of them. Eight of them belong to the staff, and twelve are rented out. But this is an island. Room service is the only way to get food. There's a little convenience shop in the lobby, a boutique…but, honestly, I think it would be pretty hard for someone to hide out in one of the cottages. Maid service is in and out, engineering…. I'm pretty sure she wasn't here. We're off the Middle Keys, and there are lots of secluded places on the other islands. Maybe she's on one of them. I'm sorry to disappoint you—were you really trying to get a story on her?"

"I am doing an article on Moon Bay," he told her. "You know how it is, though. Lots of times, reporters get wind of a bigger story while they're in the middle of something more routine."

"So if you'd run into Alicia Farr here, that would have been nice, right?"

"It would have been interesting," he said. "You do know what she looks like, right? You'd know her if you saw her?"

"Sure. I've seen lots of articles on her. And I've seen her on television," Laurie said with a shrug.

She yawned suddenly, and quickly covered her mouth with her hand. "Sorry." She was. He was appealing in his lanky way, but he wasn't interested in her—only what she might know. And she had no intention of telling him anything. She'd been ordered not to mention Alex's certainty that she'd seen a corpse, and she wouldn't.

She rose. "Please excuse me. Saturdays are very long here. People coming down from Dade County, locals who just like to come eat at the restaurant. The place is always busy."

He had risen along with her. "Thanks," he told her quietly.

"Sure. This place really is wonderful. I'm not lying, or just trying to keep my job by saying that. And Alex… well, there's no one better."

"So they say," he murmured, then asked politely, "Can I walk you to your cottage?"

"I don't rate a cottage—not yet," she told him with a shrug. "I just take the trail back to the fork in the road and head for the staff quarters. I'll be fine." She grinned to take the sting out of her next words, moved a step closer to him, and whispered, "Feel free to go question another employee. You'll find out every word I said was true."

He had the grace to flush. She gave him a wave and made her way past two couples on the dance floor, both a little inebriated, but heck, they weren't driving anywhere. If you were going to feel the influence of alcohol, this was the place to do it.

She could hear the band long after she had left the Tiki Hut behind. She started off thinking nothing of the night or the shadows, the trails were lit by torches—not like the ones at the Tiki Hut, which were real, but electrical torches made to give the grounds an island feel. Still…

Once the Tiki Hut was well behind her and the noise from it had dimmed, she thought the night seemed especially dark. Strange, because her dad had shown her once before how the glow that radiated from Miami—sixty or seventy miles away, still extended this far when the sky was clear. But clouds were out tonight. It was storm season, of course. They'd had several nice days in the last week, though, she mused.

Nice days. A few with calm seas, a few others when the water was choppy. But then, the water didn't have to be wild to carry something—like a corpse—to the shore.

She stopped dead suddenly and instinctively, some inner defense aware of a rustling noise. She felt the hair rising at her nape.

She spun around. Nothing. But the bushes seemed to be very, very dark.

She had a sudden, vivid and ridiculous image of a corpse stalking her along the trail….

"Don't be ridiculous," she said aloud to herself.

But then…a rustling in the bushes…

She stared in the direction from which the noise had come, her heart racing a million miles an hour. Slowly, she made a circle where she stood, looking around.

The noise came again. She spun sharply, staring into the brush once again.

Then…a fat possum waddled out from the bushes and moved slowly across the path.

She let out her pent-up breath and giggled.

Then she turned, ready to set out along the path again. Instead she plowed into something dark and solid, and before her numbed mind could react, arms reached around her.

"Alex, for the love of God!"

David's voice was muted by the glass, but his impatience was evident. She was so relieved to realize that he was the figure on the porch that she didn't really think. She opened the sliding-glass doors, but she had to yell.

"You son of a bitch! What the hell are you doing out there? You nearly scared the life out of me."

He pushed his way in. It was dark, only the lights in front of the house illuminating the area around them. She could see that he still looked like a million bucks, dressed in dark chinos, a red tailored shirt and a light jacket.

She rued the fact that she was wearing a tattered T-shirt with the words "Moon Bay" embroidered in powder blue against a deep aqua background. She was equally sorry that it was very short. Silly. Even if they hadn't been married and she didn't have every inch of his anatomy etched into her memory forever, they spent their lives in bathing suits. She wondered why the T-shirt made her feel so naked. And vulnerable.

He walked through the cottage, checking the front door, looking around. "Is there any other way in here?" he asked, turning around slowly and studying the living room.

"Abracadabra?" she suggested.

"Cute, Alex. Is there any other way in here?"

"Front door, back door, as you can see."

He ignored her and headed for the small hallway that led to the bedrooms and bath.

"Hey!" she protested. She started to follow him, then paused, determined that the last place she wanted to be with him was a bedroom.

A moment later, he was back.

She frowned slightly, realizing he looked as if he had

been running his fingers through his hair. She turned on the kitchen lights and stared at him once again. He looked tense. He reminded her of a shark, giving the impression of deceptive ease, while eyeing his prey to strike.

"What the hell are you doing?" she demanded.

"There was someone walking around your cottage, looking in the windows. I chased him around one side… and lost him," he told her.

"If there's anyone slinking around here," she said softly, "it's you."

He threw up his hands. "Alex, I'm serious."

"And I'm serious, too."

"Get this straight—I'm concerned."

Crossing her arms over her chest, she said firmly, "David, get this straight. You don't need to be concerned about me. I don't care about a technicality. We're not married anymore. I might not have been here alone."

"Actually, knowing you, you do care about a technicality," he informed her.

He was far too relaxed. "You followed me," she accused him. "You followed me when I was with another man, who was more than capable of taking care of me if I'd been in any danger."

"Alex, I don't really know that guy, and neither do you, and most important," he said very softly and seriously, "we are talking about a life-and-death situation."

She suddenly saw the man she knew from television, interviews and even, once upon a time, her personal life. The ultimate professional. Reeking of authority and command. Absolute in his conviction.

And for some reason, she shivered.

The woman on the beach had been dead. No matter

what anyone tried to tell her. There had, beyond a doubt, been a corpse.

And it had disappeared.

"Maybe you'd like to explain it to me," she said.

He stared at her for a long moment. "I keep thinking you're better off, the less you know," he said quietly.

"Why? You already think I'm in some kind of danger."

"Yes, I do."

"Why?"

"You found a body on the beach. A body that disappeared."

She shook her head, watching him warily. "We've been through this. Jay and the sheriff were both certain I was duped."

"But you know it was real."

She wished so badly that she didn't feel such a desperate desire to keep her distance from him at all costs. Because she did know him. And she knew that he believed her. It wasn't necessary for him to have been there—he believed her.

"If you're so convinced, there must be a reason," she said flatly.

"Want to put some coffee on?" he suggested.

"No."

"Mind if I do?"

"Yes." Even as she spoke, she knew he would ignore her. He gave her a glance as if she was behaving like a spoiled child and moved into the kitchen. His arm brushed hers as he strode past her, and she felt as if she'd been burned.

Apparently he hadn't even noticed. He was heading for the cupboard above the coffeepot.

"Would you stop making yourself at home here, please?" she said, walking past him and shoving him out of the way. "I'll make coffee. You talk."

"What did she look like? The woman on the beach. What did she look like?"

She turned around and stared at him. "Like…a woman. Blonde."

"You didn't recognize her?" He stepped past her, impatiently taking the carafe and starting the coffee.

"Recognize her?" Alex said, startled.

"Yes, did you know who she might be?"

"No. She was at a strange angle. And she had long… or longish hair. It was covering her face. I touched her throat, looking for a pulse. And then…I don't know how to describe it exactly, but there was no way not to know she was dead."

"But you let them convince you that she couldn't have been, that you were wrong, and she just got up and walked away?" he demanded.

There was a note of disappointment in his tone.

"The sheriff was there," she told him sharply. "He doubted me. There was no body. What the hell was I supposed to do?"

He turned his back on her, opening a cupboard door.

"Cups are over here," she said impatiently, producing two from another cabinet.

He poured the coffee. He drank his black, so she was startled when he went to the refrigerator, absently taking out the milk to put a few drops into hers.

She accepted the coffee, watching him, feeling again an embarrassed awareness of his crisp, tailored appearance and her own tattered T-shirt. Ridiculous to think about such things when they were talking about a corpse, she told herself.

"Did you mention your discovery to lover boy?" he inquired, sounding casual as he put the milk back in the refrigerator.

"I don't like your tone," she told him.

"Sorry, I don't like what's happening."

"Are you actually jealous?" she demanded.

"I'm not trying to run your life, if that's what you mean," he assured her. "I just don't like what's happening here."

"You haven't explained a damn thing yet, David."

"Did you tell him?" he persisted.

She let out a sigh of irritation. "No, but that doesn't mean I won't. For tonight…tonight I'm waiting. The sheriff will get back to us, let us know if anybody's missing from one of the ferries or the Middle Keys. He and Jay might have made me feel a little foolish today, but Nigel Thompson is a good man and no fool. And I could accuse you of many things, but being a total idiot isn't one of them. So get to it. What's going on?"

"I'm afraid I might know your corpse," he said quietly, his eyes a strange cobalt by night, and steady upon her.

Her heart seemed to skip a beat.

"Who?"

"Alicia Farr."

"Alicia?" she exclaimed. "Why…why would she be around here? There's not much to attract a woman of her reputation at a place like Moon Bay…but then again, there's not much here for you." She stopped speaking suddenly, staring at him. "I see. Great. You would have told me about this 'technicality' in the divorce, but only because it would have been convenient while you were here. You came to meet Alicia."

"No," he told her.

"You liar," she accused him softly. "Get out—now."

"I didn't come here just to meet her."

"David, I'll call security if you don't leave."

He arched an eyebrow, fully aware that "security" at Moon Bay meant two retired cops who were happy to putter around the grounds at night in retooled golf carts. There had never been serious trouble at Moon Bay—until today. And then they hadn't bothered with security; they had called the sheriff's department immediately.

"David, get the hell out."

"Alex, will you listen to me—I think Alicia is dead."

An eerie feeling crept along her spine. How could she be jealous of a corpse?

But she had been jealous of Alicia. The woman was—or had been—a free spirit, intelligent, beautiful and filled with knowledge, curiosity and a love of dangerous pursuits that nearly equaled David's own.

Could she be dead? That would be terrible.

But it wasn't sinking in. At the moment, Alex felt betrayed. She had to admit, it had felt nice to have David following her as if he was desperate.

"Alex?" he said, and his tone seemed to slip under her skin, no matter how numb she was suddenly feeling.

Then he walked over to her, put his cup down, and his hands went to her shoulders again, the whole of his length far too familiar against her own, his eyes piercing hers in a way she remembered too well. "Damn it, Alex, believe this—I don't want you ending up dead, as well."

They were talking about life and death, and all she

felt was the texture of his jacket, the heat emanating from him. She breathed him in and remembered the way his hands could move. He was almost on top of her, and she felt a physical change in herself, a tautness in her breasts, with way too much of her body pressed there against his.

She wanted to shove him away—hard.

She managed to get a hand between them and place it firmly on his chest, pushing him away from her, and slipped from the place where she had been flush against the counter.

"Talk, David. Do it quickly. I have a nine o'clock dive in the morning, which means I have to be at the docks at eight."

Her voice sounded tight and distant. She wasn't sure if it was the effect she wanted or not. She should have been concerned, she knew, about Alicia. She had known the woman, after all, even admired her. But she hadn't liked her.

But that didn't mean she would have wanted harm to come to her. So why wasn't she more emotionally distressed? She was just too numb, unable to accept the possibility.

"Alicia called me a few weeks ago. Do you remember Danny Fuller?"

"Of course. He came here frequently, and he was charming." He had been. An octogenarian, the man had been in on the early days of scuba diving and helped in the later development of some of the best equipment available. He had loved dolphins, and that had naturally endeared him to Alex. "Yes, I knew Daniel fairly well. I was very sorry to hear he died about a month ago, at a hospital in Miami. Of natural causes."

"I know."

"They were natural causes, right?"

"Yes. But Alicia was with him a lot at the end."

"I can see it—him dying, and Alicia quizzing him about everything he knew until he breathed his last breath," Alex murmured. She hesitated. Alicia Farr was—or had been, if any of this was true—everything that she had not been herself. She found herself remembering the woman and the times they had worked together. Alicia was the epitome of a pure adventuress, courageous beyond sanity, at times. She was also beautiful.

Even before the last year, she had frequently appeared at David's side on TV and in magazines. He, naturally, thought the world of her.

He'd slept with her, certainly. But before or after the divorce? Alex had never been certain.

That must be why she was feeling so icy cold now. Good God, she didn't want the woman to be dead, but still…

"It's probably true that she pursued him mercilessly," David admitted. "But he also sent for her, so I guess she was the one he wanted to talk to in the end. At any rate, soon after he died, she called me. She said she was on to the biggest find of the century, and that she wanted me with her. And something she discovered had to do with Moon Bay." He seemed to notice the way Alex was staring at him. "Actually, I had already been toying with the idea of coming here, so it sounded fine to me. She set a date, and said that she would meet me here. Whether she made that same arrangement with anyone else or not, I don't know. But when I tried to get back to her, to confirm, I couldn't reach her. Then, when I got here, she was a no-show. I figured she'd gone ahead to check things out. You know Alicia when she's got the bit between her teeth. I still thought she'd show, though. But I did notice that the place seemed to be crawling with a strange assortment of visitors, including Seth Granger, Hank Adamson and your new friend—John Seymore. And then…I heard that you'd found a body on the beach."

For several long moments, Alex just stared at him, not at all sure what to think, or where to start. She felt chilled. She had found a body, and it could have been Alicia's.

No. Easier to believe Jay had been right. That she'd seen someone playing a sick—and very convincing—trick on someone else.

"Maybe Alicia just decided that she didn't want you in on her fabulous find after all. Maybe she's already off on her expedition," Alex said, her voice sounding thin.

"And maybe someone else found out what she had and killed her to get it—or before she could set up an expedition to recover the treasure, so they could get it for themselves."

"If there was really a body, it's gone now," Alex said. "And Sheriff Thompson—"

"I've spoken with him. He hasn't seen Alicia, and your corpse hasn't reappeared."

"Then…then you don't really have anything," Alex said.

"What I have is a tremendous amount of fear that a friend and colleague is dead—and that someone may now be after you. Alex, maybe there's someone out there who thinks you saw something, and that could put you in danger."

Alex shook her head. "David, I'm not going to start being paranoid because of the things that might be. If Alicia is dead, and someone was willing to kill her for what she knew, wouldn't you be in far more danger than I am? What about your own safety?"

"I can handle myself."

"Great. Handle yourself doing what? Waiting? Watching people?"

"I have friends looking for information now."

She stared at him. He had friends, all right. P.I.s, cops, law enforcement from around the world. And he was serious.

A slight shiver raked along her spine. If all this was true…

"All right, David. I appreciate your concern for my welfare. And I'm very sorry if Alicia is…dead. I know what she meant to you."

"No, actually, you don't."

He walked up to her, angry again, and she tensed against the emotion that seemed to fill him, though he didn't touch her.

"There was never anything intimate between Alicia and me. She was a good friend. That's all."

She didn't look up at him as she raised her hands. "Whatever your relationship…was, it's none of my business. As I said, thanks for your concern. I'll be very careful. I'll keep my eyes open, and I swear, if I hear anything, I'll tell you. Now, may I please go to sleep? Or try, at least, to get some sleep?"

"I can't leave you."

"What?"

"I can't leave you. Don't you understand? If someone out there thinks you can prove that Alicia is dead, that you might have seen…something, you're in danger of being murdered yourself."

She shook her head. "David, my doors lock. Please go away."

They were both startled when his phone suddenly started to ring. He pulled it from his pocket, snapping it open. "Denham," he said briefly.

She saw him frowning. "Sorry, say again. I'm not getting a great signal here."

He glanced at Alex in apology and walked out back, opening the sliding door, stepping out.

She followed after a moment. He was on the porch rocker, deep in conversation. She hesitated, then shut and locked the glass door. She was going to try to get some sleep. But how? Her mind was spinning.

Before she could reach the hallway, she heard a pounding on the glass. Then David's voice. "Damn it, Alex, let me in!"

"David, I'm fine. We'll talk tomorrow. Go away!"

"I won't leave you."

"Well, I won't let you in."

"I'll have to sleep on the porch then."

"Feel free."

She let the curtain fall closed. He slammed the glass with a fist. She was afraid for a minute it would shatter, despite the fact that it was supposedly hurricaneproof.

She stared at the drapes a long time. He didn't speak again, or hit the glass.

Maybe he had actually gone away. She forced herself to walk to her bedroom, lie down, close her eyes.

At some point, she finally slept.

Her alarm went off at six. She nearly threw it across the room. She felt as if she'd never actually slept, as if her mind had never had a chance to turn off.

After a second, she jumped out of bed and raced to the back, hesitated for a second, then carefully moved the curtain to look out.

David was just rising. To her absolute amazement, he had spent the night with his tall, muscular form pretzeled into the rattan sofa on the porch.

Suddenly she was afraid. Very afraid.

Chapter 5

David wasn't feeling in a particularly benign mood toward Alex, even after he had showered, gone back to his own cottage, downed nearly a pot of coffee, shaved and donned swim trunks, a T-shirt and deck shoes for the day. She'd really locked him out.

And gone to sleep without letting him back in.

He should have slept in his own bed. His cottage was next to hers—it just seemed farther because of the foliage that provided privacy and that real island feel that was such an advertised part of Moon Bay.

He hadn't gone to his own cottage, though, because he had seen someone snooping around her place. And the phone call he'd gone out to take hadn't been the least bit reassuring.

With that in mind, he pocketed his wallet and keys, and left his cottage. Wanting to get out on the water ahead of the resort dive boat, he hurried down to the marina to board the *Icarus*.

As he started to loosen the yacht's ties, he heard his name being called.

Looking up, he saw John Seymore walking swiftly down the dock toward him. Hank Adamson and Jay Galway were following more slowly behind, engaged in conversation.

"Hey," he called back, sizing up Seymore again. For someone who had been spending his time diving the Pacific, he was awfully bronzed. That didn't mean anything in itself. The water on the West Coast might be cold as hell, but the sun could be just as bright as in the East.

"You're heading out early," John Seymore said. "Anywhere specific?"

"Just the usual dive sites," he replied. He realized that Seymore was angling for an invitation. Why not? "Are you booked on the resort's boat?"

"Couldn't get in—she was full," Seymore said cheerfully. "Hank had the same problem. We tried to weasel our way in through Jay, but he suggested we come down here to see what you had in store."

Just what he wanted. Jay Galway, Hank Adamson and Mr. Surf-Blond All-Around-Too-Decent-Guy out on the *Icarus* with him.

On the other hand, maybe not such a bad idea. He would know where the three of them were, and he might just find out what each of the men knew.

He shrugged. "Come aboard."

"I really appreciate the invitation," Seymore said. "Guys!" he shouted back loudly. "We're in!"

"Hop in, grab a line," David said.

John Seymore came on first, followed by Jay Galway, who hurried ahead of Hank Adamson. "Hey, thanks, David. Sincerely," Galway said. David nodded, figuring that Jay hadn't been happy about having to tell the writer that he couldn't get out for the day, even though it must look good for the resort's programs to be booked.

"This is damn decent of you," Adamson said, hopping on with agility. "Need some help with anything?"

"Looks like Jay has gotten the rest of the ropes. Make yourself at home."

"Want me to put some coffee on while we're moving out?" Jay asked.

"Good idea," David said.

"Sorry, I should have thought of that," John said, grimacing. "I always think of being on a yacht like this and drinking beer and lolling around on the deck."

"Oh, there's beer. Help yourself to anything in the galley." Just stay the hell out of my desk, he thought.

David kept his speed low as he maneuvered the shallow waters by the dock, then let her go. The wind whipped by as the *Icarus* cut cleanly through the water. Adamson and Seymore had remained topside with him, and both seemed to feel the natural thrill of racing across the incredible blue waters with a rush. When they neared the first dive spot on the reef, he slowed the engine.

"Trust me to take the helm?" Seymore asked him.

"Sure," David said, giving him the heading briefly, then hopping down the few steps that led to the cabin below.

He glanced around quickly, assuring himself that his computer remained untouched and it didn't appear Galway had been anywhere near his desk, which was in the rear of the main cabin in a mahogany enclave just behind the expansive dining table and the opposing stretch of well-padded couch.

"Good timing. Coffee's ready," Jay told him. Jay knew the *Icarus*. He'd once gone out with David on a salvage expedition, when he'd been going down to the wreck of a yacht lost in a storm, the *Monday Morning*. The boat had been dashed to pieces, but she'd carried a strongbox of documents her corporate owners had been anxious to find. It had been a simple recovery, but Galway had been elated to be part of the process.

"Thanks," David said.

Jay handed him a cup of black coffee. "For a good-looking son of a bitch, you look like hell this morning," Jay told him.

"I didn't sleep well."

Jay poured himself a cup. "Me neither."

"Dreaming about corpses?"

Jay didn't look startled by the question. "There was no corpse," he said flatly.

"Not when you got there," David suggested.

Jay shook his head. "I asked Alex not to say anything—since we didn't have a body."

"She didn't."

"Then?"

"It's an island, a very small one," David reminded him.

"I was sure Laurie would have the good sense to keep quiet when I asked her to," Jay said disgustedly.

"Laurie didn't talk. Things…get around."

"So you're not going to tell me where you got your information?" Jay asked.

"Nope."

"Like I said, there was no body," Jay told him. He frowned. "How far do you think it's gotten around?"

"Who knows?"

Jay groaned. "If the guests start to hear this…"

"I don't think it'll get around to the rest of the guests," David assured him. God, the coffee was good.

"It was Len, wasn't it? And don't deny it."

"Doesn't matter how I know. And I haven't said a word to anyone else. I know Alex hasn't either, and I'd almost guarantee Laurie hasn't. I do have a question for you. What makes you so convinced Alex was duped?"

Jay looked at him. His surprise seemed real. "There was no body there. And corpses don't get up and walk."

"They can be moved."

"I'm not an idiot. I was looking around just like the sheriff. The sheriff. We didn't just call security and forget it. We called the sheriff. There was no sign of a body ever having been there or being taken away. There were no footprints and no drag marks."

"What the hell does that mean? Someone strong enough could throw a woman's body over his shoulder—and there are palms fronds around by the zillions. Footprints on a beach could easily be erased."

"There couldn't have been a body," Jay said.

David watched him for a few minutes. Jay wasn't meeting his eyes. Instead he seemed intent on wiping the counter where nothing had spilled.

"You look like you're afraid there might have been. And worse, you look as if you're afraid you know who it could have been," David said softly.

Jay stared at him then. "Don't be insane! I'd never kill anyone."

"I didn't say you would. You know, I asked you before about Alicia Farr. You assured me that she hadn't checked in to the resort."

"She hasn't," Jay protested.

"She was supposed to be here."

"She called about a possible reservation, but she never actually booked. I didn't think she would. It's not her cup of tea. Anyway, that was it. She called once, made sure I had the dates available that she wanted, then said she'd get back to me. She didn't. That's the God's honest truth. She never called back."

It sounded as if Jay was sincere, but David couldn't be certain.

Jay gasped suddenly, staring at David. "I know what you're thinking! Believe me, there couldn't have been a corpse. And if there was...it couldn't have been Alicia. I mean, she didn't check in. She was never on the island."

"Well, if there wasn't a corpse, it couldn't have been anyone, right? But I should tell you, Alicia was in Miami a week ago, where she rented a boat and said she was heading down to one of the small private islands in the Keys."

"Do you know how many small private islands there are down here? Maybe she intended to come here but changed her mind. She must have arranged to go somewhere else—maybe a place that belongs to a friend or something." His eyes narrowed. "Were you...with her? In Miami?"

David shook his head.

"How do you know what she was doing, then?"

"She called me. Then when I called back and couldn't reach her I had a friend do a trace on her."

"Alicia is independent. She knows her way around."

"When she called me, she asked me to meet her here, at Moon Bay. The way she talked, she was excited about seeing Moon Bay. She seemed very specific. When she called you, she didn't say anything about her reason for coming?"

"I swear, she didn't tell me anything. She was pleasant and asked about available dates, and that was all," Jay assured him, then frowned. They could both see Hank Adamson's deck shoes, then his legs, as he descended into the cabin.

"Mind if I take a look around her?" he asked David.

"Hell no. I'm proud of my girl and delighted to give you a tour. Jay, how about relieving John at the helm, so he can get a good look at the *Icarus*, too?"

"Sure. I already know my way around," Jay told Adamson. There was a note of pride in his voice. David watched him thoughtfully as he headed topside.

Jay Galway had been sweating when they talked. A little sheen of perspiration had shown on his upper lip.

So…

Either he was afraid, or he was lying.

Or both.

Alex had expected Zach to be a problem.

He wasn't. The teenager duly handed her his dive card, then sat through her reminders and instructions like an angel. His mom had decided to stay on shore, despite the fact that they were going to make a stop on one of the main islands before returning that night.

Doug Herrera was captaining their dive boat, and Mandy Garcia was Alex's assistant. They all switched between dive excursions and the dolphins. Gil and Jeb were dealing with the morning's swim, and Laurie was taking her day off. Actually, Alex had expected to see her friend at the docks anyway—Laurie loved to dive, and she especially loved a day when the boat was scheduled to make a stop on one of the main islands when she wasn't working. It was a chance to check out the little waterside bar where they had a meal and after-dive drinks, for those who chose, before returning to Moon Bay.

But Laurie had still been at the Tiki Hut when Alex left, so maybe the late night and the excitement of the day had caused her to sleep in. And maybe she had decided not to come because Seth Granger was on the dive, and he always made things miserable.

At Molasses Reef, their first dive, Alex noted that the *Icarus*, David's yacht, was already anchored nearby. They never anchored on the reefs themselves. Most divers were aware of the very delicate structure of the reef and that it shouldn't be touched by human hands, much less bear the weight of an anchor, and wouldn't have moored there even if there hadn't been laws against it. David was close though, closer than they went themselves.

"Now that's a great-looking yacht," Seth commented, spitting on his mask to prep it.

"Yes," she agreed. The *Icarus* was a thirty-two footer, and she looked incredible under full sail. Today, however, David wasn't sailing her. He'd apparently used the motor. The yacht moved like a dream, either way. Inside, the mahogany paneling and rich appointments made her just as spectacular. The galley had every possible accessory, as did the captain's desk. She was big enough to offer private sleeping facilities for up to three couples.

"You should have asked for the yacht," Seth said, eyeing the *Icarus.*

"I beg your pardon?"

"In your divorce settlement. You should have asked for the yacht. She's a beauty. But, hey, you've got another chance to ask for her now. Heard you're not really divorced," Seth said.

"Where did you hear that?"

He laughed again, or rather, bellowed. "People talk, you know. Moon Bay is an island. Small. People talk. About everything."

He stared at her, which gave her a very uncomfortable feeling. What else was being discussed?

"I don't want her. She belongs to David. Now, if you'll excuse me, I have to get in the water. And so do you. The tour group is waiting."

Her people were buddied up the way she'd arranged them after she'd duly studied their certificates and discussed their capabilities. She'd decided to buddy up with Zach herself.

In the water, leading the way, even though she was checking constantly to assure herself that her group indeed knew what they were doing and how to deal with their equipment, she found a certain peace. The sound of her own air bubbles always seemed lulling and pleasant. As yet, no cell phones rang here.

Zach stuck with her, amazed. A Michigan kid, he'd gotten his certificate in cold waters and was entranced by the reef. It was a joy to see his pleasure in the riot of tropical fish, and in the giant grouper that nosily edged their way.

This was an easy dive; most of it no more than thirty feet. When she counted her charges again, she saw that Seth Granger had wandered off. His "buddy," the mother of the girls from the day before, was looking lost.

Alex motioned to Zach, then went after Granger. He seemed hostile, but, to her relief, he rejoined the group.

Back on deck, he was annoyed. "I saw David out on the reef. I was just going over for a friendly underwater hello."

"Mr. Granger—"

"Seth. Come on, honey, we've seen enough of each other."

"Seth, if you'd wanted an unplanned, individual dive, you should have spoken with David earlier—and gone out on the *Icarus* with him. I'm sure he'd have been happy to have you."

"Don't be ridiculous. You know I know what I'm doing in the water."

"Guess what, Seth? I don't go diving alone. Too dangerous. Now, I can have the skipper take the boat back in and drop you off at Moon Bay, or you can stay with the group and abide by our rules."

He pointed a finger at her. "I'll be talking to your boss tonight."

"You do that."

At the next two stops, he still wandered, but not as badly as the first time, pretending he had become fascinated by a school of tangs and followed them too far, and then, on the last go-round, that he had seen a fantastic turtle and been unable to resist.

When the last dive was completed, Alex allowed herself a moment's pleasure. Zach was in seventh heaven, and her other divers were exuberant over the beauty they had witnessed. They were ready, when they reached the main island and the little thatch-roofed diner, to eat, drink and chat.

"Good job, boss lady!" Jeb commented to her, a sparkle in his eye, as they went ashore themselves. "How about you have a nice dinner, and I'll keep Seth out of your hair?"

Jeb was great. A college senior, he was only hers for the summer. He was a thin kid, with flyaway dark hair, and a force and energy that defied his bony appearance. He never argued with her, watched her intently all the time, and was one of those people who seemed intent on really learning and absorbing all the information they could. When she wasn't working with Laurie, she was happiest with Jeb, though all her assistants were handpicked and great.

"You're on," she told him gratefully.

Leaving the dive boat to her captain, Alex made certain all her charges were comfortable at the Egret Eatery, as the little restaurant was called.

Zach had already found the video games located at the rear of the place. The adults had settled in at various tables.

She saw Jay, Hank, John and David at a table and felt a moment's wary unease. The four of them had obviously spent the day out on the reef together. She'd known the *Icarus* was a stop ahead of her all day. She just hadn't realized how full the yacht had been.

She was about to venture toward their table, but then she saw Seth Granger moving that way, so she steered clear.

"Hey, guys," Seth bellowed. "Mind if I join you? Drinks on me. What'll it be?"

"A pitcher of beer would be appreciated," Hank told him.

"Coke for me," David said.

"Come on. You're not going to crash after one beer, buddy."

"No, a Coke will do fine for me." David looked up and caught Alex's eyes across the room. She felt a chill leap across the open space. For a man so determined to see to her safety, he looked a lot like he wanted to throttle her. Apparently he hadn't enjoyed his night on the porch.

But he had stayed there. And he believed her, believed that the body she had discovered was Alicia Farr's, and that she herself might well be in real danger.

But from who?

Since she wasn't captaining any boat, she turned to the bar and asked Warren, the grizzled old sailor who owned the place, for a beer.

"Sure thing, Alex. How's it going over there? It's been a little slow around here."

"Really? I'm not sure about the hotel, but the dives and swims have been full," she told him.

Setting her glass down, he pointed at the television. "Storm season."

"Summer is always slower than winter. Northerners stay home and sweat in their own states during the summer," she reminded him.

He grinned. "Maybe, but we usually get a bigger Florida crowd around here than we've been getting lately."

She glanced at the TV above the bar. "Is something

going on now? I haven't seen any alerts. The last tropical storm veered north, right?"

"Yep. Now there's a new babe on the horizon. She just reached tropical-storm status, and she's been named Dahlia, but they think she's heading north, too. They think she might reach hurricane status sometime, but that she'll be off the Carolinas by then. Still, people don't seem to be venturing out as much as usual. Thank God you bring your guests over here. Right now, frankly, you're helping me survive."

"Don't worry. I'm sure business will pick up," she assured him.

"I see your ex is here. It's always good for business when he shows up here. Word gets out, makes people feel like they're coming to a real 'in' place. Still, it's kind of a surprise to see him. You all right?"

"Of course. We're still friends on a professional level," Alex said.

"You know what I think?" Warren asked her.

"What?"

He leaned low against the bar. "I think he came here for you."

"Mmm," she said. Me, and whatever excitement and treasure Alicia had in store, she thought, but she remained silent on the subject.

Then she asked, "Warren, you know who Alicia Farr is, right? Has she been around?"

"Nope, not that I've heard about."

"Well, thanks."

"Who's the blond Atlas with your ex?" Warren asked.

"Tourist."

"Not your typical tourist," Warren commented, wiping a bar glass dry.

"No, I agree." She shrugged. "Thanks, Warren," she told him. The place was thatch-roofed and open, but she suddenly needed more air. She took her beer and headed outside. She walked along the attached dock, where the dive boat had pulled in, came to the end and looked out at the water, studying the *Icarus*.

She wasn't docked; David had anchored her and come in by way of the dinghy. A moment's nostalgia struck her. She had really loved the *Icarus*, and she did feel a pang that the beautiful sailing vessel wasn't a part of her existence anymore.

She had fair compensation in her life, she knew. Diving, here off the Florida coast, would always be a joy, no matter who was on the tour. And she had her dolphins. They might actually belong to the corporation that owned Moon Bay, but they were her babies. Shania, especially. Wounded, just treated and beginning to heal when Alex had come on board, the adolescent dolphin was her favorite—though, naturally, she'd never let the other dolphins know. But she felt as if she and Shania had gained trust and strength at the same time. She had noticed that Shania followed her sometimes. One night, sipping a drink at the Tiki Hut, she had looked up to find the dolphin, nose above the surface, watching her from the lagoon.

And she had learned to live alone. By the end of her whirlwind one-year marriage to David, she had been alone most of the time anyway. Her choice, she reminded herself in fairness. But he never wanted to stay in one place, and she had longed to establish a real base, a real home. Too many times, he had been with a woman who shared his need for constant adventure. Like Alicia Farr. And she had let the doubts slip in and take over. When she had filed the papers and he hadn't said a single word, she had forced herself to accept the truth—she wasn't what he wanted or needed. He had Alicia, and others like her.

He had been planning on meeting Alicia at Moon Bay. And now he suspected she was dead.

With that thought, she dug into the canvas bag she'd brought ashore, found her cell and called the sheriff's office. She was certain she was going to have to leave a message, but Nigel Thompson's assistant put her right through.

"Hey, Alex."

"Hey, Nigel. I'm sorry to bother you, but…I'm concerned."

"Of course. But listen, I checked all the ferry records. No one's missing. Everyone who checked into Moon Bay is alive and well and accounted for. And all the day-trippers and people who checked out of Moon Bay were on the ferries out. Usually there are people in their own boats who come by way of the Moon Bay marina, but not yesterday."

"Thanks, Nigel," she murmured.

"Alex?"

"Yeah."

"I don't think you're easily fooled. I sent some men out last evening to walk the grounds. But they didn't find anything."

"Thank you, Nigel. I guess…I don't know. Thank you anyway."

"Sure thing."

She snapped the phone closed.

She nearly jumped a mile when a hand fell on her shoulder. She spun around, spilling half her beer.

It was just Jeb.

"Sorry," he said quickly. "I didn't mean to startle you. I saw you go out, so I followed. Want to wander into a few shops with me? I need a tie."

"You need a tie?"

He grimaced. "A friend is getting married up in Palm Beach next week. I've got the makings of a suit, but I don't own a single tie."

Her own thoughts were driving her crazy, but she couldn't think of a rational step she could take to solve any of her dilemmas. Might as well go tie shopping.

"So…where's that new girl of yours, David?" Seth asked.

They hadn't been there long; but Seth Granger had already consumed five or six drinks—island concoctions made with three shots each.

David had never particularly liked the guy to begin with, and with a few drinks in him, he was pretty much completely obnoxious.

"New girl?" David asked.

"Alicia Farr. Fair Alicia. Since the wife threw you over after all those pictures of the two of you came out, I figured the two of you were an item. She isn't here with you, huh? I heard tell she had something up her sleeve and was going to be around these parts. Word is she learned something from that old geezer who died a while back. Danny Fuller."

David wondered if Seth Granger was really drunk or was just pretending to be. He'd spent the day listening, waiting for one of his guests to ask the right question, make the right slip. No go. They might have been any four good old boys out for a day on the water.

But now…

"Sorry, Seth. Alicia and I were never an item. We team up now and then for work. We have a lot of the same interests, that's all. There's no reason for her to be at Moon Bay."

"Actually, there was an article about her in the news a few weeks back. Of course, it was in one those supermarket tabloids, so… Anyway, the headline was something like Dying Mogul Gives Secrets to Beauty Who's a Beast. The writer seemed to think she'd been hanging on him hoping to get news on any unclaimed treasure he might know about. There was a definite suggestion that she was coming to the Keys."

Jay Galway thumped his beer stein on the table a little too hard. "So why do you think she was headed for Moon Bay? There are two dozen islands in the Keys."

"That's true enough," David said, eyeing John Seymore. "So you're up on the movements of Alicia Farr, too, huh?" he inquired, forcing a bit of humor into his voice.

"I'm a wannabe, I admit," John said ruefully.

"I know what it takes to be a SEAL," David commented. "I can't imagine you're a wannabe anything."

"Not like me, huh?" Seth Granger demanded, giving David a slap on the back that caught him totally unaware and awakened every fighting reaction inside him.

He checked his temper. "Hell, Granger, with your money? I doubt you're a wannabe anything, either."

"The wannabe would be me," Jay said dryly.

"Jay, you're running a four-star resort, and your vacations are pure adventure," David assured him.

"Yeah, but I bust my butt for all of them—and I'm still on the fringes. But you know…I spent a lot of time with Danny Fuller. I'm sure he had a dozen treasure maps stored in his head, things he learned over the years, and Alicia had the looks—and the balls. So…"

"Looks like we're all here looking for Alicia," Seth said. "And she's blown us all off."

"I don't actually know her," John Seymore reminded them.

"That's right—Seymore's just here to get warm and cuddly with the sea life," David said.

"And your ex-wife," Seth commented.

A tense silence suddenly gripped the table.

Then David's phone rang, as if on cue. "Excuse me, will you?" he said to the others. "Reception is better outside."

He rose, flipping open the phone as he walked out, then paused in the alleyway outside the little restaurant, shaded by a huge sea grape tree.

"Can you talk?" his caller asked.

"You bet," David said. "I've been hoping to hear from you."

"I spent some time at the hospital where Danny Fuller died. Seems Alicia was in on an almost daily basis. One of the nurses heard her swearing to Danny again and again that she wasn't after money, just discovery. And whatever Danny told her, it had to do with dolphins. Apparently the words *dolphin* and *lagoon* came up over and over again. And there was one more thing I think you'll find of interest." The man on the other end paused.

"What's that?" David asked after a long silence. Dane Whitelaw didn't usually hesitate. An ex–special-forces agent, he had opened his own place in Key Largo, where he combined dive charters with a private investigation firm. Sounded a bit strange, but it seemed to work out well enough. He avoided a lot of the big city slush and came up with some truly interesting work, a lot of it to do with boats lost at sea and people who disappeared after heading out for the Caribbean.

Some of them wanted to disappear.

Some of them were forced to do so.

But if he needed information of any kind, David had never met anyone as capable as Dane of finding it out.

Dane was still silent.

"You still there?" David asked.

"Yeah."

"Well?"

"Apparently, according to the old guy's night nurse, your ex-wife's name kept coming up, as well."

"What?"

"She said the two kept talking about an Alex McCord."

David digested the information slowly. Finally it was Dane's turn to ask, "Hey, David, you still there?"

"Yeah, yeah. I need another favor."

"What's that?"

"Look into a guy for me. If he's telling the truth at all, you should be able to dig up some stuff on him."

"Sure. Who's the guy?"

"An ex–navy SEAL. John Seymore."

Jeb had his tie. Alex wasn't certain what it was going to look like when combined with a dress shirt and a jacket, but it was certainly a comment about the lifestyle he loved. Light blue dolphins leaping against a cobalt background.

Alex had purchased one of the same ties. Reflex action, she decided. The darker color was just like David's eyes, and she used to buy all kinds of little things just because they might appeal to him.

"Damn," she murmured as they walked back to the restaurant.

"What?"

"Oh…nothing. I guess I don't really want to go back in and see our…group." Nor did she want to pass the alley. She could see David. He was bare chested, wearing deep green trunks and deck shoes, leaning against the wall. He hadn't noticed them yet, because he was too deeply engrossed in a telephone conversation.

"Our group? Oh, you mean Seth Granger," Jeb suggested.

She shrugged. "Right. Seth." Seth was just a pain in the butt, though. Annoying to deal with, but once she was away from him, she forgot all about him.

She really didn't want to see David. She was furious with herself for having instinctively bought the tie.

"Just walk on by then, Alex. The boat is at the end of the dock. Wait there. I'll go in and gather up the forces. Hopefully anyone who wandered off shopping is back. And hopefully those who did more drinking than eating won't be too inebriated."

She smiled and thanked him, then started down the dock. The sunset was coming in, and she believed with her whole heart that nothing could compare to sunset in the Florida Keys. The colors were magnificent. If there was rain on the horizon, they were darker. On a bright day like today, the night came with a riot of unparalleled pastels.

It was her favorite time of day. Peaceful. Especially when she had a few moments alone, as she did now.

The dock was empty. The other boaters docked nearby were either on shore or in their cabins. The evening was hers.

She strolled the length of rustic wood planks and, at the end, stretched and sat, dangling her feet as she appreciated the sky and tried not to think about the corpse she had seen.

Or the husband she had so suddenly reacquired.

"Who's missing here?"

David had just reentered the restaurant in time to hear Jeb Larson's question.

"Mr. Granger," Zach called out helpfully.

"Mr. Denham," Jeb asked, spotting David. "Have you seen Mr. Granger?"

"Sorry, I went out to make a call. He was at the table when I left."

Jay Galway came striding in at that moment, a bag bearing the name of a local shop in his hand. He arched an eyebrow at Jeb. "Got a problem?"

"Just missing a diver," Jeb said, never losing his easy tone. "Mr. Granger."

Jay seemed startled as he looked around. "He was here twenty minutes ago," he said. "David?"

"Don't know. I was on the phone."

"He said something about going out for a smoke," Hank Adamson called. He was standing at the end of the bar. David was certain he hadn't been there a minute ago.

He looked around. John Seymore seemed to be among the missing, as well, but just then he came striding in from around back.

"Excuse me, Mr. Seymore," Jeb called. "Have you seen Mr. Granger?"

"Nope," John Seymore said.

"Leave it to Granger."

The words were a bare whisper of aggravation, but David was close enough to Jay Galway to hear them.

"Well, relax…we'll find him," Jeb said, still cheerful.

"Maybe he went shopping," Zach suggested.

"Yep, maybe," Jeb said, and tousled the boy's hair.

"You know," David said quietly to Jay, "they can take the dive boat on back. We can wait for him."

Jay cast him a glance that spoke volumes about his dislike for the man, but all he said was, "We can wait a few minutes."

Alex stared at the lights as they played over the water. The lapping sound of the sea as it gently butted against dozens of hulls and the wood of the dock pilings was lulling. The little ripples below her were growing darker, but still, there was a rainbow of hues, purple, deepest aqua, a blue so dark it was almost ebony.

She frowned, watching as something drifted out from beneath the end of the dock where she sat.

At first, she was merely puzzled. What on earth…?

Then her blood ran cold. She leaped to her feet, staring down. Her jaw dropped, and she clenched her throat to scream…caught the sound, started to turn, stopped again.

No. This body wasn't disappearing.

And so she went with her first instinct and began to scream as loudly as she could.

* * *

"We all have to wait here for just one guy?" one of the divers complained.

"My Mom will be getting worried," Zach said.

"Don't worry, you can use my phone," David assured the teen, handing it to him. "Don't you have a cell phone?" he asked the boy.

Zach grinned. "You bet. But Mom wouldn't let me take it on the boat. Said I might lose it overboard. She doesn't dive," he said, as if that explained everything about his mother.

"Leave it to Seth Granger," Jay said, and this time, he was clearly audible. "Go ahead," he instructed Jeb. "You and the captain and Alex get our crew back. David has said he doesn't mind waiting for Granger." He turned to David. "You're sure?" he asked.

"Sure. We'll wait," he said, and he hoped to hell it wasn't going to be long. Now, more than ever, he didn't want Alex out of his sight.

The others rose, stretched and started to file out.

And that was when they heard the scream.

Somehow, the instant he heard it, David knew they weren't going to have to wait for Granger after all.

Chapter 6

Everyone came running.

Alex wasn't thrilled about that, but after her last experience, she'd had to sound an alarm—she wasn't letting this body drift away. Before the others came pounding down the dock, though, she dived in. Though the man was floating face downward and sure as hell looked dead, she wasn't taking any chances.

The water right by the dock was far from the pristine blue expanse featured in tourist ads. She rose from a misty darkness to grab hold of the man's floating arm.

With a jolt, she realized it was Seth Granger.

By then the others had arrived. David was in the lead and instantly jumped into the water to join her. He was stronger and was easily able to maneuver the body. John Seymore, with Jeb at his side, reached down as David pushed Seth upward; between them, they quickly got

Seth Granger lying on the dock, and, despite the obvious futility, Jeb dutifully attempted resuscitation. Alex heard someone on a cell phone, telling a 911 operator what had happened. By the time she and David had both been fished out of the water and were standing on the dock, sirens were blaring.

Jeb, youthful and determined, kept at his task, helped by John, but Seth was clearly beyond help.

He still reeked of alcohol.

Two med techs came racing down the dock, and when they reached Seth Granger, Jeb and John stepped aside. The men from Fire Rescue looked at one another briefly, then took over where John and Jeb had left off.

"Anyone know how long he's been in the water?" one of them.

"Couldn't be more than twenty minutes," John Seymore said. "He was definitely inside twenty minutes ago."

"Let's get him in the ambulance, set up a line...give him a few jolts," one of the med techs said. In seconds, another team was down the dock with a stretcher, and the body was taken to the waiting ambulance.

Then the sheriff arrived. He didn't stop the ambulance, but he looked at Seth Granger as he was taken away, and Alex noted the imperceptible shake of his head. He took a deep breath and turned to the assembled crowd.

"What happened?" Nigel Thompson demanded.

"Well, he was drinking too hard and too fast, that's for sure," Hank Adamson commented.

"We were at a table together," Jay told Nigel. He pointed around. "Seth, John, Hank, David and myself. David's phone rang, and he decided to take it outside.

I needed to pick up a few things, so I headed down the street, and then…" He looked at the other two who had shared the table.

"I went to the men's room," John Seymore said, and looked at Hank Adamson.

"I walked up to the bar."

"When did Granger leave the bar?" Nigel asked.

His answer was a mass shrugging of shoulders.

"Hell," Nigel muttered. "All right, everyone back inside."

David was already on his feet. He reached a hand down to Alex, his eyes dark and enigmatic. She hesitated, then accepted his help.

She realized, as she stood, that John Seymore was watching. He gave her a little smile, then turned away. It seemed that day suddenly turned to night. She shivered, then regretted it. David slipped an arm around her shoulders. "You all right?" he asked.

"Of course," she said coldly.

"Alex, you don't have to snap," he said softly.

She removed his arm from around her shoulders and followed the others. She meant to find wherever John was sitting and take a place beside him.

Too late. Zach was on John's left, Hank Adamson on his right. There was one bench left, and there was little for her to do other than join David when he sat there.

She suddenly felt very cold, and, gritting her teeth, she accepted the light windbreaker he offered. She instantly regretted the decision. It felt almost as if she had cloaked herself in his aura. It wasn't unpleasant. It was too comfortable.

The sheriff's phone rang. "Thompson," he said briefly as he answered it. A second later, he flipped his phone closed. "Well, it's bad news but not unexpected. He was pronounced dead at the hospital."

"Mind if we go over Mr. Granger's movements one more time?" Nigel asked.

"He came, he drank, he fell in the water," a businessman who'd been on the dive said impatiently.

"Thanks for the compassion, sir," Nigel said.

"Sorry, Sheriff," the man said. "But the guy was rich and being a rude pain in the you-know-what all day."

"Well, thank goodness not everyone who's rude ends up drowning," the sheriff said pointedly. "I'd have myself one hell of a job," Nigel commented.

"Sorry," the man said again. "It's just that…we're all tired. I only met the man today on the dive, and he wasn't the kind of person to make you care about him. And I'm on vacation."

"Well, then, I'll get through this just as fast as I can. First things first—those of you from Moon Bay. Anyone checking out tomorrow?"

No one was, apparently. Or, if so, they weren't about to volunteer the information.

"Good. Okay, I'm going outside. One by one, come out, give me your names, room numbers and cell-phone numbers, and I may have a quick question or two. Then you can reboard and get going."

Squeaky wheels were the ones oiled first, Alex determined. Nigel asked her whining diver to come out first.

"This is kind of silly," a woman who had been on the dive complained. "A pushy rich man got snockered and fell in the water. That's obvious."

"Nothing is obvious," David said, his eyes focused on the woman. Alex felt the coiling heat and tension in his body before he continued. "Nigel Thompson is top rate. He's not leaving anything to chance."

The woman flushed and fell silent.

Alex felt as if she were trapped, so aware of David in the physical sense that she was about to scream. In this room full of people, in the midst of this tense situation, she found herself focusing on the most absurd things. Like her ex-husband's toes. His muscled calves. Legs that were long and powerful. When he inhaled, his flesh brushed hers.

She forced herself to look across the room at John Seymore, instead.

In the room, conversations began. David turned to Alex suddenly. "You all right?" he asked softly.

"Of course I'm all right," she said. He was studying her gravely. Then a slight smile curved his lips. "Why?" she asked cautiously.

His head moved closer. His lips were nearly against her ear. When he spoke, it seemed that his voice and the moisture of his breath touched her almost like a caress. "You've been undressing me with your eyes," he told her.

"You are undressed," she informed him. "And what I'm thinking about is the fact that a man drowned."

"Did he?"

"Of course! Damn you, David, we were both there."

"We were both there to pull the body out of the water, but we weren't there when he died."

"He drowned," she insisted.

"Isn't this getting to you just a little bit?" His voice lowered even further. "You're in danger."

"And you're going to protect me?" she demanded.

"You bet."

"Are you going to keep sleeping on my porch?"

"No, you're going to let me into the cottage."

"Dream on. I don't know what this absurd obsession with me is, but do you really think you're going to scare me into letting you back in my bed?"

"Only if you insist, and if it will make you feel better."

In that moment she hated him with a sudden intensity, because she had been so secure, so ready to explore a relationship with another man, and now…

David had played on her mental processes. She knew he could make her feel secure…that his flesh against her own could feel irresistibly erotic, compelling…. She wanted to curl against him, close her eyes, rest, imagine.

"You've got some explaining to do, too," he informed her. Suddenly his eyes reminded her of a predatory cat.

She stiffened. "I have to explain something to you?"

"About Danny Fuller."

"Danny Fuller?"

They both fell silent.

As more people filed outside, those waiting to be questioned began to shift around. Alex saw her opportunity and rose, placing as much distance as she could between herself and David.

And then, with nothing else to do, she found herself pacing the room. Danny Fuller? What the hell was he talking about?

She was idly walking in front of one of the long benches when she nearly collided with Jay. He caught hold of her shoulders to steady her, then she sighed, turned and took a seat on the bench right behind him.

She gazed at him where he sat. His hands were steepled prayer fashion in front of him, and he was looking upward. "Thank you, God," he barely whispered. "Thank you for making this happen here and not on Moon Bay."

"Jay!" she gasped, horrified.

He looked up at her and flushed. "Well, he was a mean old bastard, and he'd lived out most of his life," Jay protested. "He liked to drink way too hard, and never believed the sea could be stronger than he was. Well, you can't turn up your nose and think you're better than the Atlantic."

"This is still horrible."

"Yeah, I'm sure all his ex-wives are going to be crying real hard," Jay murmured.

She started to say something, then fell quiet. Without her noticing, the room had been emptying out.

It was just her and Jay left to speak with the sheriff, and Nigel was coming toward them.

"Well, it's a miracle, but no one in this place saw Seth Granger walk out. No one. Not the bartender, not a single waiter, waitress, busboy, cook or floor scrubber, none of the locals, and certainly none of your guests from Moon Bay."

"Nigel, the guy was drunk," Jay said wearily.

Nigel shook his head. "Seth Granger was always drinking, from what I've heard. Strange that he would just walk into the water, though. Stranger still that no one saw him do it. Never mind." He pointed a finger at Alex. "I want to talk to you at some length. Tomorrow. Got it?"

"Me?"

"Two days, two bodies," Nigel said.

"But…you told me there was no second body. Or first body. Other body."

"Alex, I already told you, I did all the checking I could—and I sent men out to walk the grounds. You know I didn't discount your story entirely. Anyway, we'll talk. I'll be out to see you tomorrow. For now…well, I've got some crime-scene people taking a look around here. At this point, it looks as if Seth got a bit too tipsy, took a walk, met the water and then his maker. There's going to have to be a hearing, though, and an autopsy. The medical examiner will have to verify that scenario."

Jay nodded glumly. "Still," he murmured, "at least it happened here, not at Moon Bay." The other two looked at him. "Hey, I'm sorry, but it matters."

"Well, take your guests home, Jay," Thompson said. "You." He pointed at Alex. "I'll see you tomorrow."

"Sure," she murmured.

They left, bidding Warren goodbye. Alex hoped the restaurant wouldn't end up paying for Seth's alcohol consumption. She knew Warren usually watched his customers and had been known to confiscate keys from any driver he thought shouldn't be on the road. His staff was equally vigilant.

From what she had seen, there had been a pitcher of beer on the table. Seth had probably been downing pitcher after pitcher himself, but the waitress had undoubtedly assumed the beer was being consumed by a party of five.

As they walked along the deck toward the boat, Jay stopped Alex. "I'll go back on the dive boat," he told her. "Damage control," he said with a wince.

"There's room for us both," she said.

"Take a break. Go back on the *Icarus*," he said. "That's okay with you, right, David?" Jay asked, turning slightly.

She hadn't realized that her ex—or not quite ex—husband had been right behind them. "Sure," he said.

Great. A ride back with David, John Seymore and Hank Adamson.

Still, she didn't want to make a draining evening any worse, so she shrugged. At least the ride wouldn't take long.

Along with a sympathetic smile, John Seymore offered her a hand down into the little dinghy that would take them back to the *Icarus*. She wound up sitting next to Hank Adamson, while David and John had the oars. Once again, it was John who gave her a hand on board the *Icarus*, but once there, she hurried aft, hoping to make the journey back alone.

No luck.

She had barely settled down on the deck, choosing a spot she had often chosen in years past, when David joined her.

She groaned aloud. "Don't you ever go away?"

"I can't. Not now."

She stared at him. "You know, I'm trying to have a relationship with someone else."

"I don't know about him yet."

"What don't you know about him?"

He looked at her, blue eyes coolly touching hers. "I don't know if he's in on what's going on or not."

She groaned again. "David, he hasn't been out of the

military that long. He's from the West Coast. He's not into salvage."

"He's into things connected with the sea, that's for certain."

"So?"

"So I still don't know about him."

"How about letting me make a few judgments on my own?"

"Did you see a corpse on the beach or not?" he demanded.

She looked away, silently damning him. "Yes."

"And are we absolutely positive that Seth Granger just got up, left a bar, fell into the water and drowned?"

"No," she admitted after a moment. "But it's the most likely scenario."

"'Most likely' doesn't make it fact," he said flatly. "The body that you found—and yes, I'm convinced you found a body—was Alicia's. I'm certain of it."

"How do you know that?" she demanded, but then she knew. One of his best friends, Dane Whitelaw, worked in Key Largo, leading his version of an ideal life, running a dive service and an investigations business. "Never mind. You've had Dane looking into it."

"Yup. So do you understand now?"

"Understand what?"

"Why I need to keep you under my wing for the time being."

"Under your wing?" she snapped.

"Don't get bristly," he protested. "After all, we're still married."

"A technicality."

"Even if we weren't, I'd be damned if I'd allow anyone to hurt you."

"John Seymore doesn't intend to hurt me," she said. Then she couldn't resist adding, "Unless I want him to."

He glared at her, eyes hard. "You just won't take this seriously, will you?"

"How do I know you haven't suddenly turned into a murderer in your quest for treasure?"

"Quit fighting me, please. I really don't want to sleep on your porch tonight. It will just make me harder to get along with. And if I'm cranky, I won't go to see a lawyer with you. And once I find out what's going on here…well, I could just take off again and leave you in limbo for a very long time."

"You wouldn't!" she said.

"I didn't file the papers in the first place," he said with a shrug, then rose. "We're nearly back. I've got to go dock her."

Left alone, Alex felt her temper rising, but she wasn't as furious with him at that moment as she was with herself. She shouldn't be making a terrible problem out of things. Let the idiot sleep on the couch. Under the circumstances, she needed to take everything slow. If John Seymore was really interested in her, he would wait around.

Even with her ex-or-almost-ex-husband in the cottage?

They had docked. She rose slowly, all too aware of why she was so upset. Having David on the couch should be no big deal.

Except she would know he was there. And now, with each passing moment, she was more and more aware of why she had been so attracted to him from the beginning, why she felt a strange flush of excitement when he was around, and why she found herself so annoyed that he ran around shirtless so often.

"We really do need to talk," David murmured as they went ashore, following Hank Adamson and John Seymore off the *Icarus*.

"I really need to see to my dolphins," she told him, and purposely walked as quickly as she could along the docks, aiming straight for the dolphin lagoon and praying, for once, that she wouldn't be followed. By anyone.

"Come to the Tiki Hut with me?" Jay said to David. He'd waited at the end of the deck. He was trying to sound casual, but there was an edgy note in his voice.

Damage control, David thought.

"I really need a shower," David told him.

"And I don't think anyone actually wants a drink," Hank Adamson said.

"What the hell, I'll go for a few minutes," John Seymore said.

"We'll all go," David determined. He wanted to keep an eye on the guy. He wasn't sure if he was suspicious because a man like Seymore was in a place like this, or because he was interested in Alex. Interested in her? He'd had his tongue halfway down her throat the other night.

"Apparently the sheriff doesn't believe that Seth Granger just fell in the water and drowned," Hank said as they walked.

"What makes you say that?" Jay asked him sharply.

"He questioned everyone pretty closely."

"He's the sheriff," Jay said uneasily. "He has to cover all bases. Why the hell would anyone want to kill Seth Granger."

The silence that followed his question was telling.

"For being a crass, overbearing windbag, for one," Hank offered dryly.

They reached the Tiki Hut. The employees rushed for Jay as he appeared, and he calmly explained the situation. No one seemed to be terribly sad, David noted. They were amazed, though, and maybe even a little titillated. The drowning of such a wealthy man was bound to excite gossip.

The four men took a table. David admired Jay's determination to deal with the situation. He wanted to be visible, to answer any questions. That was damage control, yes, but at least the guy wasn't shrinking from his responsibility.

Zach's mother, Ally Conroy—the one person who had seemed to be getting on with Seth the night before—was in the bar without her son, and it appeared she'd had a few herself. She rose, walked to the table and demanded, "Are they really saying he just…got up and drowned?"

"That's what they think right now, yes," Jay told her.

"I don't believe it. I didn't know him that well, but I don't believe it," she said, slurring her words. "Everyone was there, right with him. How come no one saw?" Ally demanded. Her voice was strong, but she was shifting from foot to foot as she spoke.

"Probably because none of us was expecting anything to happen," David told her, rising. "Mrs. Conroy, you seem…distraught. Would you like me to walk you to your room?"

"Why? Because I might fall into the water and drown?" she said with hostility.

"Because I wouldn't want you to hurt yourself in any way," David said.

Suddenly her eyes fell. She sniffed. "He liked me. Liked Zach and liked me. You don't know how hard it is to raise a kid by yourself. And he was…not the kind of man who'd get drunk, fall in the water and drown."

"The sheriff will be investigating," David assured her gently. "In fact, he'll be here tomorrow. You can talk to him yourself."

She suddenly seemed to deflate, hanging on David's arm. She looked up at him, a little bleary-eyed. "Hey, you're all right, you know?"

"I'll walk her to her room," David told the others.

They nodded.

Ally Conroy was definitely stumbling as she clung to David. "We've got one of the cottages," she said. "It was an Internet deal. Cool, huh? I'm paying a lot less than most people. Have to watch my money, you know?"

"Of course. I'm glad you got a good deal."

By the time they reached her cottage, he was ready to pick her up and throw her over his shoulder, she was stumbling so badly. He damned himself for taking the time to go with her, was even now missing something being said at the Tiki Hut, some piece of the puzzle that had to come together soon.

Because he didn't believe, not for a minute, that Seth Granger had just fallen into the water and died.

They reached the cottage at last. She couldn't find

her key, so David knocked on the door, hoping Zach would hear.

"He was onto something. Onto something big," Ally said suddenly.

"What?"

"He told me about some ship."

"What ship?"

"Where is that damn key?" Ally Conroy said.

David strove for patience and an even tone. "Mrs. Conroy, what ship? Please, think for me."

"The…ship. He was going after a ship. Said he had a friend who needed help, and he intended to help her, because it might be the best thing he'd done in his life. Will you look at this purse? It's an absolute mess."

"Don't worry, there's a key in there somewhere, and if not, Zach will open the door. Mrs. Conroy, you could really help me out here. Did Seth know the name of the ship he wanted to find?"

"The name of the ship…" she repeated.

"The name."

"Oh…yes! The *Anne Marie,* I think he said." Her eyes brightened, and she smiled, forgetting her quest for her key for a moment. "He was very excited about it. He said there was more fantasy written about her than fact. That the legend had it all wrong. No, history was wrong, legend was right." She shook her head and gave her attention back to her purse. "Where is that damned key?"

The door opened. Zach looked at them anxiously.

"I thought I should walk your mom to your cottage," David said.

Zach looked amazingly world-weary, understanding and tolerant. "Thanks, Mr. Denham."

"No problem, and call me David."

The kid nodded, taking his mother's arm.

"I'm okay," Ally said, steadying herself. She cupped Zach's face, then gave him a kiss on the forehead. "I guess we have to take care of each other, huh? I'm sorry, hon."

"It's okay, Mom."

"I'm going to lie down," Ally said.

"Good idea," Zach told her.

Ally paused, looking at David. "I…thank you," she said.

"Not at all."

"I'll try to remember anything else I can," she told him. "After an aspirin and a night's sleep," she added dryly.

"Thanks again."

Ally walked inside. Zach looked at David. "She liked Mr. Granger," he said with a shrug. "I was sorry, but…I didn't want her getting all tied up with him. I know she was thinking it would be great for me to have a dad, but he was a loudmouth. And rude. I didn't want my mom with him. I didn't make him fall in the water, though."

"I never thought you did, Zach," David said.

"Thanks," Zach said. As David started to walk away, he called him back. "Hey, Mr. Denham? David?"

"Yes?"

"Maybe sometime, if you're not too busy, you could show me the *Icarus?*"

"I'd be glad to," David said. "Maybe tomorrow. Ask your Mom. Maybe we can have coffee together, or breakfast, and I'll take you both out on her."

In all honesty, he liked the kid. Especially after tonight.

And he damn sure wanted to talk to Ally Conroy when she was sober.

Before anyone else did.

Chapter 7

Len Creighton was off work, and he considered his free time as totally his own. He sat nursing a double stinger at the Tiki Hut. He needed it.

He'd been behind the desk when a news brief had interrupted the television program in the lobby with the stunning information that millionaire tycoon Seth Granger was dead, apparently by drowning. There was little other information at the time, but he'd heard more about it once the boats had returned to Moon Bay. It had been pretty much the only topic of conversation in the Tiki Hut.

He was still hearing the buzz about it from other tables when Hank Adamson sat down in front of him.

"Long day, huh?" Adamson said, indicating Len's drink.

"Longer for you, I imagine, Mr. Adamson."

"You can call me Hank, please. Yeah, we were there

a long time. The sheriff asked everyone if anyone had seen Seth go out or fall in the water. No one had."

"No one saw him? How sad," Len said.

Hank lifted a hand to order a drink. After giving his order, he told Len, "Sad thing is, I don't think anyone cared."

"I care," Len said in protest. He shrugged sheepishly. "He always tipped well."

"He was rude as hell to the waitress today. You don't think she pushed him into the drink, do you?"

Len smiled, but knew he had to be careful with Hank Adamson. "I'm sure he was just tipsy and fell in himself."

"That old sheriff...he's something, though. Ever had a homicide in this area?"

"Not since I've been here."

"Well, there you go. A local-yokel sheriff just trying to make a name for himself."

"Nigel's a good guy," Len defended.

"So you think he really thinks there was foul play?" Hank asked, smiling at the waitress and accepting a beer from her.

"He's no yokel," Len said.

Adamson leaned toward him. "Why would someone murder Granger? They aren't going to be blaming it on any ex-wife. If he was killed, it had to be someone who was with us at that bar. Someone on the staff at Moon Bay?"

"No way!" Len protested.

"Your boss admits he wants in on a lot of action," Hank said. "He'd love to get into the salvage operations business."

Len stood up. Writer or no, Hank Adamson had crossed the line.

"Jay is as honest as the day is long," Len said firmly.

"Hey, an honest man can be driven to murder," Hank said, smiling as he took another sip of beer straight from the bottle. "Sit down. I like your boss. In my opinion, the jerk just fell off the pier. Finish your drink, and I'll buy you another."

Len hesitated. Then, looking across the dance floor, he noticed Jay, who saw him, and motioned that he'd be over momentarily.

Len smiled. "Jay will be joining us in just a minute," he told Hank. He sipped his drink, then was embarrassed to experience a huge yawn before he could suppress it. "Sorry. It's been a long day."

"Way too long. I don't guess many of us will be hanging around here too late tonight," Hank said.

A few minutes later, when Jay came over, Len rose, stifling another yawn, and bade the two good-night.

There was no sign of Laurie Smith at the lagoons, but she wasn't required to be there—it was her day off, for one thing. Still, Alex was surprised. Laurie really loved the dolphins and tried to spend time with them every day.

She hesitated, then pulled out her cell phone and tried Laurie's room. There was no answer. She dialed Laurie's cell-phone number next, but got voice mail.

Strange.

Mandy and Gil were both there, though. They'd already heard what had happened but she gave them the full story of how she'd found him.

"Man, imagine that. A guy can have everything in

the world, and still…" Gil said, shaking his head. "Just last night, he was flirting and drinking half the beer in the place. He had one hell of a capacity for liquor."

"I guess so. That seems to be what everyone says," Alex said.

"Tragic when anyone dies like that," Mandy said, shaking his dark head. "He was coming on to that Ally woman last night, and she was eating it up. He was boasting about something really big he was into. I thought the guy was a jerk, myself."

"Hank Adamson was there when it happened, right?" Gil said, rolling his eyes.

"He was there. One of the last to see him alive," Alex said.

"Bet he'll love telling that story," Gil said. "Anyway, I know you want to hear about these guys," he told her, indicating the dolphins.

Mandy showed her the log book for the day. "We were bringing them their good-night snack," Gil said. "Didn't know when you'd be back. But you can take over."

"That's all right," she said.

Mandy laughed. "No, it's not. We know you like to tuck them in."

She smiled. "You two do fine without me," Alex said.

"Hell, the swim was a piece of cake next to your day," Mandy said. "Seth Granger dead. Go figure." He made a face. "And you found him floating. I'm glad it wasn't me."

"You look all done in. We'll take off and leave you to your babies," Gil said. "I'm sure you don't want to replay the afternoon anymore."

"It's okay, but you're right. Truthfully, I don't want to talk about it anymore. Not now, anyway," she agreed.

"Good night, then," Gil said.

"Hey, wait!" she called. They stopped, looking at her expectantly. "Has either of you seen Laurie today?" she asked.

"I haven't," Gil said, looking at Mandy.

"I haven't either. But it is her day off," Mandy said.

"I haven't seen her since last night. She left the Tiki Hut kind of late. She'd been talking to Hank Adamson. She was holding her own against him, too, and the guy can be a real pain," Gil said.

"Yeah, he can. Did he grill either of you?" Alex asked.

"Nope," Gil said. "I was at the Tiki Hut after she left, but…I don't remember seeing Adamson after that, either, actually. But hey, I'm a bald guy with a gold earring, and Laurie is a cute girl. I'd grill her, too, if I were Adamson." He frowned suddenly. "Are you worried about her?"

"No. Not really. It's her day off. She's free to come and go as she pleases," Alex said.

"Actually, come to think of it, Len was looking for her earlier, too," Mandy said.

"Why?"

"I think he had mail for her. Or maybe he just knew that she'd been talking to Hank Adamson, and wanted to make sure she hadn't said anything she shouldn't." He shrugged.

Gil let out a snort. "Adamson is going to write what he wants, no matter what any of us say. Only thing is, now he's going to have an awful lot more to write about, having been there when Seth Granger bit the big one."

"Gil..." Alex said with a groan.

"I'll take a walk by Laurie's room and knock," Gil said. "But maybe she just doesn't want to be disturbed."

"Yeah. She could have a hot date," Mandy agreed.

"You think?" Alex said. She shook her head. "She would have told me. She hated that Date Tournament thing she went on."

"Yeah, but...she sure was impressed by your ex-husband," Mandy said.

"And the blond guy chasing you around the last few days," Gil commented.

"Well, they were both there today when Seth—as you so gently put it—bit the big one," Alex said.

"I'm sure she's fine," Gil said. "I'm sure she'll turn up by morning. Maybe she's somewhere right now, hearing all about Seth Granger. Jay must be having fits. That kind of publicity, connected to his precious Moon Bay."

"Haven't you heard? There's no such thing as bad publicity. We'll probably get more people hanging around. In another year, Warren will be advertising that he has a ghost," Mandy said.

"Hey, the guy is barely cold!" Alex protested.

"Sorry," Mandy told her.

"Let's get out of here and let the boss have her private time," Gil said to him. "Night, Alex."

The two walked off. Alex suddenly felt very alone.

For a moment she felt a chill, but then realized that the Tiki Hut was blazing with light and music, and she was just across the lagoon from it. She didn't need to feel alone or afraid, she assured herself. And she wouldn't.

* * *

The time was now. And there wouldn't be much of it.

Using the pass key he'd obtained, he slipped it into the front door of the cottage, quickly closing it behind him, then locking it again.

If someone should arrive, there was always the back door.

Where to look…?

The bedroom. He'd been there before.

He went straight for the dresser, staring at the things on top of it. He picked up the dolphin again, studying it, shaking it. Perfume sprayed out at him. Choking, he put it down.

There was a beautiful painting of a dolphin on the wall. He walked over to it, lifted it from its hook, returned it.

Anger filled him. He didn't have enough information, and despite all he'd done, he couldn't get it. Hell, everywhere he looked, there were dolphins around this woman. Live ones, stuffed ones, ceramic ones.

He heard footsteps coming toward the cottage and hurried for the back door. As long as he wasn't caught, he could come back and take all the time he wanted to study every dolphin in the place.

And he wasn't going to be caught. He would make sure of that this time.

Outside the cottage, he swore. He could have had more time right then. It was just one of the damn maids, walking down the trail.

He smiled at her, waved and kept going.

Back toward the lights and the few people still milling around at the Tiki Hut.

* * *

David's phone rang as he headed back along the path. When he saw Dane Whitelaw's name flash on the ID screen, he paused, taking the call.

"What did you find out?"

"I'm fine, thanks," Dane said dryly. "How are you?"

David paused. "Sorry, how are you? The cat, the dog? Wife, kids…the tropical fish?"

Dane laughed on the other end. "I researched your navy boy. Seems he's telling you the truth. He left the military a year ago May. Was married to a Serena Anne Franklin, no kids. They split up right about the time he left the service. He's in business for himself, incorporated as Seymore Consultants—there are no other consultants listed, however. There is one interesting thing. He was in Miami for a month before coming down here."

"So…it's possible he met up with Alicia Farr there?"

"It's possible, but there are millions of people in the area."

"Great. The guy may be legit—and may not be."

"I'll tell you one thing, he has degrees up the kazoo. Engineering, psychology, geography, with a minor in oceanography."

"Don't you just hate an underachiever?" David muttered.

"Bet the guy made a lot of contacts over the years. Men in high places. Foreign interests, too, I imagine."

"So just what are you saying? Does that clear him, or make him more suspicious?" David asked.

"In a case like this, I can tell you what I'd go by. Gut instinct."

"What does your gut instinct say?" David asked.

"Nothing. You have to go by your own gut instinct. You know him. I don't. Hey, by the way. I see it's getting even more tangled down there. I saw it on the news."

"Seth Granger?"

"You bet. Millionaire drowns and it's on every channel in the state. What happened? What aren't they saying?"

"I don't know."

"You were there."

"I was talking to you when he walked out and went swimming."

"Curious, isn't it? A guy who could—and would—have financed the whole thing goes down."

"Yeah, curious," David agreed, then added slowly, "Unless someone knows more than we do."

"Like what?"

"Like the ship being somewhere easy to reach. Where someone in a little boat could take a dive down and get a piece of the treasure before the heavy equipment—and the government—moved in. For someone who isn't a millionaire, grabbing a few pretty pieces worth hundreds of thousands before the real discovery was made could be an enticing gamble."

"You might be on to something," Dane agreed. "I'll keep digging on your navy man. Keep me posted. And be careful. There's a storm out there, you know."

"Small one, heading the other way, right?"

"Who knows? Small, yes, but still tropical-storm status. And they think it might turn and hit the Keys after all. Anyway, give a ring if you need anything else."

"Thanks."

David closed the phone, sliding it back into his pocket. The tangles were definitely intensifying. And there was only one person he could really clear in Alicia's disappearance and probable death.

Seth Granger.

Who was now among the departed himself.

Hearing a rustling in the trees, he turned, a sharp frown creasing his forehead. Long strides took him straight into the brush.

There was no one there.

But had there been? Someone who had been walking along, heard his phone ring…

And paused to listen in on the conversation?

Alex sat at the edge of the first platform with her bucket of fish and called out, though she knew the dolphins were already aware she was there. "Katy, Sabra, Jamie Boy!"

They popped up almost instantly, right at her dangling feet. They knew the time of day and knew when they got treats. She stroked them one by one, talking to them, giving them their fish. Then she moved on to the next lagoon and the platform that extended into it. "Shania, get up here," she said. "You, too, Sam, Vicky."

She gave them all the same attention, her fingers lingering just a shade longer on Shania's sleek body. The dolphin watched her with eyes that were almost eerily wise. "You're my children, you know that, guys? Maybe

I shouldn't be quite so attached, but, hey…when I had a guy, he was at sea all the time anyway."

"Was he?" The sound of David's voice was so startling, she nearly threw her bucket into the lagoon.

She leaped up and spun around. "Must you sneak up on people?"

"I didn't sneak up, I walked," he told her.

"You scared me to death."

"Didn't mean to. Still, I couldn't help hearing what you said. So…was that it? I was away too much?"

"David, there wasn't one 'it.' My decision to ask for a divorce was complicated. Based on a number of things."

"Was one of them Alicia?"

"No. Yes. Maybe. I don't even know anymore, David."

"I asked you to go on every expedition I took," he said.

"But I work with dolphins. They know when I'm gone."

"So you can never go anywhere?"

"I didn't say that. I just can't pick up and leave constantly. And I don't want to. I like a trip as much as the next person, but I like having a home, too."

"You had a home."

"We had a series of apartments. Several in one year. There was always a place that seemed more convenient. For you."

He was silent for a minute, then asked, "Was I really that bad?"

"Yes. No. Well, you're you. You shouldn't have changed what you were—are—for me. Or anyone else. It just didn't work for me."

"There is such a thing as compromise," he reminded her.

"Well, I didn't particularly want to be the reason the great David Denham missed out on the find of the century."

"There are many finds—every century," he told her. "Are you through here? I came to walk back to the cottage with you."

"What makes you think I don't have other plans?" she demanded.

He grinned. "I know you. There's nothing you adore more than the sea—and your children here, of course—but you're also determined on showering the minute you're done with it."

"Fine. Walk me back, then. I definitely don't want to get dragged into the Tiki Bar," she said wearily, aware that she no longer felt alone—or afraid.

"Want me to take the bucket?"

"Wait—there's one more round for these three."

"May I?" he asked.

She shrugged. David sat on the dock. As she had, he talked to each of the dolphins as he rewarded them with their fish. Spoke, stroked.

She was irrationally irritated that they seemed to like David so much. Only Shania hung back just a little. It was as if she sensed Alex's mixed feelings about him and was awaiting her approval.

David had a knack for speaking with the animals. He understood that food wasn't their only reward, and that they liked human contact, human voices.

Shania, like the others, began to nudge him, asking for attention.

Traitor, Alex thought, but at the same time, she was

glad. Shania was a very special creature. She needed more than the others, who had never known the kind of injury and pain that Shania had suffered.

When the dolphins had finished their fish, Alex started down the dock. He walked along with her in silence. She moved fast, trying to keep a bit ahead. No way. He had very long legs.

"If you're trying to run away, it's rather futile, don't you think?"

She stopped short. "Why would I be running away?"

"Because you're hoping to lose me?"

"How can I lose you? We're on a very small island, in case you hadn't noticed."

"Not to mention that my legs are longer, so I can actually leave you in the dust at any time."

"Go ahead."

"You have the key."

"You have your own place here."

"But I'm not leaving you alone in yours."

His tone had been light and bantering, but the last was said with deadly gravity.

"This is insane," she murmured, and hurried on. She knew, though, that she wasn't going to lose him. And in a secret part of herself—physical, surely, not emotional—she felt the birth of a certain wild elation. Why? Did she think she could just play with him? Hope to tempt and tease, then hurt…?

As she felt she had been hurt?

No, surely not. Her decision to file the papers hadn't been based on a fit of temper. She had thought long and hard about every aspect of their lives.

But wasn't it true, an inner voice whispered, that jealousy had played a part? Jealousy, and the fear that others offered more than she ever could, so she couldn't possibly hope to keep him?

Despite his long legs, she sprinted ahead of him as they neared the cottage. She opened the door, ignoring him. She didn't slam it, just let it fall shut. He caught it, though, and followed her in.

Inside, she curtly told him to help himself to the bath in the hallway, then walked into her own room. She stripped right in the shower, then turned the water on hard, sudsing both her hair and body with a vengeance. Finally she got out, wrapped herself in a towel and remembered that the maid never left anything but hand towels in the guest bath.

Cursing at herself, she gathered up one of the big bath sheets and walked into the hallway. He was already in the shower. She tapped on the door. No answer.

"David?"

"What?" he called over the water.

"Here's your towel."

"What? Can't hear you."

Why was she bothering? She should let him drip dry. No, knowing David, he'd just come out in the buff, dripping all over the polished wood floors.

"Your towel!" she shouted.

"Can't hear you!" he responded again.

Impatiently, she tried the door. It was unlocked. She pushed it open, ready to throw the towel right in.

The glass shower door was clear, and the steam hadn't fogged it yet. She was staring right at him, in all his naked glory.

"Your towel," she said, dropping it, ready to run.

The glass door opened, and his head appeared. He was smiling. "Just couldn't resist a look at the old buns, huh?" he teased. "Careful, or you'll be too tempted to resist."

She forced herself to stand dead still, slowly taking stock of him, inch by inch. She kept her gaze entirely impassive. Then, her careful scrutiny complete, she spoke at last.

"No," she said, and with a casual turn, exited the bathroom. She heard his throaty laughter and leaned against the closed door, feeling absurdly weak. Damn him. Every sinewy, muscle-bound bit of him. But as she closed her eyes, it wasn't just the sleek bronze vision of his flesh that taunted her.

It was all the ways he could use it.

The door opened suddenly, giving way to her weight as she leaned against it. She fell backward, right into his very damp, very warm and very powerful arms.

Chapter 8

It probably wasn't strange that he refused to release her instantly.

"You were spying on me!" he said.

"Spying—through a closed door?" she returned.

"You were listening at the door."

"I wasn't," she assured him. His arms were wrapped around her midriff, and they were both wearing nothing but towels. "I was leaning against it."

"Weakened by the sight of me, right?" he whispered huskily, the sound just against her ear and somehow leaving a touch that seemed to seep down the length of her neck, spread into a radiance of sun warmth and radiate along the length of her.

"I divorced you, remember?" she said softly.

"I've never forgotten. Not for an instant." There was something haunting in his voice, and his hold hadn't eased in the least.

"Would you please let me go?"

"Damn. You're not charmed, standing there, me here, my body, your body…memories."

She fought very hard not to move an inch, certain he was just taunting her, and afraid she was feeling so much more than she should.

"I never denied that you could be incredibly charming," she said, trying for calm, as if she were dealing with a child. "When you chose."

"I'm choosing now."

"Too late."

"Why? We're still technically married, remember? Here we are…together, you know I won't leave this cottage, and I think you believe my concern for you is real. And you are my wife."

In a minute she would melt. She might even burst into tears. Worse, she might turn around and throw herself into his arms, then cry out all her insecurities and her belief that they'd never had a chance of making it.

"David, let me go," she said.

"Whatever you wish." He released her. The minute he did, she lost her towel.

She turned to face him, deciding not to make a desperate grab for it. Standing as casual and tall as she could, she shook her head. "That was a rather childish trick."

"It wasn't a trick. I let you go and your towel fell off. Not my fault."

"Well, thank God you still have yours."

He grinned and dropped his towel. And his smile, as well.

For a moment he stood there, watching her, with no apology at all for the visible extent of his arousal.

He took a step toward her, reaching for her, pulling her into his arms, hard and flush against his length. She knew, though, that if she protested with even a word or a gesture, he would let her go again.

She meant to say…something.

But she didn't. His fingers brushed her chin, lifting her face, tilting her head. Neither of them spoke. His eyes searched hers for a moment; then his mouth met her lips with an onslaught that was forceful, staggering. It took only the touch of his lips, the thrust of his tongue, the simple vibrant crush of his body, and she felt the stirring of sexual tension within her so deeply that she thought she would scream. If he had lowered her to the tile floor then and there, she wouldn't have thought of denial.

But he did no such thing. His lips and tongue met hers with a flattering urgency, and his hands moved down the length of her back, fingers brushing slowly, until they had cleared the base of her spine, curved around her buttocks and pressed her closer still. She felt the hard crush of his erection against her inner thighs, equal parts threat and promise, a pulsing within, creating a swirl of pure sensuality that possessed some core within her. Weakened, shaking, she clung to him, still intoxicated by the movements of his lips, teeth and tongue.

And his hands, of course, pressing, caressing…

She drew away as his lips broke from hers. She needed to say something. Married or not, they shouldn't be here now. She had moved on. For the first time she had felt chemistry with another man. With…

She couldn't even recall his name.

David's mouth had broken from hers, only to settle

on her collarbone, where his tongue drew heated circles, then move lower.

"David," she breathed. He didn't answer, because the fiery warmth of his caress had traveled to the valley between her breasts, and with each brush of flesh, she felt the need for the teasing to stop, for his lips to settle, for his body to…

"David…"

Her fingers were digging into his shoulder then. His tongue bathed her flesh, erasing any little drops that remained from her shower. Everywhere a slow, languid, perhaps even studied caress, everywhere, until those areas he did not touch burned with aching anticipation. Her abdomen was laved, thighs caressed, hips, the hollows behind her knees, her thighs…close…closer….

"David…"

"What?" he murmured at last, rising to his full height, still flush against her, yet meeting her eyes. "Don't tell me to stop," he said, gaze dark and volatile, "Alex, don't tell me to stop."

"I—I wasn't going to," she stuttered.

He arched an eyebrow.

"I was going to tell you that I couldn't stand, that…I was about to fall."

"Ah," he murmured, watching her for the longest moment as heat and cold seared through her, heat that he held her still, cold, the fear that had come before, that he would leave her, that her life, like her body, would be empty.

"I—I don't think I can stand," she said, swallowing, lashes falling.

"You don't need to," he said, and he swept her up, his arms firm and strong, his eyes a shade of cobalt so dark they might have been pure ebony. He moved the few steps through the hall, eyes upon her all the while, pressed open the bedroom door and carried her in. And still he watched her, and in the long gaze he gave her, she felt the stirring in her quicken to a deeper hunger, urgency, desperation. It was almost as if he could physically stroke her with that gaze, touch every erogenous zone, reach inside her, caress her very essence.

She breathed his name again. "David."

At last he set her down, and though she longed just to circle her arms around him, feel him inside her, he had no such quick intent. He captured her mouth again, kissed her with a hot, openmouthed passion that left her breathless. And while she sought air in the wake of his tempest, he moved against her again, mouth capturing her breasts, tending to each with fierce urgency. She felt the hardness of her own nipples, felt them peaking against his mouth and tongue, and then the cold of the air struck them and brought shivers as he moved his body against hers. This time he didn't tease, but parted her thighs and used his mouth to make love to her with a shocking, vital intimacy, until she no longer arched and whispered his name, but writhed with abandon and desperation, unable to get close enough, unable to free herself, ravenous for more and more.

Sweet familiarity. He knew her. Knew how to make love to her. Time had taught him to play her flesh and soul, and he gave no quarter, ignored the hammering in his own head, the frantic pulse in his blood, a drumbeat she could feel against her limbs. She cried out at last, stunned, swept away, crashing upon a wave of physical ecstasy so sweet it left her breathless once again, almost numb, the beat of her own heart loud in her ears. But before she could drift magically back down to the plane of real existence, he was with her, as she had craved, body thrusting into hers, their limbs entangled. The roller coaster began a fierce climb once again, driving upward with a frenetic volatility that made all the world disappear and, in time, explode once again in a sea of sheer sensual splendor, so violent in its power that she saw nothing but black, then stars…then, at last, the bedroom again, and the man still wrapping her with his arms. Shudders continued to ripple through her, little after currents of electricity, and as they brought her downward, she couldn't help but marvel at the sheer sexual prowess of the man and the almost painful chemistry they shared.

He rose up on his elbow, slightly above her, and used his free hand to smooth a straying lock of damp hair from her face. She was startled to see the tension that remained in his eyes as he studied her. And she was more startled still by the husky tone in his voice when he suddenly demanded, "Why?"

"Why?" she repeated.

"Why did you do it? You didn't call…you didn't write. You sent divorce papers."

She stared back at him. Why?

Because I couldn't bear the thought of you having this with any other woman—ever. Because I was losing you. Losing myself. I was happy at your side, but I needed my own world, as well. And I was sure that one day you would realize I wasn't the kind of woman you could spend forever with.

She didn't speak the words. It wasn't the time. She was far too off balance. She moistened her lips, desperately seeking for something to say.

"Sex doesn't make a marriage," she managed at last. He frowned slightly, staring at her still.

She pushed him away from her. "David…you're heavy," she said, though it wasn't true.

But he shifted off her. She rose and sped into her bathroom, where she just closed the door and stood there, shivering. Finally she turned the shower on and stepped beneath it. If they had really still been married, he would have followed her. He could do absolutely incredible things with a soap bar in his hands, with suds, with water, with teasing, laughing, growing serious all over again, heated….

He didn't follow her. She didn't know how long she stayed in the shower, but when she emerged, he had left her bedroom.

She found a long sleep shirt and slipped into it, then paused to brush out the length of her now twice-washed hair. She realized that she was starving, yet opted not to leave her room.

She set the brush back down on her dresser and noted that her array of toiletries was out of order. The women in housekeeping never touched her dresser, which she kept in order herself, or her desk and computer, in the spare bedroom. Had David been going through her things?

She had a dolphin perfume dispenser. It wasn't valuable, but it was pretty and meant a lot to her, because her parents had given it to her for her tenth birthday. It was porcelain, about five inches high and beautifully painted. She always set it in the middle and arranged the rest of her toiletries around it. Now the dolphin was off to the side and a fancy designer fragrance was in the center. By rote, she rearranged the perfumes, talcs and lotions.

No big deal. Just…curious.

She shrugged, still thinking about making love with David. One part of her wondered how the hell she had lived without him, without being together like that, for an entire year. The other part of her was busy calling herself the worst kind of fool in the world.

Then she reminded herself that she shouldn't be dwelling on personal considerations at all. A man had died today. This time there was no doubt that she had found a body.

In her own mind—and, apparently, in David's—there was no doubt that she had found a body on the beach, as well. And in David's mind, that body had belonged to Alicia Farr. His friend? His sometime lover? Either way, it had to disturb him deeply, and yet…

And yet, there they had been tonight.

She set her brush down, completely forgetting that the toiletries on her dresser had been rearranged.

Then she crawled into bed. Somehow, she was going to make herself sleep.

Alone.

She really could look like an angel, David thought, opening the door to her bedroom. She was sound asleep in a cloud of sun-blond hair, her hand lying on the pillow beside her face. Just seeing her like that, he felt both a swelling of tenderness…and a stirring of desire.

Determinedly, he tamped down both.

He had the coffee going; he'd returned to his own place in a flash for clothing, and then put out cereal and fruit for breakfast. He hadn't forgotten that he'd promised Zach that he would show him—and his mother—the *Icarus*, and mentioned to the boy that they might meet for breakfast, but it was too early to meet them, and if Alex had maintained her old habits, she would forget to eat during the day, so she needed to start out with something.

And he needed to talk with her.

He walked into the room, ripping the covers from her and giving her shoulder a firm shake. She awoke instantly and irritably, glaring at him as if she were the crown princess, and he a lowly serf who had dared disturb her.

"Breakfast," he said briefly.

She glanced at her alarm. "I don't have to be up yet," she told him indignantly.

"Yes, you do."

"No, I don't."

"Trust me, you do."

She groaned, resting her head in her hands. "Really, David, this is getting to be too much. Listen, last night was…nothing but the spur of the moment. You need an ego boost? It was just the fact that you do have nice buns and you've managed to ruin my one chance for a nice affair here. At any rate, you can stay here if you want to, so knock yourself out. But I've just about had it with you acting like a dictator."

"Then maybe you should quit lying to me."

"About what?" she demanded, looking outraged.

"Danny Fuller."

She groaned. "Now I really don't know what you're talking about."

"Get up. There's coffee. That always seems to improve your temper."

"I don't have a temper."

"I beg to differ," he told her, and added, "Come on, out here, and you can eat while you talk."

He didn't let her answer but exited the room. Just after he had closed the door, he heard the pillow crash against it.

He turned and opened it. "No temper, huh?" he queried.

She still wasn't up. Tangled blond hair was all around her face, and she was in a soft cotton T-shirt that didn't do a thing to make her any less appealing. It should have been loose, but somehow it managed only to enhance her curves.

He closed the door quickly before she could find something else to throw.

In the kitchen, he poured two cups of coffee, then hesitated where he stood, tension gripping his abdomen in a hard spasm.

What the hell had gone so wrong between them? He'd never met anyone like her. He loved everything about her, from her eyes to her toes, the sound of her voice, her passion when she spoke about dolphins, teaching, the sea, and the way she looked when they made love, the way she moved, touched him, the smell of her, sight, sound, taste….

He'd never fallen out of love with her. When he'd received the divorce papers, he'd been stunned. She hadn't said a word. But it was what she had wanted, so, bitterly, silently, he had given it to her.

He started, putting the coffeepot back as she stumbled into the kitchen, casting him a venomous gaze and reaching for the coffee he had poured for her. She took a seat on one of the counter bar stools, arched an eyebrow to him and poured cereal into a bowl and added milk.

"All right, let's get to it. What was my relationship with Danny Fuller supposed to have been? Did I have a thing going with the old guy or something?"

"Don't be flippant."

"I don't know what the hell else you want me to be. Of all the stuff you've come up with since you've been here, this is the most ridiculous. I don't know what you're talking about."

"All right, I'll tell you. Alicia Farr spent all the time she could with Danny Fuller during his last days at the hospital. And in their conversations, two things kept coming up, dolphins—and your name."

She stared at him. He couldn't believe she had been hiding anything, not the way she was looking at him.

She shook her head at last. "Danny Fuller came here, yes. I liked him. He really liked dolphins, and you know me, I like anyone who likes my dolphins. Sometimes we talked casually in the Tiki Hut. He told me about some of his adventures, but if there was something he wanted to do but never attempted, I swear to you, I don't have the faintest idea what it was."

"Did he ever mention a ship called the *Anne Marie* to you?"

Staring at him, she gave it a moment's thought, then shook her head slowly. "No. He never mentioned it, and I never heard any stories about a ship named the *Anne Marie* from anyone else."

David lowered his head. Too bad. It would have helped if Alex had known something.

He gazed up at her again thoughtfully. Either she really didn't know anything or she had added acting to her repertoire of talents. Which might be the case. He had just about forced his presence here. And last night…

Well, according to her, it had been the situation, nothing more. Too many days spent on an island.

"So?" she said. "Is that all you wanted? Is that why you were so insistent on 'protecting' me? If so, honest to God, I can't help you."

"No. You're in danger. If two corpses haven't proven it to you, nothing will."

Her eyes narrowed. "Forget that. You, apparently, have heard about a ship called the *Anne Marie*."

"Yes."

"Well?"

"She was an English ship that went down in the dying days of the pirate era, in 1715. Records have her sinking off the coast of South Carolina. But the story of her sinking was told by a pirate named Billy Thornton—a pirate who apparently expected a reprieve and didn't get one. As he was about to be hanged, he shouted out, 'She didn't really—'"

"She didn't really what?" Alex demanded.

"Well, people have mused that he was about to say she didn't really go down anywhere near South Carolina. You see, before he was caught, he claimed to have seen the ship go down in a storm that ravaged the Eastern Seaboard, but some historians believe he attacked the ship himself."

"He couldn't have attacked the ship alone," Alex pointed out.

"Some legends suggest that since he was off the Florida coast, it would have been easy for him to go ashore, and kill his own men with the intent of going back himself for the treasure."

"And what was the treasure?" Alex demanded.

"There are full records in the English archives somewhere," he said, "but basically, tons of gold bullion, and a cache of precious gems that would be worth millions today."

Alex shook her head. "I don't understand. There must be hundreds of ships with treasures that sank in the Atlantic and are still out there to be found. Why would people kill over this one?"

"Most people wouldn't kill over any treasure. But the bounty to be found on this particular ship would be just about priceless."

"Did Alicia think she knew where to find the *Anne Marie?* If so, she should have announced an expedition and gathered people around her. No matter what, she'd have to go by the laws of salvage."

"Yes. But she was afraid, I think, of letting out what she knew. Afraid that someone would beat her to it."

"Why would Danny Fuller have hidden whatever information he had for so many years? If he knew something, why wouldn't he have gone after it himself?"

"I wondered about that myself. Maybe he just found out. It's my assumption that Alicia learned something from Danny Fuller about where the *Anne Marie* went down. She intended to set up an expedition, and that's why she wanted to meet me here. But she must have talked to other people, as well. And I think someone she brought in on her secret decided that they wanted the secret—and the treasure—for themselves.

"The thing is," David said, hoping he was making an impact on her, "someone is willing to kill for that treasure. And I don't think this person wants the government involved in any way. If he—or she—thinks he can bring up a fortune without the authorities getting wind of it, then I'm assuming whatever information Danny Fuller had, suggested the vessel went down in shallow waters, and that the tides and sand have obscured her. You know, kind of like time itself playing a joke, hiding her in plain sight."

"So...you believe Seth Granger was involved—invited here to meet Alicia, too, and that he didn't just drown, but was killed?" Alex asked.

"It's a possibility," he said. "A probability," he amended.

"How? He was in the bar with everyone else. And he'd clearly been drinking too much. And if someone did kill Alicia, and it was her body that I found...how in the hell did it just disappear?"

"Obviously it was moved."

"Have you talked to Sheriff Thompson about this?"

"Not directly. I haven't had a chance. I had Dane call him, though, and give him all the information he acquired when I asked him to check into things."

"Great," Alex murmured. "Do you have any idea who this person is?"

"Someone with an interest in the sea and salvage. I thought at first that it might have been Seth, but now... apparently not."

"Who else might Alicia have invited here?" Alex asked. "Or who else might have gotten wind of what was going on?"

"Well, Seth was rich—he could have provided the funding she would need for the expedition. She invited me for my expertise. I'm not sure who else she might have invited."

"So who might have found out something?"

"Your boss, for one."

"Jay? But he isn't an expert salvage diver. As far as I know, he's competent enough on a boat, but he doesn't have the kind of money you'd need for an expedition like this and…" She paused and shrugged. "I see. You think he'd like to have that kind of money. And he would love to be respected for a discovery of that kind." She shook her head. "I can't believe it. Not Jay."

"There's Hank Adamson," David said.

She stared at him incredulously. "He's a reporter."

"And he's very conveniently here right now."

"I think you're reaching," she said.

"Maybe."

"Is there anyone else on your list of suspects?" she asked.

"Just one."

"Who?"

He hesitated before answering. "Your ex–navy SEAL," he told her quietly.

She rose, pushing her cereal bowl away. "I have to go to work," she said curtly, turning her back on him.

He went after her, catching her arm, turning her around to face him. "Please, Alex. Honestly, I'm not trying to run your life, much less ruin it, but for now… just until we get to the bottom of this, don't be alone with anyone, okay?"

"Except for you?" she asked, and her tone was dry.

"Except for me, yes," he said flatly.

She tried to pull away.

"Alex, please?"

"I have to go to work, David," she said, staring at his fingers where they wrapped around her arm. She met his eyes as he let her go and added bitterly, "You really don't have anything to worry about. Last night might have been…unintended, but still, I'd never switch around between men with that kind of speed. I like John, yes. I admire him, and I certainly enjoy his company. But I have a few things to settle with myself before… Under the circumstances—let's see, those being that we're not legally divorced and we may have two murders on our hands—I'll be taking my time getting to know anyone. Will that do?"

He hated the way her eyes were sharp and cold as they touched his. But she had given him the answer he needed from her. He nodded. She turned and headed for the bedroom, and a few minutes later, wearing the simple outfit she wore to work with the dolphins, she came back out, heading straight for the door.

She turned back and said, "Don't forget to lock up when you leave." A slight frown creased her forehead.

"What is it?"

"Nothing. Just don't forget to lock up before you leave. My keys are by the door. Please make sure you pick them up."

She walked out, and he felt as if an icy blast passed by.

Alex's actual degree had been in psychology, with a minor in marine sciences. But as far as her work went, she had learned more from an old trainer when she had interned in the center of the state. He had pointed out to her that the same theories that worked with people also worked with animals. Most animals, like most people, responded best to a reward system.

With dolphins, a reward didn't have to be fish. Like people, they craved affection.

Take Shania. She accepted fish and certainly had a healthy appetite. But she also seemed to know that her vets and the workers here had given her life back to her. The best reward for her came from free swims with the people she loved, mainly Alex and Gil. That morning, after feeding her charges with Gil, Alex entered the lagoon with them, one at a time, for a play period.

At eight, an hour before the first swim was due to begin, there was still no sign of Laurie Smith. Concerned, she called Laurie's cottage, then her cell phone, and received only her voice mail. Worried then, she called Jay.

"I don't know where Laurie is," she told him. "She isn't here, and she isn't answering her phone."

"Give her fifteen minutes, then we'll start a search. She's been talking about taking a few days to visit her family in St. Augustine, but I can't believe she'd just leave without asking for the time. Unless...she's just walking out on us," Jay said over the phone.

"She loves her job. She wouldn't just walk out," Alex told him.

"I'll send someone around to her cottage," Jay promised. "By the way, we may be evacuating our guests and the majority of our personnel soon."

"Evacuating?" she said, stunned.

"Don't you ever watch television?"

"Sorry, I just haven't seen the news lately," she murmured.

"That storm stalled. The forecasters still believe she's heading for the Carolinas, but at the moment she's standing her ground. She's still not a monster storm, and this place is equipped with an emergency generator, but we can't keep the whole place running if we lose electricity and water. We'll move everyone inland for a few days if the storm doesn't take the swing she's supposed to by tomorrow. Along with most of the staff."

Alex hesitated. "I'm not leaving," she said, and added a hopeful, "Am I?"

She heard his sigh. "No, Alex, if it's your choice, you get to stay."

"Thanks."

"You know a lot of people would want to be out of here in the blink of an eye," he cautioned.

"This place has weathered a few storms already. The storm room is perfectly safe."

"I knew you wouldn't leave your dolphins unless someone dragged you off," Jay said. "All right, let me go. I'll get someone out to check on Laurie."

"Thanks."

Alex returned to the main platform area, where all guests met before breaking into two parties, no more than eight swimmers in each lagoon. Guests began to trickle in to get flippers and masks, and she and Gil started to handing them out. She was somewhat surprised to see that Hank Adamson had joined the swim again—she'd gotten the impression that he was doing each of the resort's activities just once so he could give an assessment of it.

He shrugged sheepishly when she smiled at him. "I actually like this a lot," he told her.

"I'm glad."

"Getting close to the dolphins…well, it's a whole new experience for me. Their eyes are fascinating. It's almost as if they're amused by us. They're kind of like…wet puppy dogs, I guess."

"Much bigger and more powerful when they choose to be," she said.

"Your dolphin swim is the best program here," he told her.

"Thanks."

That day, she let Gil give the introductory speech. In the middle of it, she saw Laurie Smith at last, hurrying to the platform.

A sense of relief swept over her. She realized that, deep in her heart, she had been secretly fearing that Laurie had disappeared—that she, too, would float up somewhere in the water as a corpse.

She frowned at Laurie, but Laurie looked chagrined enough already. And Alex wasn't about to question her here.

"You're all right?" she asked Laurie briefly as her friend came up next to her.

Laurie nodded, but the look she gave Alex was strange.

"What's wrong?" Alex demanded.

"Nothing. Well, everything. Not with me, though. And we've got to be quiet. People are looking at us. And what I have to tell you… We need to talk alone."

Alex couldn't help but whisper, "I was worried about you. Where have you been?"

Laurie gave her a look again, indicating that it wasn't the time or the place. "You have to swear to keep what I say quiet."

"You know I will, if I can."

"Not if you can. You have to listen to me. And you can't say a word," Laurie whispered. "I mean it. Not a word."

"As long as you're all right. And you're not about to tell me something that will endanger the dolphins or anyone else. Where have you been?"

"Hiding out," Laurie said.

"Why?"

"There was a corpse on the beach that day. Definitely."

"How do you know?"

"Because there's an undercover Federal agent on the island."

"What are you talking about?"

Laurie didn't get a chance to answer.

"All right," Gil announced loudly. "Time to split into groups. Those of you who received green tags with your flippers, head off with Alex and Mandy. Mandy, give a wave, so your people see you. Those of you with red tags, you're with Laurie and me."

"Later," Laurie whispered. "We've got to talk. People are being murdered here." She hesitated, seeing that the groups were forming and she needed to hurry. "You've got to watch out for David, Alex."

"Watch out for David? I thought that you liked him."

"Yes, I do, but…he has a lot at stake. He…he might be the murderer."

"What?" Alex said.

"Shh! We'll talk," Laurie said. "Alone, Alex. We have to be alone."

Before Alex could stop her, she was up and heading off with Gil. Without creating a scene, there was nothing Alex could do.

Stunned, she watched Laurie walk away and pondered what she'd said. David? A murderer? It couldn't be.

Could it?

Chapter 9

"This was really kind of you," Ally Conroy told David. "I hadn't realized what a big deal you are until I started talking with Seth the other night. That you would take time for us...well, it's very kind of you." She was sitting at the helm by David. Zach, filled with excitement, was standing by the mainsail, looking out at the water as they skimmed over it.

"Not a problem. Zach is good kid."

She sighed. "Yeah, at heart. I've had some trouble with him at school. I'm a nurse, and gone too often. But...we've got to live. Anyway, thank you. I was horrible last night, and you were great. It's just, Seth might have been a blowhard to others—I've heard that term a dozen times from people talking about him—but he was very sweet to me. I was just stunned and upset. He really had a high regard for you, by the way. He was going to speak to you about something important. He said that he was waiting for the arrival of one more professional friend, then you'd all be getting down to business."

"And he talked about the *Anne Marie?*" David pressed gently.

She sighed. "He asked me not to say a word to anyone, but I guess it doesn't matter now. He told me that all his life, he had been interested in treasure hunting. People always wanted his money for their expeditions, but they didn't want him to be a part of them. The woman he was expecting was going to let him go along, not just foot the bills."

"Ally, did he know anything more about where this friend he was waiting for obtained her information?"

"An old man who died. He told her he'd hidden a copy of an old pirate map on this island."

David arched an eyebrow. "You're certain? There's an actual map, and it's hidden here?"

Ally sighed. "I'm not certain of anything, but that's what he said. That the ship went down off Florida, and that the map, the proof, was hidden here."

"Thank you, Ally, for telling me," David said gravely.

"Seth didn't know where the map was," she said. "That's part of why he was so concerned that his friend hadn't arrived yet. He didn't want to talk about it with you until she did arrive." She hesitated. "Do you think maybe...someone thought he knew more about the map than he did, so they killed him? Wouldn't that put you in danger, as well?"

"Ally, we don't know how Seth died yet. And I'm a pretty big boy, but I'll watch out, okay? Thanks to you."

She smiled, turning to watch her son. "Maybe you're right."

"Ally, if you think of anything else that Seth said before he died, will you please let me know?"

"Of course."

"And watch out for yourself, too. You haven't mentioned this to anyone else, have you?"

She shook her head.

"Don't—unless you're speaking with Sheriff Thompson. He'll be over here sometime today."

"I won't say a word," she promised.

He nodded and slowed the *Icarus*, shouting to Zach that he was going to lower the anchor, because they were out of protected waters and could do a little spear-fishing.

Moments later, he stood aft with Zach, assuring himself that the boy could handle the speargun without skewering either himself or David. "We come back on board after every fish," he told Zach.

"Right. Because of the blood and sharks. And there are a lot of sharks out here, right?"

"Yup. They usually mind their own business, but…" He shrugged. "I had a friend once who liked to stay down and try to get a lot of fish at once. He used his swim trunks for a storage area. If a shark did smell the blood, the first place it would attack would be…"

"Ouch!" Zach said, laughing.

He tousled the kid's hair, pressed his own mask to his face and made a backward dive into the water.

He meant to give Zach his day out on the boat. He was anxious, however, to return to the dock at Moon Bay before noon. Before Alex would be out of the public eye.

Before she could be alone anywhere…

With anyone.

* * *

When the swim was over, Alex rewarded her dolphins with some pats, praise and fish, then stood, anxious to hurry over to the next platform and accost Laurie.

She didn't get a chance to. Jay, in another one of his handsome suits, came hurrying along the dock.

"We're starting evacuation proceedings now," he told her.

"Now?"

She looked at the sky. It was an unbelievably beautiful day, the sky an almost pure blue.

"Don't even bother looking up. You know how fast things can change."

"The storm turned toward us?"

"The Middle Keys may get a direct hit as early as late tonight or tomorrow morning. She's not a big one, but...well, you know. A storm is a storm. The ferry is here, and the guests are packing up. I'd like you and Gil to take a walk down to the beach and make sure we haven't missed anyone."

"Sure."

"The others can rinse down the equipment and get this part of the operation closed down. Later, if the storm keeps on coming, you can go down and open the lagoon gates so the dolphins can escape to the open sea if necessary."

She nodded. The lagoons were fairly deep; her charges could ride out a storm much better than people could. Still, the facility had been planned with escape routes for the animals, should they be needed.

"Did they act strangely today?" Jay asked.

"No."

"Then I'd say we've still got plenty of time."

Jay didn't have a particular affinity for the animals, but he knew enough about them to know that the dolphins would know when the storm was getting close.

"I see that Laurie arrived fine," Jay said.

"Yes."

"She told Len she forgot to charge her cell phone."

"Well, yesterday was her day off, and she wasn't that late this morning," Alex reminded him. Until she had a chance to listen to Laurie, she certainly didn't intend to tell Jay that anything was wrong in any way. She turned around, looking toward the next lagoon. Irritated, she realized that both trainers were already off the platform.

"Where's Gil? Does he know we're going on a beach hunt?"

"I just passed him. He's at the Tiki Hut, grabbing a sandwich."

"Is Laurie with him?"

"I don't know," Jay said. "Don't worry, you'll have a chance to talk to her when you get back. You know the island better than anyone else, so I appreciate you doing this yourself with Gil."

"Sure, I'll go find him."

Alex looked around for Laurie as she walked the path to the Tiki Hut, which was almost dead quiet, despite the time of day.

"Grilled chicken," Gil announced to her, lifting a wrapped sandwich. "I got you one, too, and a couple of bottles of water."

She arched an eyebrow, amused. "The beach isn't that far."

"Yeah, but we've got a lot of trails to check, just to

make sure. The ferry's already picked up anyone who planned to check out today. It will be returning soon."

"Where did Laurie go so quickly?" Alex demanded. "She should be cleaning the equipment and battening down with Manny and Jeb."

"I don't know. She was with me right after the swim. She was pretty upset, though. She couldn't believe Jay had us finish the swim when there had been an evacuation notice. But she knows her responsibilities, and we've still got hours to get out, though I'm sure the roads will be a mess. We'll find her when we get back. Jay said you're staying, but that the rest of the dolphin team has to be on the next ferry."

"Amazing, isn't it?" she said, looking at the sky, despite the fact she knew it didn't really mean anything.

"Always a calm before a storm. Didn't your folks teach you that?" Gil teased.

"I suppose."

They reached the beach. As far as the eye could see, it appeared to be empty.

"Well, I'm sure Jay will make sure all the guests and employees are accounted for," Gil said. "But I guess we have to comb the trails anyway, huh?"

She smiled. "You go to the left, I'll go to the right, and we'll circle around and meet in the middle. How's that?"

Even as she spoke, she felt a lift in the breeze. It was subtle, but there. "I guess the storm really is coming in," she said.

"You never know. They can predict them all they want, but that doesn't mean they're going to do what they're supposed to. Had it reached hurricane status yet?"

"I don't know," she said ruefully. "I wasn't really paying attention. Yesterday was quite a day, if you'll remember."

They'd reached the fork in the trail. "You go your way, I'll go mine," he told her.

She nodded and started off.

The trails were actually really pretty. She didn't know how many of the trees were natural and how many had been planted to give the feel of a lush rain forest. Great palm fronds waved over her head, allowing for a gentle coolness along the walk and, she noted, a lot of darkness and shadow.

The fronds whispered and rustled, and she felt as if the darkness was almost eerie, all of a sudden. There was a noise behind her, and she spun around, then felt like a fool. The noise was nothing more than a squirrel darting across a path.

Still, she felt as if she had come down with a sudden case of goose pimples, and then she knew why. David had told her not be alone.

And certainly not alone walking down an isolated trail.

She was suddenly angry. She'd never been afraid here before. She had enjoyed the solitude that could be found on the island.

But that had been before people started dying.

She quickened her steps, anxious to get back to Gil. "Hello? Anyone out here?" she called. There was no reply.

Birds chattered above her head.

She looked all around herself. Not much farther and she would meet back up with Gil.

She reached the farthest point, seeing the sand on

the southern tip of the isle, and stepped off the trail to look around and call out. Nothing.

She turned back, noting that the breeze was growing stronger. In the shelter of the trees, though, she could barely feel it. The dive boat hadn't gone out that morning, she thought, but pleasure craft had probably been rented out. She hoped all the guests were back in.

"Hello?" she called out again, and once more paused to look around. She quickened her pace, then stopped suddenly.

And it wasn't a sound that had caused her to stop. It was a stench. A horrible stench.

And she knew what it was. The rotting, decaying, stench of death.

She started walking forward again, shouting now. "Gil! Gil!"

She started to run, and the smell grew stronger.

There was no denying it. Very near them, hidden in the foliage, something—or someone—lay dead.

"Gil!"

She nearly collided with him.

"What the hell is it?" he asked.

"Something dead," she told him.

"Yeah…that's what I thought. But where is it coming from?" Gil asked.

"It's gotten stronger as I've come toward you," Alex told him.

"Then it's here somewhere."

She stood still, surveying their immediate surroundings.

"Alex."

"What?"

"Let's get out of here," Gil said.

"Gil, we can't. We have to find out what it is."

"Or who it is," he said uneasily. "Alex, this is a matter for the sheriff."

"No! Yes, I mean, but not now. I am not letting anyone else disappear."

"What are you talking about?"

"We have to find out what it is, then call the sheriff. Gil, please?" Alex said. She took a few steps in the direction of a large clump of trees.

"Alex…" Gil said.

"It's here," she whispered. "There are a bunch of palm fronds on the ground, fallen leaves…and the smell is really strong. It's here."

He looked at her, then sighed. "All right. I'll lift the fronds."

"We'll do it together," she said.

They steeled themselves against the smell of death and set to work.

And after a moment, it was Gil who let out a sick croak of sound.

David had listened to the radio warnings and decided it was time to head back in. The water where they were was about seventy feet deep, and he'd snagged a few snapper. Zach, proudly, had speared his first fish ever, and it had been a beauty. Someone would be enjoying his catch tonight, one big beaut of a dolphin—or mahimahi, as the restaurants called it, afraid that otherwise diners would think they were serving big cuddly marine mammals.

They hadn't taken the spearguns down this time; they'd just gone for a last look around. Far below them, a few outcrops of coral welcomed all manner of sea life.

David was just about to motion Zach back to the boat when he saw something that caused him to pause. Anemones could create the appearance of heads with waving hair, and that was what he was certain he was seeing at first. But then…

David thought there was something beneath the skeletal arms of the coral.

He surfaced, and Zach did the same, lifting his mask and snorkel. "We have to go back, huh?"

"Yes. Head on to the *Icarus*. I'll be right with you."

He watched Zach swim back to the *Icarus,* which wasn't more than twenty feet away. Then, taking a deep breath, he jackknifed in a hard, clean dive toward the depths.

He reached the coral, saw the outstretched arm, and…

Horror filled him so completely that he almost inhaled a deadly breath.

There she was.

Alicia. Or what remained of her.

Hair billowing in the water…

Features partially consumed.

Feet encased in concrete.

"That has to be the biggest, fattest, deadest possum I've seen in my entire life," Gil said, turning aside. "Phew."

"Thank God it's just a possum," Alex said fervently.

Gil looked at her, puzzled. "Okay, I know I was acting a little weird, but you seemed convinced we were going to find a person."

She shrugged, remembering that Gil had no idea she'd

already found one body on the beach. "I guess I'm just spooked because of yesterday. Let's head back."

David docked the *Icarus* just long enough to drop off Ally and Zach, then headed for dry dock on the Gulf side of Plantation Key.

There he waited for Nigel Thompson to pick him up in his patrol car.

David slid into the passenger seat, meeting Nigel's gaze.

"You're a fool, you know, going back when everyone else is evacuating. Actually, I think it's about to become mandatory. You could have taken that yacht of yours and sailed her straight north," Nigel said.

"And wound up chased by the storm anyway," David said. "And you know damn well I would never leave Alex—or Moon Bay, for that matter—until this thing is solved. I hope this storm comes in and out fast."

"I'd have divers out there now, if I could," Nigel said. "But I've got every man on the evacuation route, and since we're talking about a corpse, I can't risk living men on a recovery mission. The water is getting rougher by the minute."

"I'm afraid that by the time the storm has passed through, the body might have…hell, it might have been ripped apart," David said.

"You know there's nothing I can do right now," Nigel said firmly.

David was silent, then said, "I know. But damn the timing. There was no way to get her to the surface, and then, hell, I had a kid on the boat."

"You know the location. You won't forget?" Nigel said.

"Oh, you bet I know it. And I gave you the coordinates."

Nigel glanced at him. They were on the main road at last, just miles from the ferry platform that serviced Moon Bay, but they were creeping along. There was one road down to the Keys, and one road back, so with the exodus going on, traffic was at a crawl.

"You know, Jay Galway can refuse to let you stay," Nigel warned him.

"He won't," David said with assurance.

"And you're certain you want to stay?"

"More so than ever," David said firmly.

Nigel was quiet again, then said, "Just because you found Alicia Farr today, that doesn't mean that her remains were ever at Moon Bay. I questioned everyone about the woman yesterday, when I was asking who might have seen Seth Granger leave the bar. And not a one of them saw her, any more than they did Seth."

"Which just goes to show you that no one in the place is observant. And that someone is lying," David told him. "Did you get the M.E.'s report back on Seth, yet?"

Nigel nodded.

"And?"

"The man drowned."

"I still think someone helped him do it."

Nigel twisted his head slightly. "Maybe."

"You know more than what you've said," David accused him.

"There are some bruises on the back of his skull," Nigel said. "The M.E. hasn't determined the source of them. He might have hit his head or something. Look, they took him up to Miami-Dade. One of the best guys they've got there is working on him, all right? They deal in fact, not supposition."

"Yeah. Well, there's one dead man for certain, and I know for a fact that Alicia is dead and rotting. And fact. She didn't just drown or have a boating accident. Not unless she lived long enough to cast her feet in cement and throw herself in the water."

"All right, David, I swear, the minute I've got an all clear on the weather, I'll be out there myself with the boys from the Coast Guard, hauling her up. All right?"

"I don't know if that will be soon enough," David muttered.

"For what?"

"She was murdered—there's a murderer loose. On Moon Bay. Can't you do something? I need to get back there fast."

"What do you want me to do, plow down the cars?"

"Put your siren on."

"This isn't an emergency."

"Maybe it is."

Nigel sighed, turned on his siren and steered his patrol car onto the shoulder of the road. "If I get a flat, you're fixing it."

David shook his head, offering him a half smile. "If you get a flat, I'm going to hitch a ride in the first Jeep I see."

Still on edge, Alex and Gil returned to the resort area just as the ferry was about to leave with the last of the guests and personnel. Dismayed, Alex ran to the dock, looking for Laurie.

"Alex, you're coming?" Jeb called to her from the crowded deck.

"No, but I need to see Laurie," she called from the dock.

"She's inside somewhere," he said. "I'll find her."

Gil had run up behind her. "Damn, I hope someone got my stuff." He turned to her. "You sure you want to stay? The dolphins will be just fine. Think about it, alone in that little place with Jay, Len and a handful of others? C'mon! Just hop on board the ferry. We'll have fun in Miami."

"No, no, I can't leave," she told him.

"It's going to be like a paid vacation."

Jeb came back to the rail. "Hey, Gil, I got your wallet and an overnight bag for you."

"Great."

"Where's Laurie?" Alex asked.

"She said she was coming," Jeb said.

Alex watched nervously as the ferry's ties were loosed and she prepared to depart. She scanned the vessel for Laurie. Gil barely made it to the gangplank. An impatient seaman yelled at him, "I called an aboard five minutes ago!"

"Sorry," Gil said.

The plank was up. Alex stared at the ferry in disbelief, ready to throttle Laurie herself. How could she say what she had—then disappear without a word?

Then, just as the ferry moved away from dock, Laurie appeared at last. She looked distressed. "Alex, stick with Jay, all right? Stick with Jay and Len and…whoever else."

Alex stared back at Laurie, then whipped out her cell phone, holding it up so that Laurie would see her intention.

Laurie gave her a smile, digging in her bag for her own phone.

Then she frowned and put her thumb down. “No battery!” she shouted.

“Jeb, give her a phone!” Alex shouted.

Jeb did, and a minute later Alex’s phone rang. She answered it. “Laurie, what the hell’s going on?”

“Alex, don’t hang around David, okay?”

“Why?”

“Because something is going on. Something that has to do with salvage. Listen, you should be all right. Hank Adamson is staying on—he wants to write a story about battening down for a storm, and John will be there, too.”

“John Seymore? Why?”

“I told you about him.”

“No, you didn’t.”

“He’s the agent I told you about. He’s FBI. Well, I assume he’s FBI. Or working with them or something.”

“Laurie, how do you know this? Please, explain before the weather comes in and the phones go completely.”

“All right, I’m trying. I ran into him, so we went to his cottage and talked. Just talked. That was it. I swear.”

“I believe you,” Alex said. “Please, get to the point.”

“John said he liked you a lot, but he wasn’t stepping in when there was obviously something still going on between you and David. He was concerned, though, and wished you weren’t still emotionally involved with

David. John's afraid that Alicia Farr has disappeared. And that she's met with foul play. He was worried about me, and he's very worried about you, because apparently there's a nurse in Miami who heard Daniel Fuller talking about you, a treasure and the dolphins. Honestly, Alex, I can see why you had such a crush on John—before David showed up again. John is wonderful. I stayed at his place—just in case anyone knew I'd seen the body you discovered and thought that I might know who it was or talk. That's why you couldn't get hold of me. I stayed there even when he was out on David's boat. And last night…he told me about Seth Granger, and that he didn't think Granger died by accident. So…he knows I was going to talk to you. Alex…Alex…are you there?"

"Yes, I'm here. Why does he suspect David?"

"Who else was close to Alicia Farr? Who else is famous for his treasure hunting expeditions? Really, you should have gotten off the island. Maybe you still can. Oh, and, Alex…"

Her voice faded, and there was a great deal of static on the line.

"Alex, did you hear me? Watch…" Static. "I know because…" Static.

Then the line went dead completely.

An arm slipped around her shoulders, and she nearly jumped a mile.

"Hey!" It was Jay. He'd actually doffed his suit and was in simple jeans and a red polo shirt so he could help batten things down. "You all right?"

"Yes, of course." She wasn't all right at all, but she sure intended to fake it. "Jay, who is still on Moon Bay?"

"There's Len and me, you, the reporter—Hank Adamson. He's been incredibly helpful, and he wants to write about the storm. It's not going to be that big a hurricane, at least."

"Right. Hopefully, she'll stay small. But who else is here, Jay? Anyone?"

"John Seymore—and your ex–old man."

"You let those two stay—and made your staff evacuate?"

"David has hit storms like this at sea, he can surely weather it. And John Seymore was a SEAL. They both wanted to stay. I had the power, and I said yes. Do you have a problem with this?"

Yes.

But she couldn't explain that she doubted both men—or why. She couldn't forget her conversation with Laurie. John Seymore claimed to be some sort of agent, but was he really? Had Laurie seen any credentials?

And what about David? David, who kept warning her that she was in danger.

Had he known she had found a body on the beach because he had been the one to murder the woman?

No, surely not. She winced, realizing that she was refusing to believe it because she was in love with him. She had been since she had met him. The divorce hadn't really meant anything, and she would probably be in love with him the rest of her life.

However long, or short, a time that might be.

Where the hell was Alex? John Seymore wondered. Jay Galway had said that he'd sent her and Gil out to check the trails, but they should have been back long ago.

He went out in search of them himself.

For a small island, there were an awful lot of trails. He began to understand what had taken them so long.

As he walked, he was easily able to assure himself that everyone else had gotten off the island. He called out now and then, looked everywhere and didn't find a soul.

But, returning, he smelled a foul odor on the air and instantly recognized it. The smell of death.

As he hurried forward, his heart shuddered hard against his chest. He stood still, looking around for any sign of company.

After a moment, convinced he was alone, he stepped forward to examine the source of the odor.

A moment later, he stepped back, relieved to have discovered only a dead possum, then hurried along the rest of the trails. When he reached the Tiki Hut, it was empty. Walking around to the docks, he saw no one, and far out to sea, the last ferry was just visible.

He turned, hesitating for a moment. Alex might have gone to the lodge. But though the winds had picked up a great deal, growing stronger by the minute now, so it seemed, they were still hardly in serious weather.

He heard a distant splash.

The dolphin lagoons.

With quick steps, he hurried toward them. He arrived in time to see Alex on the second platform, talking to her charges and handing out fish. He started along the path to the platforms. Halfway there, she met him, empty fish bucket in her hand. She stopped short, staring at him.

"Alex." He said her name with relief.

She still looked at him suspiciously.

"Alex, you…you have to be careful."

"Yes, I know," she said, sounding wary. Then she stiffened. "I hear you're an agent."

"You hear I'm what?"

"An agent. A government agent. An FBI man—or so Laurie assumes."

"I'm not on the payroll, but yes, I work with the FBI."

"If you're working for the government, then why not just announce it?"

"Because there are those who shouldn't know—just yet. Because I don't know what has really happened—or might happen."

"So you're accusing David of being willing to kill to get what he wants?"

John Seymore sized her up quickly and shook his head. "I'm not accusing anyone of anything. Not yet. But Alicia Farr has disappeared. And a man died under mysterious circumstances yesterday. Your name was mentioned by a dying man who supposedly held a secret worth millions."

"I see…. So I shouldn't trust David, and your only interest in me was because a dying man kept saying my name?" she asked skeptically.

He sighed, feeling his shoulders slump. "I want to protect you."

"Gee, everybody wants to protect me."

"Alex, you know that my interest in you was real."

"What I know is that there are six of us together here for a storm. Together. I won't be alone. And by the way, I don't know a damn thing about the treasure, where it is, or what it has to do with dolphins, so you don't need to draw me into casual conversation about it."

"Alex, I really am with the authorities."

"Want to show me some credentials?"

He pulled out his wallet, keeping his distance, showing her his identification.

"Consultant, right," she said with polite skepticism.

"I'm a civilian employee, working special cases."

"This is a special case?"

"I was a navy SEAL. This is a sea-related investigation."

"Well, as we both know, IDs can be easily faked."

"I'm telling the truth," he said.

"So you went after Laurie?" she said, still polite, but her tone conveying that she didn't believe a word.

"I didn't go after Laurie. There was nothing personal between us. Besides, you were back with your ex-husband," he said flatly, then added a careful, "And far too trusting of him, far too quickly."

"Well, rest assured, I'm not sure if I trust anyone anymore. And now I see Jay. I have to lock up a few things and get up to the lodge. Excuse me, please."

She walked by him as if she had all the confidence in the world. His eyes followed her, and he could see that she hadn't been lying. Jay Galway was there.

Was he to be trusted?

There was little else he could do but hurry back for his own things and get to the storm room to join the others.

He looked at the sky just as the rain began.

Chapter 10

As soon as David got back to Moon Bay, he raced to look for Alex at the dolphin lagoons. The dolphins were swimming around in an erratic manner, but there was no sign of Alex.

He decided that she might have gone to her cottage. Jay had ordered that the six of them remaining on the island had to gather in the storm room by ten that night, when the worst was due to hit, but it was nowhere near that late, and she might well have gone to her cottage for a bath, clothing and necessities.

But she wasn't at the cottage when he arrived. Running his fingers through his hair and taking long, jerky strides, he went through the little place, room by room.

Then he heard the door open and close. He hurried from her bedroom, relief filling him.

"Alex!"

"Hey," she murmured. She didn't sound hostile, just tense—and wary.

"Are you all right?" he demanded.

She frowned. "Of course." She eyed him up and down. "You don't look too good."

"Yeah, well, I've been worried about you. I told you to stay in a crowd."

"I was with someone all day," she said, still watching him carefully. "I've been busy…just opened the lagoon gates. Uh, I think I need a shower. So if you'll excuse me…"

Was she suggesting that he leave her? Not on her life. Maybe literally.

"I'll be right here. Hey, want coffee? Tea? The electricity will probably go out soon. Of course, there's a generator in the storm room. I guess it's not like you can't have tea later, if you want. But I think I'll make some coffee, anyway." He turned his back on her, walking to the kitchen area, reaching into the cupboard. He could feel her watching him. It wasn't a comfortable feeling.

After a minute, he heard her walk to the bedroom. Her behavior was disturbing. She wasn't fighting him or arguing with him—it was almost as if she were afraid to.

She reappeared just a minute later, obviously perplexed.

"When did you get here?" she asked him.

"About two minutes before you walked in. Why?"

"Did you…move things around in here today?"

"No, why?"

"Oh, nothing. The maids seem to be getting a little

strange, that's all. The maid's been in, right? Bed is made, towels are all fresh," she said.

"Then the maid must have been in. I didn't clean up," he said without apology.

She shrugged and stared at him. Studied him. As if she could find what she was looking for if she just kept at it long enough.

"All you really all right?" he asked her.

"I'm fine. But you really look like hell."

"I need a shower, too. I took Zach and Ally out on the *Icarus*. Then I took her around to the dry dock on the Gulf side and had to get back here."

"You didn't have to get back here," she corrected him. "You don't work here."

"I knew you'd be staying with your dolphins, and I wasn't about to leave you here alone with… Alone."

She nodded. Suddenly, to his surprise, she walked up to him, put her arms around him and pressed against him. Instinctively, he embraced her, smoothing back her wet hair. "What is it?" he asked, at a loss.

"I do know you, don't I?" she whispered.

"Better than anyone else," he said. "Alex, what is this?"

She pulled away slightly, a strange smile on her lips. "You're not good husband material, you know."

That hurt. "You were the best wife any man could have," he told her.

"You do love me, in your way, don't you?"

"In my way?" he said, finding it his turn to seek an explanation in her eyes. "In every way," he said, passion reverberating in his tone, his words vehement. "I swear, I never stopped loving you, Alex. Never. I would die for you in a heartbeat."

She slipped from his arms. “I have to shower,” she murmured. “Get a few things together.”

She walked into the bedroom. Five minutes later, he couldn’t stand it anymore and followed.

The water was streaming down on her. Here, as in the other bath, the glass doors were clear. He should give her space, so that she wouldn’t decide to send him away. Now, when he needed so desperately to be with her.

You look like hell, she had told him.

Hell yes. Because I found your disappearing body, and it is Alicia Farr, and, oh God, what the sea can do to human flesh…

There was no way he would tell her about his discovery now. Not until the storm had abated and the sheriff had come. They were all alone here now, at the mercy of the storm. And maybe of a murderer.

Her head was cast back as she rinsed shampoo from her hair. Back arched, limbs long, torso compelling in its clean-lined arc. He felt the sudden shudder of his heart and the iron tug on his muscles.

Taking a step forward, he opened the glass door. She looked at him and waited.

“I told you, I need to shower, too.”

“There is another shower.”

“But you’re not in it.”

He was startled to see her smile. Then her smile faded and a little shudder rippled through her. She backed up, inviting him in. He stripped in seconds and followed her.

“Shampoo?” she offered.

“That would be good.”

“On your head?” she asked.

"Where else?"

"Should I show you?"

Her tone was absolutely innocent, and still strange.

And then he realized that she wanted him—and was afraid of him.

He set the shampoo down on a tile shelf and took her into his arms, ignoring the blast of the hot water on his shoulders. "Alex, what's wrong?"

"I'm in danger. You told me so yourself," she assured him, eyes amazingly green in the steamy closeness of the shower.

"But not from me," he whispered.

She stared back at him. Then, suddenly, she shuddered once again, moving into his arms. He held her there while the water poured over them. He felt the delicious surge of heat sluicing over his body, felt himself becoming molten steel, abs bunching, sex rising, limbs feeling like iron, but vital, movable….

She knew his arousal. Knew it, sensed it, touched it. Her fingers slid erotically down the wet length of his chest and curled around his sex. She ran her fingers up and down the length of him, creating an abundance of slick, sensual suds. Spasms of arousal shuddered through him, and he lowered his lips to her shoulder, her throat, then caught her mouth with his own, tongue delving with sheer erotic intent. He ran his hands down her back, massaged his fingers over the base of her spine, cupped them around her buttocks and drew her hard against him. He was only vaguely aware of the pounding of the water. He was keenly cognizant of the feel of her flesh against his, and the heat rising between them. Catching her around the midriff, he lifted her, met her eyes and slowly brought her down, sheathing himself inside her, and finally, when her limbs were wrapped around him and they were completely locked together, he pressed her back against the tile and began to move. She buried her head against his neck, rocking, riding, moving with his every thrust, her teeth grazing his shoulders, the water careening over them both. It wasn't enough.

Without letting her go, he used one hand to reach for the door. Opening it, he exited the slick shower with her still enfolding him and staggered to the bedroom, then fell down on the bed with her, drenching the neat spread and not caring in the least. They rocked together in a desperate rhythm that seemed to be echoed by the rise of the wind and spatter of the rain beyond the confines of the cottage. He moved, and his lips found her throat, her breasts, her mouth, once again. He brought them both to a near frenzy, withdrew, and then, despite her fingers in his hair and her urgency to bring him back, he kissed the length of her soap-slicked body, burying himself between her thighs, relishing her words of both ecstasy and urgency, at last rejoining her once again, his force rising with his shuddering thrust, until they climaxed in a sweet and shattering explosion.

They lay together afterward, damp and panting. His arm remained around her, but strangely, she suddenly seemed detached. So passionate, so incredible…

And then…

"It's getting late. I've got to get dressed. Grab a few things…did you want to go to your cottage? You could do that while I pack a few things."

He stared down at her, definitely taken aback. "Wham, bang, thank you, sir?" he inquired politely.

She flushed. "There's a storm on the way."

"Of course, excuse me, let me just get out of the way."

He rose, baffled, heading for his clothes. Then he stopped, turning back to her. "Alex, there's always a storm on the way."

"What are you talking about?"

"You—there's always something. You won't talk."

"There is a storm out there!" she exclaimed.

"If you'd ever called me, ever talked about the thoughts going through your mind—"

"I called you a number of times, David. There was always someone there to say that you'd get back to me, you were in the water, you were working with a submersible…you were…well, God knows what you were doing," she told him.

He started to walk back toward her. Strangely, she backed away from him.

"David, there is a storm out there. And worse," she added softly.

"We both should have gotten off the island," he said angrily, and started to leave again. Then he spun back on her, letting her edge away from him until she came flat against the bedroom wall. Then he pinned her there.

"Get this straight. Whatever you're feeling, whatever I did, whatever you think I did, I would defend you with my last breath, I would die to keep you safe, and I will love you the rest of my life. Turn your back on me and never see me again when this is over, hell, don't even send a Christmas card, but for the love of God, trust me now!"

He didn't wait for a reply. She had been too passionate, then too stubborn and distant, for him to expect a response that made sense. It was as if she had suddenly decided that she didn't trust him.

He was dressed before she was, wearing the swim trunks and T-shirt he'd had on all day. In a few minutes she was dressed as well, a small duffel bag thrown over her shoulder. "I thought you were getting your things?" she said.

"I'm not leaving you," he told her. "Come on; we've got to stop by my place."

The wind had really picked up, and rain was pelting down. Alex started out, then stepped back, telling him she had macs in the cabinet. They were bright yellow. They certainly wouldn't be hiding in those, David thought grimly.

When he opened the door again, the wind nearly ripped it from its hinges. "Let's go!" he shouted. "This thing is coming in really fast."

They ran along the path. Thankfully, David's cottage was close. Inside, he didn't bother dressing, just grabbed fresh clothing and toiletries, then joined Alex again in minutes. They started along the trail toward the lodge. Just as they neared the Tiki Hut and the lagoons, a flash of lightning tore across the sky, almost directly in front of them.

They heard a thunderous boom. Sparks seemed to explode in the sky.

The island went dark, except for the generator-run lights from the lodge.

In the dark, David took her arm. Together, they began to hurry carefully across the lawn to the main lobby, where Jay was waiting for them impatiently.

He led the way through the reception area, the back office and through a door that led down several steps.

It wasn't a storm cellar, since it would be impossible to dig on an island that had been enhanced by man to begin with. Rather, the ground had been built up, so they were actually on a man-made hill.

The storm room was just that—one big room. There were ten cots set up in it, others folded and lined up against a wall, and doors that were labeled "Men" and "Women." There was a large dining table, surrounded by a number of upholstered chairs, and a counter that separated a kitchen area from the rest of the room. A battery-operated radio sat on the counter.

"Nice," David commented.

"Very nice," Hank Adamson said, rising from where he'd been sitting at the foot of one of the cots. "It's great, actually."

"If you like being closed in," Len said, shrugging. It was clear that he had remained only out of deference to Jay. But he offered a weak grin.

"The kitchen is stocked, we've got plenty of water, and as you can see, the generator has already kicked in," Jay said. "The brunt of the storm is due at about 4 or 5 a.m. She's still moving quickly, which is good. And her winds are at a shade less than a hundred miles an hour, so she's not a category four or five."

"With any luck, it will be all over by late tomorrow morning," Len said.

"And the damage, hopefully, will be minimal," Jay said. "The trees, though…and the foliage. They always go. No way out of it, we'll have one hell of a mess."

"But here we all are," Hank said cheerfully. "So… what do we do?"

John Seymore had been in one of the plush chairs, reading a book. His back had been to them. He rose.

"We can play poker," he suggested. "Someone saw to it that there are cards, chips, all the makings of a good game. There's even beer in the refrigerator." He was speaking to everyone in the room, but he was staring at David.

David assessed him in return. "Poker sounds good to me," he said.

"Right," John said. "We can see just who is bluffing whom."

"Sounds like fun," Hank Adamson said. "Deal me in."

Outside, the wind howled. The sound of the rain thundering against the roof was loud, and Jay had turned the volume high on the radio to hear the weather report.

The poker game continued.

It might have been any Friday night men's crowd—except Alex was playing, too. She liked poker and played fairly well. But in this group…?

They'd set a limit, quarter raises, no more. And yet it seemed that every round the pot got higher and higher.

Neither John nor David ever seemed to fold, or even to check. Between them, they were winning eighty percent of the time. When one of them dealt, there were no wild cards, and it was always five-card stud. Their faces were grim.

Thank God for Len and Jay. As the deal came around to Jay for a second time, he shuffled, calling his game. "Seven cards. One-eyed jacks and bearded kings wild."

"One-eyed jacks and bearded kings?" John Seymore said, shaking his head.

"What's wrong with that?" Len asked defensively. "Adds some spark to the game."

"I think our friends are used to hard-core, macho poker," Hank Adamson said, grinning at Alex across the table.

"Sounds like a fine game, right, John?" David asked.

"You bet," John said.

There was a slight discrepancy over one of the kings—whether he actually had a beard or if it was only five o'clock shadow. It was Alex's card, and she said she didn't need for it to be wild. For once, she had a hand. A royal flush, with the king being just what he was.

It seemed to be the only hand she was going to take. Watching David and John, she had a feeling they would both do well in Vegas.

It was difficult to sit there. She wondered how she could have spent the time she had with David, how she could have gone to her cottage, felt the overwhelming urge to make love, while still feeling that little tingle of doubt. But watching John Seymore and the subtle—and not so subtle—ways he challenged David, she had a difficult time believing that he could be an out-and-out liar or a murderer, either.

Jay's third turn to deal, and he called for Indian poker.

"What?" David asked.

"You must have played as a kid. We all get one card and slap it on our foreheads. We bet on what we think we have," Jay explained. "You can try to make faces, bluff each other out."

"It's fun, do it," Alex advised.

The cards went around, and they all pressed them to their foreheads, then stared at one another.

"Hey, there aren't any mirrors in here, are there?" Hank Adamson asked.

"Don't think so. And no one is wearing glasses, so we should be all right."

"What do we do now?" John asked.

"You're next to me. You make the first bet," Alex said.

John shrugged and threw in a quarter chip.

He had a three on his forehead. Jay had a seven; Len had the queen of diamonds, Hank a ten, and David the queen of hearts. "Big bet, buddy, for a guy with your card," Len warned him.

"Oh, yeah?" John said. "You should fold right now."

"You don't say? My quarter is in."

"You really should fold," David told John.

"You think? I'm pretty sure you shouldn't even have bothered to ante," John told him.

Betting went around twice, with each of them saying some things that were true and others that weren't.

In the end, Len folded, followed by Hank, and then Jay. The pot rose, and Alex was amazed in the end to find out that she'd been sitting with the queen of spades on her head, enough to beat David's queen of hearts.

"I don't think I should play against you guys. You're going to lie about every hand, and I'm going to fall for it," Len said.

"Len, at most, you're going to lose about twenty-five dollars tonight," Alex told him. "Start bluffing yourself."

"I never could lie," he murmured, shaking his head.

"Ah, an insinuation that the rest of us can lie with real talent?" Hank asked him.

"Careful—anything you say can and probably will be used in a column," Alex warned Len.

"Hey, I'm wounded," Hank protested. "Seriously, I'm having a blast, and I'm going to write this place up as the next paradise."

"Let the man win a few, will you, guys?" Jay said, pleased.

"Yeah, Alex, quit winning," Len said.

"Me? Look at those two," she said, indicating the piles of chips in front of David and John.

"Right. Quit winning, you two," Jay said.

"Hey! I can bluff with the best of them. Don't anyone dare let me win," Hank protested.

"Storms are funny, huh?" Len said a few minutes later, passing the cards to John. "My sister's in-laws all have boats and live right on the water. Years ago, Andrew was supposed to hit the coast. They all asked to come in and stay with my sister inland. Well, that's where the storm came in, and they all got mad at her when their cars were flattened and they had to spent the night praying in a bathtub! This is better, huh?" he said to no one in particular.

"Who would have figured we'd be here tonight?" Jay said, shrugging.

"Who'd have figured?" David echoed. He was staring at John.

"Yeah, odd isn't it, how the best-laid plans can be interrupted by nature?" John Seymore responded.

It was enough for Alex. She had to get away from the table and all the dueling testosterone or she was going to scream.

She yawned. "I'm going to beg out of this. I'm going to make a cup of tea, and then I'm going to sleep."

"But you just won a huge pot. That's not legal," Len said.

"You can split my pot among you. I think I can spring for the ten bucks," she told him, pushing her pile of chips toward the center.

"I can cash you out," Jay said. "That's not a problem."

"And not necessary. Quit worrying and take the chips." Grinning, Alex left them. She walked to the kitchen area, amazed that the storm could be raging all around them, the electricity was out—probably all through the Middle Keys, at the least—but thanks to the generator, she still had the ability to see and make tea. She turned up the radio and heard the newscaster. They were taking a pounding. It could have been much worse, if the storm had been able to pick up more speed.

"Anyone else want anything?" she called, expecting them to ask for a round of beers.

"Naw, thanks," Jay said.

His polite refusal went all around. Alex found it very strange. Poker and beer always seemed to go together, along with an assortment of snacks. None of these guys wanted anything.

It was as if they were all determined to keep a totally clear head.

The game continued as she made her tea. Though on the surface it appeared as if they were just playing cards, she had a feeling that for John and David, it was much more. They challenged one another at every turn.

She sipped her tea, half listening to the game, half to the radio. In a minute, she was going to try to sleep.

When she woke up, the storm would be over. The islands would be in a state of wreckage, but hopefully, it would be more trees and foliage than homes and buildings.

But what then? Would she finally get a chance to talk to Nigel? Would they find the truth behind Seth Granger's death?

And what about Alicia, the treasure and the dolphins?

She finished the tea and stretched out on one of the cots. Her eyes closed, then opened suddenly.

Because someone in the room was doing a great deal more than bluffing at poker. Alicia Farr was dead. And Seth was dead, and…

Very likely, someone in the room had committed murder.

David.

No.

Why would he kill Alicia? He had plenty of money from his own enterprises. Of course, he spent it, too. His excursions were costly, and not everything he did was financed by a major corporation. But why kill Alicia? He couldn't go after treasure alone.

And she herself was still in love with him. No matter what had happened, she'd been eager to sleep with him again. Even now, she was sure he was using her. She was apparently the key to something, somehow. Damn Daniel Fuller, even if he had passed on! Why had he dragged her into this?

Then there was John Seymore. Claiming that he, too, had come to protect her. Said he was working with the FBI, even had a great-looking ID. And hey, why not try to seduce the woman he was there to protect? He'd used her, too. But until she'd talked to Laurie tonight, she had liked him, really liked him. And she'd believed he was genuinely interested in her, too, because her instincts had said so.

So much for instincts.

And now…

How could she trust either of them?

She was never going to get to sleep.

"Hey!"

She jumped at the sound of Jay's voice. She rolled over to look at him. He was listening intently to the radio.

"We'll be in the eye of the storm in about half an hour."

He was right. Listening, Alex realized that the brutal pounding of wind and rain was easing somewhat.

"When it comes, I wonder if I should take a peek at the damage," Jay said.

"It's going to be the same damage in the morning," David advised him.

"Yeah, but we'll have at least twenty minutes before it starts up hard again," Jay said.

"This storm is a fast mover," David reminded him.

"He's losing. He just wants to opt out of the game himself for a few minutes," Len said.

"I think we'll all be opting out in a few minutes," Hank said. "Looking at our sleeping beauty over there, I'm feeling the yawns coming on myself."

"We should all get some rest," David said. "I have a feeling it's going to be a real bitch around here after it lets up."

"It will take a few days to get our little piece of the world up and going again, sure," Jay said. "Depending on the damage the main islands face. They'll have electric crews out first, then road crews...we'll have people out next. It's just a matter of repair and cleanup. We've done it before, we'll do it again."

"Actually, I wasn't referring to the storm damage," David said.

"Oh?" Jay said. "Then what?"

"Nigel was supposed to be coming out today to talk to people about Seth Granger," David said.

Len exhaled a snort of impatience. The others must have stared at him, Alex thought, because he quickly said, "Look, I'm sorry. I don't know if it's the right term for a man or not but he was one hell of a prima donna. He thought money could buy him anything, and he was rude to anyone he thought was beneath him. He drank like a fish. If he hadn't drowned, he would have died soon of a shot liver anyway. I'm sorry a man is dead. But I can't cry over the fact that he got drunk and fell in the water."

"But what if he didn't just fall in the water?" David said.

"You were all there with him. What the hell could have happened? He stepped out for air, lost his balance and fell into the drink. Case closed."

"I'm not sure Nigel sees it that way," David said. "Besides, there's more."

"And what would that be?" Jay asked, groaning.

"Oh, come on, Jay. We all know Alicia Farr was supposed to be here. I have the feeling Hank never really came here to do a story on the island. He was hoping to find Alicia and get the lead on whatever she knew," David said.

"You certainly came here to find Alicia," John told him politely.

"Yeah?" David said. "You supposedly didn't even know her—but I'm willing to bet you came here because of her, too. And maybe you actually found her."

"What the hell does that mean?" Len asked.

No one answered him.

"You know, David, you've sure as hell been acting strange today. Starting out your day with the mom and the kid, then dropping them off and moving your yacht."

"He dry-docked his yacht," Jay put in. "If I had a vessel like the *Icarus*, I'd damn sure do the same thing."

"But he came back," Len noted, his tone curious, as he studied David.

"Did you find something out in the water today?" Jay asked. "Is that why you're acting so strange?"

Hank's voice was eager. "Oh my God! You did. You found...oh my God!" he repeated. "You found the body! The body that disappeared from the beach."

"No!" Len exploded. "You couldn't have! This is getting scary. Bodies everywhere."

"Where did you find the body?" John Seymore asked sharply.

"Another drowning victim?" Jay asked, sounding confused.

"I don't think so," David said. "I sure as hell didn't mean to bring this up during the storm, but since it seems you're all going to jump to conclusions, anyway, I might as well tell you the simple truth. No, not a drowning victim. Drowning victims aren't usually found with their feet encased in cement."

Where she lay, Alex froze.

"This is quite a story," Hank said.

Jay groaned. "You just had to bring this up in front of Hank, right, David?"

"I didn't bring it up!" David said sharply. "But maybe it doesn't matter. When the storm is over, the news will break anyway. As soon as he can, Nigel is sending someone out to bring her up."

"Where did you find the body?" Hank asked.

"Out beyond the reefs. I was spearfishing with Zach. Couldn't bring it up myself, because I didn't have the equipment to bring up any weight. Plus I'd already pushed the envelope on getting the kid and his mom back in, and the *Icarus* out of the storm. Nigel couldn't send anyone right away, because his people were all involved in the evacuation, and the water was growing too dangerous, too fast. But once the storm has passed, he'll get the Coast Guard in and bring her out."

"Jeez," Hank breathed.

"Did you know her?" Jay asked.

"Yes, I did. It was Alicia Farr," David said.

The moan of the wind outside was the only sound then as every man at the table went dead silent.

"Alicia Farr—dead," Hank Adamson said at last.

The others turned to stare at him, and he continued, "All right! I did come out here to get a story on her. I'd heard she was on to some incredible find."

Alex heard something make a clunking sound. She turned to look, but quietly, not wanting them to know she was awake, not when she was chilled to the bone just listening.

The clunking sound had been made by Jay as he allowed his head to fall on the table. She was sure it wasn't an emotional response to a woman being dead, though, and maybe she couldn't blame him. He hadn't really known Alicia Farr.

He was worried about Moon Bay.

David had known Alicia, and now Alex understood why he had been so tense.

He'd found Alicia's body.

Someone hadn't wanted the body to be found, so that someone had gone back for her, hidden her, then packed her in cement and thrown her back in the water, sure that this time she wouldn't wash back up.

Had that someone been David, and was he saying this now just to cover his own actions? Of course, he could find the location of the body, because he had put it there himself. The timing was certainly in his favor if he had. The storm could move the body, hide it, even destroy it. The cause of death might become almost impossible to discern. Any physical evidence could be completely compromised.

No, David couldn't be a killer. She wouldn't believe it. He had his talents, but he had never claimed acting to be among them.

And yet, at that table, they had all been bluffing.

Anger against herself welled in her heart. No, how could she believe in her soul that she loved someone so much that she had been so afraid of losing him that she had pushed him away, and then believe him capable of deception and murder?

"On that note, I think the game is over," John murmured. "Hell, I can't believe you kept quiet until now."

"I meant to keep quiet all night," David said irritably. "There's nothing anyone can do until the storm passes.

Then the body will be brought up, and Nigel will get to the bottom of what's going on."

"Maybe," Jay said dully. "And maybe he won't find out a damn thing and we'll all be walking around afraid forever."

"I don't think so," David said. "I'm pretty sure that whoever killed Alicia might have helped Seth Granger into the water. And that person will, eventually, give himself away. Until then, just be careful."

"Great, David, thanks a lot," Len said. "Now none of us is going to be able to get any sleep."

"Why?" David said. "Hey, it's just the six of us on the island. We stick together, nothing goes wrong," he said flatly.

A strained silence followed his words.

"No one sleeps, that much is evident," Len said at last.

The sound of the wind suddenly seemed to die out completely.

The eye of the storm was just about on them.

"Hell," Hank Adamson swore. "This is ridiculous. I'm going to sleep. Alicia Farr is dead, and you found her," he told David. "That doesn't make any of us guilty of anything. You're right. Tomorrow, or as soon as he can, Nigel will come out and take care of things."

He pushed his chair away from the table. Alex kept her eyes tightly closed, not wanting any of them to know she had heard their conversation.

"We're in the eye," Jay said suddenly. "Len, come with me. I'm going out. Just for a minute. Just to take a quick look around." He sounded strained.

"You shouldn't go out, Jay," David said.

"I have responsibilities here. I have to go out,"

Jay said. "The rest of you stay here. Len will be with me. Everyone will have someone keeping an eye on them."

"Just you and Len together?" John said.

"All right, then. Three and three. Hank, you come with us for a minute," Jay said.

Hank groaned.

"Please. Three and three," Jay repeated.

With a sigh, Hank rose and joined them. Jay unbolted the door, stepping out into the dim light of the world beyond the shelter. "We'll just be a minute."

Alex didn't believe for a minute that he was going out to check on the damage. They kept a gun in a lockbox behind the check-in counter. He was undoubtedly going for it.

"What the hell are you doing on this island?" David asked John.

"The same back to you," John said.

Then, out of the blue, the radio went silent as the room was pitched into total blackness.

Chapter 11

The hum of the generator was gone.

Something had gone terribly wrong.

For a moment David sat in stunned silence, listening to the absolute nothing that surrounded him in the pitch darkness. Then he heard a chair scraping against the floor.

John Seymore. The man was up, and Alex was sleeping on a cot just feet away. Seymore could be going after her. Fear—maybe irrational, maybe not—seized him. He couldn't seem to control his urge to protect Alex, no matter what.

He sprang up, hearing the scrape of his own chair against the floor. He heard movement, tried to judge the sound, then made a wild tackle, going after the man.

He connected with his target right by the row of cots. His arms around his opponent's midsection, together they crashed downward, onto the cot where Alex had been sleeping.

Dimly, as Seymore twisted, sending a fist flying, David became aware that the cot was empty. Alex had fled. She might still be in the storm-shelter room somewhere, or she could have found the door and escaped.

Seymore's fist connected with his right shoulder. A powerful punch. Blindly, David returned the blow. He thought he caught Seymore's chin. The man let out a grunt of pain, then twisted to find David with another blow.

They continued fighting for several minutes with desperate urgency, until suddenly an earsplitting gunshot rocked the pitch-dark room.

Both of them went still. The shot had come from the doorway.

Instinctively, they rolled away from one another.

"Alex!" David shouted.

There was no answer.

After the explosion of sound, silence descended again. He wasn't sure where Seymore had gone.

With a sudden burst of speed, he picked himself up and raced toward the open door. Insane or not, instinct compelled him to do so.

Alex was certain that John and David were going to tear each other apart. Damn Jay! They were supposed to stay together, watching one another, and instead he'd gone for a weapon. What the hell did he intend to do? Hold everyone at gunpoint until the authorities came? Shoot them all?

Could Jay be the killer? No! She refused to believe

it. And yet… As soon as he'd left, the generator had gone off.

What the hell had happened?

She had no idea. All she knew for certain was that David and John had suddenly become mortal combatants. Did they know something she didn't? Was one of them telling the truth—and the other not?

She had to get away, in case the wrong man triumphed. Not that she had any idea which one was the wrong one.

She'd already deserted her cot before they toppled over on it. She immediately made a dash for the door, nearly killing herself in the process, the darkness was so complete. She burst into the office and stood dead still, listening. Once she was certain the office was empty, she made her way to the reception area, inch by inch, using the furniture as a guide.

She meant to head for the lockbox herself, just in case she'd been wrong and Jay hadn't gone for the gun after all. Then became aware of breathing near her. She held dead still, holding her own breath.

Waiting, listening.

Aeons seemed to pass in which she didn't move. She nearly shrieked when she realized someone was moving past her, heading for the storm room. Once he had gone and her heartbeat had returned to normal, she tried to move around the reception counter.

Her footsteps were blocked. She kicked against something warm. Kneeling, feeling around, she realized that she hadn't stumbled against a thing but a person.

She recoiled instantly, fought for a sense of sanity, and tried to ascertain what had happened—and who it was. The form was still warm. She moved her hand over the throat, finding a pulse. Feeling the face and clothing, she decided she had stumbled upon Jay Galway, and he was hurt!

Either that, or…

Or he was lying in wait. Ready to ambush the unwary person who knelt down next to him to ascertain what had happened.

Fingers reached out for her, vising around her wrist. She screamed, but the crack of a gunshot drowned out the sound. She wrenched her wrist free and rose, determined to get the hell out of the lodge. The storm might be ready to come pounding down on them again, but she didn't care. There had to be a different place to find sanctuary.

As she groped her way out of the lodge, tamping down thoughts of Jay and whether or not he was hurt or dangerous, she was certain that her survival depended on escape. She lost several seconds battling with the bolts on the main door, then got them open and flew out.

Everything in her fought against believing Jay was the killer. He definitely hadn't been the one shooting the gun.

If Jay was on the floor, where were Len and Hank?

This was all insane!

The night was dark. Thick clouds covered the sky, even in the eye of the storm. Still, once outside, she could see more than she had before.

She hurried along the once manicured walkway, heading not toward the dock but around to the Tiki Hut, on the lodge side of the dolphin lagoons.

As she rushed forward, she was aware of a few dark dolphin heads bobbing up.

She never passed without a giving an encouraging word to her charges. Despite the darkness, she was certain the dolphins could see her, and they would instinctively know something was wrong when she didn't acknowledge them.

She should say something to them.

She didn't dare.

She was determined to make her way to the cottages. Not her own—that would be the first place anyone would look for her—but she was sure she would find a door that hadn't been locked. The cottages were nowhere near as secure as the storm room, but at least they'd been built after Hurricane Andrew and were up to code.

But as she veered toward the trail that led toward the cottages, she saw another form moving in the night ahead of her.

Panic seized her. There was no choice. She had to head for the beach.

She turned, then heard footsteps in her wake.

She was being pursued.

David was desperate to get to Alex. He damned himself a hundred times over for the announcement he had been forced to make. For not beating the crap out of Jay, rather than letting him leave the room.

But had Jay—or anyone—destroyed the generator? Or had technology simply failed them when it was most desperately needed?

Didn't matter, none of it mattered.

Out of the room, he stumbled, swearing, as he made his way through the inner office and out to reception.

He hesitated. Somewhere on the wall was a glass case that held a speargun. It was a real speargun, one that had been used in a movie filmed on the island a few years earlier. He'd passed it dozens of times, giving it no notice.

Now he wanted it.

Groping along the wall, he found the case. He smashed the glass with his elbow, grabbed the weapon, then heard movement behind him.

David streaked for the front doors, praying that nothing would bar his way.

He found the door, which was slightly ajar.

Yes, Alex had definitely gone outside.

He swung the door open, leaving the lodge behind.

It occurred to him to wonder just how much time had passed since the eye had first come over them.

And just how much time they had left.

There had to be a way to double back and find a place to hide and weather the storm.

Alex ran along the path toward the beach, then swore. There was no branch in the trail here, but if she crawled through the foliage, she could reach one of the other paths. All too aware that someone was following and not far behind, she caught hold of an old pine tree and used it for balance as she entered into the overgrowth.

Already, much of it was flattened. Even if she had found a path, it wouldn't have been worth much. The storm had brought down hundreds of palm fronds already. Coconuts, mangoes, and other fruits littered the ground. She tried to move carefully, then paused, wondering if she had lost her pursuer.

She stood very still, listening.

She could hear the sea. The storm might not be on them again yet, but the water was far from smooth. She could hear the waves crashing, could imagine them, white capped and dangerous. And beneath the water's surface, the sand and currents would be churning with a staggering strength.

Had the wind begun to pick up again yet?

Footsteps.

Whoever had been behind her was pursuing her now with slow deliberation, as if he was able to read the signs of her trail in the dark. Maybe he could.

Who was he? Had Jay been an enemy, just waiting in the darkness, or a victim? If not Jay, who could it be?

She froze in place, stock-still with indecision. Which way to go?

There was a rushing in her ears. Her own pulse. She ignored it. She had to listen above it.

Yes, there was another sound in the night. Footsteps, not the beat of her own heart.

Her pursuer. Close. Too close.

As silently as possible, she edged forward, then came to a dead stop once again. There was a new noise, coming from in front of her.

Where to go?

Only one choice.

She headed toward the beach.

She was ahead of him, so close it was as if he could still smell her perfume, on the air. And still she was eluding him.

She knew the island, and he didn't.

David didn't dare call out her name. Someone else might hear him. Once again, he damned himself for the bombshell he had dropped that night. Now the killer knew. He had hidden Alicia's body and now he knew he'd failed a second time. For a moment his mind wandered to the spot where he'd found the body. It wasn't an area where he had believed it would be found, where dive boats brought scores of people daily, but it wasn't impossibly far from the beaten path, either.

So what did that mean? What did the placement of the body mean?

He couldn't worry about it now. He had to use every one of his senses to find Alex.

Before it was too late.

He paused and listened. The rustle of the trees was eerie in the strange breeze that gripped the island. It was as if the storm was gone…and yet still there.

She was moving again. The sound was so slight, he nearly missed it. He started tearing through the bushes again, following.

She was heading for the beach.

He saw her as she raced forward, then stumbled and fell. Seconds later, he burst out of the bushes behind her.

"Alex!"

He saw then what she was seeing. Just feet from her, Len Creighton was facedown in the sand. In the night, David couldn't make out anything else, whether the man was injured, unconscious…dead.

He couldn't see Alex's reaction to her discovery, but he could tell she'd heard him. She was on her feet again, and she was staring at him, and even in the dark, he could see the fear in her eyes.

"Alex!" he cried. "Alex, come here."

She kept staring at him. As he waited, afraid to move closer, lest she run again, he surveyed the area as best he could in the dark.

Where had Len come from? How had he gotten here? Where was the danger?

He stared at Alex again. "Alex, you've got to trust me. Come with me—now. Quickly!"

He was dimly aware of leaves rustling nearby; he knew someone else had reached them even before he heard a deep voice protest, "No!"

John Seymore. Damn. He'd been on his trail the whole time. Now, David realized, he'd led the bastard right to Alex.

John Seymore stared at David with lethal promise. He had a gun. Apparently he'd been armed all along and never let on. He could kill the other man, and he knew it. But whether or not he could kill him before David sent a spear into his heart was another matter.

"Alex!" Seymore shouted, keeping a wary eye on David. "Come to me. Get away from him."

"Alex!" David warned sharply.

It seemed as if they stood locked in the eye of time, just as they were locked in the eye of the storm, forever.

Alex stared from one man to the other, and back again. Her gaze slipped down to Len Creighton, who was still lying on the beach, then focused on the two men once again.

Then she turned and dived straight into the water.

"Alex, no!" David shouted.

He couldn't begin to imagine the undercurrents, the power of the water, in the wake of the storm. And he didn't give a damn about anything other than getting her back. He even forgot that a bullet could stop him in his tracks in two seconds. He dropped the speargun and went tearing toward the water.

A dim line barely showed where water and sky met. As he plowed into the waves, he saw something shoot through the water. For a moment he thought Seymore had somehow managed to move quicker than he had and had gotten ahead of him in the violent surf.

Then he realized that whoever was ahead of him was huge, bigger than a man. David plowed on, fighting the waves to reach Alex, heedless of who else might be out there. He broke the surface.

Then he saw.

Alex was being rescued. And not by a man, not by a human being at all. One of her dolphins had come for her. Where the animal would go with her, he didn't know.

"Alex!" he screamed again.

But she had grabbed hold of the dolphin's dorsal fin, and the mammal could manage the wild surf as no man possibly could.

She was gone.

He treaded the water, watching as the dolphin and the woman disappeared in the night. The danger hadn't abated in the least; it was increasing with every minute that went by. He was losing to the power of the water himself. Fighting hard despite his strength and ability, he made it back toward the beach. When he reached the shore, he collapsed, still half in the water.

A second later, someone dropped by his side.

Seymore. Apparently he had ditched his weapon, as well, equally determined to rescue Alex from the surf.

Both men realized where they were and jerked away

from one another. Then both looked toward the weapons they had dropped. David could see Seymour's muscles bunching, and he knew his were doing the same.

But Seymore cried out to him instead of moving. "Wait!"

David, wary, still hesitated.

"You had plenty of time to kill her," Seymore said.

"You could have shot me," David noted warily.

"You'd have shot back. But the point is…you dropped the speargun and went after Alex."

"Of course I went after her! I love her."

Seymore inhaled. "Listen to me, I didn't kill anyone. I know you think it's me, but I'm working with the FBI—"

"Yeah, yeah, sure. Now you're a G-man."

"No, I'm a special consultant. I thought *you* were killing people—until two minutes ago."

David found himself staring at the man. His basic reaction was to distrust him, but there was something about the man he believed. Maybe the fact that the Glock had been a guarantee, the speargun a maybe.

Seconds ticked by. Alex was in the care of a creature that could survive the darkness and the elements better than any man. But she was still out there somewhere. And the greatest likelihood was that the dolphin would bring her back to the lagoon. It wouldn't take the animal long.

There was also the matter of the man lying on the beach just feet away from them, possibly dying.

"I'm not the killer," Seymore said.

"And neither am I," David said harshly. More seconds ticked by.

Gut reaction. Dane had told him to go by his gut reaction.

He let another fraction of time go by. Then he moved.

Ignoring Seymore, he got to his feet quickly and walked over to the prone body of Len Creighton. There was blood on the man's temple, but he still had a pulse.

"He's alive," David said. Hunkered down, he tried to assess the man's condition quickly. Concussion, almost certainly. Shock, probably.

If they left him there, he would certainly die in the next onslaught of the storm. But if he was burdened with the man, Alex could die before he got back to her.

David's back was to Seymore. The man could have picked up the gun and shot him, but he hadn't.

David turned back to him. "He's got to be taken to shelter."

Seymore picked up the gun, shoving it into his belt. He stared at David, but, like him, he knew that time was of the essence.

"Alex is out there," John said.

"Yes."

"She'll trust you before she trusts me, though she doesn't seem to have much faith in either of us at the moment," he said at last. "Go after Alex. I'll take Len." Then, true to his word, he bent down, lifting the prone man as if he were no more than a baby.

David hoped to hell the guy was really on his side. As an enemy, he would be formidable.

Was he wrong? Was this all part of an act? Were they all supposed to die tonight, but on Seymore's own terms? He might be leaving Len to face instant death.

There wasn't time to weigh the veracity of John Seymore's words.

"Cottage eight was Ally and Zach's. It's probably open," David said.

"Meet me there," John Seymore said briefly.

There was nothing left to do. David turned, scooped up the speargun, and started running back toward the Tiki Hut and the dolphin lagoons.

At first Alex had thought she had signed her own death warrant. It wasn't that she didn't know the power of the waves. She'd been out in bad weather before. She'd seen people flounder when the waves were only four feet. She couldn't begin to imagine how high they were now, but desperation had driven her into the water.

Even with everything she knew, she still hadn't imagined the battering she was going to take, the impossibility of actually swimming against the force of the sea.

She had thought she was going to die.

Then she had felt the smooth, slick, velvet sliding by her. Her mind had been too numbed at first to comprehend. The animal had made a second glide-by, and then she had known.

When Shania returned for her that time, she was ready, catching hold of the dorsal fin, just as she taught tourists to do on a daily basis.

She caught hold, though, and knew that she was doing it for her life. Still, despite her fear and panic and the waves and the desperation of the situation, she was awed. She had heard stories about dolphins performing amazing rescues. She worked with them on a daily basis, knew their intelligence and their affection.

And still…she was in awe. For a moment she wondered where the dolphin would go, and then she knew.

Safe haven.

The dolphin lagoon. Shania's home, the place where she found shelter. Where she had gone when she had been sick and injured. Where she had been nursed back to health.

The dolphin moved with astounding speed. As they neared the submerged gates to the first lagoon, Alex was afraid that she would be crushed against the steel. Shania had more faith in her own abilities. She dove low with her human passenger and raced through the opening, and they emerged in the sheltered lagoon.

"Sweet girl, sweet girl, thank you!" Alex whispered fervently to the dolphin, easing her hold and stroking the creature. "I owe you so many fish. I won't even slip vitamins into any of them," she promised.

Soundlessly, Shania moved off. Alex swam hard to the platform, crawling out of the water, shaking.

She was cold, soaking wet, barefoot, and no better off than when she had begun.

The winds would whip up again, and she had not found shelter.

Out there, somewhere, were two armed men. David and John.

And then there was Jay…. Would he have left Len to die on the sand? Oh God, she'd forgotten in her panic. And Hank? Where had he gone?

Her heart felt as numb as her fingers. There was nowhere to go, and no one to trust.

What the hell to do now? She started to rise, but a sudden wind gust nearly knocked her over. The storm was on its way back.

She headed back around the lagoon, creeping low, her goal now the Tiki Hut. The bar was solid oak. If she wedged herself beneath it, with any luck she would survive the winds and get only a minimal lashing from the rain.

Another gust of wind came along, pushing her forward. She was going to have to wedge herself tightly in. She could and would survive the night, she promised herself.

But when morning came…what then?

David raced along the path, pausing only when he neared the lagoons, trying desperately to see in the darkness. The rain was becoming heavier; the wind had shifted fully and was now beginning to pick up speed.

Trying to utilize the remaining foliage for cover, he searched the area surrounding the lagoons, then the water. The darkness was deceptive, but he thought he saw dark heads bobbing now and then.

He had no idea which animal had come for Alex, how it had known she was in trouble, or where to find her. Dolphins had excellent vision; he knew they sometimes watched people from deep in the water. But how a dolphin had known where to look for Alex, he would never know.

Even though he couldn't see Alex, he was certain the dolphin had brought her back to the lagoon. Unless something had happened along the way.

He wouldn't accept such a possibility.

David sprinted around the lagoons to the platforms. He felt he was being watched. He searched the closest pool, then the farther one. At the second lagoon, one of the dolphins let out a noise. He brought a finger to his lips. “Shh. Please.”

Assuming that John Seymore had told him the truth, and taking into consideration the fact that Len Creighton was definitely out, there were still two more men on the island, one of whom obviously posed a deadly threat. “Where did you bring Alex, girl?” he asked the dolphin. Intelligent eyes stared back at him, but the animal gave no indication of Alex’s direction in any way.

As he retraced the path back toward the resort, David thought he saw a movement in the Tiki Hut.

Alex?

He set the speargun down against the base of a palm, knowing that for the moment, he needed his hands free.

What if the person seeking shelter in the hut wasn’t Alex?

It had to be.

And if not…he had to take the chance anyway.

Slowly, crouching low, he started to move in that direction. He crept with all the silence he could manage and with the cover of a growing wind.

There she was, seeking shelter under the bar of the Tiki Hut. A good choice.

Still, he didn’t show himself. She would scream, run, perhaps make it to the lagoons, and with her animals certain she was in danger, they would protect her once again. They were powerful animals, and knew their power. They could be lethal, taking a man to the bottom of a pool, keeping him there.

He moved very, very slowly. Then froze.

There was a sound from the brush nearby.

A bullet exploded, the sound loud even against the howl of nature.

David made a dive, crashing down against Alex and clasping a hand over her mouth before she could scream.

She panicked, tried to fight him. "Shh, Alex, it's me. You have to trust me," he mouthed as her eyes, luminous and huge, met his. She remained as tense as a stretched rubber band, staring at him.

Then another shot sounded in the night. He felt her flinch, but he couldn't release her mouth nor so much as shift his weight. If she drew attention to them now…

Forcing his weight hard against her, his hand still pressed against her mouth, David remained dead still. Listening. Waiting. It was so difficult to hear over the storm, to separate the natural moan, bend and rustle of the foliage from the sounds that were man-made.

He waited.

Then…yes. Someone was going off down one of the paths. He could hear the barely perceptible sound of receding footsteps.

He eased his hand off Alex's mouth. She inhaled fiercely, staring at him with doubt and fury and fear.

"Please, Alex," he begged. "Trust me."

Her lashes fell. "Trust you?" she whispered. "What about John Seymore? Did you kill him?"

She sounded cold, almost as if she were asking a question that didn't concern her.

"No."

"So you're not the killer? He's not the killer?"

"I don't think so."

"You don't *think* so?" she said, her voice rising.

He clamped a hand over her mouth again. "Shh."

She stared up at him with eyes of pure fire. He eased his hand away again. "Damn you, Alex, I love you. I'd die before I'd cause you any harm. Don't you know that about me?"

Her lashes fell again. "Actually, it's hard to know anything about you," she said.

That was when the lightning flashed. Struck. The boom of thunder was instantaneous, as the top of the Tiki Hut burst into flames.

For split seconds, they were both stunned.

Then David made it to his feet, seizing her hand, dragging her up. "We've got to move!" he urged. Without waiting for her assent, he dragged her quickly through the debris of branches and foliage that now littered the floor.

They headed down the trail toward the cottages as the rain began to pelt them.

"Where are we going?" Alex gasped, pulling back. "Our cottages are the first place anyone would look."

He didn't answer; the night had grown so dark again that he was barely able to make his way through the trails. All his concentration was on finding their way.

"David?"

"Shh."

He longed to pause, to listen.

He dared not.

Moments later, they reached the cottage where he had delivered Ally Conroy the night before. The door was closed, but when he set his hand on the knob and turned, David found it unlocked.

Then he paused at last.

Seymore could have been lying. The guy was military, experienced. He could kill them all off, one by one. He would never be found. Before relief crews could make it to the island, he could head out, move Alicia Farr's body once again, then disappear. He would know how to do that.

Gut instinct.

And no choice.

David opened the door.

Chapter 12

Alex blinked, colliding with David's back as he entered the cottage, then stopped dead.

She peered past him.

The darkness was broken by the thin beam of a flashlight in the kitchen area of the cottage.

They heard the click of a trigger, and a face appeared in the pale light.

John Seymore.

For a moment his features were as macabre as the eeriest Halloween mask. And for a moment she and David were as frozen as ice.

John Seymore took his finger off the trigger, shoving the gun back into his belt. "Alex. You're all right," he breathed.

"Yes," she said stiffly.

"Where's Len?" David asked.

"I've got him on the floor in the kitchen. I cleaned the

wound. He's got a concussion, I'm sure. There's nothing else I can do for him now," John said.

"He's alive?" Alex breathed.

"Barely. His only chance is for us to get him across to medical care the minute we can," John said.

Alex moved around from behind David, still wary as she passed John Seymore, heading for the kitchen.

Len was stretched out there. John had covered him with blankets from the beds and set his head on a pillow. She touched Len's cheek and felt warmth. His pulse was weak but steady, his breathing faint, but even.

She sat back, leaning against the refrigerator, allowing herself the luxury of just sitting for a minute, appreciating the fact that she was alive.

Then her mind began to race. The wind was howling again. She could hear it rattling against the doors in the back. She winced, afraid they would give way, then reminded herself that they were guaranteed to withstand winds up to a hundred miles an hour.

She began to shiver, then started as a blanket fell around her. She looked up. David was standing there; then he hunkered down by her side. A minute later John Seymore sat down across from them, on Len's other side.

"Who did this to him?" Alex demanded, looking from one man to the other.

David stared directly at John Seymore as he answered. "Either Jay Galway or Hank Adamson," he said.

She shook her head. "Jay cared about Len too much."

"Did he?" John asked dryly. "Jay is the manager here. If Alicia had ever shown up, he'd be the one to know it.

Especially if she wanted to arrive in secret. Jay could have met her on the beach and killed her."

"No," Alex said. "Jay's hurt—I nearly tripped over him up at the main building, and then he—never mind. It had to be Hank."

"A reporter? Without any special knowledge of boats or the sea?" David asked quietly.

She stared across Len's still form at John Seymore. "So...you're FBI but not exactly an agent?" There was wariness in her voice, and she knew it.

John sighed. "Look, if I hadn't been so suspicious of David, I would have identified myself from the beginning. But I didn't know who could be trusted. For all I knew, you were in on it somehow, Alex."

"What I want to know," David said, "is how the FBI became interested in Alicia Farr, and why?"

"The government always wants its cut," John said simply. "Different agencies, at different times, had their eyes on Daniel Fuller. He liked to talk. According to his stories, the ship went down in American waters. No way was the government going to let a treasure hunter get to her secretly."

"So...you followed Alicia?" David said.

John shook his head. "I'd been in Miami. We knew Daniel Fuller was dying, but he refused to see anyone but Alicia. I'm sorry she lost her life over this, but she was a fool. She didn't exactly hide her visits. She was overheard calling Moon Bay. So I came to see what would happen when she arrived. My job was just to find out what she knew about the *Anne Marie*. But Alicia didn't show up. You did, David. And Seth Granger, who talked way too much. And the reporter. Then Alex found the body on the beach."

Alex felt David's fingers curl around hers. She swallowed hard. There was something so instinctively protective in that hold.

For a moment, the gravity of their situation slipped away.

If John Seymore suddenly pulled out his gun, she knew David would throw himself between them. He *did* love her.

Maybe he had always loved her.

But the sea would always come first.

"How did you know Alex found a body on the beach?" David demanded sharply.

John shrugged. "I made a point of meeting up with Laurie Smith. She's a very trusting individual. Too trusting, really. It was risky, telling Laurie the truth. But it also seemed important that she lie low, since someone might know she had been with Alex and seen the body."

"Laurie is on the mainland, or at least the main island, if she didn't head out of the Keys entirely," Alex murmured. "So she knows. She knows everything that's going on. It's insane for someone to be trying to kill us all now. The authorities will know."

David was staring at John again. "Maybe not so insane. Whoever killed Alicia also helped Seth Granger to his death. That means they didn't care about financing. We've got someone on our hands who means to get to the wreckage of the *Anne Marie*, bring up the treasure without equipment or an exploratory party, then disappear."

Alex looked from one man to another. "All right, for the sake of argument right now, David, you've decided it isn't John, and, John, you've decided it isn't David.

And it's obviously not Len or Jay." She frowned. "I told you, when I ran out of the storm room, I tripped over Jay."

"He was dead?" David asked sharply.

Both men were staring at her.

She shook her head. "No," she admitted. "He…he tried to grab me."

Their silence told her that they both believed Jay was guilty.

"He was the one who insisted on going out," David said to John.

"He'd know how to kill the generator," John agreed.

"Wait!" Alex protested in defense of her boss. "He didn't attack me. I was afraid, so I ran, but…but he could have been hurt," she said guiltily, "and just trying to get me to help him."

"Alex," John said seriously, "you know that you're the one the killer really wants. It was your name Daniel Fuller mentioned over and over again. Are you sure you don't know why?"

She felt David's tension, his fingers tightening around hers. She knew what he was thinking. If you actually know something, for God's sake, keep quiet now!

He might have decided to trust John Seymore, but John's question had set off sparks of suspicion in his mind once again.

So why did she trust David so implicitly? Maybe he had been so determined to save her because he, too, believed she knew something.

"I don't have a clue. He never talked to me about the *Anne Marie*. Ever. He rambled on, told lots of stories about the sea, and he loved the dolphins. That's all I know," she said. Her words rang with sincerity, as they should have. They were true.

"Well, hard to hide anything on a dolphin," David said. He was staring at John Seymore. Sizing him up again?

"What do we do now?" she murmured.

As if in answer, the wind howled louder.

"Wait out the storm," John said.

"You have a gun," Alex said, pointing at John. "The doors lock. We can just wait until someone comes from the main island, until the sheriff gets here. Even if the killer comes after us, well…there are three of us, not counting Len, and one of him."

"Or two," David said grimly.

John cocked his head toward David. "You think Hank and Jay are in on this together?"

"I don't think anything. I'm just trying to consider all the possibilities," David said.

"Once the storm is over, we can't really sit around waiting to be attacked, anyway," John said.

"Why not?" Alex asked.

"Because," David said, not looking at her but at John Seymore, "even if Nigel was the first one to show up after the storm, he could be shot and killed before he ever got to us. If only one man is behind this, it's likely the other one is dead already. And we know the killer's armed."

"We need a plan," John murmured.

"Whatever the plan, Alex stays here," David said. "Locked in, when we go out."

"Great. I'll be a sitting duck," Alex murmured.

"Locked in," David repeated sternly.

"And what are you two going to do?" she demanded.

"This isn't a big island, but there are all kinds of nooks and crannies where someone could hide. How are you going to find him—or them?"

"Well, we've got a few hours to figure it out," John said grimly. "No one will be moving anywhere in this wind."

Toward dawn, Alex actually drifted off, her head on David's shoulder. He was loathe to move her, not just for the silky feel of her head against him, but for the trust she had displayed by allowing her eyes to close while she was next to him.

Trust, or exhaustion.

"It's over," John said.

Seymore hadn't dozed off. Neither had David. They had stared at one another throughout the night. Now it was morning, and the storm was over.

They had their plan.

David roused Alex. "Hey," he said softly.

She jerked awake, eyes wide.

"We're going," he told her. "Remember, you don't open the door to anyone once we've gone. Not John, and not me."

"I don't like this," she protested. "The sheriff could be far more prepared than either of you think. He's not a bumpkin. You should both stay put, right where you are. That leaves us as three against one, remember?" She was pleading, she realized.

"You'll be all right if you just stay locked in," David said.

"I'm not worried about me, you idiot!" she lashed out. "I'm worried about the two of you. Going out as if you—"

"Alex, let us do this," John said.

"Don't forget, no one—*no one*—comes in," David warned her sternly again. This was going to be difficult for Alex, he knew. She was accustomed to being the one in charge, accustomed to action.

And they were asking her to just sit tight.

"I've got it," she said wearily. "I heard you. But I still don't understand what the two of you are going to do."

"We're going back together for the speargun," David said. "Then John is going to watch the trail, and I'm going to wait at your cottage."

"You know, whoever this is could come here and we could ambush him. Or them," she tried.

"Alex, he—or they—may never realize we came to this cottage," David said. "In fact, we're praying that he doesn't."

He got to his feet. John joined him. He reached a hand down to Alex, drawing her to her feet and against him. His voice was husky when he said, "No one." He moved his fingers against her nape, sudden paralysis gripping his stomach.

Seymore looked away.

David kissed Alex. Briefly. But tenderly.

"Follow us to the door and bolt it immediately, don't just lock it," John told Alex. "If it's Jay, he's got a master key."

"Bolts, on both doors," David said. "Front and back."

"Yes, immediately," she said.

They stepped out cautiously.

The world seemed to be a sea of ripped-up palm fronds and foliage. Small trees were down all over.

"Close the door," David told Alex.

Her beautiful, ever-changing, sea-colored blue-green

eyes touched his one last time. She went back in, and he heard the bolt slide into place behind them.

"This way for the speargun," he told John Seymore.

The other man nodded grimly and followed his lead.

Alex's diving watch was ticking.

Five minutes, ten minutes.

Fifteen minutes.

By then she was pacing. Every second seemed an agony. Listening to the world beyond the cottage, she could at first hear nothing.

Then, every now and then, a trill.

Already, the birds were returning.

Her stomach growled so loudly that it made her jump. She felt guilty for feeling hunger when David and John were out there, in danger, and Len Creighton still lay unconscious on the kitchen floor.

With that thought, she returned to his side. He hadn't moved; his condition hadn't changed. She secured the blankets around him more tightly.

That was when she heard the shots.

She jumped a mile as she heard the glass of the rear sliding doors shatter.

Alex didn't wait. She tore through the place, closing doors so that whoever was out there would be forced to look for her. Then she raced into the front bedroom, opened the window and forced out the screen, grateful they hadn't boarded up the place. As she crawled out the window, she wondered if the shooter was Jay Galway or Hank Adamson.

Then it occurred to her that maybe they didn't know the truth about John Seymore.

And he was the only one of them who she knew had a gun.

* * *

In the stillness of the morning, the bullets hitting the glass, one after another with determined precision, sounded like cannon shots.

David had been waiting by the door of Alex's cottage. He'd left it ajar, standing just inside with the speargun at the ready as he watched the trail. No one would be coming through the back without his knowledge—he'd dragged all the furniture against it.

But at the sound of the gunshots, he started swearing. What if John Seymore was the shooter?

No, couldn't be. Gut instinct.

Someone was shooting, though, and David felt ill as he left the cottage and raced dexterously over the ground that was deeply carpeted in debris.

What if his gut instinct had been wrong?

He'd left Alex at the mercy of a killer.

Heedless of being quiet, he raced toward Ally's cottage, heading for the back door.

Instinct forced him to halt, using a tree as cover, when he first saw the shattered glass. He scanned the area, saw no one, heard no one.

Racing across the open space, the speargun at the ready, he reached the rear of the cottage.

He listened but still didn't hear a thing.

The broken glass crunched beneath his feet, and he went still. Once again he heard nothing. Slowly, his finger itchy on the trigger, he made his way in and moved toward the kitchen.

There, lying under a pile of blankets, just as they had left him, was Len Creighton. Then, before he could even ascertain whether Len was still alive, David heard a noise, just a rustling, from the front bedroom.

Silently, he moved in that direction.

* * *

The door to her cottage was open.

Alex had run like a Key deer from the other cottage and, without even thinking about it, had come here.

Because David would be here.

The front door was ajar.

She hesitated, found a piece of downed coconut and threw it toward the open doorway. Nothing happened.

Cautiously, she made her way to the door. She peered inside. No one. Logic told her that once he'd heard the bullets, David would have run to her assistance.

She entered her cottage, thinking desperately about what she might have that could serve as a weapon. The best she could come up with was a scuba knife.

She kept most of her equipment at the marina, but there were a few things here.

She raced into her bedroom, anxious to pull open the drawer where she kept odds and ends of extra equipment, reminding herself to keep quiet in case she had been followed. But she was in such a hurry that she jerked the entire dresser.

Perfumes and colognes jiggled, then started to topple over. She reached out to stop them from crashing to the floor and instead knocked them all to the floor with the sweep of her hand.

The sound seemed deafening.

She swore, returning attention to the drawer, but then something caught the corner of her eye.

She paused, looking at the pile of broken ceramics and glass.

The little dolphin had broken, and she could see that a piece of folded paper had been hidden inside the bottom of the ceramic creature.

Squatting down, she retrieved it.

Ordinary copy paper.

But as she opened it, she realized just what had been copied. A map. The original had been very old, and there was an X on it, and next to that, three words: *The Anne Marie.*

She stared at it numbly for a second, then remembered the day when she had found her things out of order. Someone must have hidden the map that day. Returning her mind to her predicament. Rising, she opened the drawer, heedless now of making noise. She found the knife she had been seeking and quickly belted it around her calf.

Then she heard a noise as someone came stealthily toward the front of the house.

Once again, she made a quick escape through a bedroom window.

David burst into the bedroom of Ally's cottage, speargun aimed.

But no one was there.

He immediately noticed the open window and the punched-out screen lying on the floor.

Silently, he left the bedroom, then the house, and hurried on toward Alex's place.

Now the door was wide open. Cautiously, he entered.

He hurried through the cottage.

This time, it was her own bedroom window that was open. A punched-out screen lay mangled on the floor.

He heard a shot.

The sound had come from the area of the Tiki Hut.

He raced from the house and toward the lagoons.

* * *

"Stop, Alex. Stop!"

She had simply run when she left her place. Away from the front door. Her steps had brought her to the lagoons and the Tiki Hut. She made it to the lagoon on the outskirts of the Tiki Hut, which was little more than a pile of rubble now. She spared a moment's gratitude that she hadn't spent the night under the bar after all.

The voice calling to her gave her pause.

It was John Seymore. And she knew he had a gun.

She turned, and he was there, closing in on her.

"Wait for me," he said. But as she stared at him, another man burst from the trees.

It was Hank Adamson. And he, too, was armed.

"Alex, it's all right!" Adamson called out. "I've got him covered. Seymore, put down the gun or I'll shoot you."

"Alex, let him shoot me," John said. "Get the hell away from him."

"Alex, don't be an idiot. Don't run," Hank Adamson insisted.

At that moment, David burst from the foliage, his speargun raised. "Alex, get the hell away from here!" David roared, but then he paused, seeing the situation.

"Hey, David," Hank Adamson called. "I've got him!"

"Yeah, I see that," David said. For a moment his eyes met hers. Then they turned toward the lagoon before meeting hers again. She realized that he was telling her to escape. Shania had helped her once. The dolphin would surely take her away again.

But she didn't dare move.

"Yeah, you've got him, all right," David said, walking to Seymore's side. "Hank, where's Jay?" he asked. "It's all right, Alex. It's okay...Hank has got this guy covered."

She knew from his eyes that he didn't mean it.

But how was he so sure that John Seymore wasn't the bad guy?

"Hank, where's Jay?" David repeated.

"This guy must have gotten him during the night," Hank said, indicating John.

And then Alex knew. Amazingly, David looked dead calm, and earnest, as if he were falling for every word Hank Adamson said. He was gambling again, she realized. Bluffing. In a game where the stakes were life or death.

His life.

She could see what he was doing. He was going to go for Hank Adamson and take the chance of being shot. He was risking John Seymore's life, as well, but she could see in that man's eyes that he was willing to take the risk. The guy was for real.

"Now!" David shouted.

His spear flashed in the brilliant morning sunlight that had followed the storm.

John Seymore made a dive for her, and they crashed into the lagoon together.

As they pitched below the surface of the water, Alex was aware of the bullet ripping through it next to them. She heard the concussion as another shot was fired.

In the depths of the lagoon, the bullets harmlessly pierced the bottom. She and Seymore kicked their way back to the surface. Heads bobbed around them. Dolphin heads. Her charges were about to go after John.

"No, no...it's all right!" She quickly gave them a

signal, then ignored both them and John Seymore as she kicked furiously to reach the shore.

Two men were down.

"Careful!" John was right behind her, holding her back when she would have rushed forward.

He walked ahead of her.

Hank Adamson, speared through the ribs, was on top. Blood gushed from his wound.

"David!"

She shrieked his name, falling to the ground, trying to reach him as John Seymore lifted Hank Adamson's bleeding form.

"David!"

He opened his eyes.

"David, are you hurt? Are you shot?"

"Alex," he said softly, and his voice sounded like a croak.

"Don't you die, you bastard!" she cried. "I love you, David. I was an idiot, a scared idiot. Don't you dare die on me now!"

He smiled, then pushed himself entirely free of Hank Adamson and the pile of leaves and branches that had cushioned them both when they fell. He got to his feet.

"She loves me," he told John Seymore, smiling.

Seymore laughed.

Alex couldn't help it. She threw a punch at David's shoulder. "That doesn't mean I could live with you," she told him furiously.

"Actually, we have another worry before we get to that," David said, looking at John. "We've got to find Jay. And pray that help gets here soon, or we'll lose Len for certain."

They found Jay near where Alex had stumbled into him the night before. He was groaning, obviously alive. From the doorway, they could see him starting to rise. When he heard them, he went flat and silent once again.

"It's all right, Jay," Alex said, racing to his side. "It's over."

He sat up, holding his head, fear still in his eyes as he looked at them.

"It was Hank," he said, as if still amazed. "It was Hank…all along."

"We know," Alex told him.

"Len?"

"He's alive. We have to get him to a hospital as soon as possible," John said.

"Thank God," Jay breathed. He looked at them all. *"Hank,"* he repeated. "How did you figure it out?"

John looked at David. "How *did* you figure it out?"

Alex stared at David, as well.

David shrugged. "Two things. Seth Granger was killed. The man with the money, and Hank would fit into that category. That meant it had to be someone who didn't need money or backing. Someone who meant to get what he could, then get out."

"You said two things," John Seymore told him.

David stared at John. "Gut instinct," he said at last. He angled his head to one side for a moment, listening, and said, "There's a launch coming. Thank God. Nigel Thompson can take over from here."

Epilogue

She hurried along the trail. She knew she was being pursued, but now, the knowledge brought a smile to her face.

They would be alone. Finally, after all the trauma, all the hours.

Still, there was something she had to do first.

Hank Adamson wasn't dead; he, like Jay and Len, had been taken aboard a helicopter and airlifted to Jackson Memorial in Miami. All three men were expected to make a full recovery.

It was chillingly clear that the reporter had intended to use the storm as cover to kill them all, Alex last, so that he could find out what she knew by saving one victim for the end and pretending he would let him live if she would just talk.

He would never have believed that she didn't know anything. Until the end, of course. Before Nigel arrived, she had given the map to David, then smiled in relief when he had turned it over to Nigel Thompson.

She didn't give a damn about the whereabouts of the *Anne Marie.* And even if David did, people were still more important to him than any treasure.

She reached the first platform, and fed Katy, Sabra and Jamie-Boy, aware she was being watched.

As she sat down at the next platform, David, who had come after her, sat down beside her. "I have to butt in here," he told her. "I owe Shania, too. I owe her everything. Do you mind?"

Alex shook her head, and watched him for a moment as he fed and touched every dolphin, talking to them all, giving Shania special care.

"You know," she said softly, "I was jealous of Alicia, but I'm truly sorry that she's dead."

"So am I." He looked at her. "You were wrong, though, to be jealous. We never had an affair."

"She was just so...perfect for you," Alex said.

"No, she wasn't. I was always in love with you. *You* were perfect for me. I was an ass. I didn't show it. You loved your training, I loved the sea. I didn't know how selfish I had gotten."

"Well, since we're still married," she mused, "I guess we'll just have to learn how to compromise."

"Alex?"

"What?"

"I lied," he admitted. "I saw you with Seymore, and I had to think of something. Because this much is true. I love you, more than anything on earth, with every bit of my heart, my soul, and my being."

"You lied to me?" she said.

He shook his head, looking at her. "Alex, I've learned

to never, ever take someone you love for granted. We can compromise. I don't need to be in on the find of the century. For me," he added softly, "*you* are the find of the century. Any century. Don't throw us away again, please."

"David, that's lovely. Really lovely. But are you saying we're not still married? That's what you lied about?"

"Forgive me. I didn't know what else to do. Well?"

She smiled. "Actually, I'm thinking that we should be remarried here. Right here. By the lagoons. A small ceremony, with just our closest friends here. I mean, we did the big-wedding thing already."

He gazed at her, slowly giving her a deep, rueful grin.

Then he pulled her into his arms and kissed her.

* * * * *

There are people in our lives we encounter who make their marks. Those who leave some indelible influence on who and what we will become. But if we're really lucky, there are those whose presence in our lives makes a difference that goes so much deeper than the skin that our life would not have been what it was destined to be without them. This book is dedicated to one such person with whom I have had the pleasure of love and laughter and the overwhelming sorrow of loss and grief.

To my baby brother, John Brashier.
You are my soul's twin.
Never forget how very much I love you.

PERSON OF INTEREST

Debra Webb

DEBRA WEBB

wrote her first story at age nine and her first romance at thirteen. It wasn't until she spent three years working for the military behind the Iron Curtain and within the confining political walls of Berlin, Germany, that she realized her true calling. A five-year stint with NASA on the space shuttle program reinforced her love of the endless possibilities within her grasp as a storyteller. A collision course between suspense and romance was set. Debra has been writing romantic suspense and action-packed romantic thrillers since. Visit her at www.DebraWebb.com or write to her at P.O. Box 4889, Huntsville, AL 35815.

Chapter 1

Finished.

With a satisfied sigh, Dr. Elizabeth Cameron surveyed the careful sutures and the prepatterned blocks of tissue she had harvested from inconspicuous donor sites. For this patient the best sites available had been her forearms and thighs which had miraculously escaped injury.

The tailored blocks of harvested tissue, comprised of skin, fat and blood vessels, were tediously inset into the face like pieces of a puzzle and circulation to the area immediately restored by delicate attachment to the facial artery.

Lastly, the newly defined tissue was sculpted to look, feel and behave like normal facial skin, with scars hidden in the facial planes. In a few weeks this patient would resume normal activities and no one outside her immediate family and friends would ever have to know that she had scarcely survived a fiery car crash that had literally melted a good portion of her youthful Miss Massachusetts face.

She would reach her twenty-first birthday next month with a face that looked identical to the one that had won her numerous accolades and trophies. More important, the young woman who had slipped into severe clinical depression and who had feared her life was over would now have a second chance.

"She's perfect, Doctor."

Elizabeth acknowledged her colleague's praise with a quick nod and stepped back from the operating table. With one final glance she took stock of the situation. The patient was stable. All was as it should be. "Finish up for me, Dr. Jeffrey," she told her senior surgical resident.

Pride welled in her chest as she watched a moment while her team completed the final preparations for transporting the patient to recovery. Yes, she had performed the surgery, but the whole team had been involved from day one, beginning with the complete, computerized facial analysis. This victory had been achieved by the entire team, not just one person. A team Elizabeth had handpicked over the past three years.

In the scrub room she stripped off her bloody gloves, surgical gown and mask, then cleaned her eyeglasses. She'd tried adjusting to contacts, but just couldn't manage the transition. Sticking to the old reliables hadn't failed her yet. She was probably the only doctor in the hospital who still preferred to do a number of things the old-fashioned way. Like working with a certain team day in and day out. She'd worked with Jeffrey long enough now that they could anticipate each other's moves and needs ahead of time. It worked. She liked sticking with what worked.

Exhaustion clawed at her. The muscles of her shoulders quivered with fatigue, the good kind. This one had been a long, arduous journey for both patient and surgical team. Weeks ago the initial preparations had begun, including forming a mold of a right ear to use in building a replacement for the one the patient had lost in the accident. The size and symmetry had worked out beautifully.

No matter how painstakingly Elizabeth and her team prepared, she wasn't fully satisfied until she saw the completed work…until the patient was rolled to recovery. The time required to heal varied, but in a couple of weeks the swelling would lessen, the red lines would fade. And the new face would bloom like a rose in the sun's light, as close to nature's work as man could come.

As Elizabeth started for the exit, intent on going straight home and crashing for a couple of hours, the rest of the team poured into the scrub room, high-fives and cheers of elation rumbling through the group. Elizabeth smiled. She had herself a hell of a team here. They were the best, each topping his or her field of expertise, and they were good folks, lacking the usual "ego" that often haunted the specialized medical profession.

"Excellent work, boys and girls," she called to the highly trained professionals who were quickly regressing to more adolescent behavior as the adrenaline high peaked and then drained away. "See you in two weeks."

Elizabeth pushed through the doors and into the long, white sterile corridor, still smiling as the ruckus followed her into the strictly enforced quiet zone. She inhaled deeply of the medicinal smells, the familiar scents comforting, relaxing. This place was her real home. She spent far more time here than inside the four walls of the little brownstone on which she made a monthly mortgage payment. Not really a good thing, she had begun to see. She didn't like the slightly cynical, fiercely focused person she was turning into.

A change was definitely in order.

Two weeks.

She hadn't taken that much time off since—

She banished the memory before it latched on to her thoughts. No way was she going to dredge up that painful past. Two months had elapsed. She clenched her jaw and paused at the bank of elevators. Giving the call button a quick stab, she waited, her impatience mounting with each passing second. She loved her work, was fully devoted to it. But she desperately needed this time to get away, to put the past behind her once and for all. She had to move on. Regain her perspective…her balance.

The elevator doors slid open and Elizabeth produced a smile for the nurses who exited. Almost three o'clock in the afternoon, shift change. The nurses and residents on duty would brief those arriving for second shift on the status of their patients. Orders would be reviewed and the flow of patient care would continue without interruption.

Dr. Jeffrey would stay with her patient for a time and issue the final orders. There was nothing for Elizabeth to worry about. She boarded the elevator and relaxed against the far wall. Her eyes closed as she considered the cruise she'd booked just last week. A snap decision, something she never, ever did. Her secretary had insisted she could not spend her time off at home or loitering around her office. Which, in retrospect, Elizabeth had to admit was an excellent idea. Hanging around the house or office, organizing books and files or personal items that were already in perfect order, would not be in her best interest. The last thing she needed in her life was more order.

Making a quick stop at the second-floor staff lounge to pick up her sweater and purse, more goodbyes were exchanged with coworkers who couldn't believe she was actually going to take a vacation. Elizabeth shook her head in self-deprecation. She really had lost any sense of balance. Work was all she had, it seemed, and everyone had taken notice. One way or another she intended to change that sad fact.

Hurrying through Georgetown University Medical Center's expansive lobby, she made her way to the exit that led to the employee parking garage. She could already see herself driving across the District, escaping everything. As much as she loved D.C., she needed to get away, to mingle with the opposite sex. To start something new and fresh. To put *him* out of her mind forever. He was gone. Dead. He'd died in some foreign country, location unspecified, of unnatural causes probably, the manner also unspecified. His body had not been recovered, at least, as far as she knew. He was simply gone. He wouldn't be showing up at her door in the middle of the night with an unexpected forty-eight-hour furlough he wanted to spend only with her.

Stolen moments. That was all she and Special Agent David Maddox had really ever shared. But then, that was what happened when one fell in love with a CIA agent. Covert operations, classified missions, need-to-know. All familiar terms.

Too familiar, she realized as she hesitated midstride on the lower level of the parking garage, her gaze landing on her white Lexus—or more specifically on the two well-dressed men waiting next to the classy automobile.

One man she recognized instantly as Craig Dawson, her CIA handler. All valuable CIA assets had handlers. It was some sort of rule. He'd replaced David when their relationship had gotten personal. There were times when Elizabeth wondered if that change in the dynamics of the interaction between them had ultimately caused David's death. His work had seemed so much safer when he'd been her handler.

Stop it, she ordered. Thinking about the past was destructive. She knew it. The counselor the Agency had insisted she see after David's death had said the same. Face forward, focus on the future.

Her new motto.

Time to move on.

If only her past would stop interfering.

What did Agent Dawson want today of all days? Annoyance lined her brow. Whenever he showed up like this it could only mean a ripple in her agenda. She couldn't change her current plans. It had taken too long for her to work up the courage and enthusiasm to make them.

Her irritation mounting unreasonably, her attention shifted slightly. To the man standing next to Dawson. Another secret agent, no doubt. The guy could have been a carbon copy of Dawson from the neck down, great suit, navy in color, spit and polished black leather shoes. The only characteristics that differentiated the two were age and hair color.

Well, okay, that was an exaggeration, the two looked nothing alike. Dawson was fifty or so, distinguished-looking, with a sparkling personality. He'd never performed field duty for the CIA, was more the "office" type. The other guy looked younger, late-thirties maybe, handsome in a rugged sort of way, and his expression resembled that of a slick gangster. At least what she could see of it with him wearing those dark shades. The five o'clock shadow on his lean jaw didn't help. Her gaze lingered there a moment longer. Something about his profile…his mouth seemed familiar.

She rarely forgot a face, and this one made her nervous. She looked away, settling her gaze back on Dawson and the kind of familiarity she could trust. Maybe she had run into the other man before. But that didn't seem likely since her dealings with the CIA had always come through David or Agent Dawson, discounting her rare command performance with the director himself. A frown nagged at her brow. It was doubtful that she knew the other man, yet something about him seriously intimidated her. Not a good thing in a CIA agent, to her way of thinking.

But then, what did she know? She was only a part-time volunteer agent whose existence was strictly off any official records. And she hadn't even been subjected to the training program. Calling herself an agent was a stretch. She actually had no dealings whatsoever with the CIA other than performing the occasional professional service for which she refused to accept pay. To date, she had provided new faces for more than a dozen deep-cover operatives. It was the least she could do for her country—why would she allow payment for services rendered? Elizabeth saw it as her patriotic duty. The covert sideline was her one secret…her one departure from the dull routine of being Dr. Elizabeth Cameron.

"Dr. Cameron," Dawson said when she made no

move to come closer, "the director would like to see you."

Elizabeth hiked her purse strap a little farther up her shoulder and crossed her arms over her chest. "I'm going on vacation, Agent Dawson," she said firmly as she ordered her feet to move toward her car. It was her car, after all; he couldn't keep her from getting in it and driving away. At least she didn't think he could.

"The meeting will only take a few minutes, ma'am," Dawson assured quietly while his cohort stood by, ominously silent, doing the *intimidation* thing.

She considered asking Craig if he was training a new recruit or if he'd worried that he might need backup for bringing her in. But she doubted he'd get the joke. She wouldn't have gotten it either until about a week ago. That's when she'd made her decision. The decision to put some spontaneity into her life. She was sick of being plain old quiet, reserved Elizabeth who never varied her routine. Who stuck with what worked and avoided personal risk at all cost. She got out of bed at the same time every morning, showered, readied for work and ate a vitamin-enhanced meal bar on the way to the office. After ten or twelve hours at the office and/or hospital, she worked out at the fitness center and went home, took a relaxing hot bath and fell into bed utterly exhausted.

Same thing, day in and day out.

She couldn't even remember the last time she'd gone to a movie much less had a simple dinner date.

But no more.

Still, she had an obligation to the CIA. She'd promised to help out when they needed her. Right now might be inconvenient but it was her duty to at least listen to what they needed. Growing up a military brat had taught her two things if nothing else: always guard your feelings and never, ever forget those who risk their lives for your freedom. Guarding her feelings was a hard-learned skill, the knowledge gained from moving every two to three years and having to fit in someplace new. The other—well, patriotism was simply something every good American should practice.

"All right," she relented to Mr. Dawson's obvious relief. "I'll see him, for a few minutes only." She held up a hand when Dawson would have moved toward the dark sedan parked next to her car. "Anything else he needs will have to wait until I get back from my cruise," she said just to be sure he fully grasped the situation. "Even doctors take vacations."

"I understand, ma'am," Dawson confirmed with a pleasant smile. But something about the smirk on the other man's face gave her pause. Did he know her? She just couldn't shake that vague sense of recognition. Maybe he was privy to what the director wanted and already knew she was in for a battle if she wanted this vacation to happen.

She was still a private citizen. She accepted no money for her work and she had never refused the Agency's requests. But this time she just might.

Elizabeth settled into the back seat of the dark sedan and Dawson closed her door before sliding behind the steering wheel. The other man took the front passenger seat, snapped the safety belt into place and stared straight ahead. Elizabeth was glad he hadn't opted to sit in back with her. She didn't like the guy. He made her feel threatened on some level. A frown inched its way across her forehead. She had to admit that he was the first Agency staff member she'd met who actually looked like one of the guys depicted in the movies. Thick, dark hair slicked back. Concealing eyewear, flinty profile. She shivered, then pushed the silly notion away.

She wanted spontaneity in her life, not trouble. This guy had trouble written all over what she could see of that too handsome face. Upon further consideration, she decided it was his mouth that disturbed her the most. There was a kind of insolence about it…a smugness that shouted *I could kiss you right now and make you like it.*

Another shudder quaked through her and she reminded herself of what falling for a spy had cost her already.

CIA agents did not make for reliable companions. She knew better than most. A pang of old hurt knifed through her. She'd made a mistake, veered too close to the flame and she'd gotten burned.

Never again.

If she fell in love a second time, which was highly doubtful considering her current track record, it would be with someone safe, someone predictable.

Safe.

At one time she'd considered David safe.

But she'd been wrong.

He'd felt safe and comfortable, but it had been nothing but an illusion.

David Maddox had been every bit as dangerous—as much of an adrenaline junkie—as all the rest in his line of work. CIA agents were like cops; they thrived in high-tension situations, on the thrill of the hunt. No matter how quiet and reserved David had pretended to be, he'd been just like the rest of them.

Just like Craig Dawson and his companion.

Men willing to risk it all for their country, who broke hearts and left shattered lives.

She didn't want that kind of man.

Never again.

Elizabeth focused on the passing landscape, refused to dwell on the subject. The skyscrapers and bumper-to-bumper traffic of the D.C. area eventually gave way to trees and only the occasional passing motorist. It seemed odd to Elizabeth that the CIA's headquarters would be nestled away in the woods, seemingly in the middle of nowhere, like a harmless, sprawling farm. But there was nothing harmless about the vast property. Security fences topped with concertina wire and cameras. Warnings about entering the premises with electronic devices. Armed guards. Definitely not harmless in any sense of the word.

Dawson braked to a stop and flashed his ID for the guard waiting at the entrance gate while another guard circled the sedan with a dog trained to sniff out explosives and the like. Even now she imagined that high-tech gadgets were monitoring any conversation that might take place inside the vehicle. Every word, every nuance in tone scrutinized for possible threat.

The recruits here were trained to infiltrate, interrogate, analyze data and to kill if necessary. Their existence and proper training were essential to national security, she understood that. Respected those who sacrificed so very much. But she couldn't bring herself to feel comfortable here. It took a special kind of human being to fit into this world. Her gaze flitted to the man in the front passenger seat. A man like him. Dark, quiet, enigmatic. A man fully prepared to die…to kill…for what he believed in.

A dangerous man.

But not dangerous to her…never again. No more dangerous men in her life, she promised herself as she did her level best to ignore the premonition of dread welling in her chest. Safe. Occasionally spontaneous maybe, but safe. She had her new life all mapped out and the dead last thing it included was danger.

Chapter 2

The main lobby of the CIA headquarters always took Elizabeth's breath away. The granite wall with its stars honoring fallen agents. The flags and statues…the grandeur that represented the solemn undertaking of all those who risked their lives to make the world a safer place. The shadow warriors.

Elizabeth looked away from that honorary wall, knowing that one of those stars represented David. Though she would never know which one since his name would not be listed. *Anonymous even in death.*

For the first time since his death she wondered if she'd known him at all. Was his name even David Maddox?

Her heart squeezed instantly at the thought. This was precisely why she had promised herself she would not think about the past. Not today, not any day.

She had to get on with the present, move into the future.

Like David, the past was over. She was thirty-seven for Christ's sake. Her fantasy of someday having a family was swiftly slipping away. Never before had she been so keenly aware of just how much time she had wasted. Though she loved her work, she didn't regret for a moment the sacrifices she had made to become the respected surgeon she was; it was time to have a personal life as well.

The rubber soles of her running shoes whispered against the gleaming granite floor where the CIA's emblem sprawled proudly, welcoming all who entered. The guards and the metal detectors beyond that proved a little less welcoming, reminding Elizabeth of the threat that loomed wherever government offices could be found. Even in her lifetime the world had changed so much. Maybe part of her sudden impatience to move forward was somehow related to current events as well as the recent past. Whatever the case, it was the right thing to do.

Dawson led her to the bank of elevators and depressed the down button. Uneasiness stirred inside her again. Somehow she doubted that the director's office had been moved to the basement. Before she could question his selection the doors slid open and the three of them boarded the waiting car.

When he selected a lower level, she felt compelled to ask, "Aren't we going to the director's office?"

Agent Dawson smiled kindly. He'd always had a nice smile, a calming demeanor. She was glad for that. "We're meeting in a special conference room this time. The director is there now waiting for your arrival."

Elizabeth managed a curt nod, still feeling a bit uneasy with the situation despite her handler's assurances. The fine hairs on the back of her neck stood on end the way they did whenever she sensed a deviation in the status quo of a patient's condition. She could always predict when things were about to go wrong. This felt wrong. For the first time since she'd agreed to support the CIA from time to time, she felt seriously uncomfortable with the arrangement. That premonition of dread just wouldn't go away though it refused to clarify itself fully.

The other agent, the one whose presence added to her discomfort and who hadn't been introduced to her as of yet, shifted slightly, drawing her attention in his direction.

He still wore those confounding sunglasses. Elizabeth found the continued behavior to be rude and purposely intimidating. Fury fueling an uncharacteristic boldness she opened her mouth to say just that and he looked at her. Turned his head toward her, tilting it slightly downward and looked straight at her as if he'd sensed her intent. She didn't have to see his eyes. She could feel him watching her. Something fierce surged through her. Fear, she told herself. But it didn't feel quite like fear.

Who the hell was this man?

She swung her attention back to Agent Dawson, intent on demanding the identity of the other man, but the elevator bumped to a halt. The doors yawned open and Dawson motioned for her to precede him. Pushing her irrational annoyance with the other man to the back burner, she stepped out of the car and moved in the direction Dawson indicated. She would likely never see this stranger again after today, what was the point in making a scene?

On some level she recognized him. Special Agent Joe Hennessey couldn't jeopardize this mission by allowing her to recognize him before the decision was made. He'd kept the concealing eyewear in place to throw her off, but he had a feeling she wouldn't be fooled for long. He'd been careful not to speak and not to get too close.

But there was no denying the chemistry that still sizzled between them…it was there in full force. He could only hope that she was disconcerted with the unexpected trip to Langley and was off balance enough to give a commitment before the full ramifications of the situation became crystal clear.

The long corridor stretched out before them, the occasional door on one side or the other interrupting the monotonous white walls. Tile polished to a high sheen flowed like an endless sea of glass. Surface mounted fluorescent lights provided ample lighting if not an elegant atmosphere. He could feel her uneasiness growing with each step. She didn't like this deviation from the usual routine.

Hennessey knew this was her first trip to the bowels of the Agency and she probably hoped it would be the last. The adrenaline no doubt pumping through her veins would make the air feel heavier, thicker. It didn't take a psychic to know she was seriously antsy in the situation. Didn't like it one damned bit.

Dawson stayed to her right, a step ahead, leading the way. Hennessey stayed to her left, kept his movements perfectly aligned with hers, not moving ahead, never falling behind. If the overhead lights were to suddenly go out and the generators were to fail, he would still know she was there. He could *feel* her next to him. For someone who loved clinging to a routine, her energy was strong…her presence nearly overwhelming. With every fiber of his being he knew she was even now scrolling through her memory banks searching for what it was that felt familiar about him.

Thankfully they reached their destination. Dawson stopped at the next door on the left. "The director is waiting for you inside, Dr. Cameron." He reached for the door and opened it.

Elizabeth looked from him to Hennessey and back. "Aren't you coming in, Agent Dawson?"

She didn't like this at all. Hennessey could feel the tension vibrating inside her mounting.

"Not this time, ma'am."

She didn't like this. Her frown deepening, Elizabeth pushed her glasses up the bridge of her nose and moved through the open door. She had been briefed long ago about the various levels of security clearances within the CIA. Some were so secret that even the designation was classified. In most cases, the rule that every agent lived by was the "need-to-know" rule. One knew what one needed to know and nothing more.

Clearly Agent Dawson and his friend didn't need to know whatever the director was about to discuss with her. The door closed behind her with a resolute thud and she shivered. The sound echoed through her, shaking loose a memory from months ago. It had been dark… she'd scarcely seen his face, but she had known his reputation. The man who'd been sent to protect her that night had held her there like a prisoner in the darkness for hours insisting that it was for her own safety. He'd been rude and arrogant, had overwhelmed her with his brute strength…his absolute maleness. And then he'd been gone.

He'd almost taken advantage of her—she'd almost let

him—and then he'd disappeared. Like a shadow in the night…as if he'd never been there at all. She'd known what he'd done. He'd reveled in pushing her buttons, in making her weak. But she'd resisted, just barely. If she hadn't, he would have taken full advantage, even knowing that she belonged to David. She wondered if David had ever suspected that the friend he'd sent to protect her from a threat the nature of which she hadn't been authorized clearance for had almost succeeded in seducing her with his devastating charm. Some friend.

But then that was Special Agent Joe Hennessey. He might be a superspy of legendary proportions, but she knew him for what he was: ruthless and with an allegiance only to himself. The guy waiting with Dawson in the corridor reminded her of Hennessey.

"Elizabeth, thank you for coming."

Elizabeth shoved the distracting thoughts away as Director George Calder rounded the end of the long conference table and made his way to her. A second gentleman she didn't recognize rose from his chair but didn't move toward her.

Present and future, forget the past, she reminded her too forgetful self. Like David, Joe Hennessey was a part of her past that was gone forever. Face forward. Focus on the here and now…on the future. Director Calder took her hand in his and shook it firmly.

"I hope you'll forgive my intrusion into your vacation schedule," he offered, his expression displaying sincere regret.

George Calder was a tall, broad-shouldered man, not unlike the two agents waiting outside the door. Nearly sixty, his hair had long ago silvered and lines drawn by the execution of enormous power marred his distinguished face. He'd presented himself as nothing less than gracious and sensitive each time he'd requested Elizabeth's presence. But there was more this time. Something else simmered behind those intelligent hazel eyes. The sixth sense that usually centered on her patients was humming now, urging her to act.

"Technically," Elizabeth said succinctly, ignoring her foolish urge for fight or flight, "my vacation doesn't start until tomorrow so you're still safe for now."

George laughed, but the sound was forced. "Let me introduce you to our director of operations." He turned to the other man in the room. This one was slightly shorter and thinner, but looked every bit as formidable as Director Calder.

"Kurt Allen, meet our talented Dr. Elizabeth Cameron."

His fashionable gray pinstripe suit setting him apart from the requisite navy or black, Allen rushed to shake her hand, his smile wide and seeming genuine. "It's an honor to finally meet you, Dr. Cameron. Your work is amazing. I can't tell you how many of my best men you've spared."

Elizabeth realized then that Director Allen was in charge of the field agents who most often needed her services.

"I'm glad I can help, Director Allen," she told him in all sincerity. It felt odd now that she'd never met him before. Need-to-know, she reminded herself.

There was an awkward moment of tense silence before Calder said, "Elizabeth, please have a seat and we'll talk."

The director ushered her to the chair next to the one he'd vacated when she'd entered the room. Allen seated himself directly across the table from her.

The air suddenly thickened with the uneasy feel of

a setup. This was not going to be the typical briefing. There was no folder marked *classified* that held the case facts of the agent who needed a new face. There was nothing but the high sheen of the mahogany conference table and the steady stares of the two men who obviously did not look forward to the discussion to come.

To get her mind off the intensity radiating around her, Elizabeth took a moment to survey the room. Richly paneled walls similar to those of the director's office several floors overhead gave the room a feeling of warmth. Royal blue commercial-grade carpet covered the floor. The array of flags surrounding the CIA emblem on the rear wall and the numerous plaques that lined the other three lent an air of importance to the environment. This was a place where discussions of national significance took place. She should feel honored to be here. Whatever she could do for the CIA was the least she could do for her country, she reminded herself.

Elizabeth clasped her hands atop the conference table, squared her shoulders and produced a smile for Director Calder. "Why did you need to see me, Director?" Someone had to break the ice. Neither of the gentlemen appeared prepared to dive in. Another oddity. What could either of these men, who possessed the power to start wars, fear from her?

Calder glanced at Allen then manufactured a smile of his own. "Elizabeth, I think you understand how important covert operations are here at the CIA."

She nodded. Though she actually knew little about their actions, she did comprehend that covert field operatives risked their lives in positions deep undercover and generally in foreign countries.

"The men and women who make up the ranks of our

field operatives are the very tip of the spear this agency represents," he went on, verifying her assumption. "They are the forerunners. The ones who provide us with the data that averts disaster. They risk more than anyone else."

Again she nodded her understanding. The knot in her stomach twisted as she considered why he felt the need to tediously prepare her for whatever it was he really wanted to say. Every instinct warned that things were not as they should be.

"During the past two and a half years we've counted on you more than a dozen times to provide a means of escape for our operatives. Your skill at creating new faces has allowed these men and women to avoid the enemy's vengeance while maintaining their careers. Without your help, a number of those operatives would certainly have lost their lives."

"There are other surgeons in your field," Allen interjected with a show of his palms for emphasis. "But not one in this country is as skilled as you."

Elizabeth blushed. She hated that she did that but there was no stopping it. She'd never taken compliments well. Though she worked hard and recognized that she deserved some amount of praise, it was simply a physical reaction over which she had no control. Her professional life was the one place where she suffered no doubts in regards to her competence. If only she could harness some of that confidence for her personal life.

"I appreciate your saying so, Director Allen," she offered, "but I can't take full credit. My ability with the scalpel is a gift from God." She meant those words with all that made her who she was. A God complex was something she'd never had to wrestle with as so many of her colleagues did. She made it a point to remind her residents of that all-important fact as well. Confidence was a good thing, arrogance was not.

Director Calder braced his hands on the table in front of him and drew her attention back to him. "That's part of the attitude that we hope will allow you to see the need for what we're about to ask of you, Elizabeth."

She didn't doubt her ability to handle whatever he asked of her. In that vein, she dismissed the uneasiness and lifted her chin in defiance of her own lingering uncertainty. There was only one way to cut to the chase here—be direct. "What is it you need, Director Calder? I've never turned you down before. Is there some reason you feel this time will be different?"

Two and a half years ago the CIA had, after noting her work in the field of restorative facial surgery, approached her. They needed her and she had gladly accepted the challenge. She would not change that course now.

"We are aware of the relationship you maintained with Agent Maddox," Allen broached, answering before Calder could or maybe because he didn't want to bring up the sensitive subject. "I believe the two of you were… intimate for more than a year before his death."

The oxygen in Elizabeth's lungs evacuated without further ado. She swallowed hard, sucked in a necessary breath and told her heart to calm. "That's correct." To say she was surprised by the subject would be a vast understatement. But, within this realm, there was no room for deception or hedging. Those traits were best utilized in the field. And the fact of the matter was Elizabeth had never been very good at lying. She was an open book. Subterfuge and confrontation were two of her least favorite strategies.

Just another reason she had no life. Real life, emotionally speaking, was too difficult. If she kept to herself, she wasn't likely to run into any problems.

But you're about to change that attitude, a little voice reminded. She had made up her mind to dive back into a social life…to take a few risks.

If only she could remember that mantra.

Director Calder picked up the conversation again, "Three months before his death Agent Maddox was involved in a mission that garnered this Agency critical information. He was, fortunately, able to complete the mission with his cover intact."

Elizabeth imagined that maintaining the validity of a cover would be crucial for future use. She nodded her understanding, prompting him to carry on.

"Though the group he infiltrated at the time was effectively eliminated, two members have moved into another arena which has created great concern for this agency."

Outright apprehension reared its ugly head. "I'm not sure I know what you mean." She did fully comprehend that there were certain elements she would not be told due to their classification, but she had to know more than this. Tap dancing around the issue wasn't going to assuage her uneasiness.

"The two subjects involved have relocated their operation here. On our soil," Allen clarified. "They have an agenda that we are not at liberty to disclose, but they must be stopped at all costs."

Elizabeth divided a look between the two men. Both wore poker faces, giving away nothing except determination. She hated to say anything that would make her look utterly stupid but her conclusion was simple. "If you know they're here, why don't you just arrest them or…or eliminate them."

Made sense to her. But then she was only a doctor, not a spy or an assassin. She felt certain they had some legitimate reason for taking a less direct route to accomplish their ultimate goal, though she couldn't begin to fathom what the motivation could possibly be.

"I wish it were that simple," Calder told her thoughtfully. "Stopping the men they've sent won't be enough. We have to know how they're getting their information to ensure the threat is eliminated completely. Otherwise the root cause of the situation will simply continue generating additional obstacles."

Now she got it. "You need these two members of the group David infiltrated to lead you to their source," she suggested. She'd seen a crime drama or two in her life.

"Exactly," Allen confirmed. "If we don't find the source, they'll just keep sending out more assassins."

Assassins. That meant targets.

"How does this involve me?" Her heart rate kicked into overdrive. She moistened her lips as the silence stretched out another ten seconds. This could not be good.

Director Calder turned more fully toward her, fixing her with a solemn gaze that reflected nearly as much desperation as it did determination. "In order to infiltrate this group we need someone with whom they'll feel comfortable. Someone familiar. We have an agent prepared to take the risk and infiltrate the group, but we need to make a few alterations."

Her head moved up and down in acknowledgement. She was on the same page now. "You want me to give him a different appearance? A new face?" That's what she usually did. No big deal. But why all the beating around the proverbial bush?

"Correct," Calder allowed. "But just any face won't work. We'll be requesting a specific look."

"Someone these assassins know, feel comfortable with," she echoed his earlier words.

"Precisely," Allen agreed enthusiastically. "This part is crucial to the success of the mission. If the targets think for even a second that our man isn't who he says he is they'll kill him without hesitation. There is no margin for error whatsoever, Dr. Cameron. That's why your help is critical."

She looked expectantly from Calder to Allen and back. "What is it you need, *exactly?*" she asked, focusing her attention on Allen since he loved to throw around those extreme adverbs. The requirements sounded simple enough.

"What we need," Allen told her bluntly, "is David Maddox."

Her breath trapped in her throat and shock claimed her expression. She didn't need a mirror, she felt her face pinch in horrified disbelief. Her fingers fisted to fight back the old hurt. "David is dead," she replied with just as much bluntness as he'd issued the requirement. What was this man thinking?

Calder reached across the table and put his hand on hers. Echoes of the anguish she'd felt two months ago reverberated through her. "I know this is difficult, Elizabeth. You must believe that we wouldn't ask if there was any other way."

He was serious.

"Oh my God." She drew away from his comforting touch. Shook her head to clear it. This was too much. "How can you ask me this?"

"Dr. Cameron, there is no other option," Allen said flatly, his tone far cooler than before but his eyes reflected the desperation she'd already seen in Calder's. "We need David Maddox, but as you pointed out, he is dead. So we need a stand-in. We need you to do what you do best and give our agent David Maddox's face."

Tears stung her eyes, emotion clogged her throat, but somehow she managed to say the only thing she could. "I can't do that."

Director Calder leveled a steady gaze on hers. "I'm afraid my colleague is right, there is no other option, Elizabeth."

Chapter 3

Joe Hennessey waited with Craig Dawson in the corridor outside the conference room. He didn't have to be in the room or even watch the proceedings to know that Elizabeth Cameron would not like the idea. Not that he could blame her if he looked at it from her position but there were things she didn't know…would never know.

"She'll be okay with this," Dawson said quietly as if reading his mind.

Hennessey shrugged one shoulder. "She's your asset, you should know." His indifference might seem cold, but he had serious doubts where this whole operation was concerned. What the hell? He had a reputation for being cold and ruthless.

Dawson cut him a look that left no room for further discussion. He had faith in the woman even if he didn't have any in Hennessey.

Though Hennessey hadn't known David Maddox particularly well, he had met the woman in his life once. And once had been enough. Elizabeth Cameron had cool down to a science. Maybe she was hot between the sheets, but in Hennessey's estimation, a woman that reserved and uptight usually thought too much. Good, hot sex was definitely no thinking matter. It either was or it wasn't.

In his line of work he'd learned to take his pleasure where he could and not to linger for too long. Dr. Elizabeth Cameron was not the type to go for a thorough roll in the hay and then walk away. She was one of those women with a commitment fetish. She didn't do casual sex. Probably didn't even understand the concept. From what Hennessey had seen, the woman was all work and no play. Completely focused.

If she agreed to do the job, that would be a good thing. He damn sure didn't want a lesser surgeon screwing up his face. Not that he considered himself the Hollywood handsome type but he got his share of second looks. Including one or two from the good doctor. Though he doubted she would admit it in this lifetime. Just like before, she wanted to pretend there was nothing between them. In reality, there wasn't, not really. Just that one night. The night he'd saved her life but she would never own up to it. She would only remember his manhandling and overbearing attitude. But something had sparked between them that night…in the dark.

The chemistry had been there. Strong enough to startle him almost as much as it had her. She'd hated it and her extreme reaction had only made bad matters worse. But then, he loved a challenge. He'd felt the electricity between them again today. But like before, she'd wanted to ignore it. What did all that attraction say about the relationship she'd had with Maddox? Maybe there was a little bit of the devil in all of us, he mused, even the straitlaced doc.

Well, she might prefer to ignore him, but if the director had his way, she might as well get used to having him around. They would be spending the next three weeks in close quarters. Not that it would be a hardship. He thought about those long, satiny legs hidden beneath that conservative peach-colored skirt. The lady had a great body. She worked out. He'd watched her. She kept a hell of a boring routine. Yet there was no denying that blond hair and those green eyes were attractive even if she did make it a point to camouflage those long, silky tresses in a bun and those lovely green eyes behind the ugliest black rimmed glasses.

Well, attractive or not, hot in bed or not, Elizabeth Cameron held the key to his future. He hoped by now she understood that. His survival in the upcoming mission depended upon his ability to fool the enemy.

The idea of sporting another man's face held no real appeal, but if it got the job done Hennessey could deal with it. He could even manage to put up with the doc's company for a couple of weeks and maintain the necessary level of restraint. What he wasn't at all sure he could handle was her constant analysis.

He recalled quite well the way she'd studied him that one time. Her lover had apparently related a number of tales about the legendary Joe Hennessey, none of which had sat well with Miss Prim and Proper.

Half the stories were exaggerated and the other half were nobody's business. But that wouldn't keep her from holding his past, real or imagined, against him.

Hennessey put his life on the line for his country all the time. The last thing he deserved was some holierthan-thou broad, however talented, treating him like he was the scum of the earth. Throw that in the mix with the undeniable physical attraction and he came up with distraction.

He'd learned the hard way that if a guy thought with his privates in this business he ended up dead. He'd had his share of ladies along the way, but he never let one distract him from the mission.

He didn't intend to start now.

The door swung open and Hennessey came to attention. A leftover habit from his days in Special Forces. Anytime a superior officer was about, he came to attention as was expected.

Directors Calder and Allen moved into the corridor, closing the door behind them. A frown pulled at Hennessey's mouth. Where was the woman? He'd thought the plan was for him to be called in once they'd broken the news to her. Had she outright refused to do the job?

That would be just his luck. Damn. He wanted the best. And she was it.

"Agent Hennessey," Calder announced without preamble, "Dr. Cameron would like to see you now."

Hennessey blinked. "Alone?" He didn't relish the idea of the confrontation with no one else around to temper it.

Calder nodded. "She hasn't committed to the request. She insists on speaking to the operative assigned to the mission first. If she continues to resist, you have my authorization to enlighten her." He qualified his statement with a warning, "Her participation is essential, but she doesn't need to know any more than absolutely necessary."

With a heavy exhale and a nod of understanding, Hennessey stated for the record, "Yes, sir."

As he reached for the door, Dawson stopped him with a hand on his arm. "I know your reputation, Agent Hennessey," he cautioned quietly. "Don't do anything you'll regret. Dr. Cameron is a nice lady."

"I think Agent Hennessey is aware of proper protocol," Director Calder suggested, his tone as stern as his expression. He would tolerate no roadblocks now or later. The reprimand was meant for both Dawson and Hennessey.

For the first time since going to the hospital to pick up the good doctor, Hennessey removed his eyewear. He'd worn the dark glasses inside purposely, to remain anonymous until the decision was final. Apparently there was going to be no help for that now. He hoped like hell she wouldn't let that one night influence her decision.

Hennessey leveled an unflinching stare on Dawson. "I have never jeopardized a mission or an asset."

"Just remember," Dawson persisted despite the director's warning, "that she is a very valuable asset."

Hennessey shoved his sunglasses back into place and opened the door. He didn't need Dawson telling him how to do his job. He had no intention of getting tangled up with Dr. Cameron. There might be some sexual energy bouncing back and forth between them, but she definitely was not his type.

Opinionated women were nothing but a pain in the ass.

Like he'd said before, some things don't require thought.

Elizabeth couldn't shake the idea that she knew the other agent. There was definitely something familiar about him. That mouth…the way his presence overwhelmed the atmosphere around him.

It couldn't be *him*.

She would remember if it was him. It wasn't like she could forget that night. That one night. She shivered. She'd tried not to think about it, but every now and then it poked through the layers of anger and guilt she'd piled on top of the memory. He'd practically held her hostage. He'd made her feel things she hadn't wanted to feel. A hot, searing ache, a yearning deep down inside her. It had been wrong. A betrayal. And with *him* no less. David had told her all about Special Agent Joe Hennessey. His dark, alluring charm that the ladies couldn't resist; his ruthless single-mindedness. An agent like no other.

She wondered if David would have spoken so highly of him if he'd known how close his supposed friend had come to seducing her…how close she'd come to allowing it?

Heat infused her cheeks, rushed over her skin at even the memory of those few hours. He'd cast a spell on her. Made her want to forget everything and everyone else. Thank God she'd come to her senses.

Chafing her arms she banished the disturbing memories. She had to figure this out…had to find a way to make them see that she could not do this. She simply couldn't do that to David's memory.

Only, David would want her to help.

If lives were in danger he would want her to do whatever was necessary to help his fellow agents. But she needed more information. Surely they couldn't expect her to do this without further clarification.

And, dear God, could she do it?

Could she re-create David's face on another man?

* * *

She stood on the far side of the room, her back to the door. For about three seconds Hennessey hesitated, admiring the view. She might be a pain in the ass, but he could look at hers all day. Nice. All those hours on the stair-stepper clearly made a difference.

He closed the door, allowing it to slam just enough to get her attention. Startled, she whirled to face him.

The frown of utter confusion telegraphed her first thought loud and clear: *What the hell do you want?* She had no doubt expected the directors to return with their man in tow. The last person she'd expected to enter the room was him.

"Dr. Cameron, I'm Special Agent Joe Hennessey." As he moved toward her he reached upward and removed his concealing eyewear. "If you'll recall we met once before."

Her eyes rounded and that cute little mouth dropped open. "You!" The single word was cast like an accusing stone.

He tossed the glasses onto the conference table and propped a hip there. "You remember me," he offered, his smile infused with all the charm in his vast ladies' man repertoire.

She pointed to the door then to him, her confusion morphing into disbelief. "It's you he wants me to prepare for this mission?"

Hennessey flared his hands. "That's right. Is there a problem?"

Her head moved from side to side as all that confusion and disbelief coalesced into outrage. "You're nothing like David," she accused.

Well, she had that right but he saw no point in bursting her bubble where her former lover was concerned.

"I'm the same height and build. The hair color is close enough, the eyes will be an easy fix with colored contacts." He shrugged, the control necessary to hold back his own patience slipping just a little. "I don't see the problem."

She blinked rapidly, her head doing that side-to-side thing again as if the very idea was blasphemy. "You're not *like* David," she argued.

He pushed off the table and moved toward her, lowering his voice an octave, slowing the cadence of his words as he recalled the numerous taped conversations he'd listened to. "I can do anything it takes to get the job done, *Elizabeth*." Her head snapped up at his use of her first name. He said it with emphasis, the same way Maddox used to. "You'd be surprised at just how versatile I am."

Her pupils flared. She shivered. But it was the little hitch in her breathing that actually got to him, made his pulse skitter and chinked the armor he wore to protect his emotions. He shook his head and looked away. How the hell had he let that happen?

"You expect me to trust anything you say?"

Well, she had him pegged, didn't she? Apparently she'd accepted every rumor she'd heard as fact. "Bottom line, Doc, I can't do this without you." His gaze moved back to hers and he saw the concern and the hurt there. Dammit, he did not want to hurt her. Maddox had done that well enough himself, but she would never know it. "Will you help me or not?"

She tilted up that determined little chin and glared at him, a new flash of anger chasing away the doubt. "And if I refuse, what then?"

"People will die."

She blinked, but to her credit she didn't back off. "So

I've heard. Can you be more specific? I need to know what I'm getting into here." Her compact little body literally strummed with her building tension.

The question kind of pissed him off. Or maybe it was the glaring fact that he couldn't keep his mind off her every reaction, couldn't stay focused. "You know, Doc, according to Director Calder, you generally don't question his requests. I understand this is personal," he growled, "but do you really think Maddox would have a problem with me borrowing his face for a little while?"

Her fists clenched and Hennessey had the distinct feeling that it was all she could do not to slap him. Good. He wanted her responses to be real, wanted to clear the air here and now. He didn't need her hesitation coming back to bite him in the ass down the line.

"David would probably say it's the right thing to do," she said tightly. "It's me who has the problem."

He resisted the urge to roll his eyes at her misplaced loyalty. He couldn't help wondering if, when he died, anyone would think so highly of him. Not very damned likely. He was far too open to lead anyone that far off track. Well, except for his targets and that was his job.

In his personal life he kept things on the up-and-up. He never lied to anyone, most especially a woman.

He liked women. Before he could put the brakes on the urge, his gaze roamed down the length of her toned body, admiring those feminine curves, before sliding back up to that madder-than-hell expression on her pretty face.

He liked women a lot. They knew what they were getting with him. If he and the doc did the deed there would be no questions or doubts between them.

But that wasn't going to happen.

Mainly because it would be stupid.

Not to mention the fact that she looked ready to take off his head and spit down his throat.

Fine. If she wanted to play hardball, he was game. "You want to know specifics?" He leaned closer, so close he could see the tiny flecks of gold in those glittering green eyes. "You've completed makeovers on fourteen operatives in the past thirty months. Two of those operatives are dead." One being the man who taught him everything he knew, but he didn't mention that. He had no intention of giving her any personal ammunition. In addition, holding on to control was far too important for him to let his personal issues with this mission get a grip right now. He kept those feelings tightly compartmentalized for a later time. "If I don't stop these guys the rest of those operatives will end up dead as well."

"That's…that's impossible," she stammered, some of the fight going out of her. "How could they know who and where these people are? Who has access to that information?" Her gaze dropped to his lips but quickly jerked back up to his eyes. She looked startled that she had allowed the weakness.

Hennessey laughed softly, allowing his warm breath to feather across those luscious lips. Damn, he was enjoying this far too much. Maybe he should just cut loose and say what was on his mind. That he would do this with or without her help, but that if she had a couple of hours he would show her what she was missing if she really wanted to know how well he lived up to his infamous reputation.

Dumb, Hennessey. Focus. Apparently she was experiencing almost as much trouble as he was.

In answer to her question, he tossed her a response she was not going to like. "You want to know who has access to those names and faces? Directors Calder and Allen, of course, the president, your former boyfriend, me and *you.*" He said the last with just as much accusation as she'd thrown at him earlier.

She shuddered visibly, inhaled sharply, the sound doing strange things to his gut, making him even angrier or something along those lines. "Could someone else have gained access to the files?" she demanded, hysteria climbing in her voice.

He shook his head slowly and prepared to deliver the final blow. "Not a chance. Since Maddox is dead and, well, the president is the president, I'd say that narrows down the suspect list to the two directors outside that door." He hitched his thumb in that direction. "And you and me."

Fury whipped across her face, turning those green eyes to the color of smoldering jade. "If you think this tactic is going to pressure me into a yes, you're sadly mistaken, Agent Hennessey."

"Suit yourself." He straightened, a muscle in his cheek jerking as he clenched his jaw so hard his teeth should have cracked. It took a full minute for him to grab back some semblance of control. "Then consider this, *Dr. Cameron.*" He glared down at her, his own fury way beyond reining in now. "If you don't do this most likely my mission will fail, then those operatives will eventually be found and murdered, one by one."

She held her ground, refused to look away though he knew just how lethal his glare could be. "You said two are already dead?" she asked. Her voice quavered just a little.

"That's right," he ground out, ignoring the twinge of regret that pricked him for pushing the jerk routine this far. "And so are their families." He fought the emotion that tightened his throat. He would not let her see the weakness. "You see, Doc, these people aren't happy with just wiping out the list of agents who've gone against what they believe in, they play extra dirty. They kill the family first, making the agent watch, and then they kill the agent, slowly, painfully."

Her eyes grew wider with each word. The pulse fluttered wildly at the base of her throat. She didn't want to hear this, didn't want to know. Too bad. It was the only way.

"So, it's your choice," he went on grimly. "You can either help me stop them or you can try to sleep at night while wondering when the next agent will be located and murdered."

She did turn away this time. Hennessey took a deep breath and cursed himself for being such an idiot. Saying all that hadn't been necessary. But, on some level, he'd wanted to rattle her—to hurt her. He wanted to get to her when the truth was she'd already gotten to him. He'd lost control by steady increments from the moment the director ordered him to start watching her weeks ago.

He had to get back on track here, had to keep those damned personal issues out of this. If the director got even a whiff of how he really felt, he would be replaced. Hennessey couldn't let that happen. He had to do this for a couple of reasons. "I shouldn't have told you," he said, regret slipping into his voice. As much as he'd needed her cooperation, he'd gone too far.

When she turned back to him once more, her face had been wiped clean of emotion, and her analytical side was back. The doctor persona was in place. The woman who could go into an operating room and reconstruct a face damaged so badly that the patient's own family couldn't identify her. No wonder she walked around as cold as ice most of the time. It took nerves of steel and the ability to set her emotions aside to do what she did.

He should respect that.

He did.

It was his other reactions that disturbed him.

"What do you want from me?"

The request unnerved him at a level that startled him all over again.

He focused on the question, denying the uncharacteristic emotions twisting inside him. "I need you to do your magic, Doc." His gaze settled heavily onto hers. "And I need you to work with me. You knew Maddox intimately. Help me become him…just for a little while. Long enough to survive this mission. Long enough to do what has to be done."

For three long beats she said nothing at all. Just when he was certain she would simply walk away, she spoke. "All right." She rubbed at her forehead as if an ache had begun there, then sighed. "On one condition." She looked straight at him.

The intensity…the electricity crackled between them like embers in a building fire. She had to feel it. The lure was very nearly irresistible.

"Name it," he shot back.

"When this is over, I give you back your face. I don't want you being *you* with David's face."

He wanted to pretend the words didn't affect him… but they did. He'd be damned if he'd let her see just how much impact her opinion carried. "I wouldn't have it any other way," he insisted.

"Then we have a deal, Agent Hennessey. When do we start?"

Chapter 4

Elizabeth sat in her car as the purple and gray hues of dawn stole across the sky, chasing away the darkness, ushering forth the new day.

She'd managed a few hours sleep last night but just barely. Her mind kept playing moments spent with David, fleeting images of a past that had, at the time, felt like the beginning of the rest of her life.

How could she have been so foolish as to take that risk? She had known that a relationship with a man like David was an emotional gamble, but she'd dived in headfirst. The move had been so unlike her. She'd spent her entire life carefully calculating her every step.

She'd known by age twelve that she wanted to be a doctor, she just hadn't known what field. As a teenager, pediatrics had appealed to her, in particular helping children with the kind of diseases that robbed them of their youth and dreams. But at nineteen her college roommate had been in a horrifying automobile accident and the weeks and months that followed had brought Elizabeth's future into keen focus as nothing else could have.

Watching her friend go from a vibrant, happy young woman with a brilliant future ahead of her to a shell of a human being with a face that would never be her own had made Elizabeth yearn to prevent that from ever happening again…to anyone.

She'd worked harder than ever, had thrown herself into her education and eventually into her work. That burning desire to do the impossible, to rebuild the single most individual part of the human body, had driven her like a woman obsessed.

Elizabeth sighed. And maybe she was obsessed. If so, she had no hope of making it right because this was who she was, what she did. She made no excuses.

She dragged the keys from her ignition and dropped them into her purse.

But this was different.

Though she had changed faces for the CIA before, a fact for which she had no regrets, this was so *very* different.

Elizabeth emerged from her Lexus, closed the door and automatically depressed the lock button on the remote. The headlights flashed, signaling the vehicle was now secure.

She inhaled a deep breath of the thick August air. It wasn't entirely daylight yet and already she could almost taste the humidity.

"Might as well get this done," she murmured as she shoved her glasses up the bridge of her nose and then trudged across the parking lot.

The CIA had leased, confiscated or borrowed a private clinic for this Saturday morning's procedure. She noted the other vehicles there and, though she recognized none of them, assumed it was the usual team she worked with on these secret procedures. Of course, she would prefer her own team, but the group provided by the CIA in the past were excellent and, admittedly, a sort of rhythm had developed after more than a dozen surgeries.

A guard waited at the side entrance. His appearance made her think of the Secret Service agents who served as bodyguards for the president.

"Good morning, Dr. Cameron," he said as she neared. Though she didn't know him, he obviously knew her. No surprise.

"Morning."

He opened the door for her and she moved inside. It wasn't necessary to ask where the others would be, that part was always the same. Most clinics were set up on a similar floor plan. This one, an upscale cosmetic surgery outpost for the socially elite, was no different in that respect. The plush carpeting rather than the utilitarian tile and lavishly framed pieces of art that highlighted the warm, sand-colored walls were a definite step up from the norm but the basic layout was the same.

Agent Dawson stepped into the hall from one of the examination rooms lining the elegant corridor. "The team is ready when you are, Dr. Cameron."

"Thank you, Agent Dawson." Elizabeth didn't bother dredging up a perfunctory smile. He knew she didn't like this. She sensed that he didn't either. But they both had a duty to do. An obligation to do their part to keep the world as safe as possible. She had to remember that.

The prep room was quiet and deserted and she was glad. She wanted to do this without exchanging any sort of chitchat with those involved, most especially the patient.

As she unbuttoned and dragged off her blouse in one of the private dressing rooms, glimpses of those no-longer-welcome flickers of memory filtered through her mind once more. The last time she'd undressed for David. The last time they'd kissed or made love.

So long ago. Months. Far more than the two he'd been dead.

Her fingers drifted down to her waist and she unzipped her slacks, stepped out of her flats and tugged them off. The question that had haunted her for months before David had died, nagged at her now.

Had he found someone else?

Was that the reason for the tension she'd felt in him the past few times they were together?

Would she ever know how he'd died? Heart attack? Didn't seem feasible considering his excellent health, but healthy men dropped dead all the time. Or had he been killed in the line of duty?

She shook off the memories, forced them back into that little rarely visited compartment where they belonged. She did not want to think about David anymore, didn't want to deconstruct and analyze over and over those final months they had spent together.

None of it mattered now.

After slipping on sterile scrubs, cap and shoe covers and then washing up, she headed to the O.R. where the team would be waiting.

More of those polite and pleasant good-mornings were tossed her way as she entered the well-lit, shiny operating room. One quick sweep told her that the equipment was cutting edge. Nothing but the best. But then it was always that way. The CIA would choose nothing less for their most important assets.

"He refused to allow us to prepare him for anesthesia until you arrived, Doctor," the anesthesiologist remarked, what she could see of his expression behind the mask reflecting impatience.

"Hey, Doc."

The insolent voice dragged Elizabeth's gaze to the patient. "Good morning, Agent Hennessey." As she spoke, a nurse moved up next to Elizabeth and assisted with sliding her hands into a pair of surgical gloves.

"I think this crew is ready for me to go night-night," Hennessey said in that same flirtatious, roguish tone. "But I wanted to have a final word with you first."

With her mask in place, Elizabeth moved over to the table where Agent Hennessey lay, nude, save for the paper surgical gown and blanket. She frowned as she considered that even now he didn't look vulnerable. This was a moment in a person's life when they generally appeared acutely helpless. But not this man. No, she decided, he possessed far too much ego to feel remotely vulnerable even now as he lay prepared for an elective surgical procedure that could, if any one of a hundred or more things went wrong, kill him.

Those unrepentant blue eyes gleamed as he stared up at her. "Any chance I could have a moment alone with you?" he asked quietly before glancing around at the four other scrub-clad members of her team.

Elizabeth nodded to the anesthesiologist. He, as well as the two physicians and the nurse, stepped to the far side of the room.

"What is it you'd like to say, Agent Hennessey?" she asked, her own impatience making an appearance.

"Look, Doc—" he rose up enough to brace on his elbows "—I know you didn't really want to do this." His eyes searched hers a moment. "But I want you to know how much I appreciate your decision in my favor. I feel a hell of a lot better about this with you here."

She couldn't say just then what possessed her but Elizabeth did something she hadn't done in a very long time. She said exactly what she was thinking rather than the proper thing. "Agent Hennessey, my decision had nothing to do with you. I'm doing this for my country… for those agents who might lose their life otherwise. But I'm definitely not doing this for you."

Looking away, uninterested in his reaction, she motioned for the others to return.

"Let's get this over with," she said crisply.

The team, people whose real names she would likely never know, moved into position, slipped into that instinctive rhythm that would guide them through the process of altering a human face. As the anesthesia did its work Agent Hennessey's eyelids grew heavy, but his gaze never left Elizabeth. He watched her every move.

In that final moment before the blackness sucked him into unconsciousness, his gaze met hers one last time and she saw the faintest glimmer of vulnerability. Elizabeth's heart skipped at the intensity of what was surely no more than a fraction of a second. And then she knew one tiny truth about Agent Joe Hennessey.

He was afraid. Perhaps only a little, but the fear had been there all the same.

Elizabeth steeled herself against the instant regret she experienced at having been so indifferent to his feelings. She doubted he would have wasted the emotion on her, but there it was.

Banishing all other thought she took a deep breath and considered his face. Not Joe Hennessey's face, but the face of her patient. If she allowed herself to think of the patient as an individual just now then she would be more prone to mistakes related to human emotion. This had to be about the work…had to be about planes and angles, sections of flesh and plotting of modifications.

For this procedure she needed no mold, not even a picture. She knew by heart the face she needed to create. The face of the first man she'd ever loved. The only man actually. She'd been far too busy with her education and then her career for a real social life.

"Scalpel," she said as she held out her hand.

With the first incision Elizabeth lost herself in the procedure. No more thoughts of anything past, present or future. Only the work. Only the goal of creating a certain look…a face that was as familiar to her as her own.

Elizabeth stripped off her gloves, quickly scrubbed her hands and then shed the rest of the surgical attire. She cleaned her glasses and shoved them back onto her face.

Exhaustion weighed on her but she ignored it. When she'd donned a fresh, sterile outfit she went in search of coffee. Breakfast had been a while ago and she needed a caffeine jolt.

A cleanup team had already arrived to scrub and sterilize the O.R. Not a trace of the patient would be left behind. It was a CIA thing. Elizabeth knew for a certainty that the clinic would have its own personnel for that very procedure that would be repeated before business hours began on Monday, but the CIA took no chances. Nothing, not a single strand of DNA, that could connect Joe Hennessey to this clinic would be left behind.

For now he was in the recovery room with the nurse and one of the assisting physicians.

Elizabeth sat down in the lounge with a steaming cup of coffee. Thankfully Agent Dawson had a knack with coffee. A box of pastries sat next to the coffeepot. She forced herself to eat a glazed donut when she wasn't particularly hungry, just tired.

Dawson had explained that as soon as Elizabeth considered Hennessey able to move they would relocate via a borrowed ambulance to a safe house. She would oversee his recovery for the next three weeks, ensuring that nothing went wrong. Meanwhile some of the agents whose faces she'd already changed were in hiding, unable to move forward into whatever missions they had been assigned until it was safe for them to return to duty. Some, however, were already deep into missions. Their safety could not be assured without risking the mission entirely.

Her cruise had been canceled and an additional week of leave had been approved. Director Calder had assured her that the Agency would reimburse her loss which was most of the cost of the cruise. No surprise there. Canceling this close to sail date came with certain drawbacks.

When Elizabeth felt the sugar and caffeine kicking in she pushed up from the table and headed to recovery to check on her patient.

In the corridor Agent Dawson waited for her. "You holding up all right, Dr. Cameron?"

She suppressed the biting retort that came instantly to mind. Dawson didn't deserve the brunt of her irritation. The problem actually lay with her. She'd fallen in love with the wrong man. Had assumed the fairy tale of marriage and family would be hers someday. Two mistakes that were all her own. This particular favor for the CIA had simply driven that point home all over again.

"I'm fine, Agent Dawson."

He nodded. "Agent Hennessey can be a bit brash," he said, his gaze not meeting hers. "But he's the best we have, ma'am. He won't let our people down. He'll get the job done or die trying."

Elizabeth blinked. It was, incredibly, the first time she'd considered that Hennessey might actually lose his life while carrying out this assignment. Clearly, she should have. The business of field operations was hazardous to say the least. David had explained that to her when he'd opted to go back into the field after their relationship had turned personal. She'd tried to talk him out of the change, but he'd been determined and she'd been in love.

End of story.

"I'm glad we can count on him," she said to Dawson, somehow mustering up a smile.

"The transportation for moving to the safe house is ready whenever you are, Doctor Cameron."

She nodded and continued on toward recovery. This was the first time she and Dawson had suffered any tension. The meetings with him were generally brief and superficial. This intensity was uncomfortable. Just something else to dislike about this situation.

As she pushed through the double doors the nurse looked up and smiled. "His vitals are stable, Doctor."

Elizabeth nodded. "Excellent."

She moved to the table and surveyed the sleeping

patient and the various readouts providing continual information as to his status.

Heart rate was strong and steady. Respiration deep and regular.

The bandages hiding his incisions wouldn't be coming off for a few days. Even then the redness and swelling would still be prominent. After three weeks the worst would have passed. His age and excellent state of good health helped in the healing.

With some patients, especially older ones, some minor swelling and redness persisted for weeks, even months after extensive surgery. But there was no reason to believe that would be the case with this patient. The work Elizabeth had done was more about rearranging and sculpting, no deep tissue restructuring or skeletal changes. Minor alterations had been made to his nose and chin using plastic implants. Those would later be removed when she returned his face to its natural look. There would be minor scarring that she'd carefully hidden in hollows and angles. Fortunately for him his skin type and coloring generally scarred very little.

Later as Elizabeth sat alone in recovery, her patient started to rouse. The nurse and assisting physician had, at her urging, retired to the lounge. Both had looked haggard and ready for a break. She'd seen no reason, considering the continued stability of the patient's vitals, for all of them to stay with him.

Now she wished she wasn't alone. Her trepidation was unwarranted, she knew, but some part of her worried that she might see more of that vulnerability and she did not want to feel sympathy for this man. Now or ever.

He licked his lips. Made a sound in his throat. The intubation tube left patients with a dry throat. His right hand moved ever so slightly then jerked as some part of him recognized that he was restrained.

His body grew rigid then restless.

Stepping closer Elizabeth laid her hand on his arm and spoke quietly to him. "Agent Hennessey, you're waking up from anesthesia now. The surgery went well. There is no reason to be apprehensive."

His lids struggled to open as he continued to thrash just a little against his restraints.

"Agent Hennessey, can you hear me?"

He moistened his lips again and tried to speak.

Instinctively Elizabeth's hand moved down to his. "You can open your eyes, Agent Hennessey, you're doing fine."

His fingers curled around hers and her breath caught.

Blue eyes stared up at her then, the pupils dilated with the remnants of the drugs his body worked hard to metabolize and flush away.

"Everything is fine, Agent Hennessey."

"I guess I survived the knife, Doc," he said, his voice rusty.

An unexpected smile tilted her lips. "You did, indeed. We'll be moving to the safe house shortly."

"Any chance I could have a drink?" he asked with another swipe of his tongue over his lips.

"Certainly." It wasn't until then that Elizabeth noticed that his fingers were still closed tightly around hers. She wiggled free and poured some cool water into a cup. When she'd inserted a bendable straw she held the tip to his lips so that he could drink. "Not too much," she warned, but, of course, like all other patients he didn't listen. She had to take the straw away before he'd stopped.

She wiped his lips with a damp cloth. "For the first

few days we'll keep the pain meds flowing for your comfort," she said, all too aware of the silence.

He mumbled something that might have been *whatever you think, Doc.*

A few hours later, most of which Agent Hennessey had slept through, Elizabeth supervised his movement to the waiting ambulance. She had learned that her determination of when the patient was ready to be moved had less to do with their departure than the arrival of darkness. Made sense when she thought about it. Night provided good cover.

"I'll be riding in the front with the driver," Dawson explained. "The nurse will accompany you to the safe house for the night. Tomorrow his care will be solely in your hands as long as you feel additional help is no longer required."

Elizabeth felt confident that additional medical support wouldn't be necessary, but she couldn't say that she looked forward to spending time alone with Hennessey. What she had done to alter his face was only the beginning of what Director Calder expected of her.

She settled onto the gurney opposite Agent Hennessey and considered the rest of this assignment. It was her job to ensure that this man could walk, talk and display mannerisms matching those of David Maddox.

Elizabeth knew nothing of David's work, but she did know the things he talked about when off duty…when in her bed.

"Feels like we're moving."

Elizabeth stared down at the man strapped to the other gurney. His mouth and eyes were all that was visible but his voice, the cocky tone that screamed of his arrogant attitude, made him easily recognizable.

"We're on our way to the safe house," she explained.

He knew the plan, but the lingering effects of anesthesia and the newly introduced pain medication were playing havoc with his ability to concentrate.

"So I get to spend my first night with you, huh?"

A blush heated her cheeks. Though she doubted Agent Hennessey felt any real discomfort just now, she could not believe he had the audacity to flirt with her.

"In a manner of speaking," she said calmly. The man could very well be feeling a bit loose-tongued. He might not mean to flirt.

He made a sound in his chest, a laugh perhaps. "I've been dying to get you all to myself ever since that night," he mumbled.

Taken aback, Elizabeth reminded herself that he probably wouldn't even remember anything he said. Ignoring the remark was likely the best course.

"Sorry," he muttered. "I didn't mean to let that slip out."

She'd suspected as much. Swiping her hands on her thighs she sat back, relaxed her shoulders against the empty shelves behind her. "That's all right, Agent Hennessey," she allowed, "most patients say more than they mean to when on heavy-duty painkillers."

He licked his lips and groaned. The doctor in her went on immediate alert. "Are you feeling pain now, Agent Hennessey?" Surely not. He'd been dosed half an hour prior to their departure.

He inhaled a big breath. "No way, Doc, I'm flying over here." He blinked a few times then turned his head slowly to look at her. "God, you're gorgeous, did you know that?"

Elizabeth sat a little straighter, tugged at the collar of her blouse to occupy her hands. "You might want to get some more sleep, Hennessey, before you say something you'll regret."

"Too late, right?" He made another of those rumbling sounds that were likely an attempt at chuckling. "No big deal." He waved a hand dismissively. "You already know how gorgeous you are."

Maybe his hands should have been restrained. He'd been secured to ensure he didn't roll off the gurney, but his arms had been left free.

"You should lay still, Agent—"

"Yeah, yeah, I know," he interrupted. "Don't move, don't say anything. That's what I do best. But at least I'd never lie to you like he did. Never..." His eyes closed reluctantly as if the drugs had belatedly kicked in and he couldn't keep them open any longer.

Elizabeth let go a breath of relief. She checked his pulse and relaxed a little more when it appeared he'd drifted back to sleep.

Lending any credence to anything he'd said was ridiculous under the circumstances. The drugs had him confused and talking out of his head. She knew that, had seen it numerous times.

But the part about lying wouldn't let her put his ramblings out of her mind. What did he mean by that remark?

Nothing, you fool, she scolded.

She folded her arms over her chest. Then why did it feel familiar? As if he'd said what she'd thought a dozen times over. Because she'd sensed that David had been lying to her for quite some time.

Elizabeth closed her eyes and chastised herself for going down that road. David was dead. Whatever he'd said to her, lies or not, no longer mattered. He wasn't coming back. He was gone forever.

Dead.

She opened her eyes and stared at the bandaged face of the man lying so still less than two feet from her. Nothing he told her would matter. She'd loved David. He was gone. She wouldn't be taking that rocky route again anytime soon.

Nothing that Agent Joe Hennessey said or did would alter her new course.

As soon as this was over she intended to revive her social life as planned. Start dating again.

It was past time.

Chapter 5

Joe studied his reflection for far longer than the bandaged mug warranted. He didn't know what he expected to see or what it mattered. The deed was done.

Twenty-four hours had passed since he'd gone under the knife. He pretty much felt like hell. His whole head could be a puffy melon if it weren't for the pain radiating around his face in ever tightening bands coming to a point at his nose. He'd had his nose broken once, but it hadn't hurt like this.

He glanced at the table next to his bed. There was medication for the pain, except he preferred to put off taking it until the pain became intolerable.

So far this morning, he had avoided spending much time with the doc. He'd been aware of her coming in and out of his room all during the night to check the portable monitors that provided a continuous scorecard on his vitals. He'd felt her looking at him each time but he hadn't opened his eyes, hadn't wanted to talk to her. He had a bad feeling he'd already said too much.

That was part of the reason he had no intention of taking any more drugs than necessary. He vaguely recalled making a few ridiculous remarks in the ambulance on the way here.

Joe exhaled a heavy breath. He was thirty-eight years old. He'd been an undercover operative for the CIA for the past ten. He'd been tortured, subjected to all sorts of training to prepare him for said torture, and not once had he ever spilled his guts like he almost had yesterday.

"Real stupid, Hennessey."

He dragged on his shirt and decided he couldn't hide out in this room any longer. It was 9:00 a.m. and his need for caffeine wouldn't be ignored any longer.

Facing the enemy had never been a problem for him. Hiding out from the doc when she was supposed to be on his side bordered on cowardice.

Joe hesitated at the door. He could admit that. It was the truth after all. Why would he lie to himself? The next three weeks were a part of the mission. He'd simply have to get past his personal feelings. Too many lives hung in the balance for him to indulge his personal interests.

His fingers wrapped around the doorknob and he twisted, drew back the door and exited the room that provided some amount of separation. All he had to do was maintain his boundaries. No slipping into intimate territory in conversation. No touching. If he followed those two simple rules he wouldn't have a problem.

The upstairs hall stretched fifteen yards from the room he'd just exited to the staircase. Three other bedrooms and two bathrooms had been carved out of the space. Downstairs was more or less one large open space that served as living room, kitchen and dining room. A laundry room with rear exit, pantry and half bath were off the kitchen.

The house was located in the fringes of a small Maryland town. There was only one other house on the street and it was currently vacant and for sale. Twenty-four hour surveillance as well as a state-of-the-art security system ensured their safety. A panic room had been installed in the basement. Even if someone got past surveillance and the security system they wouldn't breach the panic room. Though only twelve-by-twelve, the room was impenetrable and stocked for every imaginable scenario.

The smooth hardwood of the stair treads felt cold beneath Joe's bare feet. His left hand slid along the banister as he descended to the first floor, the act taking him back a few decades to his childhood. His parents' home had been a two-story and he and his brother had traveled down the stairs every imaginable way from sliding down the banister to jumping over it. It was a miracle either one of them had survived boyhood.

Joe stopped on the bottom step and hesitated once more before making his presence known.

Doctor Elizabeth Cameron was busy at the sink, filling the carafe to make another pot of coffee, Joe presumed. A glutton for punishment he stood there and watched, unable to help himself.

She'd traded her usual businesslike attire for jeans and a casual blouse. He hadn't seen her like this. She wore generic sweats when she worked out, her scrubs or a business suit including a conservative skirt or slacks the rest of the time. He'd begun to wonder as he watched her over the past couple of weeks if she slept in her work clothes. Her cool, reserved exterior just didn't lend itself to the idea of silky lingerie no matter how much she owned.

And yet, when his gaze followed the sweet curves of her body clearly delineated by the form-fitting blue jeans and pale pink top he found himself ready to amend that conclusion.

At about five-four, she would fit neatly into the category of petite without question, but she was strong. He'd watched her work out. She could run like hell. More than once he'd wished she would wear shorts for her workouts rather than sweatpants, but he never got that lucky. He liked it a lot when she took off those unflattering glasses, which was extremely rare.

Just then she turned around, spotted him and jumped. Her hand flew to her chest. "You scared me!"

He took the final step down as she caught her breath. "Sorry." And he was, but not about startling her. He was sorry she'd caught him watching her like that. The last thing he needed was her putting together his loopy comments in the ambulance and his gawking this morning and coming up with the idea that he liked her in ways he shouldn't.

"I was just making a fresh pot of coffee." She gestured with the carafe. "There's eggs, bacon and toast. It was delivered about fifteen minutes ago."

While he was in the shower. Apparently Director Calder didn't want the good doctor to have to concern herself with preparing meals. Joe's reputation for lousy cuisine had apparently preceded him.

"Great." He crossed the room. The closer he got the more her hand shook as she poured the water into the coffeemaker. The idea that he made her nervous intrigued him just a little, though it shouldn't. He imagined she was still annoyed about his manhandling three months ago.

"I hope you like it strong," she commented without looking at him as she shoved the empty carafe under the drip basket. "At the hospital we prefer it with enough kick to keep us going."

He stopped three feet away, leaned against the counter. "That's the only way I drink it."

She glanced up at him and pushed a smile into place with visible effort. "How do you feel this morning?" Her gaze examined the bandages.

"Like hell," he admitted. "You didn't take a baseball bat to my head while I slept last night, did you?"

Worry lined her smooth complexion. "The pain meds should alleviate most of the discomfort."

Lured by the scent of the brewing coffee, he reached for a mug. She stiffened as his arm brushed her shoulder. "I guess if I took two like you ordered, they might," he confessed.

She rolled her eyes and huffed out a breath of frustration. "Men. You're all the same. You think taking pain medication makes you look like a wimp. That is so silly. The more pain you tolerate the more adrenaline your body will produce to help you cope. The more adrenaline pumping the less effective the medication you actually do take."

"Sounds like a vicious cycle, Doc." He set the mug on the counter. His gut rumbled. "Speaking of vicious." He glanced at the foam containers. "I'm starved." He'd had juice and water yesterday. A little soup last night but definitely not enough for a guy accustomed to packing away the groceries.

"You see," she snapped. "That's my point exactly."

He turned back to her. She'd folded her arms over her

chest and now glared at him through those too clunky glasses. Somehow he'd pissed her off.

"What?" he asked in the humblest tone he possessed.

"You just ignored what I said." She gestured to his bandaged face. "You've been through extensive surgery and would still be in the hospital if you were one of my *real* patients. Yet you ignore my orders regarding meds. There are reasons the medication is prescribed, Agent Hennessey. What don't you understand about the process?"

Okay, calm down, Elizabeth ordered the side of her that wanted to obsess on the subject. She'd let him get to her already and he'd scarcely entered the room. She took a deep breath, tried to slow her racing heart. How did he do this to her just walking into the room?

"Look, Doc." He leaned against the counter next to her again. "I'm not trying to be cranky. I took the antibiotics. I even took the painkiller, but only one, not two. That dosage dulls my senses. And I need my senses sharp."

Though, arguably, she could see the logic in what he said, he needed to see hers as well. They were going to be here together for three long weeks. Taking a couple of days to get past the worst of the pain from surgery wasn't too much to ask in her opinion.

"Agent Hennessey," she began with as much patience as she could summon, "it wouldn't kill you to take an additional forty-eight hours of complete downtime."

He reached around her for the coffee, taking her breath for a second time with his nearness. She hated that he possessed that kind of power over her. Men like him should come with a warning. Don't get too close. She knew the hazards, had learned them firsthand with

David. And David had been a kitty cat compared to this guy. Hennessey's unmarred record for getting the job done wasn't the only thing for which he had a reputation.

He poured himself a cup of coffee then started to put the carafe away. Elizabeth quickly scooted out of his path to avoid another close encounter.

"Trust me, Doc," he said before taking a sip of his coffee. The groan of satisfaction was another of those things she could have done without. "I'll be the first to admit it if I can't handle the pain without the second pill every four hours. Deal?"

The last time she'd agreed to a deal with him it had landed her here. But then, like him, she had a job to do. People to protect. And maybe that made her an adrenaline junkie, too, although she didn't think so. Sure, her work for the CIA was covert to a degree, but she only saw it as doing her part. It wasn't much but it was something.

Did men like Joe Hennessey look at "their part" the same way? She just didn't know. Figuring out what made him tick wasn't on her agenda. She'd thought she had David all figured out and she'd been wrong and they'd shared thoughts as well as bodily fluids for more than a year. What could she possibly expect to learn about this man in a mere three weeks?

Nothing useful.

Nothing that would add to the quality of her life or give closure to her past.

Considering those two cold hard facts, her best course of action was to steer clear of emotional entanglement in this situation.

"All right, Agent Hennessey," she agreed reluctantly. "You're correct. You are a grown man. The level of pain you can and are willing to tolerate is your call. Just make sure you take the antibiotics as directed." She looked him square in the eyes. "That part is *my* call."

"Yes, ma'am." The wink immediately obliterated any hope of sincerity in his answer.

She had to get her mind off him. Her gaze landed on the breakfast another agent had delivered. Food was as good a distraction as any. Hennessey had said he was hungry.

Each container was laden with oodles of cholesterol and enough calories to fuel an entire soccer team through at least one game. Hennessey didn't hesitate. He dug in as if he hadn't eaten in a month. But his enthusiasm waned when the chewing action elicited a new onslaught of pain.

"Sure you don't want that full dosage?" she asked casually. It wasn't that she enjoyed knowing he was in more pain than he wanted to admit, but being right did carry its own kind of glee.

"I'm fine."

She didn't particularly like the idea that her unnecessary remark only made him more determined to continue without the aid of additional medication. Maybe she shouldn't have said anything at all.

While she picked at the eggs, sausage and biscuits on her plate, he ate steadily, however slowly. Oatmeal or yogurt would have been a much better choice. She wondered if he'd been the one to order the food. There hadn't been any calls in or out. Or perhaps the agent just picked up for them whatever he'd picked up for himself.

Checking on the menu for the next few days might be a good idea.

Elizabeth dropped her fork to her plate. Why had she

done this? Why wasn't she on that cruise? She could have said no. That wasn't true.

People will die.

Saying no actually hadn't been an option.

"Agent Hennessey."

He met her gaze. "Yeah?"

As much as he tried to hide it she didn't miss the dull look that accompanied the endurance of significant pain.

She sighed and set her food aside. "Look, let's not play this game. You're obviously in pain. I would really feel a lot better if you took your medication."

"I told you I'm fine."

The words had no more left his lips than he bolted from the table and headed for the short corridor beyond the kitchen that led to the laundry room and downstairs bathroom.

Instinctively, Elizabeth followed. His violent heaves told on him before she caught sight of him kneeling at the toilet.

He'd been pushing the limits ever since he regained his equilibrium after anesthesia. This was bound to happen.

Ignoring the unpleasant sounds she moved to the wash basin next to him and moistened a washcloth. When he'd flushed the toilet and managed to get to his feet, she passed the damp cloth to him.

"I think you should be in bed."

"You know what, Doc? I think you're right."

Unbelievable. What was most incredible was that he didn't try to turn her words into something lewd or suggestive.

She followed him up the stairs and into the room he'd used the night before. He climbed between the sheets without putting up a fuss. To her surprise he even took the other pain pill she offered without argument.

"Thanks," he mumbled, his eyes closed.

When Elizabeth would have moved away from the bed his fingers curled around her wrist and held on. "What's the rush, Doc?" He tugged her down onto the side of the bed next to him.

She tried to relax but couldn't. "You should rest."

"I'm lying flat on my back. I've taken the pills. At least give me this."

If he hadn't looked at her so pleadingly, she might have been able to refuse. But there was that glimmer of vulnerability again and she just couldn't do it.

"What is it that you want, Agent Hennessey?"

"First." He moistened those full lips. Strange, she considered, his lips were awfully full for a man's. There hadn't been a lot she could do about that. The best they could hope for was that no one would notice. "I'd like you to stop calling me Agent Hennessey. Call me Joe."

His fingers still hung around her wrist, more loosely now, but the contact was there. Pulling away would have been a simple matter but he was her patient and she needed him to relax. So she didn't pull away.

"All right, Joe," she complied. "I suppose then that you should call me Elizabeth." Most anything was preferable to Doc. Although she did have to admit that he somehow made it sound sexy.

He licked his lips and said her name, "Elizabeth. It suits you."

She wasn't sure whether that was a compliment or not, but she decided not to ask.

"Talk to me," he urged, the fingers around her wrist somehow slipping down to entwine with hers. "Tell me about your relationship with Maddox. What attracted you to him?"

They were supposed to do this. That's why she was here, beyond the surgery, that is. She was supposed to make sure he knew about David's personal life—at least as much as she knew. He needed to get the voice down pat and the mannerisms. Practice would accomplish both. But the details were another matter. She had to give him the details just in case David discussed his private life with someone Hennessey—Joe, she amended—might come in contact with during the course of this undercover operation.

Elizabeth saw no point in putting off the inevitable. Getting on with it was the best way.

"He was nice," she said. And it was true. She hadn't known what to expect out of a CIA handler and his being nice was the first thing she was drawn to. All extraneous assets utilized by the CIA were assigned handlers as a go-between. She didn't say because he certainly knew this already.

"Ouch. Maybe you don't know this, honey, but nice is not a man's favorite adjective."

"Elizabeth," she corrected, feeling even more awkward with his use of the endearment though she felt confident he didn't mean it as an actual endearment.

"Elizabeth," he acknowledged.

Even then, as he acquiesced to her assertion he made one of his own. He drew tiny circles on her palm with the pad of his thumb.

She started to pull her hand away, but decided that would only allow him to see that he'd gotten to her. Pretending his little digs at her composure didn't bother her would carry far more weight. When he saw that he couldn't get to her in that way he would surely let it go.

"I liked his jokes," she went on in hopes of losing herself in the past. She worked hard not to do that on a regular basis; doing so now was a stab at keeping her mind off how being this close to Joe Hennessey unnerved her. It shouldn't, but it did.

"Yeah, he was a jokester," Joe murmured.

His voice had thickened a little from the action of the painkiller. If she were lucky he'd fall asleep soon. His body needed the rest. Whether he realized it or not his whole system was working hard to heal his new wounds which diverted strength and energy from other aspects of his existence. He didn't need to fight the process.

Something he'd said in the ambulance, about lying, pinged her memory. She'd have to ask him about that later when he was further along in his recovery.

"So he was nice," Joe reiterated, "and he could tell a joke. Is that why you fell for him?"

His lids had drifted shut now. He wouldn't last much longer. Elizabeth was glad. She stared at their joined hands. Hers smooth and pale, his rougher, far darker as if he spent most of his time on a beach somewhere.

As she watched, his fingers slackened, lay loose between hers. His respiration was deep and slow. She doubted he would hear her answer even if she bothered to give one. But he'd asked, why not respond?

"No, Agent Hennessey, those are not the reasons I fell for him." She paused and when he didn't correct her she knew he was down for the count. "I fell for him because he was like you," she confessed, her voice barely a whisper. "He made me feel things that terrified me and, at the same time, made me feel alive." As hard as she'd tried not to look back and see herself as stupid, she couldn't help it. She'd been so damned foolish.

"And look where it got me," she muttered, annoyed with herself for dredging up the memories.

With every intention of leaving the room she started to pull her hand from the big, warm cradle of his and his fingers abruptly closed firmly around hers.

"Don't stop now, Elizabeth," he murmured without opening his eyes. "You're just getting to the good part."

The only thing that kept her from slapping him was the fact that she would likely undo some of her handiwork and have to do it all over again.

Instead, she held her fury in check and went on as if he'd misinterpreted what she'd said. Tomorrow, or even after that, if he questioned her about her comment she would lie through her teeth and swear she hadn't said any such thing. Two could play this game, she decided.

Stating the facts as if they described someone else's life she told Joe Hennessey the story of how Agent David Maddox had come into her life as her handler and proceeded to lure her into temptation with his vast charm.

Hennessey would no doubt recognize the story. He probably practiced the same M.O. all the time. According to what David had told her, Hennessey left a heartbroken woman behind at every assignment. He was the proverbial James Bond. The man who had it all. A new secret life, with all it entailed, every week.

How exciting it must be to live that kind of life with absolutely no accountability to anyone. The broken hearts he left behind would certainly be chalked up to collateral damage just as the occasional dead body surely was.

Elizabeth worked hard at keeping her tone even and her temper out of the mix, but it wasn't easy. The more she talked about the past and considered her relationship with David, the more she realized how she hadn't ever really known him. She only knew what had drawn her to him.

She didn't really know David the man. She only knew David the lover.

She knew what he'd allowed her to see.

That realization was the hardest of all.

Her gaze dropped to Joe Hennessey. This time he was definitely sleeping. She couldn't help wondering if he'd done this on purpose. Made her see.

She tugged her hand free of his and admitted yet another painful truth. No. This was no one's fault but her own. She'd seen what she'd wanted to see.

Nothing more.

And now she knew the whole truth.

Her relationship with David had been based on an illusion that she had created in her mind.

Elizabeth left Hennessey's room.

She progressed down the stairs and walked to the front door. She unlocked and opened it and came face-to-face with the agent assigned to that location.

"I need to see Director Calder," she said, her voice lacking any real emotion.

"Is there a problem, Dr. Cameron?" the agent asked, his dark eyewear no doubt concealing an instant concern for the two principals it was his job to protect.

"Yes, there is," she said bluntly. "I need to go home. I've decided I can't complete this assignment. Please call the director for me."

Elizabeth closed the door. There was nothing else to say.

She'd made up her mind.

Agreeing to this part of his mission had been a mistake. Giving someone David's face was one thing but she could not do the rest. There had to be someone else who knew David's personality well enough to help Hennessey grasp the necessary elements. Surely there were videos the CIA had made, tapes of interviews David had conducted.

However they conducted this portion of the mission from here had nothing to do with her.

She wanted out.

Chapter 6

Three days elapsed before Elizabeth would again speak to him about her relationship with Maddox.

Today was his first "official" Maddox lesson. They were finally getting down to business. 'Bout time.

That first night at the safe house she had left him sleeping and called the director. Not the director of field operations. The frigging director of the CIA himself. She had demanded to be taken home, had insisted that she wanted no further part in this operation.

Somehow Director Calder had changed her mind.

Since Joe had slept through the whole thing he had no idea how the director had accomplished the feat.

At any rate, Joe had awakened the next morning to an edict from the good doctor. She refused to discuss anything about the assignment with Joe until three days had passed. She wanted him to stay on the full dosage of the medication and in bed during said time. He hadn't liked it one damned bit, but what choice did he have? It wasn't like he could disobey a direct order from Calder.

During those three days Elizabeth had attended to his medical needs. She'd changed his bandages. Thankfully at this point the bulkier gauze was gone. The swelling was still pretty ugly as was the redness. He looked like he'd been on the losing end of a pool room brawl.

"Not like that," she said, her impatience showing.

"Show me," Joe countered, his own patience thinning.

It wasn't like he'd been around Maddox that much. Getting his mannerisms down pat wasn't going to be easy without a better understanding of how he moved.

Elizabeth did the thing with her right arm that she was convinced Joe would never get right. A clever little salute of a wave Maddox had tossed her way every time he saw her. It wasn't that big a deal. He doubted Maddox waved at his targets.

Since she waited, glaring at him, Joe assumed she was ready for him to try again. So he did.

She shook her head. "That's still not right." At his annoyed look she threw up her hands. "This is impossible! You're not going to get it. You're not him!"

Enough.

Joe got right in her face. She blinked, but to her credit, she didn't back off.

"You know what, you're right, I'm not him." He grappled to regain some kind of hold on his temper. "What I need is for you to teach me what I need to know, not dog out my every attempt."

She held her ground, her arrogant little chin jutting out even further. "You know what? I think we need a break."

He straightened, shook his head. "Oh yeah. That's

what we need. We've just gotten started and already we need a break. At this rate all those agents will be dead and we won't even need to go through with this operation anyway."

Her mouth opened and the harsh intake of breath told him he'd hit his mark way before the hurt glimmering in her eyes told the tale. "Someone else is dead?"

Dammit. He hadn't meant to tell her about that. Calder had instructed him to keep quiet about the latest hit for fear she would be so shaken she wouldn't be able to continue with their work. Continue, hell, they hadn't even started. Not really.

He booted her words from the other night out of his head. He couldn't keep going over that like a repeating blog. She'd admitted, when she thought he was asleep, that he affected her and her words had affected him. Even half-comatose he'd felt a surge of want deep in his gut.

Maybe it was just the fact that he'd despised Maddox that made him want her. Then again, the truth was, he hadn't known Maddox that well. Maybe he'd despised Maddox because he had the girl Joe wanted.

And he wouldn't have ever known if it hadn't been for that one night.

That night had changed everything.

"Answer me, Hennessey," she demanded. "Who is dead?"

His hope that being on a first-name basis might bring a unity and informality to their work had bombed big time.

"Agent Motley. You may not remember him—"

"I remember him," she interrupted. "He was the first transformation."

She looked ready to crumple but somehow she didn't.

Instead she looked at him with hellfire in her eyes. "What about his family?"

Joe hated even worse to tell her this part. "His wife was murdered as well. But his daughter was away with friends so she's okay."

Elizabeth shook her head. "She isn't okay, Hennessey. She won't ever be okay again. Her parents were murdered and she's alone."

Neither of them moved for five seconds that turned into ten. He couldn't help wondering if the person Elizabeth was really talking about was her. She was alone… basically. Her father, retired Colonel Cameron, had died years ago, but her mother was still alive, at least in body. Alzheimer's had made an invalid of her and she no longer recognized her own daughter. She lived in a home especially for Alzheimer's patients. Maddox had been Elizabeth's only viable emotional attachment.

Was that why she had such trouble dealing with this operation?

"She won't be alone, Elizabeth," Joe said softly. He resisted the urge to move closer, to comfort her with his touch. "She has aunts, uncles and cousins. It won't be the same but she won't be alone."

Elizabeth wet her lips. He saw her lower one tremble just a little. "That's good." She nodded. "I'm glad she has a support system."

The way you didn't? he wanted to ask.

"Who are we really talking about here, Elizabeth? You or Agent Motley's daughter?"

Fury flashed across her face. "I don't know what you mean, Agent Hennessey. I'm perfectly fine."

"I think you haven't gotten over losing Maddox."

Judging by the horror in her eyes, completely deflating her anger, he'd royally screwed up by making that comment.

"This isn't a counseling session, Agent Hennessey," she returned coolly, too coolly. "I don't need your conclusions on my relationships."

"Relationship," he corrected, asking for more trouble.

She glowered at him. "What the hell is that supposed to mean?"

He shrugged. Hell, he was in over his head now, might as well say the rest. "*Relationship,*" he repeated. "From what I can tell that's the only long-term commitment you've been involved in. Before or since."

Her hands settled on her hips, drawing his reluctant attention to the way her jeans molded to her soft curves. Damn, he was doomed.

"Who gave you permission to look into my background? Especially my personal life?" she demanded, her tone stone cold now. She was fighting mad.

"I've been watching you for weeks, *Elizabeth,*" he said, purposely saying her name the way he'd heard Maddox say it on the few times they'd met. "It was part of my job. Get to know your routine. Get to know you. Find out who you talked to. Where you went. What you ate. Who you slept with."

She staggered back a couple of steps. "You've been watching me?"

The question came out as if the reality of what he'd been saying had only just penetrated.

"That's right. I've watched every move you've made for weeks," he replied, stoking the flames with pure fuel.

Her eyes rounded. "I haven't slept with anyone since..." Her words trailed off and something achy and damaged flickered in her eyes. Something he couldn't quite name and never wanted to see again.

"Since Maddox," he finished for her. And then he turned away, unable to look at the emotional wreckage he'd caused. It hadn't been necessary for him to push that hard. He could have stopped this before it went anywhere near this far.

"Try again."

What the hell?

He turned back to her and she stood, arms crossed over her chest, glaring at him. "What?"

"I said," she hurled the words at him, "try again. People are dying. You have to get this right."

Something shifted inside him then, made him wish he could turn back time and do those last few minutes over. He hadn't meant to hurt her but he had. But she was too strong, too determined to let him win without a fight.

Dr. Elizabeth Cameron was no coward.

Just something else to admire about her.

Elizabeth awakened that night from a frightful nightmare. David had been calling to her, begging her for help and she couldn't reach him. No matter how she'd tried he just appeared to draw farther and farther away.

She tried to get her bearings now. It was completely dark. Not home. The safe house. Joe Hennessey.

A breath whooshed out of her lungs and she relaxed marginally. The dream must have awakened her.

A soft rap sounded from her door and she bolted upright. A dozen probable reasons, all bad, for her being awakened in the middle of the night crashed one by one through her mind. She felt for her glasses on the bedside table. "Yes?"

"Dr. Cameron, this is Agent Stark. We may have a problem."

Elizabeth was out of the bed before the man finished his statement. She dragged on her robe and rushed to the door without bothering with a light.

"What's wrong?" The hall was empty save for Agent Stark. A table lamp some ten feet away backlit the tall man and his requisite black suit.

"I'm not sure there's a real problem, but Agent Hennessey has requested that we bring in something for stomach cramps. Agent Dawson insisted I check with you first."

Stomach cramps? Worry washed over her. "I'll need my bag."

Stark nodded. "I'll wait for you at Agent Hennessey's room."

Elizabeth flipped on the overhead light and rushed around the room until she determined where she'd left her bag last. She never had this problem at home. But here, with *him*, she felt perpetually out of sorts.

By the time she was in the hall she could hear Hennessey growling at his fellow agent.

"I don't need the doc, Stark. I need something for—"

"Thank you, Agent Stark," Elizabeth said by way of dismissal when she barged, without knocking, into the room. "I'll let you know if we need anything."

Judging by Hennessey's bedcovers he'd been writhing in discomfort for some time. "Why didn't you let me know you needed me?" she demanded of her insubordinate patient.

"I don't need a doctor," he grumped as he sat up.

One hand remained fastened against his gut. "What I need is Maalox or Pepto. Something for a stomachache. Apparently dinner disagreed with me."

Before Elizabeth could fathom his intent he stood, allowing the sheet to fall haphazardly where it would, mostly around his ankles, and leaving him clothed in nothing more than a wrinkled pair of boxers. She looked away but not soon enough. The image of strong, muscled legs and a lean, ribbed waist was already permanently and indelibly imprinted upon at least a dozen brain cells.

"Oh, man." He bent forward slightly in pain.

Elizabeth tried to reconcile the man who refused the proper dose of pain medication with one who couldn't tolerate a few stomach cramps without demanding a remedy.

"Are you sure it was something you ate?" Less than a week had passed since his surgery, there were a number of problems that could crop up. Before he could answer, she added, "Let's have a look."

"Come on, Doc, this isn't necessary," he grumbled.

She held up a hand. "Sit, Agent Hennessey."

With a mighty exhale he collapsed back onto the bed. She didn't really need to see the rest of his face. His eyes said it all. He had no patience for this sort of thing.

When she'd tucked the thermometer into his mouth, she moved to the door and asked Agent Stark to send for an over-the-counter tonic for stomach cramps. He hadn't mentioned any other issues that generally went hand-in-hand with cramps, but she didn't see any reason to take the risk. The medication she requested would cover either or both symptoms.

Hennessey sat on the edge of the bed, the thermometer protruding from his lips, and he looked exactly like a petulant child with an amazingly grown-up body. And a layer of gauze concealing the majority of his face.

She thought of the agent who'd died in the past twenty-four hours and she prayed that her efforts wouldn't be too little too late. She'd taken an oath to save lives. Had her support of the CIA helped or hurt? She had thought her work would save them from this very fate and now it seemed those she had helped were on a list marked for death.

How could that be?

It didn't make sense.

"Normal," she commented aloud after reading the thermometer. She set the old-fashioned instrument on the bedside table next to her bag. "Any other symptoms."

"No." He groaned. "At least not yet."

"Let me have a look at your face." She'd changed his bandages this morning and all had looked well enough. Still some redness and swelling, but that was perfectly normal.

"My face isn't the problem." He pushed her hands away. "It's my gut."

Worry gnawing at her, she reached into her bag and removed her stethoscope and blood pressure cuff. She saw no reason to take chances.

Hennessey swore but she ignored him. BP was only slightly elevated. The thrashing around in the bed and any sort of pain could be responsible for that.

She listened to his heart and lungs. Nothing out of the ordinary. His heart sounded strong and steady.

As she put the cuff and stethoscope away he said, "I told you I was fine."

"Yes, you did," she agreed. "But I would be remiss in my duties if I didn't double-check."

He made a sound that loudly telegraphed his doubt of her motives. "You probably just wanted an excuse to see me in my shorts," he said glibly.

Elizabeth tamped down her first response of annoyance and thought about that remark for a moment. Deciding he wasn't the only one who could throw curves, she sat down beside him. Tension went through him instantly, stiffening his shoulders and making the muscle in his jaw flex.

"Actually, Agent Hennessey, I've already seen most of you the day of your surgery." She produced a smile at his narrowed gaze. "Sometimes when they shift a patient from the surgical gurney sheets drop and gowns get shoved up around waists." As true as her statement was, it hadn't happened with him but he didn't have to know that. "But don't worry," she assured him, "the only person who laughed was the nurse, but don't tell her I told you."

Elizabeth would have given anything to see his face just then. If the red rushing up his neck was any indication, his whole face was most likely beet-red.

She couldn't torture him too long. He did have a problem. "I'm kidding, Hennessey."

He moved his head slowly from side to side but didn't look at her. "Very good, Doc, you might get the hang of this after all."

Feeling guilty for her bad joke, she urged him back into bed and tucked the sheet properly around him. Minutes later Stark arrived with the medication. Elizabeth thanked him and gave Hennessey the proper dose.

She settled into the chair near the bedside table and waited to see if the medication would work.

"You should get some sleep, Doc," he said, finally meeting her gaze. "If I need any more I can handle it." He gestured to the bottle she'd left on the table next to her bag.

"That's all right, Hennessey. You're my patient. I think I'd be more comfortable keeping an eye on you for a while."

Resigned to his fate, he heaved a put-upon sigh and closed his eyes.

Elizabeth glanced at the clock—two-thirty. She should go back to bed, but she doubted she would sleep now. Not after that awful dream and not with Hennessey uncomfortable.

She watched him try to lie still, his hand on his stomach, and she wished there was a way to make the medicine work faster, but there wasn't. It would take ten to twenty minutes. She thought about what they'd eaten for dinner and wondered why she wasn't sick. Then again maybe she would be before the night was through.

As if the thought had somehow stirred some part of her that had still been sleeping, her stomach clenched painfully then roiled threateningly.

She recognized the warning immediately and reached for the bottle to down a dose.

"You, too?"

Her gaze met Hennessey's as she twisted the cap back onto the bottle. "Guess so." She grimaced, as much from the yucky taste as from another knot of discomfort.

A light knock on the door and Stark stuck his head inside. "Any chance I could get some of that?"

Before the night was finished all three agents on duty had come in for medication.

At dawn Joe lay on his side watching Elizabeth sleep in the chair not three feet from his bed. She looked more beautiful than any woman had a right to. Her long hair lay against the crisp white of her robe. And those lips, well, they were pretty damned sweet, too. He would give anything right now to taste her. He would lay odds that she tasted hot and fiery, just like her spirit.

Oh, she tempered the fiery side with that cool, calm facade, but he could feel the hellion breathing flames beneath that ultracontrolled exterior.

His gaze traveled over her chest and down to her hips and then to the shapely legs curled beneath her. She worked so hard at everything she allowed herself to do. He wondered if she would work half as hard to be happy.

This was one lady who didn't fully understand the meaning of the word. He'd read what was available on her childhood. Nice family. Moved around a lot since her father had been military, but there didn't appear to be any deep, dark secrets. What had made Elizabeth Cameron so hard on herself? So determined not to fail when it came to helping others?

That was the sole reason, in Joe's estimation, that put her out of the suspect pool. No way would she do anything to endanger another human being. She simply wasn't wired that way. No amount of money—if money were even an issue for her—would entice her. He understood that completely.

Maddox was dead and Calder and Allen were directors. Joe had been filled in when he was selected for the assignment. Who else could have accessed those files?

Three months ago when he'd had to step in long enough to save this pretty lady's skin, someone had broken into her clinic. Had that been the beginning? Were the files the target then? Or had the whole exercise been about casting suspicion in a different direction?

There was no way to know. All he'd had was Maddox's urgent request for backup. Maddox claimed he'd stumbled onto a plan to go after the files of Dr. Elizabeth Cameron. Someone had evidently connected her to the CIA. Of course she had no files related to the Agency.

The only thing he did know for a certainty was how terrified she was that night. He'd held her close to him and she'd trembled. She'd had no idea what was happening, nor did she now. He was convinced. In any event, her safety was one of the Agency's top priorities.

The idea that someone might be setting her up had crossed his mind. But there was no proof as of yet. There was no evidence of anything. Only three dead agents. Still, a real player would have known the files wouldn't be in her office.

Every precaution was being taken to keep the rest of those agents safe, but some were in the middle of dicey operations with higher priorities requiring that they remain undercover.

Those were the ones most at risk.

Joe wished like hell there was a way to speed up this process, except there simply wasn't. His fingerprints could be altered with a clear substance that formed to his skin in such a way that no one could tell the difference. But his face, that had been done in the only way possible. Surgically. Until the swelling and redness were gone he had no choice but to stay right here.

Not that it was such a hardship.

He wondered if David Maddox had had the first clue that the chemistry would be so strong between Joe and Elizabeth. Surely he wouldn't have requested Joe to go to her rescue all those months ago if he'd had any idea that might be the case. Then again, he had known Joe's reputation, however exaggerated.

It was true that Joe dated often and rarely the same lady more than twice. But not all those dates resulted in sex. Not that he was complaining about the reputation. He'd always enjoyed the hype.

Until now.

That thought came out of nowhere, but when he analyzed the concept he knew it was true. Something about the way Elizabeth looked at him when she talked about his reputation didn't sit right.

He wanted her to respect him at least to some degree. Funny thing was, he'd never once worried about that before. He studied the woman sleeping so peacefully. Why was it that what she thought about him mattered so much?

His job performance had always been above reproach. He did what he had to do no matter the cost. Not a single doubt had ever crossed his mind on that score. People respected his professional ability, no question. If anyone had ever been suspicious of him personally he hadn't noticed.

Maybe that was the issue at hand here. Had the doctor's blatant distaste with his so-called reputation finally made him take a hard look at what someone else thought about him as a man…as a human being?

He closed his eyes and blocked her image from view.

He didn't want to think anymore. His stomach still felt a little queasy and his face hurt.

Why look for more trouble?

Chapter 7

Just over two weeks after surgery the bandages were gone, but some of the swelling and redness remained. All in all, Elizabeth was quite pleased with Hennessey's progress in that respect.

It was the tension brewing between them that she could have done without.

From the moment the last of the bandages had come off a subtle shift had occurred between them. Quite frankly Elizabeth couldn't say for sure whether it was her or him or if that was actually when it began. But something had changed on a level over which neither of them appeared to have any control.

Or at least she didn't.

Admittedly she couldn't read Hennessey's mind, but she didn't doubt for a second that he suffered some amount of discomfort related to the tension as well.

And to think, she could have been soaking up the sun and drinking martinis the past two weeks.

She blew out a breath and folded the last of her laundry. The Agency had delivered her luggage the day after her arrival, but a number of the outfits she'd packed for her vacation were far from what she would have preferred to wear in Hennessey's presence. The bikinis were definitely off-limits. She'd had no choice but to wear the few, more conservative outfits over and over.

Hennessey stuck with jeans and button-up shirts or T-shirts. He went around barefoot most of the time. For some reason that bothered her considerably more than it should. It wasn't that he had unattractive feet. To the contrary. His feet actually fascinated her. Large and well-formed. Like the rest of him.

She rolled her eyes and pushed aside the stupid, stupid obsession she had with the man.

Watching David's face slowly emerge beyond the swelling and redness only made matters worse. Perhaps that was even the catalyst in all of this. She just couldn't be certain of anything.

The last time she'd gotten too close to Hennessey the yearning to lean into his arms had been almost overwhelming.

Was she losing her mind or what?

Thankfully no other agents had been murdered since Motley and his wife. Elizabeth squeezed her eyes shut to block the image of the face she'd transformed for the very purpose of protecting the man behind it.

Hennessey assured her that the investigation was ongoing but all had surrendered to the idea that whoever was behind these killings couldn't be stopped any way but by infiltrating the group David had once affiliated himself with. Another week at least before that could happen.

The one other agent they had initially tried to send

undercover to infiltrate the group several weeks ago had been killed in the first twenty-four hours. Using David's face as safe entry was the only hope of getting anywhere near the truth.

Elizabeth sat down on the edge of the bed. She hadn't let herself think too much about David and the past since that night the whole lot of them—she, Hennessey and their guards—had gotten a mild case of food poisoning. Stomach cramps and a few mad dashes to the bathroom but, thankfully, nothing more disconcerting than that.

For days now she had set her emotions outside the goings-on within these walls. She had separated the bond she had shared with the man, David, from the CIA operative, David. It hadn't been that difficult, to her utter surprise. She'd turned off her personal emotions and looked at this operation as a case.

But would there be repercussions later? She was a trained physician. She understood that the human psyche could only fool itself to a certain point before reality would override fantasy.

She had far too many scheduled patients depending upon her for her to take a chance on suffering a psychotic break of any sort. Not that she felt on the verge of any kind of break, but she recognized that things with her weren't as they should be.

Scarcely a week from now her part in this would be over. Surely she could manage another five or six days. She and Hennessey had learned to be cordial to each other most of the time, had even shared a laugh or two.

But then there was the tension. She'd pretty much determined that the source of the steadily increasing tension was sexual. He was a man, she was a woman; plain, old chemistry saw to the rest.

Though she didn't dare guess how long it had been since Hennessey had had sex, she knew exactly how long it had been for her. Four long months. And that last time with David had felt off somehow. As if they were out of sync, no longer in tune with one another.

Elizabeth pushed the memories aside. Those painful recollections had nothing to do with any of this. She was a woman. She had fundamental needs that had been ignored. End of subject.

When she'd put the rest of her laundry away she went in search of her pupil. Might as well get on with today's lesson. More syntax and inflection. He wasn't that far off. She'd heard him in his room at night practicing with recordings of David's voice. She hadn't asked where they had come from. Interviews from old CIA cases or maybe from surveillance.

As she descended the stairs she wondered if he would let her listen to the recordings. Probably not, since they likely involved cases that she didn't have clearance for. Oh well, why torture herself anyway. David was gone. Listening to old recordings of his voice would be detrimental to her mental health. It didn't take a psychologist to see that one coming around the corner.

At the last step she froze. Hennessey, his back to her, had walked across the room, from the coffeemaker on the counter to the sofa in the middle of the living space. The way he'd moved had stolen her breath. Not like Hennessey at all. Like David.

Exactly like David.

She watched him sit down and take a long swill from his mug. Her hands started to tremble. When had he learned to do that? Their lessons had progressed well but nothing on this level.

Summoning her wits she took the last step down.

"Coffee smells great." Somehow she dredged up a smile.

He did the same, but it looked nothing like a David smile.

Thank God.

Wait. The goal was for him to look, act and speak like David.

"You need to work on that smile," she said as she moved toward the kitchen and the coffee. Maybe a strong, hot cup would help clear her head. Obviously she was a little off this morning.

"That smile was for you, not for the mission," he explained.

She poured herself a cup of steaming brew and decided that, as usual, honesty was the best policy. "I saw you walk across the room. It was uncanny." She turned to face him, the hot cup cradled in her hands. "How did you get so good between yesterday and today?"

Strangely, he looked away before answering. "I did a lot of practicing last night. I didn't want you to be disappointed again today."

That felt like a lie even if it sounded sincere.

She padded across the room and took the seat opposite his position on the sofa. Since he never wore shoes she'd decided she wouldn't bother, either.

"I'm glad that how I feel matters to you, Agent Hennessey." She sipped her cup as he analyzed her. Her interrogation had roused his suspicions. Just another reason for her to be suspect.

He set his cup on the table that separated them. "How you feel matters a great deal to me, Doc."

Since she had refused to call him Joe he had reverted to calling her Doc. She didn't like it but when one resolved to play dirty, one couldn't complain.

"Let's get started," she suggested, resting her cup alongside his.

"Let's," he agreed.

Well, wasn't he Mr. Agreeable this morning? Very strange indeed.

Joe ran through the steps with Elizabeth until noon brought Agent Dawson and lunch. Whenever Dawson was on duty he dined with them, so Joe had the opportunity to study his teacher.

Every aspect of her cooperation in this mission felt genuine. Even after more than two weeks in close quarters, he would swear that she was above reproach. But he had to be absolutely certain. Two days before this aspect of the mission began Director Allen had informed him of another part of his assignment: make sure Dr. Cameron hadn't been a party to Maddox's act of treason.

To say Joe had been stunned would be putting it mildly, but like any other assignment, he did his duty.

Director Calder had told her the truth about why she was needed for his operation…at least to a degree. That part Joe had known. He had also already known how to walk and talk like Maddox. He only needed a little extra help with a few of his more intimate mannerisms. More important he needed to know as many details as possible about the relationship they had shared.

Joe had hoped to go about this in a way that wouldn't cause Elizabeth further hurt, but that might prove impossible for two reasons.

Director Allen, Joe's immediate boss, still wasn't convinced of Elizabeth's innocence—despite Joe's assessment. Joe had learned that Director Calder, Allen's boss and *the* director of the CIA, was the only reason stronger measures hadn't been taken to determine her involvement, if any, with what David Maddox had done.

Maddox had sold out his country in several ways, but there was no absolute proof that he was the one who'd released the names. All indications pointed to him, but there were also a number, Allen had suggested, that pointed to Elizabeth as having been in on it with him.

With Maddox dead there was really no way to be certain.

Unless Joe could fool Maddox's primary contact from his final operation.

The only glitch was the fact that the contact was female.

Joe settled his gaze on Elizabeth Cameron and wondered if she'd had any idea that Maddox had maintained an ongoing relationship with another woman.

If she did, she hid it well.

Nothing about her demeanor over the past two weeks and some days had given him the first hint of deceit.

But she was suspicious.

She'd made no secret of it. Just another indicator that she wasn't one to hide her feelings.

"Aren't you hungry, Agent Hennessey?" she asked, drawing his attention back to the table.

Dawson's scrutiny was now on him as well. He wasn't happy with the situation at all. The more Allen pushed for information on Elizabeth, the more dissatisfied Dawson grew. Joe regarded the other man a moment and would have bet his life that the guy had a little crush on the good doctor. Of course Dawson was married with two kids and as faithful as they came in this business.

Joe pushed his plate aside. "I'm good. Let me know when you're ready to get started again."

It wasn't like he could take a walk, but he could go

to his room for a few minutes before the next session of alone time with her.

He closed the door to his room and walked over to the dresser. He stared at his face, the one that looked nothing like him and more and more like David Maddox.

In a few days the swelling and redness would be all but gone. Then he could move to the next step.

His colored contacts had already been delivered. Probably by tomorrow he would need to start getting accustomed to wearing them. He doubted it would be a problem. He'd done that part before. It was the drastic change in his face that gave him pause.

He'd been mimicking Maddox's speech and movements for weeks before this. But—he reached up and touched his face—this was different.

The counseling hadn't fully prepared him. He'd thought he would be fine with it, but the more Maddox's face emerged the less prepared he felt.

Nothing had ever affected him this way.

That the worst was likely yet to come didn't help.

He had to find a way to prod intimate details from Elizabeth. How Maddox kissed…how he made love to her was essential to Joe's success. He couldn't go into this without being fully prepared on every level.

The only question that remained at this point was how he would get the answers he needed without hurting Elizabeth with the ugly details.

A knock at his door told him his time for soul searching was up.

"Yeah?"

The door opened and Elizabeth strolled into his room. "I need to understand what's going on here, Hennessey," she demanded. “I get the feeling you’ve been hiding something from me.”

Well, here was his opportunity.

Question was, did he have the guts to take advantage of it?

Only one way to find out.

“Here’s the thing.” He moved toward her, locked his gaze with hers and let her feel the intensity. He needed her off balance. “One of the contacts Maddox had is female. I can’t be certain how close they were, considering his relationship with this group preceded the two of you.” That part was a flat-out lie but he was improvising here in an attempt to save her the heartache.

A frown furrowed a path across her brow. “How is that possible? He worked as my handler for a year prior to our…relationship. I thought the operation came later, after he’d gone back into field duty.”

This is where things got slippery.

“One of the contacts in his last operation was someone he had known for years.” He shrugged as if it was no big deal. “An on-again, off-again flame who unknowingly provided him with useful intelligence from time to time. She’s my only safe way into this.”

Elizabeth wasn’t convinced. Far from it.

“Why haven’t you mentioned this before?” The frown had given way to something along the lines of outright accusation. “No one has mentioned anything about a woman.”

“You know the drill, Doc,” he said, careful to keep the regret from his tone, “need to know. The golden rule we live by every day. You had no compelling need to know this part until now.”

“If your superiors told you that excuse would make me feel better about this new information, they were wrong," she said in a calm voice but the turmoil of emotions in her eyes belied her unyielding statement.

"We can move back downstairs to have this conversation," he suggested in deference to her comfort. He felt reasonably certain she didn't want to talk about certain details in the room where he slept.

Her expression hardened—the change was painful to watch. "Don't be ridiculous, Hennessey. I'm a doctor. Nothing you say or ask about the human body or the act of procreation will make me uncomfortable in any setting."

With that point driven straight through his chest like a knife she strode over to his bed and plopped down on the end. "What do you want to know?"

The grim line of her mouth and the cool distance in her eyes telegraphed all he needed to know.

Too late not to hurt her. He'd already done just that.

Regret trickled through him, but there was nothing to do but pursue the subject. He needed the information and the damage was done. Holding back now wouldn't accomplish a damned thing.

"We can start with pet names." He shrugged. "Did he usually call you anything other than Elizabeth?"

"What does this have to do with the other woman?"

"Maybe nothing. But I need to be—"

"Yeah, yeah," she cut in. "I get it."

A moment passed as she appeared to collect her thoughts. She stared at some point beyond him. The drapes on the windows were closed, so certainly not at any enticing view.

"Baby," she said abruptly as her eyes met his once more. "He called me *baby* whenever we…" She cleared her throat. "Whenever we were intimate."

"Baby," he murmured, committing the term to memory.

"No." She shook her head. "Not like that. *Baaaby.* With the emphasis on the first syllable."

"Baaaby," he echoed, drawing out the first syllable as if it were two.

She nodded once. "Yes. Like that."

He propped against the dresser and let her talk. She seemed to know what he needed to ask and he appreciated that more than she could possibly comprehend. She shared the sexual vocabulary Maddox used. His euphemisms for body parts and the words that he whispered in her ear as they made love. With every word, every nuance of her voice he felt closer to her…felt the need to touch her. Tension vibrated through him to the point that every nerve ending felt taut with anticipation of what she would say next.

"He liked for me to be on top," she said, careful to avert her eyes. "When I wasn't on top he was usually…" She cleared her throat. "He liked to get behind me." She fisted her fingers and hugged her arms around her middle. "He was very aggressive. Preferred to be in control other than the being on top thing."

Joe wanted to make her stop, but he couldn't. And yet with each new detail she revealed, his body grew harder, he wanted her more.

"Was there a certain…way he touched you?" he ventured, his throat so tight he barely managed to speak.

She blinked, looked away again. "My…ah…breasts. He always touched me that way a lot. Even when we were just kissing." She rubbed at her forehead, then quickly clasped her arm back around her.

He couldn't take any more of this. He'd hurt her and tortured himself physically. No more.

"Thank you for sharing such intimate—"

"Don't you want to know how he kissed me?" She glared up at him then, the breath rushing in and out of her lungs. All semblance of calm or submissiveness was gone.

Joe straightened away from the dresser. "We can talk about this some more later. There's—"

She rocketed to her feet. "He wasn't that great when it came to kissing."

Her eyes looked huge in her pale face. He couldn't tell if what he saw there was fear or humiliation. Maybe both, and it tore at his guts.

"He used his tongue too much." She paced the length of the room, then turned and moved back in his direction. "But I got used to it eventually." She shrugged her shoulders, the movement stilted. "I was so busy with my work I didn't have time to be too picky about my sex life. Really, what's a busy woman like me supposed to do?"

Her lips trembled with the last and he had to touch her. She was close enough.

"Elizabeth, I'm sorry. I—"

She drew her shoulder away from his seeking hand but didn't back off. "Are you really?" The accusation in her eyes dealt him another gut-wrenching blow. She took a step closer. "If you're so sorry then what prompted your considerable erection, Agent Hennessey?" She reached out and smoothed a hand over the front of his jeans, molded her palm to his aching hard-on.

He moved her hand away but didn't let go of her arm. "Don't do this to yourself, Elizabeth. I explained to you that the female contact was someone he knew before you came into his life."

"And I know a lie when I hear one, *Joe*."

He closed his eyes and exhaled a weary breath. Maybe he should have been up-front with her sooner. He should never have listened to Director Allen. Elizabeth Cameron was far too smart for these kinds of tactics.

"I had known something was wrong for a while," she said, her voice soft, the fierce attitude having surrendered to the hurt. "We hadn't made love in two months when he died. I'd only seen him two or three times. He called, but never talked for long. I guess I knew it was over. I just didn't know why."

It took every ounce of strength Joe possessed not to tell her the truth about David Maddox. He'd used her. He'd cheated on her all along. The latter came with the territory. No man who hoped to keep a clean relationship with a woman stayed in field operations. It simply wasn't feasible.

"You don't know that," he argued, hoping to salvage her feelings to whatever extent possible. "There could have been a lot of things going on that prevented him from coming to you. Your safety for one thing," he offered, grasping at straws. "Remember he sent me in to rescue you that one night when he was too far away to do it himself."

She nodded distractedly as if her heart was working overtime to justify what her brain wanted to reject.

"I would certainly have taken precautions to protect you if I had been in his shoes. Think about it, Doc. He cared about you. You were and still are a valuable asset to the Agency."

Her eyes met his then and something passed between them, a sense of understanding.

"I'm certain you would have, Hennessey." She inhaled a big breath and then let it out slowly. "But you see I've been lying to myself for a while now." She offered a halfhearted shrug. "I guess it made me feel less gullible."

Joe tightened his hold on her forearm, but carefully avoided pulling her closer as he would very much have liked to do. "Sometimes we believe what we want to believe, Doc, even when we know better."

She searched his eyes for so long, he shifted in hopes of breaking the contact. Didn't work.

"Are you really any different from him, Agent Hennessey?"

He wasn't sure how to answer the question.

"I mean," she frowned in concentration, "if having sex with a contact would garner you the information you needed, would you go that far?"

When she put it that way, it sounded like the worst kind of sin. "I wish I could say no, but I'd be lying."

An "I see" look claimed her expression. "Well, at least you're honest."

"I won't lie," he told her in hopes of making the point crystal clear, "unless there is no other way, Doc. Lying is not something I enjoy, but it's part of my job more often than not."

She stared up at him then, puzzled. "Did you know I would give you the information you needed without your having to seduce me?"

"Doc, this situation isn't the same. You came into this knowing the mission."

Her gaze narrowed ever so slightly. "Did I really?"

He had to smile. "To the extent you needed to know, yes."

"But you didn't answer my question," she countered, refusing to give an inch. "Would you have resorted to seducing me if necessary?"

"I had my orders, Doc, and seducing you wasn't included." When she would have turned to leave, he caught her wrist once more and drew her back. "Had I not been restrained by my orders, I can't say I wouldn't have tried. But the effort wouldn't have been about the mission."

She searched his eyes again…as if looking for answers to questions she couldn't voice. He wanted to lean down and brush his lips across hers. Just for a second, just long enough to feel the softness of hers.

But she walked away before he'd mentally beaten back his deeply ingrained sense of duty and did just that. He closed his eyes and cursed himself for the fool he was. He should have kissed her, should have shown her what a real kiss was like. Not some egotistical bastard's sloppy attempts.

He'd had that moment and he'd let it slip away. Part of him had felt certain for just a fleeting instant that she wanted him to kiss her.

"Oh."

He looked up, discovered her waiting at the door as if she'd only just remembered something of utmost importance and had decided to tell him before she forgot.

"I suppose I should tell you that you might have a bit of a problem with the female contact."

Confusion joined the other tangle of thoughts in his head. "What kind of problem?"

"I believe I would avoid making love to her if at all possible, otherwise I'm certain she will recognize you as an imposter."

His delayed defensive mechanism slammed into place. What the hell was she trying to say? "You noticed a difference between Maddox and me?" he challenged. He knew where this was headed. She'd gotten a good feel of him fully aroused. He wondered if she would actually have the guts to cut him off at the knees, which was, in her opinion, what he imagined he deserved.

She nodded somberly. "I'm afraid so, Agent Hennessey. David was considerably—"

He held up both hands, cutting her off. "I don't think I want to hear this." And here he'd been feeling sorry as hell for her.

"I was just going to say," she went on as she planted one hand firmly on her hip, "that David was way, way *smaller* than you and I doubt any woman still breathing would fail to notice."

Chapter 8

Elizabeth lay in bed that night and considered what Hennessey had told her. Her initial response had been to deny all of it. But she had known he was telling the truth. If she'd had the first reservation, his genuine regret would have allayed any and all.

Joe hadn't lied to her. He'd tried to protect her.

She closed her eyes and remembered the way he'd looked at her as she'd given him the details of her intimacies with David. That the connection had made her restless to the point of becoming moist in places she'd thought on permanent vacation startled her. Just watching him react to her words had set her on the verge of sexual release.

No man had ever managed that…not for her.

All this time she'd considered herself somewhat lacking in the libido department, but Hennessey made her feel alive and on fire. How could that be?

From a purely psychological standpoint she understood that she had been celibate for longer than usual and she was still hurting from those final months before David had died. She'd known something wasn't right. Now she knew what.

There had been another woman.

Maybe his involvement with her had been purely business, but that didn't make her feel any better. Then again, Hennessey could be correct in his suggestion that David had been trying to protect her. But that would be giving him far too much of a benefit of the doubt. Even she wasn't that gullible.

She and David had been over at least two months before his death.

So why had he kept coming back? Why those final calls? Why hadn't he just told her it was over? It wasn't like he had made any sort of major commitment.

Like any other woman, she had considered he might be the one. That the two of them could perhaps move to the next stage. Get married and start a family. But deep down, especially those last few months, she had known it was going to end.

She banged her fist against the mattress. Why on God's green earth would she get involved with another man like David Maddox?

Evidently she was just as gullible as she'd thought. And seriously out of touch with her education level.

For goodness sakes, plain old common sense screamed at the utter stupidity of this move.

And still she couldn't help how she felt.

Yes, Hennessey was CIA just like David had been.

Yes, he was handsome and charming and sexy.

Just like David.

But there was one significant difference.

She thought of the way she'd touched him. Couldn't imagine how she'd ever worked up the nerve to make that bold move. She hadn't actually. She'd acted on instinct. Without thought.

Her heart bumped into a faster rhythm even now at the memory. There was no comparison between the two when it came to matters below the belt. Joe Hennessey was far more well-endowed than David. No way would a former lover *not* notice that disparity.

Elizabeth flopped onto her side and pushed away the confusing thoughts. She refused to get involved with another man until she knew all the facts related to her last relationship.

Was it possible that David had used her for more than mere sex?

She chewed her bottom lip and let the concept penetrate fully. Didn't banish it immediately as she did when she was first asked to be a part of this. David knew the identities of the agents she'd transformed the same as she did. At least he had until the last year. They hadn't discussed the last three she'd done because there had been no reason. He was no longer her handler and like any good member of CIA personnel, she hadn't told.

Nor had he asked.

If he'd wanted to know, why didn't he bring up the subject? Never, not once did he ever, ever ask any questions. He hadn't even appeared interested.

But was that a front to keep her fooled?

She sat up, slung off the covers.

The conspiracy theories were rampant now.

She'd never get any sleep at this rate.

Could he, if he were guilty of this heinous betrayal, have listened in on her conversations with Agent Dawson?

Impossible. Dawson always picked her up and took her to a secure location before giving her any details.

They never talked in her car, on her phone, landline or cell, or at her house.

It simply wasn't done.

And David would have known those hard and fast rules far better than her.

A cold, rigid knot of panic fisted in her stomach.

He would also know how to bug her clothing, her purse, her body for that matter, in such a way that no one could tell.

"Oh, God."

Wait. Maybe she'd seen one too many spy movies.

The whole idea was ridiculous.

But people were dead…more might die.

She had to know for sure.

The only way to do that was to go home and look for herself. She would never voice those thoughts about David without some sort of confirmation. It just wouldn't be fair. She had loved him. She couldn't betray him like that simply because Joe Hennessey planted the seed in her mind.

Yes, things had been wrong somehow between her and David those last few months but did that mean he had done anything wrong? She didn't know. One thing was certain, Hennessey had said there were only a handful of people who knew the names of those agents who were being picked off one by one.

David Maddox had been one of them.

Not giving herself time to change her mind, she slipped on her clothes and shoes, grabbed her purse and headed for her door.

Holding her breath she opened it.

The hall was clear.

After taking a moment to gather her courage she eased out into the hall and moved soundlessly to the stairs.

Ten seconds later she was in the laundry room at the rear exit.

Now for the real test.

The house was watched twenty-four/seven.

There was really no way to leave without being caught.

That left only one option.

She dug her cell phone from her purse and called the one person she knew without doubt she could trust.

"Hennessey won't be happy about this." Her driver wagged his head side to side resignedly.

"Just get me into my house, Agent Dawson," she urged. "If anyone learns we sneaked out I'll take full responsibility."

Dawson exhaled loudly. "I don't think that'll keep me out of trouble, Dr. Cameron, and it definitely isn't necessary. When it comes to your safety I'm the one who is responsible."

"I'm sorry, Agent Dawson," she relented. He was right. "I don't know what I was thinking. I don't want to get you into any trouble."

He didn't slow to turn around. He just kept driving through the darkness toward Georgetown proper and her brownstone.

"It's all right, Dr. Cameron." He glanced at her, let her see his determination in the dim glow from the dash lights. "If it means this much to you, then I'm more than willing to take the risk."

Why were all the good ones taken?

Elizabeth sank back into her seat.

Just her luck.

The image of Joe Hennessey zoomed through her thoughts and she immediately exorcised him. Whether or not he was one of the good guys was yet to be seen. Just because he made her pulse leap and her heart stumble didn't mean he was right for her. All it meant was that she needed to recoup some semblance of a healthy sex life. As Hennessey would no doubt say, she needed to get laid. Come to think of it, he would probably be happy to oblige her if she were to suddenly turn stupid again.

And she had zero intention of doing that.

As they neared Elizabeth's home, Agent Dawson said, "We'll park on the street behind your house and enter from the rear if that'll work for you."

She nodded, then remembered he probably wasn't looking at her. "That'll definitely work."

"Once we get out," he went on, "we need to move quickly."

"I understand." Her heart started to beat a little faster at the idea that she might very well be in danger. She'd told herself that being exiled to the safe house was about protecting Hennessey's transformation, but maybe that wasn't all there was to it.

She shivered. Maybe that's what Dawson was worried about more than getting into trouble.

Surely he would tell her if that was the case.

Something else she didn't need to worry about.

The street was still and dark save for a few streetlamps posted too far apart. Agent Dawson parked his sedan behind another lining the sidewalk and they got out.

"Stay behind me," he instructed.

Elizabeth did as he asked, following right behind him as they moved through the side yard of the house directly behind hers. On this street the homes were small, single bungalows with postage-stamp-sized yards. A tall wooden fence lined the rear boundaries, separating these private yards from the shared space behind the brownstones. She and Agent Dawson stayed outside the fenced area, wading through the damp grass.

Her home, like the ones on either side of it, was dark, but the area around the back door was lit well enough by moonlight that she could unlock the door without the aid of a flashlight.

"Let me check it out first."

She stood just inside her kitchen while he checked out the rest of the house. When he'd returned and given her the go-ahead she took his flashlight, his assertion not to turn on any lights in the house unless absolutely necessary ringing in her ears, and went straight to her room while he guarded the rear entrance.

Though she and Agent Dawson had taken a number of journeys together in the past year, this was her first ever covert adventure with the man. She was quite impressed with his stealth and finesse.

He hadn't dragged her into an alley and held her clamped against his body as Agent Hennessey had, but admittedly, the circumstances were different so there could be no actual comparison.

"Focus, Elizabeth," she ordered, putting aside thoughts of Hennessey and his muscular body.

If David had wanted to learn about her work for the CIA he would have had to "bug" her. She felt confident that the CIA regularly monitored the vehicles they used and, certainly, Agent Dawson would keep himself bug free. But she, on the other hand, had no idea about such things. Hadn't even anticipated the need.

First she checked through every single undergarment she wore to work. Nothing. She ran the beam of light over her room and located the jewelry box. Jewelry really wasn't something she cared to accessorize with but occasionally she did wear a necklace or bracelet.

Nothing unexpected there.

That left only her clothes and her purses.

She did regularly change bags.

And each time Agent Dawson picked her up she had already changed into her street clothes. She wasn't like a lot of the medical professionals who lurked around in public while wearing scrubs. Not that it was such a bad thing, she supposed. She simply wasn't comfortable doing so.

She pulled the door to her walk-in closet almost completely shut, leaving just enough room to reach out with one hand and flip on the switch. Once the door was closed, she set Agent Dawson's flashlight aside and started her search.

Every jacket, skirt and pair of slacks had to be examined from top to bottom, inside and out. She didn't know that much about electronic listening or surveillance devices but, again, plain old common sense told her they could come in virtually any shape or form.

Before diving into her clothes, she went through her

bags. There were fewer and they were certainly easier to rummage around in.

Nothing suspicious. A few crumbs from the packs of snack crackers she carried in one. A couple of dollars in another. Wow! A peppermint breath mint from her favorite restaurant in the last one she picked up.

She unwrapped the mint and popped it into her mouth before moving onto her clothes.

This would take forever.

If Hennessey woke up she would be in serious trouble. She wondered if Dawson had told the other agent on duty about their little excursion. He hadn't mentioned it and she hadn't asked.

Hurry! Hurry!

Her hand stilled, backed up and moved over the pocket of her favorite slacks. A tiny bump. Her heart thundering, she reached inside and withdrew a small wad of chewed gum wrapped in tissue.

"Great," she huffed.

The door to her closet suddenly opened and Elizabeth wheeled around to identify her unexpected guest.

Not Dawson.

For several moments she couldn't breathe.

David.

Then the lingering redness and swelling crashed into her brain.

Hennessey.

"We've already done this, Doc," he said calmly but those startling blue eyes gave away the fury brewing behind that laid-back exterior. "Our technicians didn't find anything. You're not likely to, either."

"This wasn't Agent Dawson's idea," she said quickly. "I forced him to bring me here." She smoothed her suddenly sweaty palms over her thighs. "I threatened to come alone if he didn't bring me."

"Dawson and I have already spoken."

"Oh." She looked around at the wreck she'd made of her closet. And she'd thought the worst thing she had to worry about was falling prey to Hennessey's charm. Look at what she'd done. She wasn't equipped to play this kind of game. "I guess I'll just clean up this mess." She manufactured a shaky smile for him. She refused to admit that coming here had been too dumb for words. She'd needed to come. "You don't have to hang around. Dawson will bring me back."

"I sent Dawson back already."

She blinked, tried to hide her surprise. "Okay." She reached for a jacket lying in a twist on the floor. "I'll be quick."

"I'll be waiting."

He exited the closet, closing the door behind him.

Elizabeth stood there for a time, grappling for composure.

David had cheated on her. She didn't need any evidence. She *knew.*

The CIA obviously thought he'd used her as well or they wouldn't have been nosing around in her house. There was no arguing that conclusion. A part of her wanted to be angry, wanted to scream, but what was the point? It was done. David had done this to her.

Elizabeth closed her eyes and fought back the tears. She would not cry for or about him. He was gone. He'd been gone for a long time before he died.

Any other emotional wringers she put herself through related to him were a total waste of energy.

Slowly, piece by piece, she put the contents of her closet back to order, purses and all.

She thought about snagging a few items to take back with her, but she wouldn't be there much longer. There was no need.

As soon as she opened the door she flipped off the closet light. It took several moments for her eyes to adjust to the darkness. She thought about turning on the flashlight but there was really no reason since she knew her way around her own bedroom.

"You finished with what you came here to do?"

She stumbled back, gasped, before her eyes finally made out the image of someone sitting on the bench at the foot of her bed. The voice left no question as to identity.

Hennessey.

"Yes, I guess so."

Since he made no move to get up she sat down next to him.

Joe told himself to get up, to get the hell out of her bedroom, but he couldn't.

He kept torturing himself over and over with the images her words evoked even now. He knew with certainty that Maddox had made love to her in this room. With her on top...with him behind her. His hands on her breasts.

Every breath he drew into his lungs carried the scent of her. Her room, her whole house, smelled of her. Nothing but her. She was a doctor. She was never home long enough to cook. Only to soak in a tub of fragrant water. To shower with her favorite soap and shampoo.

She didn't wear perfume. Only the soap or maybe the subtle essence of the lotion sitting on her bedside table. He hadn't needed to turn on a light since arriving to see any of this. He'd been here with the techs when they'd gone through her things. He'd touched the undergarments she wore next to her skin. Had inhaled the scent of her shampoo.

And then he'd watched her. Twenty-four/seven for weeks. Until he'd thought of nothing but her.

"He used me, didn't he?"

The fragile sound of her voice carried more impact than if she'd screamed at him from the top of her lungs.

"Yes, we believe so."

Silence.

"For how long?"

"That we don't know."

"That's why you said you wouldn't lie—" she swallowed "—like he did."

"Yes."

"So…" She sucked in a ragged breath, tearing the oxygen out of his with the vulnerable noise. "Maybe it was real in the beginning?"

"Maybe."

More silence.

"I loved him, you know."

He squeezed his eyes shut against the tears he heard in her voice. "I know."

"Do you know how he died?"

That information was off-limits to her…but how could he let her wonder. "He died in the line of duty. That's all I can tell you."

"Will you take me back now?"

"Yes."

Joe stood. He reached for her hand and led her from her room, along the short hall and down the narrow staircase. He'd been in her home enough times to know the layout probably as well as she did.

He locked the door for her when they'd exited the rear of the house. Then they walked quietly through the moonlight until they reached his sedan.

Nothing else was said as they made the trip back to the safe house.

Joe took several zigzagging routes to ensure they weren't followed.

Daylight wasn't far off when they finally parked in the garage.

She got out and went inside. He didn't follow immediately.

He needed to walk off some of the tension shaking his insides. He'd alternated between wanting to yell at her and wanting to kiss her. Managing to get by without doing either was a credit to his sheer willpower.

He'd wanted to make her forget that bastard Maddox, but he'd resisted.

She didn't need him taking advantage of her vulnerability.

He might be a lot of things, but that kind of jerk he wasn't.

Inside the house he trudged up the stairs. He dreaded lying down again knowing sleep would not come. Their earlier candid discussion had kept him awake the greater portion of the night as it was.

He'd known when she left the house.

He'd followed but hadn't interfered at first, only when she'd stayed too long he'd had no choice.

The time he'd given her had been enough. She'd come to her own conclusions in her own time which was best. Anything he'd said or asserted would only have been taken with a grain of salt, would have put her on the defensive.

He didn't bother with the light in his room. Just kicked off his shoes and peeled off his shirt, inhaling one last time the smell of her where her arm had brushed against him as they'd sat on the bench in her room.

He stripped off his jeans and climbed into the bed. He was tired. Maybe he'd catch a few winks after all.

The instant his eyes closed her voice whispered through his head. Every intimate detail she'd relayed today echoed through his weary mind. He fisted his fingers in the sheet, tried his best not to think about how her nipples would feel against the palms of his hands. He licked his lips and yearned for her taste.

He could have gotten up and taken a cold shower. Probably should have. Instead he lay there and allowed the sensuous torture to engulf him. Didn't resist.

He was too far gone for that.

Elizabeth lay in her bed, her knees curled up to her chest. Director Calder had known the truth. Hennessey had known. Maybe even Dawson.

She was the only one who hadn't had any idea that David was using her.

How could she have been so blind?

She clenched her jaw to hold back the fury. How could he do that to her? He'd professed his love for her and all along he'd been using her.

How long had he planned his little coup?

At least one thing was for sure, he hadn't gotten to enjoy the fruits of his evil deeds.

A part of her felt guilty for thinking about his death that way, but the more logical part of her reveled in it.

He might have used her, but he'd paid the ultimate price in the end. Along with three of the agents she'd given new faces.

Her stomach roiled with dread.

Who else would die before Hennessey could stop this?

Was there nothing she could do?

Give them new faces?

But if it were that easy the CIA would have suggested it.

No.

It would never be that simple.

Hennessey would have to risk his life to get close enough to the devils behind this to take them out.

One was a woman.

A woman who would undoubtedly expect him to make love to her as David likely had. And then she would know that Hennessey was an imposter.

Heat rushed through Elizabeth in spite of her troubling thoughts. She just couldn't help the reaction. She needed him—wanted him.

But that would be yet another monumental mistake on her part. She didn't need to make any more mistakes far more than she needed to indulge in heart-pounding sex with Hennessey.

But she could dream about him. And how it would feel to have him kiss her and hold her close.

There was no rule against fantasies.

She remembered that night three months ago when he'd held her against him in the darkness. His body had felt strong, powerful. His muscles hard from years of disciplined physical activity and maybe from the feel of her backside rubbing against him.

When she'd touched him tonight…felt the size of him

against her palm, she'd wanted to rip off his clothes and look at all of him for a very long time. Just look. Then she wanted to learn all there was to know about him on a physical level.

How he tasted…how his hands would feel gliding over her skin…

She drifted off to sleep with that thought hovering so close she could have sworn it was real.

Chapter 9

Director Calder remained seated at the table but Joe was far too restless to stay in one place. He poured himself a fourth cup of coffee and grimaced at the bitter taste.

"You're absolutely certain you're ready to do this?" Calder asked once more. "Any further delay could be detrimental to our chances, but I'm not willing to run the risk of sending you in too soon."

"Do I look ready?"

Joe faced the man the president himself had chosen to oversee one of the nation's most important security agencies and let him look long and hard. He'd put the colored contacts in this morning. He'd wanted to try them out while Elizabeth was preoccupied going over dates with Dawson.

Calder moved his head slowly from side to side. "You look just like him." He blew out a breath. "It's uncanny, Hennessey."

Joe nodded. "I know." Even he had been shaken this morning. As he'd gone about the morning ritual of going to the john, he'd caught a glimpse of his reflection in the mirror and done a double take. His tousled hair had looked like it always did first thing in the morning, but his face…well, suffice to say it wasn't his.

The swelling and redness was gone entirely—at least as far as he could tell. It was as if he'd gone to bed last night with a little of both and then this morning *poof.*

He'd gone back to his room and called Dawson. He needed a distraction for Elizabeth until he could get used to the change himself.

She'd mentioned a day or so ago that sometimes this sort of abrupt change happened, but he wasn't prepared. He seriously doubted that she would be either.

Once he'd put the contacts in he'd had to brace himself on the counter to keep from staggering back from the mirror. The transformation had been incredible.

He, for all intents and purposes, was David Maddox.

"We knew Elizabeth was good," Calder went on, "but this is beyond our greatest expectations."

Joe had been watching this new face emerge from the aftermath of surgery and he'd known the transformation would get him by, but this was far more than that. This was almost scary.

He thought about Elizabeth and the way she'd sneaked back to her home the other night. He'd wanted to comfort her. To hold her until she came to terms with the way Maddox had used her. But he'd held back. She hadn't needed any more confusion. She'd needed someone who understood…someone to listen and he'd done both those things.

In the three days since she'd been distant. Not that he

could blame her. She'd just learned that the man she'd loved had cheated on her, used her. Had likely never really cared about her. That was a hard pill to swallow, even for a fiercely intelligent woman who was also a skilled surgeon.

Learning the truth had, in a way, facilitated what had to be done. Elizabeth had focused more intently on their work and so had he. A lot had been accomplished.

He was ready for this mission.

"Where is she now?"

"She's with Dawson. He's going over significant dates with her to see if she recalls anything relevant."

Calder frowned. "Haven't we already done that?"

"I needed her distracted for this meeting." Joe leaned against the counter and forced down more of the coffee.

"You're still convinced she had nothing to do with this," Calder wanted to know.

"Totally convinced." Joe set his cup in the sink. He'd had all of that brew he could stomach. He moved to the table. Though he still felt too restless he needed Calder to see just how convinced he was. "She had no idea what Maddox was up to. I think you know that."

Calder nodded. "I do. It's Allen who's still not on the same page with us. But I'll take care of him."

Joe breathed easy for the first time since this operation started. He knew what Maddox had done. No way would he stand idly by and let Elizabeth take the fall for anything that bastard did.

"Is it essential that we wait the next three days before I go in?" Joe ventured. He knew the plan as well as anyone, but he wasn't sure staying here with Elizabeth for seventy-two more hours was a good idea.

"We have to trust our intelligence, Hennessey," Calder

said, telling him what he already knew but didn't want to hear. "Word is that she'll be in-country in just over forty-eight hours. We don't want to rush this thing."

The director was right, no question. But Joe's instincts kept nagging at him to get into position. There was nothing specific he could put his finger on. The best analysts in the world were processing new intelligence every hour of every day. If anything had changed, Joe would know it right after Calder.

The fact that Calder was literally sitting in on this one personally made it the highest priority mission. So far three agents had been ambushed, two while involved in an ongoing mission. Stopping those assassinations was imperative. Additionally, Dr. Elizabeth Cameron had been Calder's brainchild. He had personally brought her into the Agency's family. He and Dawson, discounting Maddox, were the only ones allowed to approach her, until this operation. Joe had a feeling that Calder felt responsible for the woman's safety as well as her actions, good, bad or indifferent.

When Calder had gone, Joe went back to his room to study his reflection in an attempt to grow accustomed to the face staring back at him. It wasn't easy, considering he would have liked to rip Maddox apart himself if someone hadn't beat him to the punch. That the bastard's body hadn't been recovered only infuriated Joe all the more. But three credible eyewitnesses had testified to what they had seen. The shooter had been found but he'd refused to talk and ended up offing himself the first chance he got.

Whoever had sanctioned Maddox's termination was powerful enough that his reputation alone had ensured the shooter wouldn't turn on him.

The remaining questions were about Maddox's associates. Who had wanted the list of agents with new faces? Even if Joe infiltrated the group, could he be sure they would talk? Not even the CIA could stop a nameless entity. A name, a face; they needed something to go on.

Before more bodies piled up.

"I'm sorry, Agent Dawson," Elizabeth said finally. "That's everything I remember. If there was anything else during that time frame I can't recall."

"That's all right, Dr. Cameron." He closed the document on the computer. "What you remembered will be useful." He stood then. "We should probably get back."

Elizabeth followed him from the borrowed office in the rear of the downtown library. She wasn't sure why he had insisted they review all the newspaper reports from the three months prior to David's death. Maybe to prod her memories. She hadn't remembered anything she hadn't told them already. But she hadn't minded taking another shot at it. She was only human. It was just as likely as not that she could have forgotten something relevant.

But she hadn't.

If she were honest with herself she would admit that getting away from the safe house for a few hours was a good thing. Other than her one excursion back to her brownstone she hadn't left in three weeks. She was thankful for the respite.

The other night when she'd had to face the reality of what she'd denied about David for months she'd almost asked Hennessey to sleep with her. She'd so desperately needed someone to cling to, she'd resisted that crushing need by the slimmest of margins. Thank God he'd had his head about him. All he would have had to have done was touch her, in the most innocent fashion, and she would have surrendered without a fight.

For the past three days she had felt pretty much numb. Empty, really. Everything she'd thought to be true about David was nothing but lies. Learning that truth had hurt, but not so much as it would have had she not suspected that there was someone else months before his death.

But just beneath the numbness she had felt these last few days lay something else that simmered steadily. She told herself it was nothing, but that was a lie. She'd been attracted to Hennessey since that first night three months ago when he'd shown up to play bodyguard. That attraction hadn't abated. Not in the least. But with David's death and the idea that agents she had given new faces were dying, she hadn't been able to think about that for any length of time. Even now, maybe it was the exhaustion or just the plain old emptiness still hanging on, her developing feelings for Hennessey were too far from the surface to analyze with any accuracy.

And why in the world would she even want to go there?

Hennessey was the furthest thing from what she needed as a man could get. He represented everything wrong she'd done in her last relationship.

Why couldn't the irrational part of her that wanted to reach out to him see that?

He was one of those dangerous types. A man who risked everything, every single day of his life. She couldn't count on him any more than she had been able to count on David, excluding his various and sundry betrayals.

What she needed was safe, quiet, bookish.

A man who spent his days behind a desk reviewing accounts or reports. Not some gun-toting, cocky hotshot who kicked ass at least twice before lunch most days.

She closed her eyes and tried to clear her mind as Dawson took the necessary clandestine route back to the safe house. Thank God no more agents had died.

And although she hadn't seen Hennessey this morning she knew the time was close at hand for his departure. The swelling and redness had been all but gone yesterday. She'd struggled with focusing on the work rather than the end result.

It was far less painful to look at each feature individually rather than to look at his face as a whole. But the one saving grace was his eyes.

Joe Hennessey had the most amazing blue eyes. Even with his face changed, those startling blue eyes made it virtually impossible to notice anything else.

His flirtatious personality emanated from those eyes.

The deep brown of David's still haunted her dreams occasionally, but lately the only man she'd been dreaming about was Hennessey.

Such an enormous mistake.

Why couldn't she get that through her head?

She saw it coming. If she could just hold out a little while longer.

Three more days and she would go back to her life. He would go wherever it was David's associates were suspected of being and most likely they would never again see each other. The end.

She squeezed back the emotion that attempted to rise behind her eyelids. She'd done her job, had prepared Hennessey for the operation. There was nothing else she could do. Nothing else she should do until this was over. Then she would reverse the procedure, assuming he survived.

Getting on with her life was next on her list. She could not wallow in the past or pine after a man who would do nothing but bring her more heartache.

She had to be smart. Making the right decisions about her future had to be next on her agenda. Her career was everything she'd hoped it would be. Now if she could only say the same about her private life.

There was only one way to make that happen.

Put David Maddox and anything affiliated with him out of her head. Move forward and never look back.

It was simple.

But before she could do that she had to be sure she had passed along every tidbit Joe Hennessey would need to survive the coming mission. Even though she fully understood that a relationship between them would be a mistake, she didn't want him hurt. Whatever she could do to facilitate his efforts was not only necessary but nonnegotiable.

By the time she and Dawson had reached the safe house it had started to rain and a cloak of depression had descended upon her despite her internal pep talk. The sky had darkened, much like her mood.

When the garage door had closed, ensuring no one who might be watching had seen her emerge from the vehicle, she got out and went inside. She shook off the nagging weight that wanted to drag her into a pit of regret and dread. This wasn't the end, she assured herself, this was a new beginning.

Hennessey would move on with what he did best and she would refocus some of her energy into her personal life. She'd neglected that area for far too long.

Life was too short to spend so much time worrying

about all the things she'd done wrong. All the mistakes she'd made. She had to look ahead, move forward.

How many times did she give her patients that very advice? All the time. The kind of devastation that wrought physical deformities more often than not was accompanied by chronic clinical depression. At times, even after full recovery, a patient would linger in the throes of depression's sadistic clutches. Patients had to make a firm choice, to wallow in the past or move into the future.

She had to do the same.

No more dwelling on yesterday. Time to move forward.

Elizabeth hesitated at the door, pushed her glasses up the bridge of her nose and took a long, deep breath.

"Your future begins now," she whispered.

Without looking back, Elizabeth pushed through the door and into the laundry room of the safe house.

The smell of Chinese cuisine alerted her to the time. Lunch. Stark must be on duty. Whenever he was the agent in charge of bringing in meals, his food of choice was Chinese. Not that she minded, she liked fried rice, a lot.

Agent Stark looked up as she entered the kitchen section of the large living space. "You're just in time, Dr. Cameron."

She inhaled deeply. "I noticed."

"I see you made it back, Doc."

Elizabeth looked up at the sound of Hennessey's voice. Her chest seized and her eyes widened in disbelief. She closed her eyes and reopened them in an effort to clear her vision. It was still him…*David.*

"I started wearing the contacts," he said as he tapped

his right temple. "The change in eye color definitely put the finishing touch on the look."

He said the words so nonchalantly. She blinked again, told herself to breathe. She couldn't. Managing a nod was the best she could do.

Hennessey gestured to the counter. "You hungry?"

He moved like Hennessey. He spoke like Hennessey. But no matter that she told herself that what she saw was an illusion she, herself, helped to create, she just couldn't get past it. Pain twisted in her chest, radiated outward, encompassing her entire being.

"I'll…" She swallowed against the lump in her throat. "I'll have something later."

She rushed past him, couldn't bear to look a moment longer. This felt so wrong…so damned wrong.

Taking the stairs as fast as she dared she made it to her room in record time. She closed the door and slumped against it.

A full minute was required for her to catch her breath, to slow her heart rate. To form a coherent thought.

She should have been prepared for this moment. David's face had emerged a little more each day. She'd watched the features move from discolored and distorted to smooth and glowing with the tint of health.

All those things she'd expected…she'd been prepared for. But this…

It was the eyes she hadn't been fully equipped to see…to look into.

David's eyes.

As dark as a moonless night.

She'd gotten lost in them so many times. Not once had she been able to read his intentions. Whether it was the deep, murky color or just his skill at evasive tactics she couldn't be sure. But the mystery had been part of the attraction. He'd drawn her in so easily.

How in the wide world could she have believed she could do this?

Elizabeth closed her eyes and blocked the tears; forced away the images.

She couldn't do this.

And why should she?

She'd done her part.

There was no reason for her to stay a minute longer.

A light rap on the door behind her made her breath hitch again. She pressed a hand to her chest and reached for some semblance of calm.

She had to get her composure back into place.

All she needed to do was tell Agent Dawson she was ready to go home. Her work here was finished.

No one could argue that infinitely valid point.

Steeling herself against the turmoil of emotions attempting to erupt inside her she straightened away from the door, then turned to answer it.

It would be Hennessey.

It would be tough.

But she was strong.

She smoothed her damp palms over her skirt and pulled in another much needed breath.

Then she opened the door.

David's eyes stared down at her.

Not David, she reminded herself.

Hennessey. Agent Joe Hennessey.

"We should talk about this."

She looked away, let his voice be her buoy. Hennessey's voice. Low, husky, shimmering with mischief just beneath the surface. Not the slow, deep cadence of David. Why was it she'd never realized how very calculating his voice had been? It wasn't until she'd come here with Hennessey that she'd understood what sexy really was.

David hadn't been sexy…he'd been bawdy.

Elizabeth squared her shoulders and did what she should have done days ago. "Agent Hennessey, clearly I've contributed all to this operation that I have to offer. I'm certain you won't be needing my services any longer. With that in mind, I'm sure you'd understand if I chose not to have this discussion." She braced to close the door. "Please let Agent Dawson know I'll be ready to go in ten minutes."

She had expected him to argue.

She'd even expected him to try to stop her.

But the last thing she'd expected was for him to kiss her.

He took her face in both his hands and pulled her mouth up to meet his.

Just like that.

His lips felt firm but somehow more yielding than she had expected. His mouth was hot…ravenous, as if he was starving and she was dessert. She melted against him, couldn't help herself. The sweet feel of her body conforming to his made her shiver with a need so urgent she moaned with the intensity of it.

Sensations cascaded down from her face, following the path of his hands as he stroked her cheeks with his long fingers then slipped lower to caress her throat.

Her heart beat so hard she couldn't breathe…couldn't think. She just kept kissing him back—kept clinging to his strong body, hoping the moment would never end.

"Elizabeth," he murmured against her lips. "I'm sorry. I…" He kissed her harder….

She tried to pull away…tried to push against his chest.

But she couldn't bear the thought of taking her hands away from his chest. Even through the cotton shirt she reveled in the feel of the contours of his body. She suddenly wanted to touch all of him. To see if the rest of him was as amazing as his chest and the other part she'd already examined.

His arms went around her and for the first time in months she felt safe in a way that had absolutely nothing to do with professional success or inner strength. She wanted this as a woman…and she didn't want it to end.

But it had to end.

She couldn't do this again.

Her hands flattened against his chest and she pushed away from him, not taking her lips from his until it was impossible to reach him anymore.

He opened his eyes and her heart lurched.

"I have to leave now."

She stumbled back from his reach.

"Elizabeth, I can take out the contacts. We can talk."

She closed her eyes, tried to block the visual stimuli. Told herself to listen to his voice. Joe Hennessey…not David. Not David.

"Please." She forced her eyes open again. "I need to go now. There's nothing more I can do."

He looked away, displaying the profile she'd created. David's profile. The slightly longer and broader nose, the more prominent chin.

She swallowed. Looked away.

"This isn't who I am." He gestured to the face she had sculpted. "You know who I am."

She did. That was true. He was Agent Joe Hennessey

of the CIA. A dangerous man…her gaze shifted back to his…with an even more dangerous face.

"I do know who you are." The words were strong but she felt cold and hollow. "And I can't do this with a man like you. Not again. The price is too high."

She turned her back to him in the nick of time. She couldn't let him see the foolish tears.

"I'll let Agent Dawson know you're ready to leave."

She heard him walk away.

Finished.

This was finished. No reason for her to stay…to put herself through this.

All she had to do was go home and forget this assignment…forget the man.

Chapter 10

Elizabeth reviewed the day's messages, her mind on autopilot. That was the way it had been for most of the day. The only time she'd been able to really think clearly and in the moment was when she'd been with a patient. Thankfully three patients who'd been on standby awaiting appointments had been available to fill her day. So far four work-ins were scheduled for tomorrow and then she'd be back on her regular schedule.

Back to her real life.

Her concentration, such as it was, shattered yet again. Elizabeth tossed the messages onto her desk and leaned back in her chair.

This was her life.

Slowly, her heart sinking just a little more, she surveyed her chic office. Clean lines, no clutter. Diplomas and other accolades matted and framed in exquisite detail draped the smooth linen-colored walls. Short pile carpet in the same pale color padded the floor and served as a backdrop to the sleek wood furnishings. The rest of the clinic's decor was every bit as elegant; the treatment rooms equipped with the same spare-no-expense attitude.

The practice shared by herself and two other specialized physicians dominated the east corner of an upscale Georgetown address. Clientele included patients from all over the country as well as a few from abroad. Business boomed to the point that expansion would surely soon be necessary.

All those years of hard work had paid off for Elizabeth in a big way. Professionally she had everything she desired. Everything she'd dreamed about.

But that was where the dream ended.

She'd deluded herself into believing there could be more. That she could throw herself back into a social life. The chances of that doomed plan seeing fruition were about nil—she recognized that now. The cruise had been a last-ditch effort on her part to wake up her sleeping sex life. Not that she'd had any sort of exciting social life in the past. Admittedly she hadn't. But even dating hadn't crossed her mind since David's death. Absolutely nothing had made her want to venture back into the world of the living and the loving.

Until Joe Hennessey popped back in.

All those forbidden feelings Hennessey had aroused three months ago had suddenly reawakened when he waltzed back into her small world with this assignment.

Elizabeth closed her eyes and let the volatile mixture of heat and desire spread through her. He made her want to embark onto that emotional limb of love again. How could she be so dumb when all those diplomas hanging on the walls proclaimed her intelligence?

A light tap on her closed door dragged her away from the disturbing thoughts and back to the harsh reality that she was once more at square one, alone in her office at the end of the day with no place to go and no one with whom to share her successes or her failures.

She forced her eyes open. "Yes."

The door cracked far enough for Dr. Newman, one of her partners, to poke his head into her office. "You busy?"

Elizabeth tacked a smile into place. "Not at all. Come in, Dr. Newman." As long as she'd known Robert Newman—they'd worked closely for four years—they had never moved beyond the professional formalities. She suddenly wondered why that was. He was a very nice man. Safe, quiet, bookish, all the traits she should look for in a companion. That she admired and respected him was icing on the cake. Just another prime example of her inability to form proper social relationships.

His lab coat still looking pristine after a full day of seeing patients, he shoved his hands into his pockets and strolled up to her desk. "Do you have dinner plans?"

Now that startled her. Was he asking her out to dinner? They'd attended the same work-related social functions numerous times, but never as a couple. She blinked, tried to reason whether or not she'd misunderstood.

Had she somehow telegraphed her misery through the walls? Was this a pity invitation?

He cleared his throat when she remained speechless beyond a polite pause. "I thought you might not have had time to shop since you've gotten back. Your cupboards are probably bare."

Oh, yes, this was definitely a dinner *date* invitation.

Now she knew for sure just how little attention she'd paid to the men around her. If she'd had any question, the hopeful look in her colleague's eyes set her straight.

How could she have missed this? She'd had absolutely no idea.

"You would probably be right," she confessed, well aware that any continued stalling would be seen as not only a rebuff but rude. She reached deep down inside and retrieved a decent smile. "To be honest, I'm beat. I think I need a vacation to recover from my vacation." It wasn't until that moment that she realized how much her affiliation with the CIA had changed the dynamics of her other professional relationships. How many times had she lied to her colleagues about her whereabouts?

Don't go there. Not tonight.

She pushed up from her chair, glanced around her desk to ensure she hadn't forgotten anything that wouldn't wait before meeting Dr. Newman's gaze once more. Disappointment had replaced the hope. "But I'd love a rain check."

Some of the disappointment disappeared. "Sure."

After a brief exchange of war stories about the day's patients, Dr. Newman said good-night and was on his way.

At that moment Elizabeth realized just how very exhausted she felt. A long, hot bath, a couple glasses of wine and a decent night's sleep, she decided, would be her self-prescribed medicine.

After rounding up her purse she headed for the rear exit. She'd already called Agent Dawson and let him know she was ready to go. When she reached the parking lot he waited only steps from the clinic's rear entrance. He would follow her home and then maintain a vigil outside until around nine o'clock and he would be replaced by Stark.

As she slid behind the wheel of her Lexus she regarded the necessity of this measure once more. She hadn't really felt that the added security was necessary but Director Calder had insisted. She'd finally relented and agreed to one week of surveillance. If he felt that strongly, how could she ignore the possibility that he might be right? After all, ferreting out intelligence and analyzing risks was his business.

The drive to her brownstone was uneventful. Before leaving her car at the curb she couldn't go inside without asking Agent Dawson if he'd prefer to come inside. She'd spent the past three weeks holed up with Joe Hennessey; spending time alone with Dawson would be a breeze.

But Agent Dawson declined her offer.

She'd known he would. Dawson was far too much of a stickler for the rules.

Unlike Hennessey.

Or David.

Wasting her time and energy obsessing over the two men she'd allowed herself to get close to was pointless. Why put herself through the additional grief?

How had it been so easy all these years to move through life without getting her heart snagged? Work had been her focus. Until just over a year ago when David had lured her into a relationship. She'd thought it was time. Why not? Most women her age had already been involved in committed relationships. Why shouldn't she? But it had gone all wrong.

Another thought crept into her mind. Maybe she simply wasn't equipped to deal with failure. Her academic and professional life had succeeded on every level. Perhaps the fear of failure kept her from taking emotional risks.

"No more self-analysis," she muttered.

She unlocked her front door and stepped inside. Left all the questions and uncertainty on the stoop.

Home sweet home.

A long, deep breath filled her lungs with the scents of her private existence. The lingering aroma of the vanilla scented candles she loved…the vague hint of the coffee she'd had this morning.

She dug around in the freezer until she found a microwave dinner that appealed to her. Five minutes and dinner would be served. A bottle of chardonnay she'd bought to celebrate the night before departing on her cruise still sat unopened on her kitchen island. Perfect.

Lapsing back into her usual routine as easily as breathing, she set a place at the table, lit a candle and poured the wine. Just because she ate alone didn't mean she couldn't make it enjoyable.

The chicken breast, steamed vegetables and pasta turned out better than she'd expected. Or maybe she was just hungry. She hadn't realized until then that she'd completely forgotten lunch. She did that quite often. But so did most of her colleagues.

The wine did its work and slowly began to relax her. By the time she'd climbed out of the tub she was definitely ready for bed and well on her way to a serious good night's sleep.

She pulled the nightgown over her head and smiled at the feel of the silk slipping along the length of her body. Practical had always been her middle name, but she did love exquisite lingerie. Panties, bras, gowns. She loved sexy and silky. Vivid colors were her favorites.

Her bedtime apparel was way different from her day wear. David had always teased her about it.

Cursing herself, she turned out the light and stamped over to her bed. She had to stop letting him sneak into her thoughts. He was dead. Creating his face on another man had torn open old wounds once more. She needed to allow those wounds to heal. Whatever her future held she needed to get beyond the past.

She pulled the sheet back, but a sound behind her stopped her before she slid onto the cool covers. She wheeled around to peer through the darkness.

"It's just me," a male voice said, the sound of it raking over her skin like a rough caress.

She shivered. "Hennessey?" What was he doing here? Had something happened? She felt her way to the table and reached for the lamp.

"Don't turn on the light."

Elizabeth stilled, her fingers poised on the switch.

"I don't want you to see him. I want you to listen to *me*. Only me."

Her heart started to pound. What on earth was he doing here? Had he relieved Agent Dawson? No, that didn't make sense. This was Dawson's mission....

"I don't understand." She wished her throat wasn't so dry. Every part of her had gone on alert to his presence. Her hands wanted to reach out to him, her fingers yearned to touch him. She would not listen to the rest of the whispers of need strumming through her, urging her to connect with him on the most intimate level.

"I'm leaving tomorrow. I didn't want to go without..."

He didn't have to say the rest. She knew what he wanted. What *she* wanted. She could stand here and pretend that it wasn't real or that she didn't want it, but that would be a lie. Tomorrow he would be gone and if she didn't seize this moment she would regret it for the rest of her life.

Could she do that? Risk the damage to her heart?

She pushed the uncertainty away. Her entire adult life she had erred on the side of caution when it came to affairs of the heart…but not tonight.

She didn't wait for him to say anything else or even for him to move. She moved. Reached out to him and took him in her arms.

His mouth came down on hers so quickly she didn't have time to catch her breath. She reached up, let her hands find a home on his broad shoulders.

She didn't need to see his face. She could taste Joe Hennessey…recognized the ridges and contours of his muscular chest and arms. She didn't know how she could have done something as foolish as fall for this man…but she had. There was no changing that fact. The best she could hope for was to salvage some part of her heart after he'd gone.

His fingers moved over her, making her sizzle beneath the silky fabric. Wherever his palms brushed her skin heat seared through her. She couldn't get enough of his touch, couldn't stop touching him. Even the thought of taking her lips from his made her experience something like panic.

No matter what the future held for either of them, they could have this night.

His hands slid down her back, molded to her bottom. She gasped, the sound captured by his lips. He urged her hips against his and she cried out. Ached with such longing that she wasn't sure she could bear it.

Joe held her tightly against him, shook with the incredible sensations washing over him.

He shouldn't have come to her like this. He'd known better. For the past forty-eight hours he'd told himself over and over that she'd done the right thing walking away. It was the best move for all concerned.

But he couldn't leave without kissing her one last time. He'd thought of nothing else every minute he hadn't been attempting to talk himself out of this very moment.

He'd thought about that one kiss they had shared. Of the way her body had reacted to his all those months ago when he'd come to her rescue.

He needed to feel her in his arms. He'd walked away the last time without looking back because she had belonged to another man. That had been a mistake. He should have fought for her. They'd had a connection. He'd felt it. So had she, he'd bet his life on it. But he'd walked away and tried to put her out of his mind.

Impossible.

Spending the past three weeks with her had only convinced him further that they had something special. All they had to do was explore it…let it happen naturally.

He had to make her see that.

She trembled when he reached for the hem of her gown and tugged it up and off. God, he wanted to see her body, to learn every hollow and curve. But the light would ruin everything. He needed her to know who was making love to her tonight. He couldn't let Maddox's face interfere. He crouched down long enough to drag her panties down her legs. The subtle rose scent of her freshly bathed skin took his breath.

As he stood, her fingers shook when she struggled to release the buttons of his shirt. He helped, tugging the shirttails out of his trousers and meeting her at the middle button. The sound of her breath rushing in and out of her lungs made him feel giddy.

Together they worked his trousers down to his ankles, then stumbled back onto the bed with the efforts of removing his shoes and kicking free of the trousers.

He peeled off his boxers then lay on the bed next to her. He didn't want to rush this. As badly as he wanted to push between her thighs and enter her right now, he needed to make this night special. Take things slow, draw out the pleasure. Like it was their last night on earth.

He slid his fingers over her breasts, pleasured her nipples, relishing her responsive sounds. Unable to resist, he bent down and sucked one hardened peak. She arched off the mattress, cried out his name. He smiled and gave the other nipple the same treatment just to hear her call out his name again. He loved hearing her voice...so soft and sexy.

He kissed his way down her rib cage, tracing each ridge, laving her soft skin with his tongue. He paid special attention to her belly button. Sweat formed on his body with the effort of restraint. He was so hard it hurt to breathe, but he couldn't stop touching her this way, with his hands, his mouth.

He touched the dewy curls between her legs, teased the channel there and she abruptly stiffened. His body shook at the sounds as she moaned with an unexpected release.

When her body had relaxed he immediately went to work building that tension once more. He nuzzled her breasts, nipped her lips, all the while sliding one finger in and out of her. Her heated flesh pulsed around him, squeezed rhythmically. Soon, very soon he needed to be inside her.

Elizabeth couldn't catch her breath. She needed to touch him all over…needed to have him take her completely. She couldn't bear anymore of this exquisite torture. She couldn't think…couldn't breathe.

She encircled his wrist, held his skilled hand still before he brought her to climax yet again. "No more," she pleaded.

He kissed her lips, groaned as she trailed her fingers over his hardened length. She shuddered with delight at the feel of him. So smooth and yet so firm, like rock gilded with pure silk.

Her breath left her all over again as he moved into position over her. She opened her legs, welcomed his weight. His sex nudged hers and she bit down hard on her lower lip to prevent a cry of desperation.

He thrust into her in one forceful motion. For several seconds she couldn't move or speak. He filled her so completely. The urge to arch her hips was very nearly overwhelming but somehow she couldn't move. She could only lie very, very still and savor the wondrous awareness of being physically joined with Joe.

Eventually he began to move, slowly at first, then long, pounding strokes. The rush toward climax wouldn't be slowed, hard as she fought it. She could feel him throbbing inside her. His full sex grew harder as his own climax roared toward a peak.

They came together, cried out with the intensity of it.

As they lay there afterward, neither able to speak with their lungs gasping for air, Elizabeth understood that she had just crossed a line of no return.

She had allowed Joe Hennessey inside her. She, a doctor, had participated in unprotected sex. But worst of all she'd freely given over her already damaged heart.

"Elizabeth, I've wanted to make love to you since the first time I saw you," he murmured, his lips close to her temple. "No matter where I was, I couldn't close my eyes without seeing you."

Her chest felt tight. A part of her wanted to confess to the same weakness, but that would be to admit that three months ago she'd already disengaged emotionally from David. What did that make her?

She squeezed her eyes shut and blocked the thoughts. She didn't want to think right now. She just wanted to lie here and feel Joe next to her. She wanted to let her body become permeated with the scent and taste of him.

Just for tonight.

"When this is over," Joe said softly, "I want to see where these feelings take us. I don't want to let you go."

When this mission was over…then there would be another. Clarity slammed into her with crushing intensity. And another mission after that. Each time Joe would be gone for days or weeks. He could be killed in some strange place and she would never even know what really happened.

Just like before.

She had known this would be a mistake. She couldn't let herself believe in—depend on—a man who risked so much. She'd already gotten too close to him. Letting it go this far was crazy.

"I can't do this." She scooted away from him and to the edge of the bed. "You should go."

He sat up next to her. It was all she could do not to run away. But she had let this happen. She had to face the repercussions of her actions.

He exhaled a heavy breath, turned to her and began, "When I get back—"

She jerked up from the bed, fury and hurt twisting inside her. "If you come back." She hurled the words at him through the darkness, imagined his face—his *real* face.

He didn't respond immediately, just sat there making no move to get dressed. She couldn't see him really, just the vague outline but she could feel his frustration.

"I will be back, Elizabeth. I won't leave you the way he did."

A new rush of tears burned in her eyes. "How can you make a promise like that? You have no idea if you'll survive this mission much less the next one!"

"Elizabeth, don't do this." He stood, moved toward her, but she backed away.

She was too vulnerable right now. If he touched her again she might not be able to stick by her guns. She just couldn't do this to herself again. It hurt too much.

"I know you don't want me to go," he whispered, his voice silky and more tempting than anything she'd ever experienced.

Don't listen!

She had to be strong.

"I want you to go," she reiterated. "I'm not going to fall in love with another man who can't live outside the lure of danger. I won't let that happen."

She had to get out of here. Nothing he said would change how she felt. She felt around for her gown, found it and quickly jerked it on. The sooner she put some distance between them the better off she would be.

"Maybe it's not too late for you," he said causing her to hesitate at the door. She would not let herself look back. "But," he went on, "it's way too late for me. It's already happened."

She walked out.

A numbness settled over her.

What was he saying?

She shook off his words.

Nothing he said mattered.

She had to protect herself.

This was the only way.

Joe dragged on his clothes and pushed his feet into his shoes. A rock had settled in his stomach. He needed to convince her that they could do this, but she didn't want to listen right now.

A part of him wanted to track her down and make her see this his way. But that would get him nowhere fast.

Maddox had hurt her. She was only protecting herself.

Joe was the one who'd made a mistake.

He should have realized she needed more time. Especially under the circumstances. For God's sake, she'd scarcely gotten through giving him the face of her old lover and learning of the full extent of her former lover's betrayal. How could he have expected her to fall into his arms and live happily ever after?

Because he was selfish. Desperate to have her as his own. But he'd screwed up. Succeeded in pushing her farther away. Regaining that tender ground might very well be impossible.

He walked out of her room, surveyed the dimly lit hall but she was gone. If he wanted to, he could find her. She wouldn't be far away. Maybe in the kitchen or behind one of the closed doors right here in this hall. But he couldn't do that. He had to respect her needs.

Coming here had been his first mistake tonight. He wasn't about to make another. Oddly he couldn't bring himself to regret making love with her. Mistake or not, he refused to regret it for a single moment.

Not in this lifetime.

He stole out the rear exit of her brownstone and into the concealing darkness of the night.

Right now he didn't have time to work this out. He had an assignment that couldn't wait another day.

But when he got back one way or another he intended to sway her to his way of thinking. Whatever it took, he wouldn't give up.

They belonged together.

All he had to do was survive this mission.

He had as many of the facts as were possible to glean from the sparse details they had uncovered. He had the face Elizabeth had given him—his ticket into Maddox's seedy world of betrayal.

He would get this done. He would return to Elizabeth and then he would make her see that he was right.

Maybe she didn't feel as strongly about their relationship as he did, though he suspected she did. But that didn't change a damned thing as far as he was concerned.

He was definitely in love with her.

Chapter 11

Elizabeth stared at the tousled sheets on her bed. She'd done it again. Made a huge error in judgment.

She hadn't been able to sleep in here last night. Not with the smell of their lovemaking having permeated every square inch of the room. Even now she could smell the lingering scent of Joe. If she closed her eyes she could recall vividly the way he'd touched her in the dark.

And now he was gone.

She steeled herself against the fear and worry. This was exactly why she hadn't wanted to fall for a man like him again.

Who was she kidding? She'd fallen for him before she'd even known her relationship with David was over. She'd lied to herself, pretended she hadn't felt the things she felt for Joe. Denial was a perfectly human reaction to anything confusing or fearful. Just because she was a trained physician didn't make her any less human.

Or any smarter, it seemed.

Elizabeth quickly dressed, choosing her most comfortable slacks and a pale blue blouse. She needed all the comfort she could get today, including a light hand with makeup. Not that she wore that much anyway, but she just didn't feel up to the extra effort today.

As she exited her bedroom, she refused to think of Joe and the idea that he'd likely begun efforts to infiltrate the enemy. If she did she would only start to worry about where he was and what was happening to him.

Today was the pivotal test of all her work. His face, his mannerisms and speech. All of it would be scrutinized by the group of assassins he needed to fool.

God, what if these evil people had already heard somehow that David was dead?

She couldn't go there…just couldn't do it.

Work. She needed work to occupy her mind.

When she reached the door she remembered her blazer and she hurried back to her room to grab one.

Again the tangled mass of linens tugged at her senses. She got out of there, took the stairs two at a time.

Determined to put last night completely behind her, she opened her front door and stepped out into the day.

The sun gleamed down, warming her face, giving her hope that this day might turn out all right after all. A new beginning. Another opportunity to do something good and right. Maybe she would never be as smart as she should be in her personal life, but her career could be enough. It had been for a long time now. Why change a game plan that appeared to work?

"Are you ready, Dr. Cameron?"

Elizabeth smiled at Agent Dawson. Nice, safe, quiet

Dawson. Like Dr. Newman. The kind of man she should be seeking, but somehow never gravitated toward.

"Yes, I am, Agent Dawson." And it was true. She was ready to move on. And she could as long as she didn't stop long enough to think.

"There's been a change in plans this morning," he commented as they moved toward the vehicles parked at the curb. "I'll need to drive you to the clinic this morning if you don't have any objections."

She shrugged. "No problem." It wasn't like she had plans to go anywhere during the course of the day. If she had lunch she usually ate in her office. Most likely she'd spend what time she had available between patients going over files and finishing up reports.

That was the least glamorous part of her job—paperwork. Not the insurance forms or billing statements prepared by the clinic's accounting staff, but the detailed reports on patient history and recommended procedures as well as results of those performed and updates on follow-up consultations. Lots and lots of reports and analyses.

Elizabeth frowned as she glanced out the car window. Was there some reason he hadn't shared with her that dictated the necessity of an alternate route? This wasn't the way she usually drove to work.

"Agent Dawson." She leaned forward to get a better look at him if he glanced her way in the rearview mirror. "Is there some reason we're going this way rather than my usual route?"

"I can't answer that, ma'am. I have my orders."

Elizabeth leaned back in her seat, but she didn't relax. She had known Agent Craig Dawson for more than a year. Something about his voice didn't mesh with the man she knew. This was wrong somehow.

"Agent Dawson," she ventured hesitantly, "is something wrong?"

He glanced in the rearview mirror for the briefest moment and their eyes met. In that instant she saw his fear, recognized the depth of it.

"I'm sorry, Dr. Cameron," he said, his tone hollow, listless. "They have my family…they're going to kill them if I don't do what they tell me. Please believe I didn't have any choice."

Terror tugged at Elizabeth's sternum. *They.* He had to mean the people who worked with David…the ones to whom he'd sold out his fellow agents.

Her heart bolted into panic mode.

Was he taking her to them?

Or did he plan to kill her himself…in order to save his family?

She moistened her lips and marshaled her courage. "What're you supposed to do, Agent Dawson?"

His uneasy gaze flicked to the rearview mirror once more. "I have to deliver you to the location they specified. That's all." He looked away. "God, I don't want to do this."

"We should call Agent Stark." She rammed her hand into her purse, fished for her cell phone. Her heart pounded so hard she could scarcely think. "He'll know what to do."

Where was her phone? She turned her purse upside down and emptied the contents. She always put it back in her purse before going to bed after allowing it to charge for a couple of hours.

"We can't do that, ma'am."

The full ramifications of the situation struck her. He'd taken her cell phone. His family was being held hostage.

Agent Dawson was no longer her advocate.

"Stop the car, Agent Dawson." Her order sounded dull and carried little force, but she had to try.

His defeated gaze met hers in the rearview mirror once more. "I'm afraid I can't do that, Dr. Cameron."

Panic knotted in her stomach, tightened around her throat. She steeled herself against it, mentally scrambled to consider the situation rationally.

Her movements slow, mechanical, she picked up her belongings one item at a time and dropped them back into her purse. The lip balm she always carried. Hairbrush. Keys. Her attention shifted back to the keys. They could be useful. She tucked the keys into the pocket of her blazer.

She glanced up to make sure Agent Dawson wasn't watching her, then sifted through the rest. Ink pen. Another possible weapon. She slid it into her pocket as well. With nothing else useful, she scooped up the rest and spilled it into her bag.

Okay. She took a deep breath. Get a clean grip on calm and keep it. No matter what happened she needed to keep her senses about her.

She was a doctor. She'd been trained to maintain her composure during life-and-death situations. This was basically the same thing.

Only it was her life on the line.

Searching for a serene memory to assist her efforts she latched on to the sensations from last night. Smells, tastes, sounds of pleasure.

She clung to the recollection of how Joe's skin had felt beneath her palm. The weight of his muscular body atop hers. She trembled as the moments played in her mind. Their bodies connected in the most intimate manner.

But most of all she held on to the last words he'd said

to her…he loved her. He hadn't needed to utter those exact words, the message had been clear.

Whether she lived through this day or not, she could hold that knowledge close to her heart. She wished she had told him how she felt. Even if it was a mistake, he'd deserved to know. How was it that fear for one's life suddenly made so many things crystal clear?

She did have deep feelings for Joe. If she were totally honest with herself she would have to say that she loved him. She would also have to admit that it was, without question, a huge mistake. But, under the circumstances, that point seemed moot altogether.

Elizabeth turned her attention back to the passing landscape. She needed to pay attention to their destination. That ability was another thing that no doubt spelled doom for her. Didn't they always blindfold hostages in the movies so they wouldn't know where they were taken? Further proof that the outcome for her would not include a dashing hero and a last-minute escape. She would know too many details to risk her survival.

All the more reason to be prepared.

Another thought occurred to her then. "Agent Dawson." Her voice sounded stark in the car after the long minutes of silence. When his gaze collided with hers in the mirror she went on, "How can you be sure they won't harm your family anyway?"

He didn't answer, except the look in his eyes gave her his answer. He couldn't be sure, but he had to try. His work had brought danger to his family. He had to take whatever risks were necessary in an attempt to keep them safe. He wasn't a field operative. He was reacting the only way he knew how.

Elizabeth didn't readily recognize the neighborhood. It wasn't the sort of area anyone would willingly frequent. Dilapidated houses and crumbling apartment buildings. Trash lay scattered in parking lots and along the broken sidewalks. Junked cars as well as newer models, some considerably more expensive than the houses they fronted, lined the street. At this hour of the morning no one appeared to be stirring about. But she didn't have to see any of the residents to guess at the community profile. Poverty-stricken. Desperate.

Every city had its forgotten corners. Areas where the government failed to do enough. Where people survived on instinct and sheer determination.

No one here would care what happened down the street or on the next block. Survival depended upon looking the other way and keeping your mouth shut.

Elizabeth had never known this sort of hopelessness. No one should. She hoped this sad part of life wouldn't be the last thing she ever saw.

The car stopped and Elizabeth jerked to attention. Her gaze immediately roved the three-story building that sat on a corner lot. The windows were boarded up and the roof looked to be missing most of its shingles.

Dawson got out of the car and walked around to her side. He opened the car door and waited for her to get out. Vaguely she wondered what he would do if she refused. Would he shoot her? She didn't think so.

The energy would be wasted. She had no choice any more than he did. Making matters more difficult would serve no purpose. Agent Dawson wasn't her enemy. It was the people inside this ramshackle building who represented the true threat.

She got out of the car and he took her by the arm. She didn't resist, didn't see the point.

He led her to the front entrance and ushered her inside where the condition of the structure was no better than the outside had been.

Though it was daylight outside, the interior was barely lit and only by virtue of the sunlight slipping between the boards on the windows. She wondered if there was any electricity supplying power to the building. Not likely.

Up two flights of stairs and at the end of the hall Dawson hesitated. Elizabeth met his gaze, saw the regret and pain churning there.

"I'm sorry, Dr. Cameron."

The door behind him swung open and a man carrying a large, ugly gun stepped into the hall. He quickly patted down Agent Dawson and removed the weapon he carried in his shoulder holster. Then he did the same to Elizabeth. He ignored the keys and pen.

"This way," he growled.

Dawson held on tightly to her elbow as they moved into the room the man had indicated. She wished she had told Dawson that she knew he was sorry and that she understood, but there hadn't been time.

"Well, well."

Elizabeth's attention darted in the direction of the female voice. Blond hair cut in a short, spiky style, analyzing gray eyes. She looked tough dressed in her skintight jeans and T-shirt. Her arms were muscular as if she worked out with weights. She wore a shoulder holster which held a handgun while she carried a larger, rifle-type weapon similar to that of her comrade.

"I finally get to meet sweet Elizabeth," the woman said hatefully.

Elizabeth felt her muscles stiffen. This was *the* woman. She didn't have to be told. The woman referred to her in a way that David had regularly, sweet Elizabeth.

Unflinching, she lifted her chin and stared at the other woman who seemed to tower over her. "Who are you?"

The witch with the guns laughed, boldly, harshly. "I think you know who I am."

Elizabeth ignored Dawson's fingers squeezing her elbow. His concern for her was needless. She doubted either one of them would make it out of here alive.

"You must be the woman David left every time he came home to me," Elizabeth said succinctly. The transformation on the other woman's face let her know her words had prompted the desired result.

Looking ready to kill, the woman strode up to Elizabeth and shoved the barrel of the rifle she carried into Elizabeth's chest. "You think you know something about me, Miss Goody Two-Shoes?"

Elizabeth held her ground despite the terror sending tremor after tremor through her. "I know David never once mentioned you."

The woman's face contorted with anger. Elizabeth braced herself for the fallout. To her surprise the woman's attention shifted to Dawson.

"Get his wife on the line," she said to her accomplice.

Dawson tensed. "I did everything you asked. You said you'd let them go."

"That's right," Elizabeth interjected, her heart aching for the poor man, "you got what you wanted. Let Agent Dawson and his family go."

Dawson looked at her then, his expression trapped somewhere between thankful that his family appeared to be safe for the moment—since he would soon hear his wife's voice—and downtrodden because of what he'd done to Elizabeth.

The woman said nothing to Elizabeth but tossed a cell phone to Dawson.

"Hello?"

The look of relief on his face told Elizabeth that his wife was on the other end of the line.

"You're all right?" he verified. Horror abruptly claimed his expression. "No!" He stared at the woman who'd given him the phone, then at the phone. "What've you done?"

The oxygen evacuated Elizabeth's lungs and the room suddenly tilted. Had they…? Oh, God.

"Don't worry, Mr. CIA Agent," the woman taunted with a wave of her gun, "you're going to join them… right now."

The horrible woman fired two shots. Dawson jerked with the impact, staggered back then collapsed on his side into a twisted heap on the dusty wood floor. The color of blood spread rapidly in a wide circle on his shirtfront.

Elizabeth dropped onto her knees next to him. She rolled him onto his back and assessed the situation.

Before she could attempt to stop the bleeding, the man with the gun hauled her to her feet.

"He'll die!" Elizabeth screamed at him as if he were deaf or stupid.

"That's the point," he said in that low guttural growl of his.

Elizabeth felt the hysteria clawing at the back of her throat. She felt cold and numb. The urge to scream squirmed in her chest.

She thought of the keys in her pocket and how she might be able to use them. But it was no use. She recognized from the location of the wound that nothing she could do in this setting would benefit Agent Dawson.

His family was dead. Maybe he was better off that way, too. He would never have forgiven himself if he'd lived.

Elizabeth swiveled toward the woman standing only a few feet away. "What do you want?" Her voice carried its own kind of malicious intent.

For the first time in her life Elizabeth understood completely how it felt to want to kill someone. If she possessed a weapon she would not hesitate to murder one or both of those holding her hostage.

The woman grinned, an expression straight from hell. "Everything," she said with sinister glee.

The man grabbed Elizabeth's arm again and pushed her toward a door on the other side of the room. "Where are we going?" she demanded, a new kind of fear rushing through her veins.

He cut her a look but said nothing.

The smaller room he shoved her into was empty and just as unkempt as the other one. Before she could turn around he slammed the door shut. She rushed to it, knowing before she twisted the knob that it would be locked.

A surge of relief made her knees weak. At least he hadn't followed her in here.

She moved back from the door, took a moment to gather her wits. Okay, she had to think.

The events of the past few minutes reeled through her mind like a horror flick. She closed her eyes and banished the images. She didn't want to see Dawson's face when he'd heard whatever they did to his wife on the other end of that phone call. She didn't want to see him fall into a dying heap on the floor over and over.

Things like this didn't happen in her life. She was just a doctor. One who worked at a quiet, upscale clinic. She'd never had to deal with the hysteria and insanity of E.R. work. She'd never been exposed to this sort of horror outside a movie theater.

Several more deep breaths were required before she could stop her body from quaking so violently.

She reached into her pocket. Keys, ink pen. Not much that would help her in this situation.

Okay…think. First she needed to take stock of her situation. She moved to the boarded-up window on the other side of the room. Peered through the cracks between the boards. Nothing. Not a single pedestrian to call to for help, not that she was sure anyone in this neighborhood would be willing to get involved. But maybe someone would call the police if they heard screaming. She glanced toward the door. Of course if she screamed her captors would come running.

She tugged at one of the boards. The wood creaked and shifted but not enough for her to work it loose.

"Damn."

She walked around the room. Surveyed the floor. Looked inside the one other door that opened up to a tiny closet. This room had probably been a bedroom at one time. She looked up at the ceiling. No removable ceiling tiles or attic access doors. Just stained, cracked drywall.

There was no way out of here. She had to face that fact.

She propped against the wall near the window. She couldn't get out the window, but it made her feel better to be near it all the same.

Why hadn't they killed her? There had to be a reason she was still breathing.

The woman with the guns had said she wanted *everything*. What did that mean?

Had David failed to follow through with all the names of the agents she'd given new faces? That was the only marketable asset Elizabeth possessed in this lethal scenario. But why would David betray his country—and her—and then fall down on the job?

Maybe he'd been killed before he could provide the full list. Why then had it taken these goons three months to come looking for the rest?

It didn't make sense.

Did criminal activities ever make sense?

She scrubbed her hands over her face and exhaled loudly. Would Dr. Newman miss her this morning and call her house to see where she was? When he didn't get her would he contact the police?

She didn't think so. He could well assume that she'd had a personal emergency come up. She was an adult after all, one who had recently rebuffed his advances at that. He might not care to pursue the question of where she was this morning.

So what did she do?

Could she just stand here waiting for one of her captors to decide it was time to kill her? Did she dare assume that she was some sort of bargaining chip who would be kept alive for trading purposes?

She just didn't have any experience in this sort of situation. But the one thing she did know was that being a victim, to some extent, was a choice. She could stand here feeling helpless until they came for her or she could devise a way to fight back.

She'd always struggled to reach her goals, never once giving up. She had to do that now, had to find a way to help herself. She might not escape, but she would die trying.

She had nothing to lose by tackling the boards over the window again. That appeared to be her only viable means of possible escape.

After swiping her damp palms against her pants she grabbed hold of a board and pulled with all her might. It didn't budge much, but it did give a little.

Even that little bit gave her hope.

She worked harder, struggled with all her might.

The first board came loose, sending her staggering backward. She barely managed to stay on her feet.

Her heart pounding with anticipation, she laid the board aside and reached for the next one.

She could do this.

She *had* to do this.

Her life depended upon it.

The door suddenly flew open and Elizabeth pivoted to face what would no doubt be one of her captors.

Her heart surged into her throat.

Joe.

She rushed across the room and into his arms. Tears streamed down her cheeks but she didn't care. She was just so damned glad to see him. How had he found her?

She hadn't heard a scuffle. Had he killed those two awful people holding her here?

"Thank God you found me," she murmured against the welcoming feel of his wide shoulders. "I'm so sorry I made you leave last night. We should have made love again."

Last night felt like a lifetime ago now, but she had to tell him the truth now, right this second. She wouldn't leave him hanging another moment.

"You were right, Joe, it's too late for me, too. I love you." She drew back and looked into his eyes. "I should have—"

Her stomach bottomed out and every ounce of relief she'd felt drained away as surely as Agent Dawson's blood had.

She knew those eyes…not contacts…recognized those lips… This wasn't Hennessey…this was…

"David." But he was dead…wasn't he?

Chapter 12

Joe's flight landed in Newark, New Jersey, twenty minutes earlier than scheduled. He grabbed his carry-on bag, the only one he'd brought with him, and waited for an opportunity to merge into the line of passengers heading for the exit at the front of the plane.

After disembarking he made his way to the terminal exits and hailed a cab. He gave the warehouse address and relaxed into the seat. It was five twenty-two. Thirty minutes from now he would arrive at his rendezvous point and the game would begin.

One call to the man on the ground here in Jersey and his contact had agreed to meet with him at six o'clock.

Ginger was her name.

She'd been expecting to hear from him weeks ago. Lowering his voice and summoning that gravelly tone Maddox used, Joe had explained that his assignment had kept him under deep cover far longer than he'd anticipated, but he was back now. He needed to touch base and get a status on how the operation was proceeding. He'd considered demanding to know why only three agents had been taken out so far but since he didn't know the ultimate reasoning behind that move, he didn't risk it. For all he knew Maddox could have dictated the dates each hit would go down.

As the scenery zoomed past his window Joe's thoughts found their way back to last night. To the way touching her had shaken his entire world. He'd known it would be that way. From the first time he'd seen her, watched her walk across the parking lot at her clinic, he'd sensed she was special. Maybe too special for him. He wasn't at all sure a guy like him deserved a woman like that.

Making love to her last night had fulfilled every fantasy he'd enjoyed since that night months ago, when he'd first held her in his arms to keep her from walking into a trap at her clinic.

Her body had responded to his as if they'd been made for each other. Every touch had ripped away yet another layer of his defenses. He'd spent his entire adult life avoiding commitment on an emotional level. His work made him unreliable in that department. He understood that. Knew with complete certainty that a permanent relationship would be unfair on far too many levels for any woman to tolerate.

But he just hadn't been able to help himself where Elizabeth was concerned. He'd wanted her more than he'd ever wanted any woman. He couldn't recall once ever being this vulnerable to need.

Elizabeth comprehended the difficulty becoming involved with a man like him entailed. She'd clearly made a promise to herself not to risk her heart to any more men like David Maddox. And as much as Joe wanted to argue that he wasn't anything at all like Maddox, he recognized the career-related similarities. Still he wanted nothing more than to convince her to let this thing between them develop naturally. He wanted to make promises. Promises he might not be able to keep.

It was too much to ask. He would be the first to admit to that glaring fact. How could he ask her to give that much?

He couldn't.

She had been right to ask him to leave.

He should never have gone to her like that. She'd already been hurt by one man like him. She deserved the chance to find someone more reliable, more available with whom to share her life.

She deserved that and more. And Calder had to find a way to protect her better. He couldn't let anyone like Maddox near her again.

She'd paid far too much for that mistake.

The taste of her lips abruptly filled Joe and it took every ounce of strength he possessed to push the tender memories away.

He had to focus now.

Staying alive had to be top priority.

Maybe he and Elizabeth didn't have a future together but that didn't mean he couldn't hope.

"Stop here," he told the driver.

The cabbie pulled the taxi over to the curb four blocks from Joe's ultimate destination. He paid the fare and got out. The air he sucked into his lungs felt thick with humidity and the smell of diesel fuel from the huge trucks and trailers still rumbling in the distance down Avenue A. At almost six o'clock things were winding down along this particular warehouse-lined street of Newark's Ironbound community. A few trailers were still being loaded. The sounds of rush-hour traffic from the surrounding streets and avenues mixed with the heavier grumbling of the trucks.

He surveyed the deserted warehouses at the far end of the street where encroaching residential developments made the old standing structures ripe for condo-izing. Not exactly a picturesque view for prospective owners.

Dressed in jeans and boots and a T-shirt beneath an open button-down chambray shirt Joe blended well with the warehouse crews headed home for the night. He used that to his benefit and moved easily toward the rendezvous point.

He fell into "Maddox" stride without thought. Focused his energy on giving off a confident vibe. This meeting was his and Ginger's and anyone else planning to be there needed to know that. Maddox never let another human being intimidate him. From watching the videos of a number of his interrogations he liked belittling his assets. Though all agents took that approach to some degree Maddox went further than most. He appeared to get off on degrading those he considered lesser forms of life, which appeared to be most other humans.

The abandoned warehouse where Ginger waited looked in less than habitable condition. He took a final moment to get into character then went inside. He carried the 9 mm Beretta in his waistband at the small of his back and a backup piece in an ankle holster. His preferred weapon of choice was a Glock but for this mission he needed to carry what Maddox would.

"It's about time."

Joe settled his gaze on the woman with blond spiky hair and immediately recognized her as Ginger from the surveillance photos on file at the Agency.

"Patience has never been one of your strong suits." He kept his gaze fastened on hers. No averting his eyes, no letting her read anything that Maddox wouldn't display in this situation.

Ginger sashayed over to him, a high-powered rifle hanging down her back from a shoulder strap. "Did you miss me?" she asked as she slid her arms up and around his neck.

He gifted her with a Maddox smile. "Occasionally."

She kissed him and he kissed her back, using all the insights that Elizabeth had shared with him. Aggressive, invasive. Ginger appeared to like it. Maybe too much.

He set her away. "We have business to attend to," he said in an icy growl that made her eyes widen in surprise. He didn't analyze her reaction in an attempt to prevent any outward response himself.

She inclined her head and studied him. "You're right. We've kept him waiting too long already."

With that ominous announcement she pivoted on her heel, the weapon on her shoulder banging against her hip, and strode toward the freight elevator.

Joe followed. From the intelligence the Agency had gathered there was at least one more scumbag working with this woman. Her known accomplice was male, twenty-seven or -eight, and seriously scruffy-looking. But then, he watched the woman pull down the overhead gate that served as a door and set the lift into motion, that didn't surprise him after meeting the enigmatic Ginger in person. She looked about as unsavory as they came. The third man was the unknown factor, but Joe imagined that he would be every bit as sleazy.

Maddox's taste had definitely altered. Of course a field operative couldn't always be selective when working undercover. However, Maddox had, so far as they had determined, continued his alliance with these three well after the mission ended. If Joe's conclusions were correct, Maddox had used at least two of this group to orchestrate the hits on his fellow agents. The question was, for whom? The why was about money. It didn't take a rocket scientist to figure out that part.

Too bad for Maddox. A guy couldn't take his hefty bank account to hell with him.

The upward crawl came to an abrupt, jarring halt on the third floor and his guide shoved the door up and out of the way. The third level appeared to be nothing but a wide-open vacant space. What could be an additional storage room or office stood at the far end and was separated from the larger space by a single door.

She glanced over her shoulder. "Stay here."

Joe snagged her by the elbow and wheeled her around to face him. "This sounds a lot like insubordination, *baby,*" he offered, his tone at once sensual and accusing.

Again her eyes widened in something like surprise, kindling his instincts once more and sending him to a higher state of alert.

"Just following orders," she said with a shrug before pulling free of his hold and heading toward the door on the other side of the space.

Joe's instincts were humming. Something was off here. A glitch he couldn't quite name. But he understood that the undercurrents he felt were tension filled.

The surprise he'd seen in Ginger's eyes. Had she recognized something a little off with her former lover?

There was always the possibility that she and her accomplice had heard that Maddox was dead but Joe doubted that. The info had been kept within Director Calder's realm alone.

Intelligence indicated that the group had been putting out feelers as to Maddox's location.

There was every reason to believe that the two leaders of this little group, Ginger and her male counterpart, Fahey, had orchestrated the three assassinations thus far. Whatever their motivation, the two wanted to hook up with their source, David Maddox, once more. There was nothing on the third party.

Maybe it was the physical relationship between Ginger and Maddox or maybe it was simply a matter of needing the rest of the names.

Joe would be the first one to admit that he'd been surprised by Maddox's duplicity. It wasn't that he hadn't suspected the guy was fully capable of that kind of betrayal. He'd simply believed him to be devoted to his work and his country, if not the people in his personal life, specifically Elizabeth Cameron.

Maybe that sticking point had been the catalyst for Joe's determination to prove that Maddox had betrayed not only Elizabeth but his country.

Almost immediately after he'd started his own investigation, one week after the first assassination, intelligence had started to pick up on activity from this group. Joe had known what that indicated.

That's when Joe had gone to Calder with his suspicions. He'd bypassed his immediate supervisor, Director Allen, and laid all his suspicions on the table for the big dog.

Allen wasn't too damned happy about it. But it had gotten things rolling. Once Calder was hooked, Allen had jumped in with both feet.

Joe hadn't really cared whether Allen got on board or not. All he'd needed was Calder's blessing.

He'd gotten that.

He moved to attention when the door opened and Ginger sauntered back into the main room where he waited.

A figure appeared in the doorway behind her and it took a full five seconds for Joe's brain to assimilate what his eyes saw.

Maddox.

He should have known, Joe thought grimly.

Faking his own death would be the perfect way to get off the hook when he had what he needed.

"It's like looking in a mirror," Maddox said as he came closer.

"Yeah," Ginger agreed.

Fury whipped though Joe. "You betrayed your own people, Maddox."

Maddox shrugged. "Everybody has to retire sometime. I always believed in cashing out when stocks are the highest."

Joe shook his head. "I hate to offer a cliché, Maddox, but the truth is you're not going to get away with it."

The sick smile that Maddox was known for slid across his face. "I already have, Hennessey, or hadn't you noticed?"

Maddox inclined his head and Ginger took a bead on Joe, dead center of his chest.

"You can't do that here!"

Joe's gaze moved beyond Maddox.

Now the puzzle was complete.

Director Kurt Allen.

What do ya know? The third party was an inside man.

He'd known Allen was a bastard but he'd thought that was just his personality.

"We have to stick with the plan," Allen snapped. "No mistakes, Maddox." Allen glanced at Joe but quickly averted his gaze.

Maddox didn't like being chastised in front of a former colleague. "This is my op," he snarled. "These are my people. They follow my commands."

"A whole army of one, huh, Maddox?" Joe couldn't resist the dig. The only player on Maddox's team he'd seen so far was the woman. Allen didn't count as a soldier. Joe hoped the dig would get him what he needed to know—where the others were and what they were up to, but asking wouldn't likely work out. He'd have to goad it out of the two traitors.

Maddox's furious gaze landed on Joe. "You don't have any idea who I've got working for me, Hennessey, so don't even try."

"Where's your boy Fahey?"

"He's babysitting your sweetie pie," Ginger sneered.

A rush of fear shook Joe but the rage that followed hot on its heels obliterated any hint of the more vulnerable emotion. He fixed his gaze on Maddox. "If anything happens to her you're going to be in need of a second resurrection."

Allen scoffed. "Why would we let anything happen to her? She's what all of this has been about."

Confusion momentarily gained a little ground over his fury. "What the hell are you talking about? This bastard—" he indicated Maddox "—has been killing off our people."

It was Maddox's turn to laugh now, sending Joe's rage right back to the boiling point. That scumbag was a dead man.

"We have no interest," Allen explained with enormous ego, "in killing off recycled agents. What we want is Dr. Cameron."

"We already have a number of excellent surgeons," Maddox added, "but not one of her caliber. Our wealthier clients deserve only the best. She is the best."

In his line of work Joe had come across the slave trade in most every imaginable walk of life, but this was definitely a first.

"You intend to make her work for you," he restated. "Giving rich criminals new faces."

"And fingerprints," Allen said smugly.

Joe had heard reports on start-up activities like this. Clinics in obscure places attempting to create the ultimate in escapism. New faces, new fingerprints, even new DNA.

It was a damned shame the Agency's own people were working against them.

"It's amazing all right," Joe allowed. "Too bad neither of you lowlifes is going to see it become a reality."

Ginger took aim once more. "Do you want me to get this over with now?"

Joe's fingers itched to go for his own weapon but that would only get him killed. He needed a distraction.

"You know she'll refuse," Joe tossed out there just to buy some time. But he was right. No way would Elizabeth willingly do this.

Maddox shrugged. "She'll come around, Hennessey. You know the techniques."

The thought of Elizabeth being tortured physically or mentally ripped him apart inside.

"She really thought you loved her," he said to Maddox in hopes of stirring some sentimental feelings.

Ginger laughed. "He doesn't love anybody."

Maddox turned his face toward her, smiled approvingly.

"Then I guess it won't matter to either of you that she's carrying your child."

The lie did the trick.

Ginger's fire-ready stance wavered for a fraction of a second.

Just long enough for Joe to react.

He whipped out his 9 mm and fired twice. Ginger dropped. Maddox and Allen dove for the floor.

Maddox was the first to return fire.

Joe rolled to the left. Pulled off another round, capped Allen in the forehead before he'd gotten a grip on his own weapon.

Maddox started firing. Didn't let up.

Joe rolled, curled and twisted to avoid being hit. With no cover it was the only choice he had.

Maddox disappeared through the door on the far end of the room.

Joe scrambled to his feet and lunged in that direction.

He burst through the door just in time to see Maddox going out the window.

Fire escape.

Damn.

At the window a spray of bullets kept Joe from following the route Maddox had taken.

With the last shot still echoing in the air he risked a look out the window. Maddox was halfway down.

Joe muttered a curse and propelled himself out onto the uppermost landing.

He ducked three shots.

That made sixteen.

In the few seconds it would take Maddox to replace his clip, Joe rushed downward. One flight of rusty metal steps, then another.

Bullets pinged against metal, forcing Joe to zigzag as he plunged down the next flight. He got off two rounds, gaining himself a few seconds' reprieve.

Maddox hit the pavement in the rear alley, landing on his feet and bolting into a dead run.

Joe was three seconds behind him.

His heart pumped madly, sending much needed adrenaline through his veins.

But he had the advantage from this angle.

Problem was if he killed Maddox he might not find Elizabeth until it was too late.

He needed the bastard alive.

Maddox was likely counting on that.

Joe stopped. Spread his legs shoulder width apart and took aim.

The first bullet whizzed right by Maddox's left ear.

The second closer still.

Maddox skidded to a halt. "Okay!" he shouted. "You made your point."

Though he held up both hands in a gesture of surrender, Joe wasn't taking any chances.

"Place your weapon on the ground, Maddox. Now!" Joe eased toward him, keeping a bead on the back of his head.

"All right. All right." He started to lower his weapon, bending at the knees in order to crouch down close enough to lay the Beretta on the ground.

Ten feet, eight. Sweat beaded on Joe's forehead as he moved closer still.

Just as Maddox's weapon reached shoulder level he dropped and rolled.

Joe almost fired, but hesitated.

That split second of hesitation cost him every speck of leverage he'd gained.

"Looks like we have an impasse," Maddox said from his position on the ground. Though he lay on his back he'd leaned upward from the waist just enough to get a perfect bead on Joe's head.

Joe shrugged nonchalantly. "The way I see it, if we both end up dead, then there won't be any report for me to file."

Maddox grinned. "You always were a cocky SOB. But this time you've met your match."

"I don't think so." Joe's trigger finger tightened. "Now put down your weapon before I have to kill you."

"A good agent never gives up his weapon, Hennessey."

The explosion of the bullet bursting from the chamber was deafening in the long, deserted alley.

It hit dead center.

Chapter 13

Elizabeth crouched in the darkest corner of the room. She squeezed the keys in her hand, letting the bite of metal keep her senses sharp.

David was alive.

The son of a bitch.

Fury boiled up inside her, leaving a bitter burn in her throat.

For weeks after his death she had wished she could have spoken to him one last time before he died. If she'd only had the opportunity to apologize for her impatience and frustration with his work. As dedicated as she had always been to her own work, how could she grow disgruntled about his loyalty to the job? And that was exactly what she'd done. She had used a double standard. It was okay for her to work long hours seven days a week, month in, month out, but when he failed to show for weeks on end she'd behaved petulantly.

She'd kidded herself and pretended they were two of a kind and his long absences didn't bother her. But they had. To say otherwise was a lie.

So when she heard about his death she'd tortured herself for endless nights. Thinking of all the things she should have said.

All that energy…all that emotion wasted on a man who wasn't worth the time it took to tell him to get lost.

If only she'd known just what a monster he was she might have killed him herself.

Okay, maybe that was an exaggeration.

But she wanted desperately for him to pay for what he had done. He could rot in prison for the rest of his life and she wasn't sure that would be punishment enough. Yet execution was far too quick and merciful.

Elizabeth closed her eyes and cleared her mind. She couldn't be distracted by her hatred and bitterness toward David. She had to focus. Finding a way to escape the man holding her was the only hope she had of saving Joe.

She knew the meeting location.

All she needed was her freedom.

Her fingers tightened around the keys once more.

If she called him in here by crying out in pain as if she were sick, she could…

Well, she wasn't sure what she would do but she could make it up as she went.

God, she prayed, *please don't let him kill Joe.*

If Joe died…there were so many things she wanted to say to him. Too late…just like before.

Determination roared through her. No. She wouldn't let this happen to her again.

She had to do something.

When David had died there had been nothing she could do. Considering what she knew now she was glad. But this was different. Joe was a good guy and she loved him.

Why was it she couldn't do anything personal right? It always seemed as if she went about her relationships backward or sideways or something.

Deep breath.

She could do this.

Pushing to her feet she gathered her courage and prepared to make her move.

As a doctor she knew his most vulnerable spots. His eyes. The base of the throat. Then, of course, there was always the old reliable scrotum.

Another deep breath.

As she exhaled that lungful of air she cried out at the top of her lungs.

She doubled over, moaned and cried, summoning her most painful memories in an effort to make it sound real.

The door burst inward.

"What the hell is wrong with you?"

Elizabeth wailed again, held her stomach as if the pain were so intense she could do nothing else.

He grabbed her by the arm and tried to pull her up. "I said, what's wrong with you, bitch?"

"God, I don't know." She moaned long and low.

He slung the rifle over his shoulder. "Stand up where I can look at you."

"Ohhhhhh!" With that savage cry she came up with her hand, stabbed the key to her Lexus into his right eye.

He screamed.

His grip on her arm tightened.

She tried to get free.

Couldn't.

His fingers wrenched her arm painfully. The keys flew across the floor.

"Don't move!" He held his left hand over his eye. But he kept her close with the other. "I could kill you!" he snarled like a wounded animal.

Her heart thudded so hard she couldn't draw in a breath. She had to get loose.

Then she remembered her one other weapon.

Her free hand went into her pocket. Her fingers curled around the ink pen.

There was only one way to get away from this man.

She reared her arm back and brought it down hard, shoving the ink pen into the soft tissue at the base of his throat.

He released her. Grabbed at his throat as he frantically gasped for air.

She bolted for the door.

He grabbed her by the waist.

She screamed, tried to twist free.

His weight slammed into her back and they went down together.

She landed in a sprawl on the floor with him atop her.

His fingers curled around her throat. She tried to buck him off. Tried to roll. But he was too heavy. Horrible gasping sounds came from his throat as he struggled to get air past the hole she'd made. Blood soaked into the neck of his T-shirt, dripped down his cheek.

The pressure on her throat cut off her airway. She bucked and gasped. Pulled at his arms. No good.

Blackness swam before her eyes.

Desperate, she clawed at his face. At his injured eye and then at his throat.

He howled and fell off her.

She scrambled away from him. Clambered to her feet and raced toward the door.

She didn't slow or look back until she was out of the small house and on the street.

Hysteria slammed into her full throttle. She stood in the middle of the street and turned all the way around. Where was she?

The drive had been hours long. She'd dozed off once. She had no idea where she was.

Her gaze landed on a vehicle up the street and she ran in that direction until she could make out the license plate.

New Jersey.

The Garden State.

New Jersey?

The air raging in and out of her lungs, she stood there and tried to think. Avenue A. She'd heard that location mentioned. Warehouse.

A phone. She needed a phone—911. Help. She needed help.

The low drone of an automobile engine sounded behind her. She spun around and her heart leaped. Help!

She ran toward the car. Waved her arms frantically. "Help me! I need the police!"

The car sped forward, hurried past her. The elderly female driver stared wide-eyed at her.

"Help!" Elizabeth cried once more.

It was no use. The woman drove away as fast as she could. Elizabeth looked down at herself then. Blood was smeared on the front of her pale blue blouse. Her hair was likely disheveled. No wonder the woman didn't stop.

Panic slid around her throat like a noose. A crashing sound had her pivoting toward the door of the house she'd escaped.

The sound hadn't come from there.

Thank God.

A phone. She pushed the hair back from her face. Concentrate, Elizabeth. She needed a phone.

She rushed toward the next house. There wasn't a vehicle in the driveway. Please, please let someone be home.

Balling her bloody fist she banged on the door. "Is anyone home?" She banged harder. "Please, I need to use your phone. It's an emergency. Please."

No one was home. If they were, fear kept them from answering the door.

She rushed back out to the street, looked both ways for a driveway with a car in it.

There had to be someone home, car or no car.

Elizabeth rushed from house to house, pounded on door after door.

Finally a door opened. An elderly man stood on the opposite side of the threshold.

"Can't you read?" he groused.

Elizabeth blinked, uncertain what he meant. She tried to calm her respiration. Tried to make herself think rationally.

"See!" He tapped a sign hanging next to his door.

No solicitation.

"No!" She stepped into the path of the closing door. "I need help. I need the police."

He seemed to really look at her then. Blinked behind the thick lenses of his glasses.

"What happened to you?"

"Please," she pleaded. "I need to call the police."

His gaze narrowed in suspicion and for a moment, she feared he wasn't going to let her inside. Finally he backed up, gestured for her to come in.

He quickly surveyed his porch and yard. "Is somebody after you?"

She shook her head. "No, I don't think so." She looked around the room. "I need to use your phone."

He shuffled toward the kitchen. "It's in here."

Elizabeth rushed past him, almost knocking him over. She didn't take the time to apologize. She had to warn Joe.

Her first instinct was to call 911. But the police might not take her word for what was happening. And she didn't have the exact location. The Agency would surely know Joe's plan for connecting with his contact.

She punched in the number she'd learned by heart long ago. A voice answered on the first ring.

"I need to speak with Director Calder." Elizabeth ID'd herself using the code name and number she'd been given when she first agreed to work with the Agency.

When Director Calder's voice came across the line Elizabeth felt the sting of tears. Thank God.

She explained about David and warned that Joe was walking into a trap somewhere in the vicinity of Avenue A here in New Jersey.

The phone cut out.

"What did you say?" She'd missed whatever Director Calder had said.

He repeated, but again the phone started cutting out and she only got a word here and a word there.

She turned to the owner of the house. "Is there something wrong with your phone?"

In the moments it took him to answer, fear surged into her throat. What if she hadn't completely disabled her captor? What if he was out there attempting to tamper with the phone line? Her heart pounded erratically.

"Damn thing won't hardly hold a charge anymore. Just put her back in the cradle for a minute and she'll be fine."

"Director Calder?" she shouted into the mouthpiece of the receiver but the line was dead.

She depressed the talk button again and again. "You're sure that's all it is?"

The old man nodded. "It's the only one I got. Being cordless lets me use it all around the house but lately it won't hold a charge for long. I guess I left it out of the cradle too long today."

Elizabeth stuck the phone back into its cradle and took two deep, calming breaths. She'd made the call. Even though she didn't know what Calder had said, he'd gotten all she needed to tell him. He would ensure help got to where Joe was supposed to meet his contact.

"You need to wash up or something?" the old man asked. He looked at her face and then her hands. "Your throat's all red and swollen. You sure you're okay, lady?"

She shuddered and considered all the diseases she could catch with that horrible man's blood all over her.

"I'd like to wash up," she managed to get past the lump in her throat. Her body shook so hard she could barely stay vertical. She recognized the symptoms. The receding adrenaline. She'd have to be careful about shock. She'd been through an ordeal.

"Down the hall." He gestured to the hall at her left.

She nodded. "Thank you."

Her legs as weak as a toddler taking her first steps, she staggered to the bathroom.

"Sweet Lord." Her reflection was not a pretty sight. Her hair was a mess. Her face had a few smears of blood but her blouse was the worst. And her throat was red and swollen. Her bloody blouse was even torn.

She shuddered again, wondered if the man who'd been holding her captive was lying in that other house dying. She should call 911.

Being quick about it, she thoroughly washed her hands and face. She ran her fingers through her hair and sighed. That was the best she could do. Before leaving the bathroom she said one more urgent prayer for God to watch over Joe.

Please let him be safe.

When she returned to the living room the old man was still in the kitchen.

"Thought I'd make you some tea," he said as she joined him there.

"Thank you." She nodded to the phone. "May I try your phone again?"

He shrugged. "Probably won't do you any good but you can try."

She picked up the phone and punched in the three digits. The operator answered and she explained about being held captive and injuring her captor to escape. She verified the address with the old man fretting over the tea cups and then hung up.

The police and paramedics would be here soon.

"Thank you," Elizabeth said as she took the tea he offered. "I'm Elizabeth Cameron." She sipped her tea and sighed. The heat felt good drenching her raw throat.

"Rosco Fedder." He sweetened his tea, stirring it thoughtfully. "Sounds like you had yourself a fright, Missy."

She nodded. "More than you can know." That was certainly the truth. She darn sure couldn't tell him that the CIA was involved. He probably wouldn't believe her anyway.

By the time she'd finished her tea she felt a little less shaky. She couldn't stop worrying whether or not Joe was all right. Maybe she should call Director Calder again. The sound of sirens intruded into her thoughts and drew her to the front door.

"They're here." Her voice came out small and shaky in spite of her much calmer state.

Rosco joined her at the door. "You think that fellow survived?"

Dread welled in her belly. "I don't know." But she wasn't worried about the awful man who'd been holding her hostage. She was worried about Joe. Had the CIA been able to get to him in time?

"I'm going over there," she told Rosco. "Thank you for your help."

"That's what neighbors do, lady," he let her know. "They help one another. Most any of the folks in this neighborhood would've done the same if they'd been home. I'm the token old man 'round here. 'Bout the only one retired."

She managed a smile for her Good Samaritan and walked out to the street. Exhaustion made her feet feel as if they weighed a ton each. But she didn't stop until she'd reached the front walk where three police cruisers and an ambulance were parked.

A sedan pulled over to the curb drawing her attention beyond the fray of uniformed personnel rushing about.

The driver's side door opened and a man emerged.

Terror exploded in her chest.

David.

Elizabeth started to run back toward Mr. Fedder's house. Her heart threatened to burst out of her chest but she didn't slow, just kept running.

"Elizabeth!"

She felt her feet stop beneath her, almost causing her to fall forward.

"Elizabeth! It's me, Joe!"

Her whole body quaking like mad, she slowly turned around in time for him to skid to a stop only a couple of feet away.

"Honey, it's me, Joe."

Hope tugged at her. It was Joe's voice. But the face…

Her gaze settled on his and her heart leaped with joy.

The most beautiful blue eyes stared back at her.

"Joe!" She threw herself against him. His big strong arms closed in around her.

"I told you I'd be back," he murmured close to her ear.

And he hadn't let her down.

She drew back and looked into his eyes again. She wanted to tell him the truth…that she loved him despite her best efforts not to.

But would love ever be enough with a dangerous man like Joe Hennessey?

Chapter 14

Elizabeth slipped on her surgical gown then scrubbed up. As she dried her hands and arms she studied her reflection. Her throat was still bruised but she'd get over it.

Incredibly the man who'd done that damage had survived and the Agency hoped to garner much needed information from him. Elizabeth didn't care how useful he could be to the Agency as long as he spent the rest of his life behind bars…far, far away from her.

She'd been stunned to learn that killing off the agents had been a ploy to lure her into a situation, both as a suspect and as an asset to be protected. David had wanted to steal her away in such a manner that an Agency operative, namely Joe Hennessey, would be blamed for her disappearance and ultimate loss. No one would ever be the wiser that David was alive and he would have Elizabeth to use in his new posh escape clinic. She would have been a prisoner, giving sleazy, however wealthy, criminals new faces in exchange for living another day.

How could she have been so completely fooled by David?

"Dr. Cameron."

Elizabeth hauled her attention back to the here and now, and away from those disturbing thoughts. "Yes."

"The patient refuses to be prepped for anesthesia until after he speaks with you."

Elizabeth sighed. "I'll be right there." She'd been through this routine before.

With the same patient as a matter of fact.

She breezed into the O.R. and strode straight up to the operating table.

"What seems to be the problem, Mr. Hennessey?" She glared down at him, resisting the urge to tap her foot.

He looked around the room at the Agency's specialized team who waited to begin. His gaze lit back on Elizabeth's. "I really need to speak with you alone."

Elizabeth rolled her eyes and huffed her exasperation. "Clear the room please."

When the last of the four had moved into the scrub room, Elizabeth, keeping her hands where they wouldn't get contaminated, glared down at her patient.

"I just wanted you to know that I didn't mean to take advantage of you."

She did not want to talk about that night again. In the past three days they'd scarcely seen each other and when they had he'd wanted to apologize for making love to her. How was that for making a girl feel like she was loved? Not once had he mentioned having treaded into that four-letter territory.

So, of course, neither had she.

It was for the best, she supposed. He would go back to his superspy world and she would return to her work.

No harm. No foul.

They were both alive.

That was the most important thing. Right?

Funny thing was, every time she asked herself that question she got no answer.

"That night—"

She held up a sterile hand. "Stop it, please. I don't ever want to talk about that night again." She hoped she managed to keep the truth out of her eyes but she couldn't be sure. The way he scrutinized her face she doubted she hid much from him.

"I guess I can understand how you feel." He heaved out a big breath.

Elizabeth watched his sculpted chest rise and fall with the action. She wanted to touch him so badly that it literally hurt.

But that would be a mistake.

Whatever crazy connection they had shared during those stressful weeks was best forgotten.

"Just give me back my face, Doc." His gaze connected fully with hers and some unreadable emotion reached out to her, made her ache all the more. "I guess that'll have to be enough."

Elizabeth called in the team and within moments they had lapsed into a synchronized rhythm.

As Joe slipped deep into induced sleep she surveyed the face she'd given him. This was the last time she would see David Maddox's face. And she was glad.

She poised, scalpel in hand, over the patient and took a deep breath. "Let's get this done."

* * *

Elizabeth closed the door of her office and collapsed into her chair. She was completely exhausted. She just couldn't understand what was wrong with her. No one could claim she didn't get enough sleep. She slept like the dead. Eight to ten hours every night! It was incredible.

And food. She ate like a wrestler bulking up to meet his weight requirements.

As she sat there marveling over her strange new zest for sleep and food, realization hit her right between the eyes.

She was late for her period. Only about ten days and that wasn't completely uncommon. Her cycles never had been reliable. She'd considered birth control pills years ago in order to regulate herself but the risks for a woman her age, though she didn't smoke, were just not worth the bother. Condoms had always worked.

But she and Joe hadn't used a condom.

Mortification dragged at her as if the earth's gravity had suddenly cubed itself.

She was thirty-seven years old. A doctor at that. And she could very well be pregnant by *mistake!*

A kind of giddiness abruptly replaced her mortification.

A baby could be…nice.

Anticipation fizzed inside her. Okay, better than nice. A baby could be amazing!

She had to know.

Elizabeth shot to her feet.

She needed a pregnancy test.

Now.

She rushed out of the clinic without a word to anyone.

It was her lunch break anyway. She could do what she wanted. Didn't need anyone's permission.

As she settled behind the wheel of her Lexus she considered the attitude she'd just taken.

Maybe she was changing.

What do you know? She might just like this new feeling of liberation. All work and no play had turned into drudgery.

She drove straight to the nearest pharmacy and bought the test. She couldn't bear to wait until she got back to her office, besides she wanted privacy from her colleagues.

Since she was a doctor the pharmacist gladly allowed her to use the employee restroom in the rear of the store.

Her fingers trembling, Elizabeth opened the box and followed the simple instruction. Then she closed the lid on the toilet and sat down to wait.

Joe popped into her thoughts. If she was pregnant, should she tell him?

She chewed her lip. If she did, he would want to be a part of the child's life. Was that a good thing?

Maybe not.

But how could she not tell him?

Elizabeth groaned. More dilemmas.

Anger lit inside her. As soon as the restoration surgery on his face was complete she'd been ushered away from the borrowed clinic. She hadn't even been allowed to stay to see him through recovery.

Director Calder had refused to give her an update on Joe the two times she'd called.

And in the four weeks that had passed she hadn't heard from him once. Joe, not Calder. He hadn't called, hadn't come by. Nothing.

Obviously when he decided to move on he didn't look back.

It was for the best, she knew.

But that didn't make it hurt any less.

She'd shed a few tears, cursing herself every time.

Heck, she'd even forced herself to go on a few dates to try and put him out of her mind entirely. But nothing ever worked.

There was just no denying the truth.

She loved him and her heart would not let her forget.

The minute hand on the wall clock moved to the five. It was time.

Holding her breath she picked up the stick and peered at the results.

Positive.

A thrill went through her.

She was pregnant!

Shoving the box and the telltale test stick into the trash, she struggled for calm. Bubbles of excitement kept bobbing to the surface, making her want to alternately laugh and cry. Don't lose it, she warned. Keep it together. She had patients to see this afternoon. She could completely freak out when she got home tonight.

After washing her hands she made her way back to the front of the drugstore, thanked the pharmacist who studied her suspiciously, then hurried to her car.

She didn't drive straight back to the clinic. She was ravenous. Two drive-thrus later and she had what her heart—stomach actually—desired. Two quarter-pounder cheeseburgers, mega fries and an Asian salad with an extra pack of dressing.

The girls in reception gawked at her as she passed through on the way to her office with her armload of bags. She just smiled and kept going. When she'd gotten into her office and closed the door she dumped her load on her desk and relaxed into her chair. After she ate all this she would surely need a nap. She glanced at her schedule. Not going to happen. Oh well, she'd make up for it tonight.

Still a stickler for neatness, she arranged her lunch on the burger wrapper, with the salad bowl anchoring one corner. The first bite made her groan with pleasure. What was it about being pregnant that made food taste so good?

She would have to get a handle on her diet…just not today.

A tap on her door distracted her from her salad. She frowned. If Dr. Newman asked her to go out with him again she was just going to have to tell him that it would be unethical. Their working relationship prevented her from pursing a personal one with him. That should do the trick without hurting his feelings.

"Yes."

The door opened and the next bite never made it to her mouth.

Joe Hennessey, in all his splendor, from that sexy jawline to that perfect nose, waltzed in.

"They told me that you were having lunch." He glanced at the smorgasbord laid out in front of her. "Looks like there might be enough for me to join you."

Elizabeth snatched up the ever present bottle of water on her desk and washed a wad of fries down.

"What do you want, Hennessey?"

He hadn't contacted her in four weeks. The director of the CIA had refused to give her an update on his condition. How dare he show up here now!

The positive results of the pregnancy test flashed in front of her eyes and another wave of giddiness swept over her. She clamped her mouth shut. Couldn't say a word about that until she knew why he was here. And maybe not even then.

He walked up to her desk but didn't sit down. "I should have called you."

That was a start. "Yes, you should have." She nibbled on a fry. She would die before she'd tell him how lonely she'd been. How badly she'd yearned to have him in her bed.

He bracketed his waist with his hands and took a deep breath. "The truth is I didn't want to see you or even talk to you until I was me again."

Stunned, she dropped the fork back into her salad bowl. "I'm not sure I'm following," she said cautiously but she knew what he meant. He wanted her to see him when they talked…*his* face.

He leaned forward, braced his hands on her desk. She inhaled the clean, slightly citrusy scent that was uniquely Joe Hennessey. Her gaze roved his face. Every detail was just as it was before.

Damn she was good.

Elizabeth blinked. Chastised herself for staring. Since he hadn't answered her question he'd obviously paused to take notice of her staring.

She cleared her throat and squared her shoulders. "You're going to have to explain what you mean, Agent Hennessey."

"Don't play games with me, Elizabeth," he warned, those blue eyes glinting with what some might consider intimidation. But she knew him better now. That was his predatory gleam. And she was his prey…he wanted her.

"Really, Hennessey, you should be more specific."

"I love you, Elizabeth. I can't sleep. I can't eat. I miss you. I need to be with you."

I...I...I, was this all about him? Let him sweat for a bit.

She shrugged indifferently. "I've been sleeping fine." She glanced at the food in front of her. "Eating fine as well."

He straightened, threw up his hands. "What do you want me to do? Beg?"

That could work, she mused wickedly.

"No," she told him to his obvious relief.

He eased one hip onto the edge of her desk and popped a French fry into his mouth. "Then tell me what you want, Elizabeth. I'm desperate here."

His work was her first concern. But she would never ask him to give up his career.

"I don't think we could ever work, Joe," she confessed. She looked directly into those gorgeous blue eyes. "You know the reasons."

He downed a swig of her water and grimaced. "What if I told you I'd gone off field duty?"

She froze, her heart almost stopped stone still. "What did you say?" She prayed she hadn't heard wrong.

"I'm taking a position with a new agency, one that compiles intelligence from all the other agencies and prepares reports for the president. I'd tell you more about it but it's top secret." He grinned. "I'm officially a desk jockey. Is that safe enough for you?"

She shook her head. Afraid to believe. "You can't do that for me. You have to do it for you."

He reached for her hand, engulfed it in his long fingers. "I did it for us, Elizabeth." He peered deeply into her eyes. "And just so you know, even if you kick me out, I'm not going back to field work. I'm done with that. So what's it gonna be?"

Elizabeth jumped to her feet and stretched across her desk to put her arms around his neck. "Yes!" She smiled so wide she was sure it looked more like a goofy grin.

His brows drew together in a frown. "Yes, what?"

She knew he was teasing by the sparkle of mischief in his eyes. "Yes, I'll marry you, you big dummy."

A grin widened on his sexy mouth. "Well, now." He reached down and nipped her lips. "I guess that means you're going to make an honest man out of me."

"Actually..."

He kissed her and for a few moments all other thought ceased. There was only the taste and heat of his mouth. God she had missed him. Never wanted to be away from him again.

She drew back just far enough to look into his eyes. "Actually," she reiterated, "I thought I'd make this child I'm carrying legally yours. You okay with that?"

It was Joe's turn to be stunned. "A father? I'm going to be a father?"

Elizabeth nodded.

He kissed her with all the emotion churning inside him. He told her how much he loved her over and over until they were both gasping for breath.

He pressed his forehead to hers. "I'm definitely okay with that, Doc," he finally murmured.

Elizabeth pulled away from him. "You'd better get out of here."

Confusion claimed that handsome face. "You're kidding about that part, right?"

She wagged her head side to side. "I have patients to see. The sooner I get through my schedule, the sooner I'll be home."

He grinned. “And we can have makeup sex.”

Now there was that naughty side peeking out. “But we didn’t have a fight,” she countered.

“We did have a trial separation,” he suggested.

He had her there.

“Go.” She motioned toward the door. “We’ll have all the makeup sex you want. Tonight.”

He backed toward the door. She couldn’t help watching the way he moved. So sexy. So chock-full of male confidence.

“I’ll be waiting at your place. I’ll even have dinner waiting.”

Before she could question that promise he turned around and strolled out the door.

Her gaze narrowed. He said he’d have it ready, he didn’t say he’d cook it.

Elizabeth pressed her hand to her tummy and smiled at the feeling of complete happiness that rushed through her.

Now she could rightfully say that she really did have it all.

And Joe Hennessey had definitely been worth the wait.

* * * * *

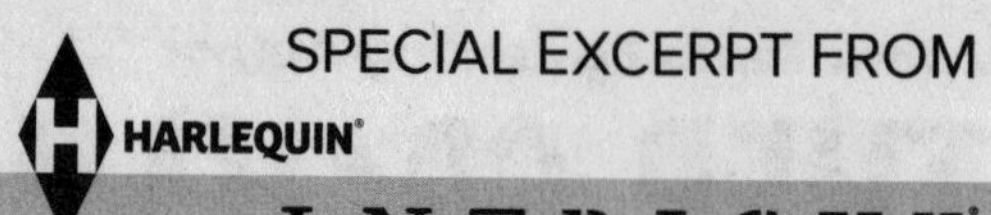

BLOOD ON COPPERHEAD TRAIL
by Paula Graves

Nothing can stop Laney Hanvey from looking for her missing sister. Not even sexy new chief of Bitterwood P.D....

"I'm not going to be handled out of looking for my sister," Laney growled as she heard footsteps catching up behind her on the hiking trail.

"I'm just here to help."

She faltered to a stop, turning to look at Doyle Massey. He wasn't exactly struggling to keep up with her—life on the beach had clearly kept him in pretty good shape. But he was out of his element.

She'd grown up in these mountains. Her mother had always joked she was half mountain goat, half Indian scout. She knew these hills as well as she knew her own soul. "You'll slow me down."

"Maybe that's a good thing."

She glared at him, her rising terror looking for a target. "My sister is out here somewhere and I'm going to find her."

The look Doyle gave her was full of pity. The urge to slap that expression off his face was so strong she had to clench her hands. "You're rushing off alone into the woods where a man with a gun has just committed a murder."

"A gun?" She couldn't stop her gaze from slanting toward the crime scene. "She was shot?"

"Two rounds to the back of the head."

HIEXP69740

She closed her eyes, the remains of the cucumber sandwich she'd eaten at Sequoyah House rising in her throat. She stumbled a few feet away from Doyle Massey and gave up fighting the nausea.

After her stomach was empty, she crouched in the underbrush, fighting dry heaves and giving in to the hot tears burning her eyes. The heat of Massey's hand on her back was comforting, even though she was embarrassed by her display.

"I will help you search," he said in a low, gentle tone. "But I want you to take a minute to just breathe and think. Okay? I want you to think about your sister and where you think she'd go. Do you know?"

Does Laney hold the key to her sister's whereabouts? Doyle Massey intends to find out, in Paula Graves's BLOOD ON COPPERHEAD TRAIL, on sale in February 2014!

HIEXP69740